The man's stark fe[...]le's chair swiveled slowly aro[...], in stone, black hair braided tight and lapping in [...] her knees. She regarded the man at her feet in awful silence.

"What did he do?" whispered Lily.

Adam shrugged, answering her in a low voice. "It's the typical story: asteroid miner comes into some station on leave, runs across a sweet adolescent je'jiri girl in full raging heat who'd slipped her clan for a night on the prowl. And of course all intelligent people are avoiding her like the plague, and trying to get calls through to whatever ship has hired out her clan. But people like him usually figure that as long as the je'jiri isn't already mated, they're safe."

At last La Belle spoke. "You knew the law." Her anger was bone deep, and implacable. "'No human will mate or have intercourse in any sexual or sensual fashion with je'jiri.' You have violated the very foundation of their culture, as admittedly alien and atavistic as it may seem to us. Yi took the hunt on. I cannot stop it."

He lay in crumpled anguish at her feet, weeping with noisy and awful terror. The bridge crew stood utterly silent, watching him without compassion. "But you are La Belle Dame," he sobbed. "*You* could stop them."

She stood up. "I am La Belle Dame Sans Merci," she said with the bite of diamond, "and I do not suffer fools gladly."

And to Lily's left, the third set of elevator doors opened.

THE HIGHROAD TRILOGY

Book Two:

Revolution's Shore

****

Alis A. Rasmussen

BANTAM BOOKS

NEW YORK · TORONTO · LONDON · SYDNEY · AUCKLAND

REVOLUTION'S SHORE
A Bantam Spectra Book / July 1990

ISBN 0-553-28544-0

Published simultaneously in the United States and Canada

Bantam Books are published by Bantam Books, a division of
Bantam Doubleday Dell Publishing Group, Inc. Its trademark,
consisting of the words "Bantam Books" and the portrayal of a
rooster, is Registered in U.S. Patent and Trademark Office and
in other countries. Marca Registrada. Bantam Books, 666 Fifth
Avenue, New York, New York 10103.

PRINTED IN THE UNITED STATES OF AMERICA

RAD   0 9 8 7 6 5 4 3 2 1

For Arnold and Edith Bodtker

Special thank-yous to Brandon Chamberlain, Jay Silverstein, and Chris Kinney for military and technical suggestions: don't blame them if you don't believe it; to Sonja Rasmussen for help fixing the worst translations; to Ruth, Milt, and Judi Silverstein for baby-sitting (again); and Carol Wolf Holtzman, Raven Gildea, Jane Butler, and Judith Tarr for their valuable feedback on this ongoing project.

Will ye gang tae the Hielands
my bonnie, bonnie lass
Will ye gang tae the Hielands
wi' Geordie?
And I'll tak' the high road
and ye'll tak' the low
And I'll be in the Hielands
afore ye.

1   Virtue's Reward

****

Obsessions are dangerous in proportion to the amount of fear they breed in their possessors: the closer the possessor to loss of control, the greater the fear.

Kyosti Bitterleaf Hakoni, professionally known as Hawk, had three obsessions. The first was his work as a physician, work denied him for almost twenty-five years but now restored. The second was his lover. But last, and encompassing the first two, he was obsessed with a fear that someday his past—not even the past people knew him for, the one that had made him and his compatriots both heroes and criminals—would catch up with him.

Of course it would. And, of course, in the way he most feared.

But at this moment Hawk sat against the sheen of one wall of his cabin, an arm, half-obscured by the riot of his pale hair, hooked behind his head. With a concentration that directly recalled his namesake, he watched his lover as she slept. His eyes seemed hooded in their intensity, as if he feared that the full force of his stare might obliterate her, flesh and soul.

She did not stir.

He watched her for a long while, silent, and finally a series of chimes, the change of watch, rang through the ship and she shifted beneath the blanket and her eyes opened.

At first she glanced around the room, recalling where she

was, but when her gaze found Hawk she relaxed, and yawned and stretched. He watched her.

"Kyosti," she said when she had finished, "what were we doing when we went through the last window?" Her voice still held the slight hoarseness of awakening, lending it an unwittingly passionate quality.

Hawk smiled.

"That's what I thought. Hoy." She sat up, her covers slipping off her to reveal the light curve of her skin and the medallion—five interlinked circles pierced by a spear—that Heredes had given her. It hung now, just as it always did, just below the hollow of her throat. She shivered, as if the memory of what they had been doing brought her both pleasure and anticipation, and rested her head on her hands, palms covering her eyes. "I could become addicted to that."

His eyes had not lost their intensity, giving his smile a disturbing blend of amorous warmth and that complete instability brought on by unquenchable thirst. Then she looked up, and his expression changed abruptly to something much more innocuous.

"Don't laugh at me," she said. "And don't even try to kiss me. I need something to drink." He stood up. "Yes," she added. "You can get it for me, please."

He left, the door sliding to behind him. For an instant his presence still seemed to be with her, and then that feeling dispelled.

"Hoy," she said again, but with more emphasis, and she lay back down. Above her on the bunk, the intercom buzzed and she reached up to flip it on. "You're through."

"Lily?" A woman's voice, tight and controlled. "Get up to the bridge. Fast. *Your* pilot—"

"I'm coming." Lily dressed and left the cabin before Hawk returned.

The corridor of the *Easy Virtue* stretched out in dimness before her: evidently Captain Bolyai had chosen to spare as much power as possible. Lily padded double-time to the elevator that gave access to the bridge. She punched an unlit button with one finger and felt the lift shudder and rise beneath her feet. Its low hum sighed to a halt and the door shunted aside to reveal the glare of the bridge.

"—and I don't care if your tupping grandmother was a saint of the Lotus Way, Tobias, you heard the radio traffic—there's a general alert on in this system and we haven't got the clearances to get past a close check. So sit down at your damned station."

Jenny Seria stood gripping the tunic of a nondescript man whose chief feature was a grimace of pure hatred directed at the wild tattoos covering the pilot Pinto's face and bare arms. Jenny herself bore a look of disgust tempered by the exasperated glance she cast over her shoulder at Lily's entrance.

"And I told you," hissed Tobias, "that I won't ship with any cursed tattoo." As he spoke, Lily noticed that his left eye was beginning to swell, mottled with a deep bruise, and that Captain Bolyai, bearing a harassed look and worried frown at the same time, had a tight but tenuous grip on Pinto's right arm. "I'll rot along with the cursed ghost fleet and all the corpses on Gravewood before I'll touch the same board as that whore's get—"

Pinto broke free from Bolyai and lunged for Tobias.

Lily met Pinto halfway, bracing herself, and stopped him dead in his tracks. He began to fight against her, realized who she was, and froze into a posture stiff with fury.

"I'll kill him," Pinto muttered, but despite the rage in his voice he did not attempt to break past Lily.

Lily looked at Captain Bolyai. "Isn't there someone else who can man that station?"

Bolyai shook his head. His eyes examined Lily with the look usually reserved for a once-trusted pet who has brought something truly disgusting in off the streets. "Th'other just went off-shift. Tobias hadn't been up before—"

"Cursed right I hadn't," began Tobias. "And if you think I'd've stayed on this boat knowing you let such filth aboard—"

Pinto jerked forward, caught in Lily's grasp, but Tobias responded to the movement by flinging himself gleefully toward Pinto. Only to be thrown hard to the ground by Jenny. The mercenary knelt over him and twisted his arm up behind his back until he cried out in pain.

"Captain!" This from the man at comm. "Military scan. One cruiser, one cutter entering oct quadrant."

Bolyai flushed. "Put it through."

"—request that you identify yourselves. Repeat, this is *Heart of Lion*. We are in control of this system. We are impounding all vessels without Central clearance. Identify yourselves."

For a long space the only sound on the bridge was the crackle of static as *Heart of Lion* waited for a reply, mixed with Tobias's gasping breaths as Jenny let up on his arm.

"Tupping idiot," she muttered, jerking him up to his feet and shoving him into his chair.

Bolyai went from pale to mottled red as he recovered from the first shock. He took three swift steps to stand behind the navigator's chair. "Get us out of here." His voice shook.

There was a second moment of silence as all attention focused on the nav chair's occupant. Maned with a glistening crest, the seated sta shook her head and hissed inaudible words to herself as her six-fingered hands tapped calculations into ship's computer. She sighed, like water flowing downhill.

"The last fix I received from the station here leads into a narrow vector. At our present course, our shift would narrow both our velocity window and our angle—no room for error. None."

The comm came to life again. "This is the *Heart of Lion*. We are under orders to fire on all hostile vessels. We repeat: identify yourselves."

Pinto tugged at Lily's arm, and she released him. He too went to stand by the nav bank, studying the three-dimensional chart that came up on the screen.

"I can do it," he said.

The sta glanced up at him, scale-rimmed eyes blinking once, slowly, before she turned her gaze to Bolyai.

He had by this time broken out in a sweat. "I'll lose my ship," he whispered.

"I can do it," Pinto repeated.

"You're not going to let that whore of a tattoo put his filthy hands on—" Tobias's words cut off as Jenny tightened her grip on him.

"Shut up." She looked at Lily. "He got us this far, after all."

Bolyai looked at Lily.

Lily nodded. "Trust him."

"Go," murmured Bolyai, as if by speaking softly he could negate the responsibility for the command.

"This is the *Heart of Lion*. We will fire if you do not—"

"And turn that tupping noise off," shouted Bolyai, gaining strength of purpose in anger.

The sta had already entered the coordinates and began to read out the numbers.

"I won't—" began Tobias.

"You will," said Jenny.

He hesitated, and she drew a pistol, laser light red, from her belt. He began to transfer coordinates through engineering.

For perhaps ten seconds all proceeded in silence. Then the sta's crest raised slightly, and she hissed out a long, nervous breath.

"Velocity out of phase," she said, almost singing in fluid nervousness. "I need a correction. Immediately. I need seven point seven eight degrees at three forty-seven, current vector."

Pinto slipped into the pilot's chair, twisting the stillstrap around his body. "Call them in." He adjusted the viewers to his eyes.

"Vector clearance," began the sta. "Window at one point five, neg three point eight, forty-two."

"That's tight," muttered the comm man.

"We're all dead," cursed Tobias in an undertone meant to carry across the bridge.

"Homing to six ought fifty-seven degrees. Three twenty-two bits."

"Shifting vector," said Pinto. The minute movements of his hands could not be seen under the stillstrap.

The sta read off her numbers, calculating as the ship shifted placement. "Six ought sixty-seven. Six ought eight five. Seven ought one. Seven ought four. Reverse." Tension invaded her fluid voice. "Cancel seven ought seven point eight. Add seven ought eight point one at three forty-eight bits."

"Check," said Pinto.

Bolyai's hands trembled as he gripped the back of the navigator's chair. Tobias cursed fluently.

"Oh, tup yourself, Tobias," said Jenny genially. "They say if you vector wrong you end up in Paradise. What are you worried about? It's the only way you'll ever get there."

"Captain!" The comm man gasped. "Cruiser is banking for fire."

"Seven ought six. Seven ought seven point eight. Three forty-six bits. Three forty-seven. Three forty-seven."

"I've got surges," swore the man at comm. "They've fired. We'll never make it."

"Three forty-seven. Closing imperative. Seven ought eight point one. Three forty-eight. Break."

"We will," breathed Lily.

They went through.

Behind, the hunter trailed her by scent, inexorable, nearing. However far she fled, however faint her trail grew, it would pursue, until at last she would turn to see its face.

And came out.

"Perfect," hissed the sta.

Lily turned. The lift door slid open to reveal Kyosti. He stared directly at her, almost as if he had been watching her even through the metal of the door. She shuddered, shaking off the vision, but as it faded she remembered with greater clarity their last trip on the *Easy Virtue*, when he had moved across a cabin inside a window.

An impossible act, and in time she had let herself believe she had imagined it. Except that now—surely he had been in the mess, or in their cabin. Could he possibly move so far in a space that lasted no more than an instant for everyone else? What if he had reached her before they had come out of the window?

He did not move out of the lift.

"I have Jungfrau beacon," said the man at comm. "Holy Void. That's the tightest vector I've ever shipped. We skipped Joch system completely." He turned disbelieving eyes on the sta navigator. "Did you know this window would skip us so far?"

The sta merely unfurled her crest so that it glittered, bronze, in the glare of the lights. "Yes," she breathed, sibilant. "I saw the Ridani's touch on the first vector we rode through. It was our only chance, but I believed." She rose, uncurling her great height, and flattened her crest as she faced Pinto. "You are a master." The gesture embodied formal respect.

Pinto unstrapped and laid a delicate hand on the softly humming board. "Thank you," he murmured.

Tobias flung himself out of his chair and shouldered past Kyosti, who was in his turn forced to step out onto the bridge as Tobias commandeered the lift and vanished from sight.

Captain Bolyai sat down in the vacant chair. He had gone pale again, and his hands were slick with perspiration. "I've never had to run before," he whispered. His breathing came ragged. "Not like that. Circumspection is all one needs." He swiveled to glare at Jenny. "I want you all off my ship. I *said* no troublemaking on this boat, and I meant it. No attracting attention. *All* of you off."

Lily glanced at Jenny, but the mercenary had fallen silent, quiet, as if only by not speaking could she keep her anger in check. "This system is no more than a beacon," Lily countered, meeting Bolyai's gaze. "With a rotating crew. They don't even have life support for so many."

Bolyai dropped his eyes to examine the boards. Pinto was smiling, a look of mocking cynicism. The sta sighed and sat back down at her station, beginning calculations anew.

"I'll drop you," began Bolyai in a low voice. "Name your system. You deserve that much at least, getting us out of Arcadia system. But all of you have to go. I won't have trouble on the *Virtue*."

"All right," agreed Lily. Bolyai let out a held breath, as if her acquiescence came as a surprise to him. "Harsh."

"I beg your pardon?"

"We want to go to Harsh."

He turned several new shades of pale. "Void, woman, that planet is a prison."

"I know."

"There are several fine Stations where a fugitive can find employment, safety, money—"

"Harsh," she repeated.

He sighed, but he did not protest further. "Very well. Harsh it is." He motioned to the sta. "Start running a route. As *short* as possible."

The sta's fingers raced over the keypad, setting a course.

"Harsh? Have you lost your tanks, Lily-hae?" Jenny sat down on the bunk in Lily's cabin, where they had retreated from Bolyai's resentment and anger.

"I'm sorry." Lily stood by the door, her attention on Jenny, but her glance resting at intervals on Kyosti, who reclined on what little floor space was left. Above, on the top bunk, the sphere that was Bach drifted a finger's breadth above the mattress. "I'm sorry," Lily repeated. "I never meant to get you and Lia and Gregori thrown off."

Jenny shrugged. "Bolyai's a coward. I'm amazed he let a

tattoo pilot the *Virtue*, but we were in such a rush to get out of Central—and no one on first shift had Tobias's idiotic objections—that he had to use what he had. Now that the shock's worn off, he'll take it out on whoever's easiest to blame. When our last pilot tried to fly on ambergloss and almost ran us into the next life, he tossed off our second engineer with her, since they were bunkmates. He looks for someone else to blame for his own nerves. We'll be all right."

"Come with us," Lily offered.

"To Harsh? Into the hands of Central's troops, who would gladly arrest us, lock Gregori and I away in the mines, and send Lia back to her family? I think not."

Bach, Lily whistled. Bach rose, lights flashing, and drifted down to hover beside his mistress. *Plug into the screen.*

Jenny raised her eyebrows, puzzled, but said nothing.

Bach began to sing in fine four-part counterpoint. Figures came up on screen and shifted to new figures as he paged through his memory.

"Master Heredes is dead, Jenny." Lily's voice came out flat, suppressing her grief. "Murdered, by Central. That's why we're going to join Jehane."

"Jehane! I never took you for a revolutionary."

Lily hesitated. "I'm not sure I am one. But Central will pay, Jenny. They're the ones who murdered Heredes. And my friend Robbie—you might know him as Pero—made me understand that Central is corrupt. They won't give up their power voluntarily. I think Jehane's revolution is the best chance, maybe the only one, that Reft space has to have a fair government."

Kyosti, unmoving on the floor, regarded Lily with no obvious expression.

"I can accept that." Jenny ran a finger over the tight nap of her hair. "But why Harsh?"

"Because according to information Heredes sent to me—to Robbie, really—" Lily shook her head. "It's a long story. But Jehane is moving on Harsh. I fully expect that when we reach there, Jehane's troops will be in control."

"Why would Jehane want Harsh? One blazing inferno of a moon orbiting a methane hell of a planet, producing ore and fuel and tell-chips with what amounts to slave labor working under killing conditions. Or at least that's what you hear over the nets."

"What do you think he wants? He wants those prisoners. They have every reason to hate Central. They'll join Jehane without a second glance."

"Fine army," muttered Jenny. "I'll remember not to turn my back on any of them."

"Does that mean you'll come with us?"

Jenny laughed. "I'm no revolutionary. But why do you want me, Lily-hae? Aliasing and Gregori are more burden than asset, much as I love them."

"There must be something Lia can do."

Jenny considered this seriously. "She can cook."

"There you are. Two reasons, Jenny. First, I have a debt to pay—a girl who got indentured to Harsh because of me. I intend to find her. And second, I'll join Jehane. You know that I met him once. It's not so much that I didn't trust him, but that he—scared me."

"*Scared* you?"

Lily could only shake her head. "I'm not sure what I mean. Maybe I don't trust my own reaction to him. He's very—powerful. In any case, when I join him, I want some negotiating power to set my own assignment. And the more people I have with me who have skills he can use, the more leverage I'll have. You're a mercenary—and trained as an Immortal, no less. Pinto's a pilot—and one of the best, tattoo or not. Kyosti's a doctor. Lia can cook. And Bach—"

Bach sang three notes and a three-dimensional star grid, interlocked by a complex interweaving of lines, came up on the screen.

"The most recent information out of Central's military intelligence computers. Jehane's movements. Interpreted by Heredes and by Bach, they suggest that he is moving to take Harsh. And I have barely scratched the surface of what Bach has accessed from Central's computer-net. I have Bach, Jenny. Therefore, Jehane wants me. That's what I'll negotiate with."

Kyosti's eyes had not wavered from Lily's face. His lips arced into the barest of smiles.

Jenny grinned and stood up. She examined Kyosti a moment, taking in the studied nonchalance of his posture that revealed instead the complete focus of his attention. Lily waited, expectant, but not tense with it—in control, rather, as if the precise situation of her body illuminated the relationship between these three people and one robot in the room.

"Lily-hae Ransome." Jenny shook her head, started again. "You've changed."

"It's Heredes now. Lilyaka Ash Heredes."

"That must be it." Jenny gave her a mock salute. "I'll go pack our bags."

As the door closed behind the mercenary, Bach began to sing

> *Schaut hin, dort liegt im finstern Stall,*
> *Des Herrschaft gehet überall!*
> *Da Speise vormals sucht ein Rind,*
> *Da ruhet itzt der Jungfrau'n Kind.*
>
> *Behold here: there in a dark stable lies*
> *the One who has dominion over all.*
> *Where, before, an ox sought food,*
> *there now rests the Virgin's Child.*

2 Old Friends

****

They swung into orbit far from the regularly trafficked routes into Harsh Station. An eerie silence had deadened the usual communications channels: what scraps of talk the *Virtue* caught on comm bore the stamp of patchworked equipment and illicit, brief messages planetside leaking out through Harsh's killing atmosphere. Other vessels littered the in-system lanes, but whether they were silent by choice, or through destruction, it proved impossible to tell, their orbits being in any case too distant for visual scanning.

The *Virtue* drifted at low power for an entire revolution of the planet, a ghost on the fringe of Station's net, and listened. At last Captain Bolyai gathered up his courage, egged on by his rapidly deteriorating nerves, and decided to shuttle Lily and her people down to the surface and leave them there.

It was a quiet group that boarded the small shuttle. Jenny came first, in full rig, weapons strapped about her and a pack on her back that contained everything she possessed. She held with one hand the small hand of her son, Gregori, who carried a small replica of her pack; behind them followed the slight figure of Aliasing, Jenny's companion, lover, and fellow fugitive. Lia wore clothing a little too rich for the *Virtue*'s faded hull, and carried not a backpack, but a finely brocaded bag of some organic fiber, an obvious relic of wealth in a past existence. Her dark hair framed her piquant face as mists frame a waterfall.

Pinto already sat at the controls of the shuttle, speaking in a low voice to the bridge several decks away. The geometric pattern of tattoos that covered his face shifted color as the lock light blinked on and off with each entry. He turned at the sound of Aliasing's soft voice, and her gaze caught his, and they both smiled: an expression that illuminated each face in turn, for a moment seeming to brighten the dim interior of the shuttle.

After Aliasing, Kyosti entered, then Bach, and last, sealing the hatch, came Lily. She went forward to sit beside Pinto, flipping on the comm-station as the engines began to rumble to life beneath them.

"Jenny," she said over her shoulder, "which is the broadband link?"

"Two interlinked circles—"

"Oh, I see. And the focused beam is the arrow, and I can patch to incoming with the—yes, I see."

"What's going to happen to the shuttle once we're down?" asked Aliasing.

Jenny shook her head. "Bolyai is cutting his losses and running as soon as we detach."

"But—" Aliasing began to speak, lost impulse to a quaver in her voice, and began again. "But what if the planet's abandoned?"

"We know it isn't abandoned," said Lily. "We've got some radio traffic—but Station is down. I don't know what's going on down there, or at Harsh Station, for that matter. We'll have to play it as it goes."

This silenced Aliasing. Kyosti finished stowing their packs and containers and belted himself in at the back.

"Detach sequence." Pinto's voice was cool, but his hands trembled slightly at the controls.

The shuttle gave a roll, yawed to one side, and then they hit free weight for the drift away from the *Virtue*. Its colorless bulk receded in the single viewport, and Pinto brought the engines to thrust and pointed the ship into its descent.

The ride through the upper atmosphere was rough. Lily monitored radio traffic, but kept broadcast silence. Abruptly they hit calm like a sheet of stillness and banked into a smoother descent. Pinto kept up a quiet murmur of altitude checks and Lily began to attempt to get a fix on Harsh Main Block, the center of Harsh's tight mesh of surveillance and prison administration.

Through static and the whirring noise of the shuttle's venting fans voices filtered, scraps of communications passing along the planet's surface.

"—sealed tunnel thirty-six from further incursions, but left five cells without—"

"—regroup to point Alpha. Their resistance may prove too difficult to—"

"We have complete control of Portmaster's functions. I repeat. Portmaster's is now under Jehanist control. Supply and transport ships may now commence landing sequence. Acknowledge."

Lily toggled the "static" switch. At the back of her mind nagged some reference, forgotten but familiar.

"Accepted. This is Vanov, on the *Boukephalos*. We will be sending an initial track of two supply boats and three transports to land at point two rev intervals. Acknowledge."

"Accepted. Block is not equipped to deal with landings at higher than point four frequency. Acknowledge."

"Accepted. Will alter the schedule. First boat in close orbit. Will enter Block instrument range in point three."

"Accepted. And out."

"Finch." Lily sat frozen in astonishment, static crackling from the speaker at her fingertips, as the voice of the Main Block's comm suddenly fell into place in her memory. "Finch!"

Pinto glanced at her, curious, but returned his attention to the controls.

"Who's Finch?" asked Jenny, alert to the tone in Lily's voice.

"How the Void did he get here?" Lily asked of no one.

In the back of the shuttle, Kyosti had been resting, eyes closed, relaxed, but now his posture changed abruptly. He sat up, not stiff, but poised on some brink, and opened his eyes to examine with tight intensity Lily's profile as she reached for a new control on her banks. She opened her stations for broadcast.

"Lily," began Jenny, "are you sure—"

"Main Block. Main Block, acknowledge."

"This is Main Block. Identify yourself. All unidentified

ships will be considered hostile. We are under Jehanish authority. Acknowledge."

"Finch."

"Who is—Lily!"

"How did you—"

"How did you—"

There was a slight delay as their signals bounced and returned off each other, and a second as they each waited for the other to speak. At last Lily spoke.

"Where can we land?"

A pause.

"Field Blue. There'll be tight security measures. Troops. But I'll meet you, Lily. I'll leave now. And out."

A different voice guided Pinto down to the flat plain where a series of low domes rose like slowly emerging boils from the ground. He landed the shuttle smoothly on a strip lined by blue lights and taxied in to the nearby blue-lit dome. Around them, the air sat free of wind but permeated by a constant downward sifting of some heavy white element, drifting constantly to meld into the sandy surface of the planet. The shuttle's wheels barely stirred this dust, but its falling made a soft drumming noise on the metal above them.

The sound of the lock change rang through the hull, and then Pinto rolled back the layer of protective sheeting and they could see the huge cargo hold they now entered.

The harsh gleam of fluorescent tubing cast unpleasant shadows onto the cluster of white-uniformed troops that had assembled by the loading dock. All of them had guns out.

Pinto coasted into the berth and turned to Lily. "Should I open the hatch?"

"Yes." She unstrapped herself. "I'll go out first. Find Finch, and explain."

"Who are they?" asked Aliasing as Lily passed her.

"Jehane's people. Bach, see if you can get any fix from communications on where Jehane himself might be. But do it surreptitiously."

Bach whistled his assent. Aliasing settled back into her chair, looking more thoughtful than apprehensive.

As Lily waited at the lock, Kyosti rose decisively to stand directly behind her. Jenny, alert as any trained mercenary must be, unbelted quickly and followed him out through the lock, loosening a strap on one of her guns as she went.

Lily descended the hatch stairs as the doors slowly lowered before her. With a sense almost of disorientation, she saw Finch standing, out alone in front of Jehane's troops, in what might have been the same posture that she had last seen him in, watching as she left Unruli.

The hatch rang on metal as it hit the floor of the hold, and she and Finch started forward together. He now had a slight grin on his face, bemusement mixed with real happiness, but tempered by some sorrow behind it all.

"Lily!" He put out his hands as he neared her. Without thinking she stretched hers out as well, so that their hands were closing, almost touching now—

She did not reach him.

The attack took her so completely by surprise, with half her attention on Finch and the other half, wary by experience, on the white-uniformed soldiers, that Kyosti was already on top of Finch, choking him with the kind of quiet conviction that is most dangerous, before Lily registered the fact that he had broken past her and thrown himself on her old friend.

For an instant, the only sounds were of Finch's struggling, growing weaker. Kyosti said not a word.

The soldiers had frozen in much the same disbelief as Lily had, their mirror opposite. Kyosti's hands, long fingered and very pale, fitted neatly about the dark turn of Finch's neck. Finch's black hair was longer than it had been; its black ends brushed Kyosti's taut wrists.

Lily's knees gave out, and she threw herself forward. There was a hissing bolt. She sensed in her peripheral vision that Jenny had stepped to one side and shot.

Kyosti shuddered, stiffened, and fell on top of Finch.

The soldiers broke forward in a wave.

Eyes wide with panic, Finch threw Kyosti's body off him and scrambled gasping away to one side. As Lily rushed up to him, he leapt up to his feet and jerked away from her, leaving her caught in between the two men.

She stopped, and turned abruptly around to kneel by Kyosti. White uniforms surrounded them, guns trained on them, and Jenny was shoved through the crowd to stand with arms raised high, away from her weapons, beside Lily's kneeling form.

"Just remember," said Jenny laconically. "I'm the one who shot him. Just stun, Lily-hae."

Lily put her hand on Kyosti's neck and felt his pulse, then rose slowly, hearing the question implicit in Jenny's tone. A few of the soldiers had lowered their guns, relaxing. Lily quickly picked out the officer.

"Let me speak with you and Finch," she said.

The officer did not take his eyes off of Kyosti's prostrate form. "He'll have to go in custody. What is he? A maniac?"

Behind, Lily could hear Finch's gasping chokes as he fought to regain his breathing. "I don't know," she replied, suddenly cold with a memory of Kyosti breaking a chair that no one of human strength should have been able to break. "But I do ask that you leave Jenny"—she nodded toward the dark mercenary—"with him."

"Agreed. Who else do you have in the shuttle?"

"Three more people and a 'bot. We're here to join Jehane."

"Right." The officer examined her skeptically and motioned to his soldiers. "Alsayid's ten take control of the ship—full custody of the vessel and contents and crew until I personally give other orders. Inonu, your ten to escort these two to a holding cell. Strict security. You four accompany me, and the rest—stay with Alsayid." With his pistol, he waved Lily forward. "We'll go to the command center, you and I and comrade Caenna."

Lily turned to see Finch's gaze fixed on her with mournful accusation. He rubbed his throat with his left hand.

"You'll understand that I take an escort with us," added the officer.

"Yes," agreed Lily. "I understand." She studied Kyosti a moment more, glanced at Jenny, at the shuttle, and then followed the officer. Finch, walking alongside, kept two soldiers between him and her the entire way to the command center.

3 Walls

****

Comrade Officer Yehoshua was a stocky man with old, white, finger-length scars on his arms that Lily recognized as the legacy of years of cable stripping on asteroid mines. Against the dusky bronze of his complexion, the lines showed doubly strong. His face had an unexpectedly lean cast, punctuated by his shrewd scrutiny of her as they settled into seats in a small room behind com-central. He had left his pistol outside, after she had been thoroughly searched.

Finch sat beside him, still shaking. Lily slumped back in her hard chair with a sigh. Yehoshua pointedly said nothing. Through the closed door, Lily could hear the desultory conversation of their four escorts. Farther, a low hum of machinery shut on and off at intervals.

"Who is that man?" Finch stood up, as if startled by his own outburst. He glared at Lily. "Who is he?"

Lily stood also and put out her hands. "Finch."

"Stay away from me." Finch retreated behind Yehoshua, who did not shift except to keep his gaze leveled on Lily's face.

"I didn't know it would happen," she pleaded. "I swear to you, Finch. I didn't know. It took me as much by surprise— Hoy. Do you think I'd have let him out of the shuttle if I'd known?"

He shook his head, infinitesimally. "Then who is he? Why did he try to kill me?"

She sat down, covering her eyes with one hand. "I don't know. I don't know who he is." Removed her hand to look at Yehoshua, who regarded her without expression. "That's not what I mean. I know who he is. Void help me, Finch, I don't know why he did it."

She halted, brought to two realizations at once. "Hoy," she said in an undertone. "That can't be. But he said—" Her gaze had drifted to the wall, but abruptly she sat up straight and looked first at Finch, then at Yehoshua.

Finch watched her warily, but with hope. Yehoshua examined her with the intent gaze of a well-trained and acute observer. She kept her expression passive as she considered Kyosti's behavior: she knew quite well that she had never mentioned Finch by name to him—and yet she knew with equal conviction that Kyosti had tried to murder Finch now because Finch had once been her lover.

Yehoshua still did not speak.

"All right," she said decisively, returning her gaze to Finch. "He's my lover, Finch. I just never realized how jealous he is. It won't happen again." I hope, her thoughts amended.

Finch blanched. "*He's* your lover. Hoy, Lily. It's easy for you to say it won't happen again. And where have you been all this time?"

"Yes, comrade," said Yehoshua quietly. "Where *have* you been? And why do you want to join Jehane?"

Lily smiled, shifting her hands to her lap to give herself a more demure, less threatening posture. "I haven't made a very auspicious beginning, have I?" she asked. The barest smile touched the line of Yehoshua's lips. As she expected, he did not reply. She returned her gaze to Finch. "But I don't understand why *you're* here, Finch. When I left Unruli . . ." she trailed off.

"Blame Central for that." His expression twisted into one akin to hatred: the Finch she had known, easygoing almost beyond belief, seemed lost in that face, as if a stranger now stood before her. "They arrested us—for helping the booters. Came down hard all across Unruli. I don't know why. Dad they let go, since he never was in on any of our system. But Mom and Grand'mam and Swann and I they shipped here— without a hearing, with nothing! An Grand'mam was sick."

His voice cracked. "She's dead, Lily. They stuck her in the twenties dig with a bunch of filthy tattoos. They knew the dig was unsafe, unstable, but they had a rich lode in the twenty-eight tunnel, so they sent tattoos, and anyone else they considered worth as little as *that*, down there. And it blew. They hit a pocket of explosive gas. The whole twenties dig had to be shut down. Almost three hundred people were killed."

"And some two thousand Ridanis as well, I believe," added Yehoshua as if in afterthought.

Finch shrugged. "If you count tattoos, I guess. But Grand'mam was down there. They never even got the bodies out." His lips twisted down with bitter anger. "They didn't want to risk any of their personnel down there. They could at least have sent some tattoos to check the—"

Yehoshua lifted a hand, a deceptively casual gesture that cut Finch off. "Comrade, I understand your grief. But it is not you who are being questioned."

"We know each other," said Lily quietly. "We grew up together. What about Swann and your mother, Finch?"

He glanced at Yehoshua, sat down, like a sigh. "Mom's in hospital. She got shot in the first fighting, but she'll live. Swann's still out in the thirties dig—the last of the old guard sealed it off and now they're waiting it out, hoping to hold off until reinforcements come. But I don't think any message has gone out, so it's just a matter of time." He grimaced. "All we know is that casualties in the thirties, prisoner and guard alike, have been high. They destroyed the access trains and tubes, just outside the peripheral living blocks. No one knows who's left."

Yehoshua frowned. "I think that is enough, comrade Caenna." He reached into his jacket and removed Lily's com-clip from a pocket and inserted the clip into a viewer on the stand to his right. "Lilyaka Ash Heredes. That *is* your name?"

Because he was looking at Lily, he missed Finch's reaction: a slight start, subsiding quickly into a neutral mask.

Lily, seeing this, merely shrugged. "Yes."

"You are registered here as an instructor at the Abagail Street Academy on Arcadia. Is that also correct?"

"I did work there, but I resigned. I worked for Pero the last months I spent on Arcadia. He's why I had to leave. Martial law was declared by Central, and they executed a man they claimed was Pero but who was not. Pero is still alive. This news I *know* is not yet known to Jehane, because only a military cruiser traveling the direct route here could have gotten here faster than we did." And they would not have had Pinto piloting, she added to herself.

"I've heard of Pero," said Yehoshua slowly. "Comrade Jehane broadcasts his speeches to the troops." He frowned. The white scars on his arms were mirrored by a few on his cheeks and at the corners of his eyes, like wrinkles, or echoes of the silver sprinkling his black hair. "Where is your ship?"

"Not *our* ship. She left. We just got passage off Arcadia because they needed a pilot so badly. They're a booter, and they dumped us here—gave up a shuttle. We've nowhere to retreat now, whatever happens." She shrugged, as if this situation was of no concern to her.

"We."

"Five adults, one child, one 'bot. My people have skills and information that will be quite valuable to Jehane. I assure you."

"*Your* people." Yehoshua's emphasis was careful.

Lily paused, thought back over the impetus that had brought them here. "Well, yes," she answered slowly, considering. "I suppose they are mine in a way. I'm responsible for them being here now."

"And why *here*, comrade Heredes? Why Harsh?"

A certain tone in his voice alerted her, and she chose her words carefully. "Two reasons. I have unfinished business on Harsh: a friend who was unlawfully imprisoned here—not you, Finch, because I didn't know—I didn't know, but if I had—" She shook her head, met his gaze fiercely, and had the satisfaction of seeing his face clear, trusting her again, as if the episode with Kyosti had, almost, never happened. "I came here to free her."

"And the other reason?" Yehoshua was still punching buttons on the terminal, scrolling out whatever information remained on her clip. She knew how little was there, fed in by Master Heredes as a screen to her real identity, and his.

"Because I knew Jehane would be here."

"You *knew*!" For the first time, Yehoshua's careful layer of disinterest cracked, to reveal astonishment. "You can't have known—we didn't even know until we got here—" He broke off.

"You'd be surprised at what I know," said Lily, and she laughed at the absurdity of her comment. "No. What I mean to say, comrade, is that I have a great deal more information that Jehane would like to have—needs to have—but that information goes to him alone. Not through anyone else. My price for recruitment. Do you understand?"

"I understand that you're pretty damned sure of yourself." He shook his head. "You can't meet with Jehane. Impossible. In hostile territory only his personal lieutenants have access to him. But it may be possible for you to speak with my superior officer." He stood up and went to the door, spoke into a band at his wrist in a low voice that she could not hear.

"Lily." Finch left his chair to kneel beside her, putting a hand on hers where they rested in her lap, reassuring, needing reassurance. "What happened to Master Heredes?"

She shut her eyes and turned her face away, felt her throat constrict. Still, found it possible to speak, fueled by anger. "He's dead. He's the one Central murdered, calling him Pero. Why do you think I'm joining Jehane? For revenge."

His hand tightened on hers, and she knew at that moment that he shared her sentiments completely.

"Who is Master Heredes?"

Lily released Finch's hand abruptly. Her gaze jumped to Yehoshua, who still stood by the door but now watched her intently, having recovered his composure completely.

"My father," she said bitterly.

This time, having both Lily and Finch equally in his sight, Yehoshua saw Finch's expression of surprise before Finch could disguise it. For a moment he merely examined the two. Finch stood up, twisting his hands nervously in front of himself. Lily stared back impassively. Then Yehoshua turned and left the room, sealing the door shut behind himself.

Lily stood up and began to pace out the dimensions of the room while Finch turned, stationary, to follow her progress around the four blank, encircling walls.

"What do you mean, 'your father'?"

"Finch." Her pace did not slacken. "They are undoubtedly listening in."

He continued to stare as she walked. "You're different, Lily. You've changed."

Now she stopped. "You're the second person who's said

that to me. Here." She shoved a chair against the wall. "Let's do kata. Do you remember first kyu?"

"Kata? Are you crazy? Hoy, Lil, no wonder you've taken up with psychopathic murderers as your—"

"Finch. I don't know how long we'll have to wait here, but I don't intend to give them the pleasure of watching me get progressively more nervous. Kata."

He laughed suddenly. "Have you spent a lot of time in holding cells, or prisons, lately?"

"Why, yes," she replied, smiling with sweet irony. "I have. This one's about the same size as the others were."

Behind her, the door shunted aside. She whirled and dropped into a fighting stance.

Yehoshua, entering, halted and regarded her thoughtfully as she straightened up. "Let's hope you really are on our side." He motioned her outside. He now held his pistol in his left hand, and the four white-uniformed soldiers stood at careful intervals in the corridor outside. "We're to take you to Records. If you can find your—friend—we're to do whatever possible to, ah, reunite you with her." He paused.

"And then?" Lily prompted.

He still did not speak for a moment, like an actor waiting for the prime silence in which to deliver his line. "And then we arrange an audience for you with comrade Jehane."

She let out her breath, more relieved than she had realized. "That was easy," she said, more to herself than to him.

"Yes, it was," he replied, drily. "You seem to interest him. He seems to think that he's met you before. Under another name."

In the corridor, the four soldiers shifted, growing restless, and one hissed some complaint to her companion. Lily felt a shiver of fear run up her back, recalling Jehane—a man who appeared mild but hid behind that facade some secret, some intense power, driving his ambition, that she did not care to discover.

"He has a good memory," she murmured as she followed Yehoshua out. Finch, still looking confused, trailed behind them.

4　Oh Frabjous Day

****

It did not take Lily long to find the record of Paisley's arrest and indenture on Harsh, or her assignment berth: EntOps; tunnel 37; op sector 30–39.

"She's in the thirties," said Lily.

Finch, sitting behind her, gave the screen a cursory glance. "She must have some good status record, then. The thirties are the best and cleanest and safest run dig on Harsh. That's why the old guard retreated there. Swann's on communications in the thirties surface com-central, tagging incoming ore boats, same job I had here at the Main Block. Or at least, she was."

"Good status record." Lily scrolled to the next page of Paisley's entry, but the incarceration charges were listed as "priority" and not accessible to her at this console. "Right. What does 'EntOps' mean?"

Yehoshua answered. "Their division of entertainment. Your friend is lucky. In general, the 'EntOps' people get the best treatment—they're the leisure-time folks. The workers have to buy entrance to entertainment with good conduct and performance."

"What does entertainment consist of?"

"Vids. News. Singers and live theater and panto. Sports. Lectures and classes. At least that's how it worked out on the mining stations."

"You were incarcerated?"

He shook his head. "House miner. In Salah-eh-Din system. Twenty years."

"How did you end up with Jehane?"

He regarded her quizzically. "Like everyone else. I saw him speak. He's very persuasive. And he's right, about Central."

"Ah," said Lily, turning back to load the information on Paisley into her clip, which Yehoshua had returned to her. "So the access tubes to the thirties tunnels were blown— completely sealing them off?"

A nod from Yehoshua, echoed unconsciously by Finch.

"Well, I owe her, and I mean to get her out, if she's still alive. Are you planning an attack?"

"Classified, comrade. You should know better than that."

"Then let me take three of my people, and I'll go in and get her."

Yehoshua laughed. "You're a cool one. Which three? Or let me guess—the mercenary and the psychotic. Who's the third?"

"My 'bot. But you haven't met him yet, or you'd have more confidence."

"Lily!" Finch spoke as the screen flicked to black, erasing Paisley's file. "You can't go in. It would be suicide."

"How many guards, and how many prisoners?" Lily asked Yehoshua.

He laid a dark hand on the records console, brushing his fingers along the smooth, pale surface as he calculated. His eyes narrowed. "Come on," he said abruptly. "I'm going to take you to see Callioux."

"Here's what we're dealing with." Comrade Officer Callioux bent over a table whose lights and illuminated lines marked out in three dimensions a map of the complex on Harsh: mines and tunnels and living blocks. "We have Main Block virtually at center, with the numbered section blocks radiating out as spokes, but also linked at underground levels one, two, and three by access tube."

"Do these tubes include ore trains?" Lily asked, examining the grid with the eye of one experienced in mining operations.

"Yes." Callioux looked up and beckoned to a slim woman covered with the profusion of tattoos that marked a Ridani out from other humans; she was dressed in a poorly fitting white uniform. "Comrade Rainbow was a guard here, and she can explain the workings better than I can."

"Do you know ya mining, min Heredes?" Rainbow asked in a diffident voice.

Lily smiled slightly at the Ridani honorific. Beside her, Finch made a gesture of derision, but Lily ignored him. "Yes. I do." She pointed to a spoke illuminated by a dull red glow. "This is the section that failed?"

Rainbow had moved forward to stand beside Lily. She nodded. "Ya twenties dig. It be abandoned now. It were ya terrible, such destruction."

"You were here?" Lily eyed her, a woman of middle years whose slightness belied the gleam of strength in her eyes. "I didn't know Central commissioned Ridani soldiers."

"Only for ya work with ya Ridani prisoners. I were stationed in ya twenties surface dome, to search ya new Ridani prisoners as come in. Here. I watched as they pulled out all ya guards and ya govinment troops, and left ya prisoners to die. That be ya time I became ya Jehanist."

In the brief silence following this quiet remark, Lily studied the green-lit outline of the 30s dig, reaching far into the depths of the planet. Red blinking lights showed the areas where the retreating guards had blown the access tubes to cut themselves off from Jehane's attack.

"Then the only access to the thirties is by the surface dome," Lily said at last.

Callioux made a negative gesture. "With this atmosphere, we can't equip our people for a ground assault, and an air assault would be decimated by the dome's stationary cannons. And we can't blast through the tubes without alerting everyone, and probably destabilizing the zone and the artificial atmosphere."

"No," Lily agreed. "But you clearly have any number of shafts in the twenties dig"—she used a pointer of white light to identify several shafts from the deep levels in the 20s tunnels that reached into and almost overlapped with equivalent shafts from the deep 30s—"that a small group could use to pierce through into shafts in the thirties. Take them from behind."

There was another brief silence.

"But the twenties dig is unstable," Callioux protested at last.

Lily shook her head. "Look at these figures for stress placement and tunnel maintenance. They couldn't have gone down eight—no, nine—levels with that structure if the rock was unstable. Finch mentioned something about explosive gas—I'd bet it was an isolated pocket, or a series of pockets. That would ruin half the operations, or even poison the atmosphere. There must be more detailed data recording the relative strength of the different veins. And in any case, if instability was known to be present, they must have easer drills that can push through with a minimum of vibration. Hoy, those were standard at the House mines."

By the door into the cavernous operations room, Yehoshua laughed. He was lounging at his ease, eight white-clad soldiers standing at intervals around the room. "House miner," he said. "Wouldn't you know."

Lily turned with a grin. "Yes, and I hated every minute of it. Funny that it's serving me well now. Didn't you say you were, too?"

"Both my cousin Alsayid and me. Filistia House."

"Ah," said Lily, suddenly mindful of her supposed identity, and she turned back to face Callioux. "Comrade Yehoshua said that you are in charge of the force barricading the thirties dig." Callioux nodded. "Then I volunteer myself to break in. I think you know my goal."

"To liberate a friend. Yes. And I know that comrade Jehane is interested in you, Heredes. Unprecedented, such interest. Well." Callioux paused to consider.

"You know, Sura," continued Yehoshua from the door, "that we are under time constraints."

"I am well aware of that," replied Callioux without looking up. "Just as I am aware that we outgun what guards are left in the thirties dig if only we could get past their topside guns."

"I think it could be done," said Rainbow abruptly, "getting through by ya shafts into ya thirties." Her uninvited comment seemed brash, coming from a Ridani, despite her mild voice and the supposed emancipatory purpose of Jehane's revolution. "Ya main drill engineer were ya indentured Unrulian, and he be in ya hospital." She swiveled to meet Lily's interested gaze. "Can you handle ya easer drill?"

"I've done it. Not with any precision, though."

"Hold on." Callioux slapped the view table buttons so that all the lights vanished except for the red and green 20s and 30s. "Do you propose to go on this expedition alone, Heredes?"

"No. I'll take two companions, both of whom are trained fighters, and a 'bot. This would be a quick strike."

"And take what information you've gained from us in to the troops holding out in the thirties? I think not."

"I'll go," said Yehoshua abruptly. "I'm familiar with mines. And I'll ask for volunteers."

"I volunteer," said Rainbow quietly.

"Lily—" began Finch.

"Finch, remember, Swann's there somewhere."

He frowned and looked down.

"But I wouldn't suggest," added Yehoshua to Callioux, "that you let the man who assaulted comrade Caenna go."

"But you must," interrupted Lily. "I need him. You have no idea how much I need him in an operation of this kind. And it won't happen again." The large room, illuminated by a vague ceiling glow, dwarfed her figure, but even in such space, sterile and contained, her resolve showed clearly in the lines of her body. "You must let me speak to him. I doubt if any of your people can reason with him."

"And you can?" Yehoshua's voice was softly mocking, but he raised his dark eyes to Callioux, questioning.

"Time constrains us, comrade," answered Callioux to Yehoshua's unspoken question. "Jehane is already preparing to evacuate the planet and system, and he means to leave behind the prisoners in the thirties if he has to."

"But that's five thousand people," cried Finch. "You can't just abandon them."

"Ten thousand," murmured Yehoshua.

"I hardly think," replied Callioux drily, "that the government will kill them for the unfortunate accident of having been left behind. They need their work force, after all, and these mines are valuable to them, and justifiably unpopular with free workers. In any case, if a small force, at little risk to us, can break through, then it will be to our credit. And if it fails"—Callioux's shrug was eloquent—"we have lost a few noble comrades, martyrs to the cause of freedom, and this woman and her associates, who are of doubtful loyalty in any case. Therefore, I am minded to let comrade Heredes have her way. After all, how many of the prisoners whom we have liberated are convicted murderers? At least her companion did not succeed"—a glance here for Finch, who paled—"and was stopped, need I add, by another one of her people. Have you already formulated a plan, Heredes?"

"Is this right?" Lily looked at Rainbow. "We have one central elevator shaft, that runs to just beneath the main control center in the surface dome, and four auxiliary shafts in each of the four spokes. And the power plant is here, beside the control center."

"Sure," agreed Rainbow, mystified.

Lily turned to Callioux. "When the main power goes the first time, bring your assault unit in close to the dome. When it goes the second time—"

"Hold on." Callioux touched the tabletop, tracing a thin thread out from the 30s dig. "They've cut all links—we can't control their power plant from Main Block anymore."

"That's good," said Lily. "That will confuse them even more. When the power goes the second time, you assault the dome."

"Perhaps you'll be good enough to explain," replied Callioux facetiously, "where you'll be at that point."

Lily pointed to the circle that marked the 30s main control center in the surface dome. "Here."

Callioux chuckled. "I see. You don't lack nerve, I'll give you that. Very well. I'll give you one rev, Heredes. Comrade Yehoshua. A strike force and attendant troop ships will wait that long, in case you can break through to the surface. Otherwise we'll leave you."

Lily smiled. "Generous, in its own way."

"Quite generous." Callioux did not return the smile.

"But Lily—" Finch stood up, distressed.

She shook her head. "I'm sorry, Finch. I've got to go. Just don't worry."

"Then I'll come with you—"

"Finch." This gently. "You'd be a liability. I'm sorry."

He sank back into his chair, letting his hands cover the thick strands of his black hair. "I'm going to lose everyone," he murmured.

Lily knelt beside him and reached forward to kiss him. Thought better of it, suddenly, seeing Kyosti's dead, set expression as he had tried to throttle him, and patted him on the arm instead. The gesture seemed remarkably weak. "Finch, think about it this way. With people like Kyosti on our side, how can we lose?"

Finch did not look up, merely shuddered. The bruising that mottled his throat had begun to purple.

"This seems to me," said Callioux, switching the view table off completely, "like a great deal of fuss over what is frankly a rather small incident within the scope of what we have seen during the course of our revolution."

"You didn't see the attack." Yehoshua motioned to his soldiers to converge on the door. "It was—eerie. That's the only word I can think of. His expression was—not quite human."

"We've all seen inhumanity. I daresay we'll see more." Callioux's gesture toward the monitor above the door seemed impatient with human foibles. "Now. I have a meeting. I leave you in charge, Yehoshua. Heredes has tactical command of her own people. I send you along as observer, and to offer support if necessary, and to watch our backs. You have—Rainbow? How much time?"

"Eighteen hours," said Rainbow.

Lily met Jenny in a holding cell adjacent to, and looking into, the high security cell where Yehoshua's soldiers had incarcerated Kyosti. From her stand by the door she could see, through a translucent window, Kyosti lying on his back on the hard plastine bench that was the room's only obvious piece of furniture. He lay perfectly still, hands cupped under the disarray of his light hair, eyes shut. The only movement discernable was the slight rise and fall of his chest as he breathed.

"He looks like he's in a coma," said Lily.

Evidently some apprehension sounded in her voice, because Jenny smiled and rested a comforting hand on Lily's tense back. "I don't think so. When he came to after the stun blast wore off, he shook—trembled, like he had a palsy—for at least fifteen minutes. No one went in. I wasn't allowed to speak to him. Then he stopped, as if he had controlled it somehow, and he took one circuit around the room, hand on the wall as if"—she raised her eyebrows in surprise—"it just occurred to me now, as if he was using touch to gain information, and then he lay down. He's been like that ever since."

"Wonderful," said Lily, running a pale hand through her straight, black hair in a gesture made nervous by the expression of worry that marked her gaze as she watched Kyosti's prostrate form. "Damn," she muttered under her breath.

"He must have an incredible memory," Jenny said a little too casually, "to have linked you saying Finch's name over comm with your former lover. How did he know he had the right person?"

"He *can't* have known. He may have known I had two lovers before him—yes—" She considered, lowering her hand. He had known, but *she* had not told him; he had told her himself. She had never discovered how he had found out. "Well, he knew that much," she went on, not ready to divulge this information to Jenny. "But I *never* told him their names or anything about them."

"Are you sure?"

"Quite sure. I never figured it was any of his business." Jenny still regarded her skeptically. "Someday when we're not under surveillance, I have a long story to tell you."

"Sure, Lily-hae." Jenny laughed, glancing at the tall man in the other cell. "I don't doubt it."

"But." In the neutral glare of the cell's lights, reflecting off the grey sheen of wall, Lily's expression hardened. "Right now I've got a new assignment. I'm going to ask you to volunteer for a dangerous job, Jenny. You *must* refuse if you have too. I know you have dependents. I can use you, because of your experience, but not to their cost. Something can be arranged—"

"Lily." Jenny let one hand indicate the empty loops on her tight-fitting mercenary's suit that usually carried weapons—weapons now in the custody of Jehane's troops. "What am I? A mercenary. No matter who I hire out to, Lia and Gregori risk losing me. I've made what provisions I can, left them with some collateral, a plan of action to follow. And Lia's more canny than she seems—she just rarely lets it show." She touched the back of her left hand to her forehead, light palm against her dark skin. "Bolyai fired me. Now you're hiring. I'm yours."

"You could join Jehane. I can't even pay you, Jenny."

"But I trust you. I'm not working in big organizations

anymore, not after—my previous experience. Bureaucracy loses you, and you lose yourself. I'm hiring on with *you*."

Lily sighed, looking up at the short cap of tight curls that crowned Jenny's head, at the handsome face, creased both by equanimity and by hard times, at the breadth of her shoulders and the muscled length of her arms. "Well, I'm not going to let you go as easily as Bolyai did. You're too much of an asset."

Jenny grinned and offered her a mock salute.

Lily sighed again, exasperated. "And I haven't even told you what the job it. And it *is* dangerous."

Jenny shrugged, almost insouciant. "*Ensha-lat*, as we used to say on Unity. 'As it is willed.' You can't fight what is fated."

For a moment Lily regarded her, not quite affronted—disbelieving, perhaps. "*I* can," she said decisively.

Jenny grinned again. "That's what I like about you, Lily-hae."

"Go on." Lily slapped her on the shoulder. "The one named Yehoshua will return your weapons to you, and you'll have a few minutes at the shuttle to talk to Lia and Gregori. And bring Bach back with you. Now I need to see Hawk." Behind, the door to the corridor whisked open as if at Lily's command.

Jenny saluted, not mocking now, as she left the cell. "Luck to you," she said, and was gone.

Lily frowned, tapped in a sequence on the keypad beside the window, and braced herself to step into the next room.

She stopped on the smooth-surfaced floor and the door sighed shut behind her. There was a moment's dead silence. Kyosti did not move, did not even seem to register her presence in the room. His eyes remained shut.

"Hello, Lily," he said.

She almost jumped, the comment came so quietly and suddenly out of the silence, without even a movement from him to presage it. She glanced around at the featureless, grey interior. "I was told this cell is sound and sight proof."

Now he opened his eyes, to reveal their piercing blue, tempered with a hint of green in the depths; like spring foliage seen reflected in water. "It is." He sat up, a lithe, relaxed movement, and lowered his hands to pat the bench beside him invitingly.

Lily did not move. "Then how did you know it was me who

came in? You weren't looking. I never took my eyes off you.
And I didn't say anything."

For a long moment he did not reply, but she felt that he
was measuring some aspect of her, closely, carefully, and with
the greatest concentration, and that whatever conclusion
he reached based on that measurement would determine
the entire course of his behavior. For an instant she felt
he trembled on the edge of his control, and then abruptly he
relaxed, visibly—when she had not even known he was tense—
and he leaned back against the wall and smiled, lazy and
sensual.

"Come sit down beside me," he said, inviting.

That she was tempted to go and take what he was offering
her—even at a time like this—irritated her. "Kyosti, stop it."

He sat watching her expectantly, as if she were the one
who had to explain. He seemed utterly calm and reasonable,
so she allowed herself to lean back against the wall, hands
loose at her side, and just looked at him: the exotic
handsomeness that had first attracted her to him was not,
perhaps, so much the component parts of simple physical
beauty but rather 'a combination of unusual yet graceful
features underlaid with a blend of mystery and, she reflected
with bitter irony now, danger.

"Even if he is dead," said Kyosti suddenly, "what possible
reason could he have had to be executed as Pero?"

The vision of Finch choking under Kyosti's pale hands
stood in Lily's mind so strongly as Kyosti spoke that she could
not at first decipher the content of his question. She felt
momentarily as if she had wandered into the wrong conversation.

"Pero—you're talking about Heredes!" She shoved herself
away from the wall and strode over to stand directly in front
of him. "*I* want to talk about *Finch*. Do you remember
him—the man you just tried to murder?"

Her anger emanated like a force off of her, but his initial
response was only to reach up and enclose her hands in his
own, drawing them to his lips. He did not kiss them, merely
held them there, as if he were trying to breathe her in.

He sank forward, off the bench, and, kneeling, embraced
her. Just stayed there, head against her abdomen, face hidden by his hair. His seeming vulnerability drained out her
anger.

"He's not my lover anymore," said Lily, grasping for outrage. "That's long past. You've got nothing—*nothing*—to be jealous about."

"I know," he murmured, although he did not relax his grasp on her.

"Jehane's people have accepted my explanation. They'll let you go. But it won't happen again. Will it?"

"As long as I'm never in the same room with him."

"Kyosti!" She put her hands at either side of his face and tilted his head back so that she could see his expression. "I just promised you that he won't be my lover again. Do you understand? All other things aside, I don't desire him in that way anymore." And she leaned down to kiss him.

It proved a more potent gesture than she intended. Somehow, with pressing and touching and the smooth flow of long practice, she found herself lying on the bench next to him in an intimate embrace. Inappropriate, surely, for such a time, and yet she thought it might be better to reassure him. And he was so close, and so nice to hold.

He was the one who pulled away. His expression bore no rage, no jealous fury, just simple resignation. "It doesn't matter," he said quietly. Deep in his voice she heard the echo of an old, wrenching sorrow. "I have to kill him. Now that you know that, you can keep me away from him."

"*Why?*"

He broke away from her and pushed up off the bench to his feet, finding refuge in the corner opposite the bench. "*Don't ask me that.* I thought I had finally escaped. *Abai'is-ssa.*" The alien word slipped out of him too naturally. "I should have known better. You should have left me on Arcadia." He did not look at her as he spoke.

"Yes," she replied sardonically as she, too, stood up. "You said something like that before. But Finch is one of my oldest friends. Do you expect me to let it go at that? Who are you going to attack next? Me?"

Now he turned. His face was set, a mask of sheer impersonal threat, like a red warning light signaling the entrance to a danger zone that is off-limits to all personnel who do not have the complete envelopment of a life suit.

"*Never suggest that to me.*" He looked so revolted by the thought that she felt suddenly embarrassed, as if she had set out to deliberately offend him. "There may be people who are that sick, to kill their own lovers. I'm not one of them."

His anger completely deflated hers. It seemed impossible, facing him now, to force the issue. She took in a single, rather shaky breath to calm herself. Once they had left Harsh, there would be time.

"I'm not suggesting," she began slowly, leaping back to his first question, as if the ensuing conversation had not taken place, "that Heredes meant to be executed as Pero, but if he was caught, and knew that they would kill him—and infiltrating their entire defense network was clearly treason—I think he would convince them that he was Pero if only to leave a trail of confusion as his final legacy. After all, Pero is free to work openly again, for a while."

"I still don't see," replied Kyosti, taking up the thread of this conversation without any hesitation, "how Heredes *could* be caught."

"'You were caught . . .'"

"By the League, a government far in advance of Central in such techniques, I assure you."

"I thought the League and all its people had forsworn any contact with the kind of espionage you and Master Heredes used to be engaged in on their behalf."

Kyosti smiled bitterly. "Forsworn, yes. But not forgotten. That would be foolish indeed. 'Beware the Jabberwock, my son!' We're dangerous, unpredictable beasts."

"Oh, what does it matter?" she cried, lifting a hand to pull at her hair in helpless anger. "How they caught him or how he came to be identified as Pero. He's dead."

Kyosti came across to her in three swift strides. "Lily," he murmured, soothing, and he cradled her against him.

"We don't have time for this," she muttered into his shirt, although she did not pull away. "Do you remember someone I talked about named Paisley?"

He considered, nodded. "A Ridani girl. Indentured to— Harsh. I see. A victim of the terrible prejudice in this area." He shook his head. "Only in such a backward pioneer culture—"

"What's 'pioneer'?" She pulled back from him. "And you needn't use that patronizing tone of voice. I've never seen League space. I've got no proof you came from there, or that Master Heredes did, or sensei Jones. You might all be making it up."

He laughed. "My dear Lily, haven't I ever told you that you speak Anglais with the most delightful, primitive accent?"

She knew perfectly well that he, and Heredes, and sensei Jones, were incontrovertibly not citizens of Reft space, that they had indeed come from far away across the old lost paths to the home planets from which humans and pygmies had long ago migrated to Reft space. So she only removed herself from his grasp and walked to stand beside the thin seam of the cell door. "Sometimes I forget about *your* accent," she said. "Although," she added thoughtfully, "Master Heredes never had one."

"That's because he used to be an actor. Now what about Paisley?"

5   Blooded

****

Through her breathing helmet, Lily could hear the slow hiss of liquid burning through plastine. A forgotten toy, perhaps, left to fall on the tunnel floor in the panic after the first explosions. They had seen the results of that panic: on leaving the central shaft at the deepest tunnel in the 20s dig, level 9, they had found on the other side of the lock a cluster of at least one hundred bodies. Most had decayed badly, eaten through by the poisoned atmosphere, though some were still recognizable as Ridanis.

At the very front of the grisly remains lay the body of a woman clutching a small child, as if she had been more desperate than the rest, with such a burden, or the others had thrust her forward in the hope that the child at least could be saved. Now, watching the drip of some acidic fluid, released by the jostle of a passing boot out of a half-broken pipe, Lily wondered if the little doughnut-shaped object that was slowly disintegrating under the touch of that liquid had been dropped by the same child.

They had paused to consult the map. Yehoshua knelt beside a Ridani man who had worked in these diggings. Behind, his subordinate Inonu stood with her ten troopers, flanked by Yehoshua's cousin Alsayid and the Ridani trooper Rainbow.

Silence hung over them, heavy and enclosing. The micro-

phones on the helmets accentuated the low voices of Yehoshua
and the miner as they discussed their route, and the light
scraping of boot on rock, hands tapping guns, as Inonu's
soldiers shifted, restless underneath so much earth. The
floors and walls and ceiling of the tunnel, although broad and
high, showed rough-hewn and incomplete in the filtered
beams lancing out from their helmets.

Jenny stood in an open door, a gap in the tunnel wall,
turning her head back and forth slowly as she used her light
to sweep the room beyond. Her hand, encased in the same
slick material that made up their standard government guard
issue coveralls and much of their helmets, tightened on an
outthrust knob of rock as she counted bodies. Ahead, Kyosti
knelt alone in semidarkness. He had shut his helmet light off.

After a moment Jenny pushed away from the doorway and
returned to crouch by Lily. She leaned forward until her head
touched Lily's. "It's enough to make you join Jehane." Her
voice sounded muffled and tinny through the mike and the
thin remains of the poisoned atmosphere. "It just occurred to
me that if what we're wearing is standard issue, then none of
the prisoners had any protective gear at all."

"Stops them from escaping."

"Right. I wouldn't attempt the surface even in *this*, and
neither would you. But why would the guards wear this gear
in the mines if they thought it was completely safe? It was a
precaution against this kind of disaster." She made a gesture
of disgust; her gloved hand, brushing the wall, caused the
dripping pipe to stop leaking, leaving the discarded toy lying
pathetically in two melted halves. "Although what else I could
expect from Central I can't imagine. The sort of people they
would indenture to Harsh certainly weren't worth the price of
one of these suits."

"How many bodies did you count?" Lily asked.

"I stopped at fifty. Say, we didn't lose the 'bot, did we?"

"No, he went ahead to sound out the thickness and stabili-
ty of the rock separating the two digs. I just input the map
and sent him off." Lily used the butt of her rifle to jostle the
pipe so that it leaked again, dissolving the toy into a lump of
unrecognizable slag.

Jenny turned her head to watch Lily's movement and then
rose abruptly. "Hey!" Her shout carried at least as far as
Yehoshua, despite the dampening hush of the tunnel. "Hawk!

Are you crazy? There're chemicals in this air that'll eat right through your skin."

In the darkness of the tunnel ahead, Lily could scarcely see Kyosti's figure, enveloped in the murky fabric of the guard suit, until a flash of pale, bare hand alerted her to his position.

"Hawk!" Jenny repeated.

Lily felt a person push past her, grabbed, and found Yehoshua in her grasp.

"I'll take care of this," she said, sweeping past him. "Are you crazy?" she asked as she came up beside Kyosti.

He turned, his tall figure outlined against blackness by her helmet light. "Probably. Why do you ask?"

"Do you want to lose that hand? You heard what they said about the atmosphere down here. You saw the bodies. Or do you think you're immune?"

He did not reply immediately, but she could suddenly tell from his posture and his eyes behind the helmet that he was smiling. "Did you know," he said at last as he slowly slipped the long glove back on his hand, "that this tunnel is almost one hundred and seventy-five years old? It's no wonder they had trouble. They doubtless did not maintain it properly."

"Doubtless," she replied brusquely, not interested in humoring him. "I didn't have time for any research except what Callioux summed up for us before we left. Come on." She waved to Yehoshua, and he and the Ridani miner came forward to lead them on. It took her some minutes of careful walking over the uneven rock floor to realize that Kyosti hadn't had time, or opportunity, for research either.

The transition from the main level 9 tunnel to a side, working shaft, came as a shock to one accustomed to the smooth-bored shafts of the Ransome House mines, built to accommodate machines and free miners who could easily choose to move on to more agreeable working conditions.

They had to crawl single file on their hands and knees over sharp, uneven rock. Now and then, the shaft opened into a pocket where seven or eight might assemble, packed tightly together, for a break or to facilitate entrance into a new series of shafts, but in these pockets the sense of claustrophobic heaviness heightened, if anything. In Ransome House, there was not a shaft but you had height enough to stand, and width enough to walk three abreast; the Sar had always believed that a well-treated worker produced the best work—a philosophy he had drilled into his children. Lily could appreciate it now.

In at least half of the pockets they had to maneuver past corpses, and once Yehoshua, at the fore, had to push a decaying corpse bodily ahead of him until there was room to shove it to one side. Two of Inonu's ten disintegrated under this confinement, and were sent back to wait at the central elevator shaft. One man was sobbing softly to himself, but could not bring himself to backtrack that ground alone.

After several stalls, and one very long wait where—the ceiling pressing into her back, her elbows scraping against the walls—she had to recite kata in her head to keep calm, Lily emerged at last into what seemed an enormous room. As rough-hewn as the others, it could contain the entire party: Inonu and her eight remaining soldiers, Yehoshua, Alsayid, Rainbow, the Ridani miner, and herself, Jenny, and Kyosti. Close, but nevertheless all of them.

Crouched beside Yehoshua, Lily trained her light on the oversize com-screen the officer held and watched as the Ridani shifted the pointer until it showed their current location and the shaft they had chosen to lead them to the 30s.

"Here it be," he said, showing a shaft that trailed into a similar grid of shafts branching out from tunnel 39. "Close enough I reckon that ya easer should sure be put together here. Won't be another such broad'ning before ya drill shall come tae use."

Yehoshua nodded, and spoke into his wrist-com to Inonu, who crouched across the pocket from him. She immediately signaled to those of her people who had packed the components in, and within a reasonable space of time the drill was assembled. It was about the length of Lily's arm and as thick as her torso.

"Hold on," said Yehoshua. "What happened to the power pack? We can't use it like this."

"Don't worry," said Lily. "Come on. We're running short of time."

"Right." Even distorted by the mike, Yehoshua's reply was sarcastic. "Inonu, follow us at the specified distance, and remain *only* until oh-four-fifteen. Then return to the surface and leave. Understood?"

Inonu hesitated, but replied in the affirmative.

"I'll take it," said Lily to the Ridani miner, but he shook his head.

"So much," he explained, gesturing with the drill, "I can do for ya people trapped in ya thirties."

She shrugged and let him precede her into the shaft. They crawled in silence. She felt more and more keenly not the incalculable weight of kilometers of rock a hand's breadth above her back, because she had known that on Unruli; here it was the tiny space through which they moved that unsettled her. Fantasies of collapse, of bodies pinned by stone—all she could hear of the others behind her was their smothered breathing and, once, a curse of pain. A conviction that she was about to crawl into a corpse in the last stages of disintegration seized her with such terrifying force that she stopped moving.

A hand touched her ankle. A helmet brushed her hip. "'For thou art my rock and my fortress; therefore for thy name's sake lead me, and guide me,'" Kyosti said. His voice seemed peculiarly clear in their confinement.

Her breath shuddered out of her. Like an echo, ahead, three small lights blinked: blue, green, and orange. A moment later the miner blocked her view, but now she started forward again.

"Bach," she whispered. "Thank you." As she neared the end of the tunnel she could hear the robot singing:

> *Mond und Licht*
> *Ist vor Schmerzen untergangen*
>
> *Moon and light*
> *are quenched for sorrow*

The miner came to a confused halt, seeing this apparition, and Lily reached forward to grasp his shoulder. "That's your power source," she said. "Let me show you." She could not whistle in the helmet, so she called out, and Bach, complaining the whole time in a low undersong about the rough surfaces of the tiny shaft which threatened to scratch his exterior polish, floated up to them and allowed her to holster him to the easer drill.

"I'll be glad to get out of here," she said, her voice a little shaky. "The mines on Unruli weren't anything like this. My father would *never* have allowed it. Imagine if this place collapsed."

Kyosti had squeezed in beside her, a very tight fit, and he chuckled. "'And the height of the rock above the head of the workmen was a hundred cubits.'"

"Cubits?" Lily asked, but Bach began at the same time to sing as the Ridani miner thrust him forward to the end of the shaft.

"What is he saying?" asked Kyosti.

"Something about—waters of Gihon." Lily shrugged. "I can't hear him."

Then the miner settled into place, about ten meters in front of them, and began to drill.

Spitting sparks of light, a sudden rise in temperature, and pressure on her eardrums were the only signs that the drilling was in progress. If it made noise, it could not be heard above the muted sound of Bach's song.

"Someplace named David," said Lily. "Where's your rifle?"

Hawk patted a long shape tucked in between his knees, briefly touched the shock grenades on his belt, and let his hand come to rest on her waist, a gesture almost protective. At her back, she felt Jenny's movements as she checked out her weapons and loosened the straps that held them against her body. Farther back, Yehoshua spoke to his cousin, but his words were lost in the muffling air. Behind them, the faint beam of Rainbow's helmet light cast a luminescent glow on the same mineral vein cut along the shaft wall, and behind her—a wall of solid blackness.

They waited.

A slight shift in pressure in her inner ear.

"Here we go," said Lily, moving past Kyosti. "He's got equilibrium."

The miner did not stop working, but the pattern of his drilling changed. Lily passed through a recent pocket, almost filled now with the rubble of the current drilling, and inched forward into the new shaft, crawling almost on her belly. The miner paused as Lily came up behind him.

"I pierced through, min," he explained. Around him, the walls gleamed as if they were hot, but she could feel nothing through her coveralls. "We be coming in at ya angle, so I

mean to bear down ya circle here, so ya last dislodging shall
make ya least stirring."

"Good."

Bach winked blue lights at her, but no longer sang as the
miner went back to work. Sparks flew, cut off abruptly as a
cracking noise shuddered the air. Flipping a switch on the
drill, the Ridani eased away a meterwide circle of rock. Lily
was amazed at how thin it was—a sure sign of the precision of
Bach's sounding and the skill of the miner.

"Thank you," she said to him as she helped him unholster
Bach from the drill, and then she looked back at her five
companions, and crawled through into the 30s.

It was like coming into another world. For a moment she
hesitated, until she realized that they had come into a dig
supervised to standards more befitting a House mine. With a
roll and a push she slipped down the side of the sloping wall,
and stood up on mercifully smooth floor. If she raised her
hands she could touch the ceiling, but she could stand, and
Bach, floating out next to her, had ample room to drift beside
her as she crouched and peered, gun raised, in both directions.

The shaft was deserted, and silent. A small antenna rose
out of Bach, and after a moment of dense quiet he gave a
four-note whistle, *All clear, one hundred meters.*

She motioned to Kyosti, and the others clambered out of
the shaft behind her. She surveyed them briefly, and then set
out to the right, toward the main tunnel.

The shaft was empty, lit by an uninterrupted string of tube
lighting. Shafts branched out at irregular intervals, and three
times they had to climb long stretches of ladder seamed into
the rock face. At last, ahead, the intensity of the light
changed, and Lily knew they were nearing the shaft's opening into the main level 9 tunnel.

She put a hand back, stopping the five people behind her,
and then reached up to tap an acknowledgment of previous
commands into Bach's keypad. He winked lights, a quick
pattern, instead of replying in song, rose to the ceiling, and
went forward alone.

Yehoshua pushed quietly past Jenny and Kyosti and crouched
beside Lily. He waited for a while in silence. Shifted once,
then spoke in an undertone.

"You really think this is going to work?"

Beneath the concealing mask of her helmet, Lily smiled. "I

think so. He'll go up the elevator maintenance ladder just like we will, only faster. And once he gets to the power plant's main console, we're free. No one will expect Bach."

Yehoshua considered this in silence for a time before replying. "I've never seen a 'bot like that. And I wouldn't have believed it if I hadn't seen it. Where did you say you got it?"

She began to reply, heard voices, crouched and poised her rifle. The voices passed, evidently guards patrolling the main tunnel.

"How many prisoners can we expect will be down here?" she asked after a suitable interval.

Yehoshua shook his head. "I can't guess. Not many. This deep the only cells are for the recidivists: violent or political repeat offenders. My great-grandmother's brother spent time on Harsh."

"What for?"

"Triple murder. Died here, too. Story is he got in a vendetta and was taken out with one of those old vibration drills."

"Hoy." Lily shuddered. "That's terrible."

Yehoshua chuckled. "Yeah. Because we're Monists, we got the body back for proper burial. My old grand-pap once told me that there wasn't much left."

"Is this true?" Lily demanded suddenly. Yehoshua inclined his head, recognizing her question, but he retreated back to stand beside his cousin without answering her. Quiet descended on the little group.

They waited.

Lily felt one foot begin to numb, shifted it. Now and again she looked back to check Jenny and Kyosti, but they both remained still and absolutely quiet. Rainbow coughed once or twice, a low sound, and Yehoshua whispered something to Alsayid, followed by a muffled laugh from the cousin.

More time passed. Inevitably, her mind wandered from the task at hand. She thought of the dead Ridanis in the shaft they had just passed through. The Sar had never employed Ridanis, but she knew him well enough to know that he would not countenance a policy that condemned them to such a horrible death. She felt a sudden and unexpected urge to tell him what she was doing now. It was strange, thinking of Ransome House after having been away so long. Perhaps he would even approve of her new life—but the chance to explain was unlikely to present itself. With a sigh, she checked her wrist-com for the hour.

Then, without warning, without any transition whatsoever, the lights went out.

Lily stood, banishing nostalgia in an instant because it was time to act. "Let's go."

They came out into the tunnel just as a low, moaning alarm began to wail, seeming to come from deep beneath the walls of the main tunnel. The beam of Lily's helmet lamp swept a sheen of smooth wall and ceiling, stopped on a dead surveillance camera, moved to Yehoshua.

"You and Alsayid and Jenny, take out the A Block guards. Kyosti, Rainbow: with me."

She set off at a lope down the straight corridor. They met no one until they had crossed the circular intersection that surrounded the huge central elevator shaft, but coming around the curve they almost ran into two guards, helmet lights still off as they stood surprised by the blackout.

Lily took one down with a sweep of her rifle, clubbing him to the floor. Turned to see Kyosti with a hard grip on the second, his rifle pressed against the guard's head. All Lily could see was the terrified widening, the plea, in the guard's eyes; the rest of his face was hidden by the breathing mask.

"Kill him," said Kyosti as she stood staring. He fired, and a blast of light streaked out. The guard collapsed.

She hesitated, still straddling the unconscious man at her feet. Kyosti swung his gun around and shot.

The stench of heat rose up to her, a fine thread. She felt sick, was afraid to look down to see what now lay beneath her. Rainbow had already moved on, up the C Block corridor, rifle raised.

"You've never killed anyone, have you," Kyosti said.

She barely managed to shake her head.

"Catch," he said, and she just caught his rifle as he tossed it to her.

"What—"

"That's yours until you've killed someone."

"But you're unarmed!"

"And I'm going straight in," he promised as he followed Rainbow.

She gasped out an unvoiced curse, moved, stumbled on

the body, and ran after Kyosti. Needing him as a vital part of
the team, it had simply not occurred to her that she might
put him in danger. Or else, she realized, as she passed him,
passed Rainbow, that when she acted, all other considerations
vanished. At the C Block lock she pounded frantically at the
door. It opened to reveal a guard, tense but unsuspecting.

"Emergency," Lily gasped out, thrust past him, past the
second open lock door, and into the main guardroom.

Opened up with her rifle as she dove behind a console.

It was over in seconds. Rainbow evidently shot the man in
the lock, because moments later, as Lily sweated and shuddered
in the silence, huddling behind the console, she saw Kyosti
enter, distinctive by the relaxed precision of his walk.

"One's still alive," he said, and she had to stand up, to
survey the five dead guards: three were half-dressed, as if
they had just woken up. Most were sprayed with blood and
gaping wounds. Kyosti just stood there as the wounded man
rolled, reached for the gun dropped by his dead compatriot,
and lifted it to aim at his nearest clear target: Hawk.

Lily shot him in the head, and he slumped forward over
the other body. Rainbow came forward and began to search
the bodies.

Lily walked to the door, paused by Kyosti long enough to
shove his rifle into him so hard that he had to take three steps
back.

"I hate you," she muttered. "Rainbow! What are you
doing?"

"Got it." Rainbow rose. "Ya manual keypad for ya cells.
Free ya prisoners."

Her voice seemed so nonchalant that Lily was filled with a
wrenching rage at the Ridani's seeming ability to kill so
casually. She whirled and stalked out. Had to wait in the
empty corridor until Kyosti and Rainbow emerged a few
minutes later.

"We checked the other rooms," Kyosti said. "They're clear."

From some deep recess of memory that she had forgotten
existed, there flashed a vivid picture of Master Heredes
sitting cross-legged on the floor of his Academy's workout
room, watching her as she did a particularly complicated
kata. "Yes," he said in this memory, "yes. In this move you
strike directly to the temple. Done so, with proper align-
ment, you kill your opponent with that single blow." His face

remained impassive, as if killing was an abstract ideal that never touched reality, as if the opponent was always an idealized shadow of one's self, echoing your own movements across space. She wondered, standing there in the light of the three filtered helmet beams, how many people Heredes had killed in the course of his very long life.

The tube lighting along the walls flickered on, off, on: low wattage power, almost grey, and the hushed, strained whirring of the auxiliary venting system kicked in.

Lily forced herself to relax her grip on her rifle, finger by finger. "Come on," she said, more to herself than to her companions.

They met the other three by the metal door that led on to the meter-square maintenance shaft that paralleled, opened out from, the central elevator shaft. The door was ajar.

"I didn't believe it." Yehoshua said as they came up. "The 'bot really did it."

"Who do you think cut the power?" Lily demanded.

"Maybe Main Block finally tapped through and cut it."

"Maybe that's what the guards will think. We can hope. Did you clear all three corridors? Good." In the distance they could hear prisoners shouting to each other across the cell tunnel. "Rainbow. Release one prisoner, and then follow us up. Lock this shaft behind you."

Rainbow paused to look up at the ceiling. "It be ya sore long way to ya surface dome, min."

"I know." Lily stepped through the door and set one hand on a ladder rung. "That's why they won't be expecting us."

6 Jacob's Ladder

****

They climbed.

Lily's hands began to hurt first, from being curled around the metal rungs, then the arch of her foot, from pushing off all the time. Eventually her back began to ache as well, right around the shoulders and between the shoulder blades.

Rainbow started to lose ground fairly soon. Yehoshua and Alsayid kept up until they passed the door marked level 6 and then their lights, too, began to recede into the vast depths of blackness that surrounded them: the empty, seemingly bottomless central shaft.

Lily had to stop just above level 5. She laced her elbows around a rung and let her hands hang open, breathing hard. Below, Jenny stopped as well, but Kyosti continued up until he was half-overlapping Lily. Letting go with one hand, he massaged each of her palms in turn.

"Hoy," she gasped. "You'd think it was three kilometers between levels instead of one-third."

"It'll get worse," replied Kyosti cheerfully.

It did. She reached a point where she could block the pain lancing through her muscles, but the halts became more frequent, and the relief they afforded less. Once she heard a curse, far below, and she trained her light down to see Alsayid dangling and pulling himself back onto the ladder

with Yehoshua's help. Rainbow's light was lost in the deep
black beneath. The air stirred around them.

"Damn it," cursed Jenny from below. "Would you turn that
light back into the wall? I'm terrified of heights."

Kyosti laughed.

Lily started up again. They had long since passed level 2
when abruptly a red light snapped on some meters above
Lily's head. She flipped off her light immediately, and the
others vanished as well.

"They've restored power," she said softly, downward. "It's
been"—she checked the gleaming numbers on her wrist-com—
"over four hours. We'll wait for the others to catch up."

"How much time do we have left?" asked Jenny. Her voice,
even at a whisper, caused strange reverberations in the shaft.

"Enough."

"Damn my eyes if I don't ache like a Senator's sore—"

Noise above, an echoing, deep click, and a heavy humming. Pressure—wind—began to increase against their faces
and shoulders, stirring the rifles slung over their backs.

"Hold on," said Kyosti. "The elevator's coming down."

Lily vised her arms around the vertical poles of the ladder
and hugged herself against the metal, hooking her knees
around a rung, pressing as flat as she could. Then she shut
her eyes.

As wind roared past, ripping at them, the elevator descended.
The hum increased until it shook the ladder itself; the rungs
vibrated as if they were trying to throw off these intruders.
Just as the noise and wind seemed unbearable, the blank wall
of the elevator slid past. Lily hugged against the ladder so
tightly that she got seams in her skin, and she felt the wall of
the elevator jostle her rifle. She held her breath until,
mercifully, it slid past and continued down.

"Hoy," she said as she started to climb, "let's get out of
here." She stopped, catching her breath, and just held on
until, after an interminable time, she heard Yehoshua hailing
her.

"Are you all three there?" she asked, in return.

"Alsayid is about fifty rungs below me, and the Ridani at
least one hundred below him, but we're still climbing."

"Just one level to go." She began the slow rung-to-rung
ascent, propelled now more by a strong desire to beat the

elevator's inevitable return trip than by that burst of strength
that comes from nearing the goal.

The last gap between level 1 and the surface seemed the
longest, but at last they were met by a pattern of blinking
lights: red, green, and blue.

When she reached Bach, she merely rested her head
against the cool sheen of his curve for long moments. She
could hear Jenny's ragged breathing, and a little later, Yehoshua
and Alsayid halted below her. Kyosti remained silent and still
at her feet.

At a brief whistle from Lily, Bach recounted his mission in
beautiful four-part counterpoint, softly serenading the climbers.

*Affirmative, patroness. None discerned my ascent or trail
unto the main computer. And lest they suspect my ploy, I did
engage the power overrides so that it might appeareth to
their technicians that an overload had occurred. Wast well
done?*

"Very well done, Bach," said Lily, unable to muster up the
breath to whistle. "And this ladder goes all the way up to the
control center?"

*Affirmative. I have ascertained that the main control cen-
ter does indeed rest upon the top of this elevator shaft, and
this ladder dost as well ascend to a door that should open
onto such center. Although such as have built this place have
also locked this door.*

"We expected that," said Kyosti, once Lily had translated.
"We'll have to send Ishmael up to set charges."

"Ishmael? Kyosti, do you make up these strange names?
Don't answer. Is Rainbow up with us yet?"

A slight voice from below. "I'm here."

"Last instructions. Alsayid, you and Bach set the explo-
sives. Jenny, you and Rainbow wait by this ladder—when the
charge goes you must be first up the ladder to the command
center. And Bach must come in right behind you."

"Check," replied Jenny, her voice flat with concentration.

"Yehoshua, Alsayid; you follow me. Hawk will be going up
the ramp alone into the control center. We wait until he's
inside, and then we hit as soon as he attacks."

"Hold on." Yehoshua sounded, for the first time, skeptical
and angry. "I don't intend to commit suicide. That's a three-
meter-wide ramp up to the control dome, with two mounted
laser guns at the top placed for cross fire."

"Change of plans," said Lily. "It'll work."

"Forget it."

Lily waited a moment, controlling her voice, and then spoke. "Hawk. Tell them."

"I have six shock grenades. Four thrown to the four corners when the ladder hatch explodes and two into the laser emplacements—which are manual, I believe—that will give you a good five seconds with most of the personnel in the dome stunned. Of course, you'll have to watch your back."

"But that will leave *you* stunned and a sitting target."

"Maybe." Kyosti's voice was colorless.

Lily began to climb. Bach rose ahead of her. "We haven't got time for this. Move it."

Alsayid passed them at the main dome-level door, and he and Bach went on up. Alsayid returned quickly, however.

"There's a lock on this side," he murmured to Lily. "The 'bot says he can blow it."

Above, she heard a faint whine, like a drill. "Hoy. Damned show-off. All right, hand me up the manual key. We're going out."

It took a moment for the small rectangular keypad to pass from hand to hand, but Lily disengaged the lock on her first try. She took a breath, let it out, and swung the door aside.

It opened out into the corridor. She stepped out, easy, as if she were meant to be there, and found herself in a narrow, empty corridor. Motioned the others out quickly.

Jenny immediately knelt by the door, and after a hesitation, Rainbow stopped beside her, rubbing her arms with one hand. Lily waited for Kyosti to disappear alone around the bend in the corridor, and then she walked forward with Yehoshua and Alsayid at her heels.

Around the bend the corridor came to an end: one door opened into a long, narrow maintenance room, a second gave onto a large, brightly lit corridor that arced around the curve of the elevator shaft. Down it, she heard voices, a few raised, and then one, angry, that she recognized.

"You idiot, we have a complete security breach in level nine—"

Lily signed Yehoshua and Alsayid forward. As they rounded the corner, they saw Kyosti berating two guards, who were wearing the same standard issue coveralls they were. The two guards, cowed by Kyosti's apparent authority, quickly turned to escort him toward the broad hall through which equipment was loaded into the elevator and which held, on one side, the long ramp that led to the central dome above.

Kyosti had pulled down his breathing mask so that, evidently, the guards could see clearly the scorn with which he kept up a constant flow of furious invective about security breaches and incompetent level supervisors. Lily could not quite hear the details. As they came out into the hall she made a small sign with her hand and split off from the other two, filtering into the restless gathering of armed guards.

"—must have been a malfunction. Damn rebels would have attacked by now."

"—keep us off guard—"

"—I heard prisoners on level seven sabotaged the—"

She moved along the wall until she stood on a level with the ramp, seeing Kyosti walking up it alone, seemingly oblivious to the muzzles of the big laser guns trained on his approach. Caught Yehoshua's eye, to her left, and began to press nonchalantly forward toward the beginning of the ramp.

A second's high, piercing whine warned her: an instant later a muffled explosion sounded from above, and she broke forward at a run as the rest of the guards were registering the sound. She reached the ramp just as a series of low *pops* betrayed the concussions of the shock grenades Kyosti had thrown. Behind, footsteps rang on the ramp, but she did not have time to turn to see whose they were, only heard the beginning of heavy shooting.

The fifteen meters up that ramp seemed, with the two muzzles of the laser guns trained straight on her, like a kilometer. A burst of light shot out at her. She hit the floor rolling, heard a scream of pain behind, came up running as, ahead, she heard Kyosti yelling her name.

Metal rang beneath her boots, and she was through the double doors. Her first sight was of Kyosti wrestling down the gunner at the laser emplacement. Opposite, a guard drew himself to his knees and aimed a rifle down the ladder shaft. It took Lily two shots to cut him down, and then she saw a head emerge from the shaft: Jenny.

People stirred at the consoles. A woman reached for a gun. Lily turned, dropping to her knees, and fired over the heads of Yehoshua and Alsayid into a line of guards pounding up the ramp. Held her fire, noticing in an abstract way that Yehoshua

was struggling behind his cousin, and that red trailed after
him.

Then one of the laser guns woke and swept fire through the
first two lines of guards. They fell back, hesitated. Lily
whirled to cover her back, dropping to her belly, but Jenny
was methodically picking off everybody left in the command
center from behind the body of the guard by the ladder.
Behind her, Rainbow fired in bursts down the shaft. And
singing—

"Bach! Shut the damn doors!"

Laser fire from the ramp. A moan. Lily moved to Alsayid,
helped him drag Yehoshua out of the line of fire. Alsayid,
bleeding from one leg, staggered up to the laser emplacement, shot the still-stunned man in the chair, pushed the
body aside, and seated himself. The fire on the ramp doubled, devastating the guards' advance. Lily knelt beside
Yehoshua. Blood leaked out of him onto the metal floor. He
writhed, coughing spasmodically.

"Jenny!"

Jenny appeared at her side.

"Take Kyosti's position. Send him out here."

Jenny moved.

Lily glanced toward Rainbow. The Ridani woman had
paused to switch rifles, taking one from a dead guard, and a
burst of fire ricocheted up from below until she stuck the
muzzle into the shaft and set off shooting again.

Without a word, Kyosti knelt beside Lily and began to strip
the suit from Yehoshua with a small, red-handled knife.

"Do you need me?"

He shook his head.

The power went out. Black. She froze in the act of standing, surprised, until Kyosti switched on his helmet light and
resumed his work.

She switched on her light and stepped over corpses to
reach Bach.

"Topside guns disabled?"

*Affirmative. Opening hangar doors. Auxiliary ventilation
systems engaging—now.*

A low whine signaled their advent.

"Now we wait for Callioux." Lily picked her way carefully
around the command center, checking each body for signs of

life. All were dead. She placed five rifles by Rainbow and returned to Bach.

Progress? she whistled, pulling the dead comm-officer off his console and seating herself in his place.

All hangar doors open. All locks on all levels sealed shut.

Lily switched on the outside channels and toggled until she caught comm.

"This is Heredes. We have control of thirties main command center. Please acknowledge main strike."

As if in reply, an explosion shook the dome. In the silence of its aftermath, Lily could hear the fire of the mounted laser guns stutter and cease.

"Assault up the ramp has stopped," called Jenny, hidden from view by her emplacement.

"We did it," Lily breathed.

"Strike acknow—"

A second explosion shuddered through the dome. Jenny fired a single burst from her gun.

"My cousin—" Alsayid's voice, strained with worry and physical hurt, came from the opposite emplacement.

"He'll live." The auxiliary lights came up, casting an eerie glow on the litter of bodies, on Kyosti's pale hair as he drew off the helmet and mask and laid a gentle hand on Yehoshua's motionless form. "But he's going to lose his right arm. I'm sorry."

Alsayid murmured a phrase, solemn as a prayer. Lily shifted her foot, accidentally nudging the bloody head of the dead comm-officer. She began to shake, gasping hard to fight it, but even so, she was still trembling when Callioux came up the ramp, hair singed by laser fire but otherwise unhurt.

7 The Mule

****

They let Callioux's soldiers take over at command central, waited first in the hall below the center until level 1 was cleared, and then waited in the extensive level 1 medical complex until the last of the guards surrendered or died. Most surrendered, once they realized how thoroughly they were breached. One squad of six managed to sneak out the way Lily and her people had come in, but Inonu's ten caught them soon enough.

Kyosti quickly stripped off his guard's uniform and threw on a white medical jacket, going to work on casualties with a physician's disregard for which side they were on. On level 7, the guards had massacred two hundred prisoners before Callioux's people arrived, but otherwise most of the injuries came from Callioux's assault on the dome.

Alsayid sat by his cousin, who had been put on a stasis couch and now, unconscious, was entirely unaware of the discussion going on above him concerning his mangled arm.

Lily had also taken off her guard's uniform, unable to stomach the constant reminder of the blood that spattered it; now she fell asleep, head resting on Bach as he sang a quiet, soothing chorale.

It seemed but minutes later that Callioux woke her up. "Level four is clear," Callioux said. "We're evacuating level two now, so if you want to find your friend before she gets lost on the transport ships, you'd better go now. All the prisoners are still locked in their cells. It shouldn't be hard."

Lily nodded, pushing herself with difficulty to her feet, and found Jenny beside her. They took the Auxiliary B elevator down to level 4. The broad tunnel was quiet, patrolled by pairs of white-uniformed Jehanist rebels. Now and again a prisoner spoke or yelled from one of the cells, but otherwise they remained silent.

They passed cell door after cell door, small entrances to small compartments.

"I was expecting something livelier then this," Jenny said in an undertone to Lily as they headed for the C Block console that would register names to cell numbers. "From what Yehoshua said, I thought this would be more like the Havliki District on Landfall; bars and stages and street tunes and dancing all hours."

"They *are* prisoners," replied Lily.

The four soldiers at C Block were expecting them and showed surprise only when Bach plugged into the console and quickly perused the level 4 records.

"That's strange," said Jenny, looking over Lily's shoulder. "Most of the prisoners on level four are in six-bunked rooms, but your Paisley is in this block of solitary cells." She shrugged, but her mouth turned down with suspicion as Lily turned to get a manual key from the officer in charge.

"I hope it was worth it," Lily muttered to herself, still seeing the carnage of the command center, as they reached the cell door and keyed in the "open" sequence.

The door slipped aside to reveal a small, shabby room, made pathetic by a tattered blanket in faded colors that was hung up to cover one grey wall. On the metal bed that doubled as a bench, seated on a thin pad of uncovered foam, Paisley stared, head bowed, at her clasped hands. Her hair in its tight braids still hung to her waist, and she wore the self-same tunic that Lily had bought for her on Unruli Station, although its colors were now muted and it was patched and threadbare in places from long and continuous use. The Ridani girl did not lift her head until, reacting to the silence as if it was unusual, she looked up.

"Min Ransome!" Her face, pensive in repose, transformed with a brilliant smile, quickly shuttered by despair. "Oh, they got you, too. I be sorry for that."

"No, they didn't get me—" Lily paused, realizing that
Jenny stood behind her, still in her guard's uniform. "This is
Jenny. She's not a guard. Paisley, we're here to free you."

"Free me!" Paisley flung herself at Lily, throwing herself to
her knees at Lily's feet. She burst into tears.

Lily let her cry for a while, and then tugged her gently to
her feet. "You're coming with us, now, Paisley," she began,
prying Paisley off of her. "You'd better get what belongs to
you here, and we'll go."

Paisley recovered her composure with an obvious effort,
dabbing at her eyes with her knuckles. "If you hadn't my
kinnas already, min Ransome, sure be you'd have it now." She
glanced up, and her expression cleared. "Sure, and glory!"
she exclaimed. "It be min Bach." She offered Bach a formal,
little bow, to which the robot replied with a quick flurry of
notes.

Heartened by this display, Paisley climbed up on the bed
and yanked down the tattered blanket that hung above it. She
sat down cross-legged in the middle of the cell, her back to
the doorway, and began with deliberate movements to rip the
blanket into shreds.

Lily glanced at Jenny, questioning, but the mercenary
merely shrugged. The blanket proved to be so worn that it
took little time for the Ridani girl to reduce it to strips, which
she placed with careful precision in the four corners of the
room, chanting a strange, tuneless little song under her
breath all the while. When she had only three strips left, she
backed out of the cell, forcing Lily and Jenny out into the
corridor, and left the last strips to mark her path.

She stopped in the corridor and looked at Lily. "I be
cleansing the room," she said, "so that ya memory of it don't
bind me."

"But don't you have anything to take with you?" Lily
asked.

"Didn't bring ya nothing here, so be it I can't take ya
nothing away. It all be in ya pattern, you see?"

"Sure," said Lily, an unconscious echo of Paisley's speech.
"I remember how that tunic hung on you. At least they fed
you well here."

"Sure, and course they fed me. I be ya entertainment,
bain't I? Had to keep me looking ya swell, didna' they?"

For the first time, Lily heard real bitterness in Paisley's

voice, and examining her more carefully now, she saw that
the beautiful adolescent from Unruli Station had somehow
matured in a way that had sharpened the edge of her beauty,
as if with a knife, or with the pain of harsh experience. Jenny
was frowning, seeing something that she, too disapproved of.

"But what did you do all this time?" asked Lily.

"Lily," began Jenny, warning.

"Sure, and what did you think they do with ya handsome
tattoos?" Paisley examined Lily as if she were sporting tattoos
herself. "Forced us as ya fancy whores for ya guards as
wanted to be slumming with dirty pleasure, and them prisoners as had ya special privileges."

"Oh, Paisley." The knowledge came as such a truly unexpected shock to Lily that she could only mouth platitudes.
"Oh, Paisley. I'm sorry. What did you do?"

Paisley shrugged. "I shut my eyes."

Lily turned away, unable to reply.

"How old are you?" asked Jenny gently.

Paisley considered, both the question and the dark mercenary, and eventually decided something in Jenny's favor. "I
begun ya bleeding ya two years back, I reckon. Thereabouts.
Ya Station time, that be. It be right at ya Festival time, too.
That be glory good kinnas."

"Fifteen, maybe," muttered Jenny, and without thinking
she put a hand out to rest on Paisley's shoulder.

"How did you stand it, Paisley?" Lily murmured, still not
looking around. "More than a year. I don't think I've ever
heard anything as awful as that."

Paisley shrugged again, a wealth of fatalism in one small
gesture. "Hadn't much choice, had I? There be also ya rule,
no hitting ya girls, and they most of them followed it, so it
weren't so bad as it could have meant." Her face brightened
slightly. "And there be also ya Mule."

"Mule?" Lily turned, caught both by the strange name and
by the tone of Paisley's voice.

"She be good to me. She be in ya tech division, and her
credit be so good, she could afford near anything, but she
asked for me—me!" It appeared that, to Paisley, this choice
was inexplicable. "Near half ya nights I be working."

"Randy bitch," murmured Jenny.

"Weren't nothing like that!" cried Paisley, pulling roughly
away from Jenny's hand. "Sure, we slept together, but she got

no—well, it were more cuddling, like. She be lonely, I reckon. Given what she be it were no surprise ya others shunned her, though they be ya Ridani and shunned themselves. It were mostly companionship. She taught me to play ya *bissterlas*. And she begun to teach me 'bout ya tech workings. Sure, she be hot ifkin on ya math, and she learned me all 'bout ya 'bots and ya motors and—" Words failed her. In the glare of the corridor tubing she seemed taller, older, scarcely adolescent at all, as if the girl from Unruli Station who had so blithely adopted Lily and tagged along behind her had been cocooned on this planet and only now emerged as a new self. "Everything! I be sure enough trained for ya tech job now."

"Who is this woman?" Lily asked. "Where is she? Was she an officer here?"

"She be no woman. Nor ya officer. Ya prisoner like me. Ya Mule. That be what we called her. I don't even know her real name."

"No woman?" asked Jenny. "Then what is she?"

"See for yourself," answered Paisley. "If you kin get me out, sure you kin get her out, too."

"But Paisley," protested Lily. "All the prisoners are being freed. Why do we need to bring this person with us?"

Paisley pursed her lips, looking stubborn. The dappling of her tattoos lent determination to her expression. "If that be so, why'd you come get me, if you trust ya new folk so sure? They be for freeing me, too, bain't they? I reckon you fair have ya little trust in such folk as would have use for ya prisoners such as be put here. That be ya truth, don't it?"

"Paisley," began Lily, warning. Jenny checked her wristcom for the time.

"Well, it be ya truth," continued Paisley recklessly. "I kin see ya meaning in ya talk that runs between ya prisoners here, and ya guards. They say Jehane hae come, and if it be true, then I reckon either you hae no trust for him 'cause he be ya Ridani, or 'cause you reckon he be not ya real Jehane."

"Well I hope I'm not so prejudiced," Lily burst out. "We have to go, Paisley. I can't just adopt every stray who comes to my attention."

"It be only fair." Paisley paused and looked pointedly at Lily. "She saved me ya much grief."

Lily looked away, aware that she was being shamelessly

manipulated on the altar of her own guilt. "All right," she said, frowning at Jenny's expression as she capitulated. "Where is your Mule? If she's not boarded onto the transports yet, I'll see what I can do."

"Bleeding heart," muttered Jenny, but she did not object as Lily led them back to the level 4 guardroom and directed Bach to plug into the console and track down this prisoner called the Mule.

Unfortunately, Bach quickly located the Mule, by a combination of name cross-reference and an audit of the EntOps transaction books, in a solitary cell on level six, deep enough that one might suspect a prisoner of some worth or some recalcitrance. Lily merely shook her head.

"Jenny, take Paisley and Bach up top. Pinto should have brought the shuttle in by now. I'll fetch this Mule, and Kyosti, and see what provisions Callioux has made for us in the fleet, and then meet you there. And Paisley"—now her tone was stern—"no more strays."

Paisley bowed meekly and followed Jenny without a word, although she began almost immediately an animated conversation with Bach as they left the guard block for the main elevator.

Lily bullied her way past the officer in charge and got the Auxiliary C elevator down to level 6. The Jehanist soldiers there did not dispute her right, carefully linked with frequent invocation of Callioux's name and authority, to remove one of the prisoners early.

As she left, she heard one whisper to the other: "Isn't that the comrade who led the strike force that opened the dome?"

Level 6 consisted mostly of solitary cells and shaft openings, and she tracked down the requisite cell and keyed it open with little difficulty.

And found herself for the second time on Harsh staring at a physical piece of her past, so unexpected that, like meeting Finch, she was at first too stunned to react.

It was impossible that she not recognize, and remember, the Mule. The name itself brought illumination with it: on the plain metal bed of the cell, which was richly furnished by the addition of a terminal hooked out from the wall, sat the sta who had been incarcerated in the cell beside her on Remote. The sta who had questioned her about kata, and shown interest in her befriending of an inconsequential Ridani girl.

But not a sta, and certainly not a woman. She—he?—looked up at her, incurious, bored, or perhaps simply rendered fatalistic by the cruel blow fate had long since dealt it.

"Hoy," breathed Lily, astonished, but capable still of keeping the rest of her thought unvoiced: that she had thought it was just some obscene tall tale, about stas and humans actually—and that in any case, it was impossible that they might actually interbreed. She shuddered, suppressed it out of pity. Caught herself and spoke. "Do you remember me?" she asked carefully. "From Remote. My name is Lily—Heredes."

The Mule regarded her with an expression all-too-humanly sardonic on its sta-ish face. "Ah, the Lily Ransome, I thought it was. I recollect you." Its voice was a sibilant hiss, but not as fluid as a sta's. "The Ridani girl was your friend. As now she is, in a fashion, mine. But she is an innocent child, and naive to the ways of prejudice."

"I'm sorry," said Lily abruptly, drawn to the reddish sheen—not skin, not scales; the lank mane that could not crest; the muzzled face, protruding not quite far enough; and most of all, resting on the terminal keys, the four-fingered, one thumbed human hands. "But I just can't believe it. How can you even exist? It's impossible."

"Clearly you have no understanding of the juxtaposition of humor and cruelty in the unformed will of the cosmos. Of course it is impossible that I exist. Therefore, I do." The sta-ish fluidity of the Mule's voice could not disguise the cutting sarcasm of its words.

"You must be lonely," said Lily simply, feeling at that moment the true horror of the Mule's situation.

The Mule stood, unflexing to a sta-ish height, lifting its human hands from the terminal in a dismissive, angry gesture. "Spare me this. What do you want?"

"I, and some people with me, came to Harsh to join Jehane, and to free Paisley. I have Paisley, and she wants you to come with us."

"Jehane? The Ridani hero? Is there really a Jehane?"

"There's a man who calls himself Jehane, and he's just liberated Harsh's prisoners, and he means to destroy the corrupt government on Central and institute a new government."

"Uplifting sentiments." The Mule considered her skeptically. "Why should I want to join Jehane?"

"I don't know," replied Lily. "Maybe you don't. I have my own reasons, and asking you to come with us is a favor I'm doing for Paisley. If you care to join us, and especially if you have talents that I can use to bargain for a good place for us within Jehane's forces, then you are welcome. If not, then please just accompany me up and explain to Paisley *yourself* that you don't want to come with us, because otherwise she'll never let me rest."

This speech reduced the Mule to silence, followed by a long, slow hiss that she recognized after a moment as sta-ish laughter. "Compared to the vistas of opportunity that have previously been brought before me, the word 'welcome' is—" It paused. "—acceptable. Very well." With deft fingers, the Mule dismantled the terminal and quickly packed a small duffel bag with sundry clothing and items stowed beneath the bed. "I will join you."

"Thank you." If Lily's tone was dry, her face hid it, and the Mule chose to ignore it. "But I can't just call you 'the Mule.' You must have another name."

"No. I was cast off the moment the nature of what I am was discovered." Lily did not school her expression quickly enough, for the Mule's mane lifted slightly, in sad parody of a sta's glorious crest of rage. "Don't pity me!" it hissed. "How I despise your pity, all of you who are whole and blithe in wholeness." It turned its back on Lily and repacked the entire contents of the duffel bag before it turned around again.

"Let's go," said Lily quietly. They left, but she was bitterly aware of the soldiers' curious stares, of laughter behind hands, as she passed with her new companion. The Mule said nothing, showed no emotion, inured to such display.

They walked into chaos at level 1, the medical personnel and patients being ferried up in lots to the waiting transports. She found Kyosti at last beside the stasis couch that held Yehoshua, who was now without a right arm. White swathed his shoulder and chest. He was unconscious, but Kyosti spoke in a low voice to his cousin, Alsayid. Hawk's white medical jacket was speckled with the almost familiar colors of human suffering.

Lily waited, impatient, checking her wrist-com, until Kyosti finished and waved to a group of soldiers, who wheeled the couch out of the complex, Alsayid following. She watched as he glanced around the empty ward, as if he were looking for something, until his gaze stopped on her.

He smiled.

Glanced at the Mule beside her, and his eyes widened in surprise. The Mule made a strange, strangled *tsshs* with its tongue. Lily looked over to see it regarding Kyosti with a similar surprised, but intent, scrutiny. Abruptly, as if with common consent, they dropped their gazes and Kyosti walked smoothly over to them as if nothing had interrupted his smile at Lily.

He kissed her chastely on one cheek and turned to her companion. "How do you do?" he said urbanely. "You must be the Mule. I'm Hawk."

The Mule acknowledged him with a little hiss of sta-ish laughter.

"We have to go," said Lily. "I need to find out how we're leaving the system and when I'm meeting Jehane."

"Callioux already told me," said Kyosti. "They want me on the hospital ship, so we'll travel with them until the rendezvous point. I need to check the last ward before we go. Come with me?" He gestured toward an open door.

"Excuse us a moment," Lily said to the Mule, and went with Kyosti. From the doorway of the ward, she watched him move from couch to couch, adjusting tubing at one bed, massaging a leg at another, shaking his head over the motionless form at a third. At the end of his tour, he spoke for a long time with the technologist supervising the twelve patients. Then he returned to Lily.

"We're leaving these. They're all guards and too badly hurt to live through a window. Two technologists to watch them. Central should send people in soon enough."

Lily stared up at him. His face had an impassive, but intent, expression as he spoke, considered and at ease. Quite the same expression he had when he had shot dead the two guards on level 9.

"I don't understand you," she whispered. "How can you kill people with one hand, and heal them with the other?"

He blinked. "How can I not?" he asked, not understanding the question.

"How can it be so easy for you to take life, and yet so important for you to save it?"

The passion of her question seemed to give him pause and, curiously, he glanced past her toward the patient, waiting figure of the Mule at the opposite side of the empty ward. "'Roses are planted where thorns grow,'" he said, "'And on the barren heath sing the honeybees.'"

"I don't understand you," she repeated, her voice constrained now as if with weariness, but she turned and led them to the elevators and up to the shuttle where the others were waiting for them.

8 Audience

****

"I said no strays," said Lily, looking first at Jenny and then at Rainbow, who had strapped herself in beside Paisley, evidently finding refuge in the fellow Ridani.

Jenny shrugged, punctuating the gesture with an ostentatious sigh, but did not answer.

"I reckoned my chances, all sides of ya pattern," said Rainbow in a soft voice, not pleading, "and I reckoned I be best off with you, min Heredes, being if you'll have me."

"Hoy. All right. I'm too tired to fight this out. But you're Jenny's—min Seria's charge. Understood?" A nod. "Jenny. She's your responsibility then." Jenny, too, nodded, but a tiny smile, only half-mocking, broke the surface of her lips. "Good. Now I'm going to take a nap until we dock at *Hospital*. Unless one of you has another surprise?"

Given the tone of her voice, no one volunteered any.

She slept until they were slung into the vast cargo hold of the merchantman renamed *Hospital*, stayed awake long enough to be assigned a four-bunk cabin with Jenny, Lia, Gregori, and Bach, and went back to sleep.

If they passed through windows, she neither woke nor had strange enough dreams to account for it. When she did wake up, she found Kyosti asleep on the narrow bunk with her. Long intimacy had allowed him to find a way to fit in beside her without waking her, or even pushing her too close to the edge of the bunk. She shifted carefully, but he remained asleep. The cabin was empty, except for Bach. The robot floated unlit next to the ceiling. Lily lay quiet for a while on the thin foam pad and watched Hawk.

His breathing had a slow, regular pulse that reminded her abruptly of a Bajii Ransome aunt's astronomical studies: she was a crazy old woman, lodged in an orbiting science lab for so much of her life that visits to the closed vistas of Ransome House left her almost hysterical with claustrophobia, but she had once in her ramblings claimed to have discovered, or glimpsed for one all-too-brief hour, the pulse of the distant heart of the universe.

Then Hawk smiled and opened his eyes, breaking the illusion.

"You slept through two meals," he said, "and unless you're quick you'll miss this one."

She sat up. "I'm starving. Where are we?"

"Some godforsaken backwater with only a pygmie-manned Station orbiting a white dwarf."

"The rendezvous point," she guessed, and stood up to smooth down her clothing so that it did not look quite so slept in.

"Callioux left a message," Kyosti went on, watching her slightest movement with unnerving thoroughness. "You're to rendezvous with the *Boukephalos* at oh-eight-oh, fleet time."

"*Boukephalos*—that's Jehane's ship?"

Kyosti chuckled. "I wonder what he'll come up with next," he murmured. "You're to go alone."

"I expected that." Lily considered Bach thoughtfully, whistled. *You will remain here and let no one but our people enter this cabin. You can control the lock?*

Affirmative, patroness. I will voice code it to thy specifications.

"Good. Be very cautious, Bach. You're my—"

"Ace?" suggested Kyosti.

Bach responded with a rippling arpeggio.

Lily merely rubbed her face with her palms. "Hoy. Where's the washing cubicle?"

"Down the hall."

She gave a last tug to her sleeves. "What time it is? And where's the mess? And everyone else?"

He swung off the low bunk and stood up, the light tips of

his hair almost brushing the ceiling. "In the mess. I told them I'd get you there by oh-six-thirty."

She checked her wrist-com and grinned. "Bless the Void. I have time for a shower. Meet me there."

Jenny had assembled everyone at a long table in the far corner of the mess hall, isolated from the other diners by several empty tables. Lily had some trouble counting, however, as she came up to the table: it was almost full. Jenny sat with Gregori and Lia; on the other side of the table sat the brilliant Ridani contingent, Pinto, Paisley, and Rainbow, taking strength in numbers, with the Mule sitting stiffly beside Paisley. But there were two more—

"Finch! What are you doing here?" With some surprise she greeted his sister, Swann. "I'm glad to see you got off okay. Your mother?"

Finch, looking mutinous, did not reply immediately, but cast a pointed and hostile glance at the three Ridanis. "*She* said," he nodded toward Jenny, "that *they* were meant to be here, but I can't believe you'd have us sit down to table with tattoos."

"Finch," whispered Swann, looking embarrassed.

Paisley regarded Finch with interest, but Pinto and Rainbow had, as if allied, fixed stares of equal contempt on Finch's angry face.

"Hoy." Rather than sitting down, Lily leaned her hands on the table and forced Finch to meet her gaze. "I never took you for a bigot, Finch. I thought you were above that."

"It's got nothing to do with bigotry," began Finch. "The fact is, it's well known the kind of foul diseases—"

Pinto started up out of his chair and grabbed across the table for Finch's shirt.

Finch jerked back, banging his chair on the chair behind him. "Is this another one of your lovers?" he asked sarcastically, out of range.

"Pinto, sit down," snapped Lily. "Finch, shut up. Hoy." She regarded the two men with disgust, but after a few long moments during which the other diners in the cafeteria whispered and glanced around and subsided back to their meals, both men did as they were told.

"Where's Hawk?" asked Jenny in a low voice before an uncomfortable silence could grow.

"He's supposed to be here." Lily glanced toward the door, then at Finch, who was too busy glaring at Pinto to be aware of this exchange. "Keep an eye out for me, Jenny."

Jenny nodded with quick understanding and shifted her chair just enough to give her a good view of the door.

"I don't have much time," said Lily, "so I'm going to make this short." She paused to survey the group, waiting until all of them watched her attentively, even Pinto, who nevertheless lapsed at frequent intervals with quick, bitter glances at Finch.

Lily let her gaze settle first on Swann. "Your mother?" she repeated.

"In *Hospital*," Swann began.

"We came with her," interrupted Finch. "We can't go back to Unruli. You know that."

"Yes, I do," replied Lily. She sighed, thinking for a moment that the closed corridors of ships were not so different from the underground tunnels of Ransome House. "I don't have much time," she said again. "I think you all know that I'm going to meet with Jehane. To offer him my services— and the services of those of you who are willing to throw your lot in with mine."

The Mule hissed, a slight but penetrating sound. "And why should this Jehane, being so powerful, want your services as anything more than another soldier?"

"I have several things he wants, and I mean to negotiate with those to get what I want."

"Which is?" asked Jenny.

Lily grinned, a private understanding between her and the mercenary. "I'm not sure yet. But I want to keep this group together, all of you who want to stay with me. You don't have any obligation to me. You can join Jehane's forces in any capacity you wish, or not. But if you do stay with me, you have to accept that I will use whatever talents you have as part of my bargaining, and you have to accept whatever assignment I choose as best suited to my goal."

She waited, but no one spoke. Pinto stared down at the geometric patterns decorating his hands, and she guessed that he surely must be thinking of his father, of the way Senator Isaiah had utterly rejected his once-loved son for the sin of being half-Ridani. Pressing her lips together, she chose and cast off words in her thoughts, not wanting to say the wrong thing.

"I'm not specifically a Jehanist," Lily continued quietly, aware of Lia's eyes going wide at the declaration. "I support his goals. I had the privilege of working with a man named Pero, on Arcadia, and I learned a great deal about selfless passion from him, and about our rights and duties as citizens of the Reft. He made me understand that we need reforms in the government of Reft space. I want to see Pero in a position to bring those reforms to the people, because I know he will. That's one reason I'm joining Jehane now. Because Pero *is* a Jehanist, and speaks for Jehane and his goals."

She considered this a moment in silence. Paisley gazed at her with rapt attention.

"But I'm really not a reformer either," she went on. "Whatever my personal feelings about Jehane or Pero or anyone who *does* work for reform, I have to admire their zeal, but I can't emulate it. So you must understand this: The main reason I am joining Jehane is to revenge myself on the people, the government, in Central, who killed my father."

"But Lily—" Finch began, while Swann, who also knew Sar Ransome, simply looked bewildered.

"Sometimes other ties are as thick as blood," said Lily softly, but with finality. Finch subsided. Swann still looked confused.

"Sure," said Paisley, enlightened. "Kinnas be ya bond as strong as ya family, if it be owed, like I owe to you. Ya man, he be ya one we meant to scam off ya spook ship, bain't he, min Ransome?"

"It's Heredes now, Paisley. It wasn't them. It was Central." She had to stop, feeling a mask of stark anger and sorrow harden on her face.

"Well, Lily-hae," said Jenny cheerfully into the silence. "You know I'm with you."

"I am too," said Aliasing, beside her, so faint a voice that it was almost lost in the harmonic buzz of the mess hall's other conversations. Gregori was playing a mathematical game on the com-screen that Lily had prudently brought along for him, and had long since ceased paying attention to the adults' discussion. Finch and Swann had their heads bent together in a whispered conversation, so Lily shifted her gaze back to the

Mule, who hissed in the affirmative, casting an ironic gaze at Paisley's determined face.

"You know I be," Paisley declared in a ringing voice, as if daring anyone else at the table to state their intentions with as much loyalty or boldness.

Lily smiled at her, looked next at Rainbow, a little questioning.

"I said before," said the Ridani woman. "And be I meant it then, too."

"Pinto?" Lily asked, pausing at the frown on his face. For the first time she realized clearly that the inherent natural beauty of his face, and of Paisley's as well, was cleverly and subtly enhanced by the patterns chosen for them at whatever early age such choices were made in the labyrinth of Ridani culture.

"You know I've got no choice," he muttered. "You possess my kinnas. What else am I supposed to do?"

At the sound of his voice, Finch looked up, first at him, then at Lily. "Swann and I both agree," he began slowly, "that we and Mom would be best off with you, Lily. We'd just get lost in Jehane's forces, and probably separated as well. But you aren't really going to mix—"

"Don't want to dirty your hands with us filthy tattoos, do you?" asked Pinto, with a sneer. "Well, maybe you never considered that we don't like mixing with *your kind* any better—"

"You can't talk to me like—"

"I can talk to *you* anyway I damn well please. You don't deserve—"

"Sit down!"

Since both men were sitting, the words had the desired effect of startling them into a brief silence. Brief enough: "Now listen. Keep your prejudices to yourself. And that goes for both of you. And all of you." Lily swept a quick glance around the table. "Unlike Jehane, I don't have any resources backing me up except my people and Bach. So you will show politeness and respect for each other. Or I will ask you to leave. Is that understood?"

"Min Heredes." Unexpectedly, it was Rainbow who spoke, tentative but with growing firmness. "Be it you know about ya one, or be it you don't." She looked at the Mule. "We all knew, in ya thirties, 'bout what it be, and some had their say as it were ya perverted—" She paused, and by the set of her mouth Lily could tell that in her own way she was attempting to be compassionate. "—ya monster. Some said it be buying ya one Ridani girl's favors for ya unnatural fashions."

The Mule began, with stately contempt, to rise. Paisley stared at Rainbow with astonished disgust.

"No, no, min," hastened Rainbow. "Be it you misunderstand me. If all know, then there's none to whisper."

"I will thank you," replied the Mule with fluid disdain, "to stay out of my affairs."

Lily saw Finch and Swann, and even Jenny and Pinto, staring at the Mule with dawning enlightenment, mingled with some revulsion and, in Lia's case, pity.

"Damn my eyes," breathed Jenny. "I thought it was just one of those wild space tales, like the old ghost ship."

"And now everyone knows." Lily tapped her hands impatiently on the table. "Which settles the question."

"Sure, and that be ya lowest run, sneaky way to tell folk—" began Paisley hotly, glaring at Rainbow.

"Paisley."

Paisley frowned, looking mulish, and clenched her hands in her lap.

"Any other surprises? Or confessions?" asked Lily sardonically. "Thank the Void. Now maybe I can eat before I go to meet Jehane."

"What about the crazy—" began Pinto with his usual caustic undertone. Responding instantly, Finch jumped to his feet with a gasp, just as Pinto said, "doctor," in a surprised voice at the sight of Finch losing all his color as he stared at the mess door in terror.

Lily whirled. Across twenty meters, she saw Kyosti halt in the door, his whole being fixing like a programmed seeker onto the paralyzed Finch. Some faint word escaped Finch's lips. He was so mesmerized by the sight of Hawk that he could not even move to flee, or to beg for help.

"Pinto, cover him," snapped Lily, already moving. "Jenny, with me."

Finch flung aside chairs as he threw himself away toward the far wall, but to Lily, the sound of their clatter and fall faded into a dull counterpoint as her concentration narrowed onto her target. She knew, incontrovertibly, that Kyosti must not, could not, reach Finch, that whatever she had thought about Kyosti's rash words about inevitability and killing, she

had erred in believing them rash. She felt more than saw
Jenny circle out to close in on his other side. Kyosti's
attention had riveted with such utter focus on Finch that he
seemed oblivious to the two women converging on him.

Jenny reached him first, and since they had all been forced
to leave their hand-pack weapons on the shuttle—security
reasons—she tackled him.

Had she not had the most ruthless hand-to-hand combat
training available in the Reft, he would have thrown her off.
Damaging her did not seem in his purpose: he continued to
stare at Finch, who had trapped himself in a corner and was
frozen in terror even as his sister and the three Ridanis
massed in front of him, trying to hide him from Hawk's sight.

Jenny tugged Hawk to his knees and was trying to force
him down, but even so he struggled up with all her weight on
him. Lily simply ran straight into him and wrapped her arms
around him and hugged him hard into her chest, as if
suffocating him. He paused in his forward momentum, distracted by her presence.

She looked back over her shoulder, gestured wildly with
chin and eyes, and Pinto grabbed Finch by the arm and
yanked him around the edge of the room and out the door.
The others crowded along behind.

Kyosti attempted to rise again, slowed, partly by his re-
straints and partly by some new information registering in his
mind. He sank back onto his knees.

There was a long pause, like a moment of opportunity lost,
or of the kind of transfer of information that interrupts a
computer's flow.

Everyone in the mess stared at them. The Mule, followed
by Lia and Gregori, picked his way past overturned chairs
and came up to them just as Kyosti began to shake.

It wasn't even trembling, in fear or anger or relief at
danger passed by. As Jenny had said, it was as if he was in the
grip of a palsy so debilitating that it took both Lily and Jenny
to support him. His face seemed shut down, emotionless, as
if he was not there at all, though his eyes remained open.
The tremors shook him for at least five minutes, while Lia
and the Mule, prompted in her case by compassion and in his
by some unknown emotion, attempted to shield the scene
from the sight of onlookers. Gregori asked if he was sick, and

an officer in Jehanish whites approached to offer to take him to one of the wards.

Lily shook her head and waved him off. At last the tremors subsided, and Kyosti lay limp. He had fainted.

"What time is it, Jenny? Hoy, I have to go. Have Pinto meet me at the shuttle. Tell Finch to lock himself in his room. No, in the room with Bach. And you'd better get Kyosti checked by a doctor."

"I don't think he'll like that," said Jenny.

"Damn what he likes," said Lily fiercely. "I've never seen anything like that in my life. Is that what happened before?"

"Yes, but the first time was worse."

"I'll carry him," said the Mule unexpectedly.

"Thank you." Lily studied the Mule with interest, and calculation, for a moment. "Can you stay by him?"

The Mule nodded and reached to transfer with remarkable gentleness Kyosti's unconscious figure from the grasp of the two women into its own. Like any sta, it was obviously stronger than a human.

"Oh, hells," muttered Lily, watching Kyosti's limp form as the Mule carried him out. Simple jealousy did not seem to her an adequate explanation for what she had just seen. She straightened out her clothing, straightened herself. "Keep them in line, Jenny. Just for as long as I'm gone."

Jenny chuckled. "Look at it this way, Lily-hae. At least it'll never be dull."

The *Boukephalos* proved to be one of Central's own class 4 military cruisers, impressed into Jehane's service by some unknown means.

Lily left Pinto in the shuttle, which was docked in the vast fighter squadron bay, and met a group of ten crisp-stepping soldiers in crackling white uniforms who escorted her through the gleaming corridors of Jehane's flagship to the upper decks. She was forcibly reminded of La Belle and her ship, the *Sans Merci*, although the utilitarian lines of the *Boukephalos* could scarcely measure up to such competition.

They showed her into a large, plain office: a desk and single molded plastine chair in front of a wall screen, facing a single plush chair that looked out of place in the middle of the expanse of marbled floor.

She sat in the plush chair and waited.

Enough time passed that she suspected the wait was meant to impress the extent of their power—*his* power—over her. She did kata in her head, concentrating, and was thus almost surprised by the abrupt slip and sigh of an opening door.

She stood up, not hasty, but in order to meet on the same level.

Jehane entered and paused as the door sighed shut behind him to examine her.

In one year he seemed to have changed not at all. The office, nondescript, gained sudden life at his entrance, as if its space needed only his presence to illuminate it. His hair still shone like a vein of gold, dazzling and attractive. His eyes, richly green, bored into her as if with his gaze alone he could penetrate to her inmost secrets.

He walked to the desk, lengthening his path by keeping to the wall, saying nothing, but all the while his attention remained clasped to her like an ornament, or a need, something she could merely reach out and, taking, be utterly satisfied with. She resisted the temptation to lose herself in his scrutiny. The sheer weight of his charisma sank onto her, although this time she did not feel the stark fear she had felt the first time she had met him—and she recognized the fear for what it was: he would be easy to lose one's self in.

He sat down, graceful and poised, and lifted a hand. "Please." His voice was gracious. "Please sit down, Lilyaka Hae Ransome."

"Heredes," she said.

"Heredes," he agreed, munificent.

She sat down.

He had the gift of being able to keep his gaze fixed on her, as if she were the most important person in his existence, and yet remain all the time aware of the room and the flashing play of the intercom and the slow circle of lights on the wall screen behind him, tracing star fields and solar systems like an echo of his vast concerns.

"You wish to join my cause," he said at last. It was neither a question nor a statement, but rather a reflection of some casual thought, intrigued but undecided.

"Yes. Together with twelve others who have let me speak for them."

"Twelve." He mused over this figure. "Most of those who come to believe in my goals join me as common soldiers and earn a more intimate place in our revolution by effort and blood and loyalty."

"Exactly," Lily agreed. "But you would be wasting me in the army, in the usual forces."

"Would I, indeed?" He considered her thoughtfully.

In any other person, man or woman, his features would have been too perfect, a little false, a little stilted. But Alexander Jehane had such force of personality, such radiant personal power, that his beauty seemed almost a secondary consideration, an accidental flaw conferred on him by unsuspecting parents.

"Would I, indeed?" he repeated, no longer a question. "Are you prepared to give me the coordinates of your voyage here from the old worlds—from Terra?"

Lily was startled into a brief laugh at this sally. "You don't really want to confront the Terran League, do you?" she asked. "You can't hope to defeat them in any military fashion, I don't think, and in any case, for what reason would you be rebelling against them?"

"Indeed," he replied smoothly, "what need for our revolution if we are reunited with our elders who will bring reform and unity to Reft space. You understand my need."

"Yes, I do," said Lily, meaning it. "And you're right—" Abruptly she wondered what Kyosti's compatriots, Anjahar and Maria, would think of Central's abuses—what would they, as law-enforcement officials, report back to the League? Had they been faster, perhaps Heredes could have been saved. "The League wouldn't condone Central's government, I don't think. But I don't know the way back, or how long it runs, or how complicated the calculations are. I told you that once before. I can't help you with that."

"Then what do you propose to help me with?"

"I believe," said Lily slowly, "that you already know."

He drew an index finger across the fine grain of the plastine desktop. "I have monitored with great interest the events on Harsh, and the liberation of the thirties dig. I am sure you are aware that I am not militarily as strong as Central—not yet. Central is aware of it, thus they are only now beginning to see the true threat I pose to them. Therefore, I must still rely on surprise and speed and subtlety for my victories, and on the careful mining of what information I can glean, and on the precise use of what forces I command, and on the constant recruitment of the oppressed and discontent who have just and good cause to rally to my aid. Thus—"

He paused, and she waited, expectant, even eager, to hear him finish. Realized abruptly that he had paused just to test the extent of her attention on him.

He smiled. For an instant she caught a glimpse of another Jehane, a man who was not so engrossed in leading a revolution that he could not briefly be amused by the very tactics he used to manipulate people, and share that amusement with her, seeing that she recognized them for what they were. Then that window vanished, collapsed back into the gravity of the task at hand. "Thus I build a special force, trained in the more arcane disciplines: espionage, commando, saboteurs..." He trailed off.

"Terrorist," she finished. "Yes, I know a bit about such disciplines."

"But you must prove to me that your skills, your people, if you mean to carry so many with you, are equal to the task. That you are, indeed, worth the effort to train and draw so close into our plans, be equal to the risk of using you in missions that must meet with success on the slimmest of odds."

"Like the thirties dig."

He shrugged. "Simple force is not always the most expedient method, and many times will fail utterly despite the mastery of surprise."

"Do you know that I worked with Pero on Arcadia?"

Now he paused without obvious deliberation. He tapped a few commands into a screen set into the desktop, and called up information that evidently satisfied him. "'They executed a man they claimed was Pero but who was not,'" he quoted, reading from the screen. "I just received information from my best and fastest source that Pero was executed and that there is riot on Arcadia and martial law."

"That information is false—well, not entirely. It's true, but it wasn't the real Pero, Robert Malcolm, who was executed. *He* is still alive."

"You sound certain."

"I am certain."

"I am glad to hear it," he said with conviction. He tapped more keys. "'Five adults, one child, one robot.' Yet you tell me now, twelve people will join with you."

It was her turn to shrug. "I gained five people, more or less accidently."

"*You* gained?"

"No, comrade Jehane," said Lily with a diplomacy that, it occurred to her, she must have learned from Sar Ransome. "*You* gained them. But some people feel safer in smaller groups."

"Indeed." The comment was utterly noncommittal, but even as the word died into the still air, his entire posture changed, tensing. "How did you know you could find me at Harsh?" he asked coldly.

"What is my assignment?"

He smiled again, and relaxed. "You wish a bargain. Very well. I know perfectly well you will be valuable to our cause, Lily Heredes. And I have no current reason to distrust your motives or your zeal." He let the unspoken threat linger a moment on silence, then went on. "Those who betray the revolution are dealt with swiftly and without mercy. Those who give of themselves for the cause of reform are rewarded each day with the liberation of new recruits, of Stations yoked under Central's bitter regime, and they will be rewarded with the restoration of a government meant for all citizens."

Lily smiled. "You sound like Pero."

"No," he said softly, not without menace, not without compassion. "Pero is *my* voice. He speaks in the prison of Arcadia, where my voice most begs to be heard. How did you know you could find me at Harsh?"

She took in a deep breath to steady herself while she chose words. Let it out. "I possess the distilled contents of Central's entire Intelligence network, on disk."

His hissed breath, stalike, revealed for an instant that she had caught him completely by surprise.

"Central's records of your movements were analyzed by the same expert who liberated the information from Central's com-net in the first place—the same man who was executed as Pero. That led me to Harsh."

"His name will be a monument to our cause," said Jehane with feeling. He stood up. "You will be under the command of Comrade Officer Callioux."

"*Callioux!*"

"Officer Callioux is in charge of the special forces, which

were, when you met them, in the final stages of planning an assault on the thirties dig."

The revelation caught her openmouthed. "Callioux told me—you let me run the whole operation, risk it, when you intended to free the thirties dig all along!"

Jehane regarded her without amusement or irony. "You wished to prove yourself. The test came to hand serendipitously. Comrade Officer Callioux will assign you, and your people, an appropriate berth on one of the special forces ships. Callioux's own, I believe."

Lily, still collecting herself, could not find words to reply.

"But first," and Jehane placed a single, precise finger on the intercom, "I will provide you with an escort to fetch this information you have brought me. After it is in my hands, you and your party will be released to Callioux."

Lily stood up. The door slipped open, and without surprise she saw the remembered figure of Kuan-yin, looking brash and vehement and not at all merciful. Kuan-yin's gaze was locked on Jehane, but at his gesture, she marched her ten soldiers across to Lily, waiting behind them with the tense readiness of a chained predator. Her glance, raking Lily, held promises of unspeakable pain should Lily not succor Jehane in every way he saw fit.

"For your protection," he said gently.

She looked at the ten soldiers and at Kuan-yin. "Who are you protecting me from?" she asked.

Jehane only smiled, softly apologetic.

9   Bleak House

****

"Hoy." Lily took the glass of ambergloss that Jenny offered her and watched as the mercenary sat down with controlled grace on the chair next to her. "Pinto got into *another* fight? That's what—the eighth he's been in in the six months we've been on this boat? Callioux will deny him Station leave now, no question. I don't see why he can't just learn to ignore the slurs like Rainbow does."

"Or ask innocent questions that make the comments sound stupid, like Paisley?" Jenny chuckled. "You have to remember, Lily-hae, that he's not really used to it, still not. He and Lia used to play together as kids. He was rich and privileged. And now—now he's just any other tattoo. Maybe he feels it's the only way he has left to distinguish himself."

"Wise Jenny," murmured Lily, sipping her drink and studying the bar they sat in with casual interest. Like all bars across the vast spectrum of human existence, this one was poorly lit and noisy. The bitter scent of spilled ambergloss permeated the air, and the floors were unswept, but otherwise the place was clean, uncluttered, and totally without character, a standard station bar servicing merchanters and soldiers. "Although I don't think Callioux is going to be so understanding."

Jenny shrugged. "It wasn't Pinto started the fight anyway. He got involved later. It was Paisley."

"Paisley!"

Jenny grinned. "We all went down there to watch Pinto play three-di—and to win a little money betting on him. And they had a *bisterlas* table going in one corner, so the Mule sat down. At first the sta already there refused to let it—him—play, as usual, but two had to go on shift, and Paisley was the only other person in the entire bar who knew the game. And she refused to play unless they let the Mule factor in as well. So." She shrugged. "You know how the sta are about *bisterlas*. They let the Mule in. And damn my eyes if I've ever seen a faster calculator. I don't think *Bach* could run those numbers as fast as the Mule did."

Lily raised her eyebrows, skeptical but not disbelieving, and crossed her legs to sit more comfortably. "And?"

"And of course some sta made a comment about perversions— it's funny how we humans make obscene jokes about sta and humans having sex, because I think sta think it's far more disgusting than we do. A real insult: your mother tupped out-species, that kind of thing. And Paisley jumped up and hit the esstavi right on the muzzle." A new gleam of amusement tipped Jenny's eyes. "Used her training, too: centered and focused. Knocked the honorable right out of his chair—of course he wasn't expecting it. Anyway, some greasy merchanter called her an ugly whore of a painted bastard, something on that line, and that sent Pinto off." A pause. "You know they're sleeping together."

Lily met Jenny's speculative gaze with a shrug. "They're Ridanis. If you believe everything that's said about Ridanis, then they must be sleeping together. And with Rainbow too."

"Frankly," Jenny replied, "that's one rumour about Ridanis I have reason to believe is true." She halted, grinning at Lily's expression. "Jealous, Lily-hae?"

"What? About Pinto?" Lily set down her glass with exasperation. "I will admit he has a handsome face, and a—what's the phrase—pleasing form, countered, of course, by a hot-tempered, but not unsympathetic, disposition, but frankly I have enough trouble arranging shift schedules so that I know Kyosti and Finch will never be in the same place at the same time. Not to mention assigning Bach to medical duty with Kyosti so that he can monitor Hawk all the time." She gave a glance at her wrist-com, but its letters and numbers gleamed a reassuring green on the tiny screen.

"I wonder," Jenny mused, "if that's what that strange phrase refers to. 'Forbidden fruit.'"

"Where did you hear that?"

"Where do you think? Hawk and I were talking one day—well, you know the way we talk. It's more arguing, really. I don't even remember what we were talking about." She looked as if she was about to say something more, changed her mind, and took a swallow of ambergloss instead. The amber liquid swayed smoothly in its glass as she set it down again. "Lily." Both her tone and expression betrayed her resolve to continue on an unpopular subject no matter Lily's preference.

"I don't want to talk about it."

"*You* don't want to deal with it," retorted Jenny. "I think you keep hoping the problem will go away by itself. The strongest team breaks at the weakest link."

"He's *not* a weak link! He's a brilliant physician," Lily exclaimed, then glanced self-consciously around the bar, aware of the heat in her voice. She met Jenny's gaze and smiled ruefully. "Maybe I'm the weak link for being afraid to—let him go."

"*Let* him go? To make him go. He won't leave you. I can understand that you might be afraid to force him to leave. I don't know how he would react. Like he did toward Finch?"

"No." Lily shook her head, sure enough of this point that she could respond calmly. "He won't hurt *me*."

Jenny considered this. "Are you afraid of him?" she asked softly.

Lily watched the still pool of her drink in the well of her glass. "I don't know," she replied, scarcely audible. "Jenny, is it"—she hesitated—"is it—queer to be attracted to that kind of wildness, that—unpredictability?"

"Sweetens it, doesn't it?" said Jenny as if she knew quite well that it was true. "You remember Mendi Mun, the Immortal who got Lia and I pregnant and escaped Central with us, and then squirreled off leaving us to get off Arcadia ourselves? He had something in him, right at his heart—if he had a heart—that you couldn't quite get at. It made him more interesting. I sometimes think Lia would have gone with him, not me, if she could have. But she didn't get the chance."

"Oh, Jenny. Surely not."

Jenny shrugged. "I'm not saying Lia doesn't love me in her

own way—" She stopped, clearly unwilling to unburden
herself further. "It's not going to come to the test anyway,
Lily-hae. It's just the kind of thought a person has when she's
in bed alone on a cold night."

"I've had my share of those." Lily's comment generated
nothing further from Jenny. "So what did the Mule do after
Paisley knocked over the sta?" Lily asked, determined now to
change the subject.

Jenny shifted in her chair, looking, for the briefest space,
relieved to be returning to this neutral topic. "Kept playing,
cool as you please, until Paisley got in over her head, and
then he rearranged a few people's positions to stop her from
getting badly hurt. Pinto and Rainbow were halfway across
the bar by that time—a person couldn't really sort out who
was with 'em and who against."

"What were you doing all this time?"

"Letting them have their fun. When it started getting too
rough I waded in and cleared things out. Even got the owner
to thank me for it. I suppose," she added, "that he didn't
suspect that I was with the ones who started it, being as they
were all Ridanis."

Lily watched Jenny consider this and smiled as she imagined the sight of a single Immortal-trained fighter taking on
an entire room of brawling soldiers and drunks and subduing
them. "Interesting," she said finally, "about the Mule, though.
Defending Paisley. He never shows her any preference on
ship."

"But I bet she still sneaks into his—its—cabin some nights."

Lily shuddered, suppressed it. "I don't have that much
compassion."

Jenny raised her glass, tipped and turned it so that the
amber liquid caught shadow and light in its flow. "Not many
do. I certainly don't. But that doesn't change the fact that the
Mule's the fastest calculator I've ever seen play *bissterlas*,
and I've seen lots of sta play in Stations all over the Reft."

"I wonder what it's like," said Lily slowly, "to be so cynical
about life—and so very alone."

They considered the Mule's fate in companionable silence
while music and images blared from the vid screen that
backed the bar, and a new swell of white-uniformed soldiers
filtered in to sit at tables and counters in the big room.

"Shift change." Jenny checked her wrist-com. "I'd better go. I've got a class to teach."

Lily stood also, but paused, hand still on her glass. "It's hard to believe we've been with Callioux almost half an Arcadian year. I can't decide whether the time has gone fast, or slow."

"I can't decide what in hell Jehane thinks he's up to," said Jenny. "A great initiative at Harsh, and now he's retreated back to Tollgate and sent half his fleet into these Hells-forsaken backwaters to achieve Void knows what. All I can say is that this sad excuse for a Station is aptly named Bleak House."

"Training?" Lily suggested. "He had all the new people from Harsh to incorporate into his forces. That takes time. And a lot of information from Bach to incorporate and sort through—most of Central's Intelligence files."

"You've been talking to Callioux."

"No," Lily admitted. "I'm guessing. And I watch Jehane's addresses now and then."

"Better you than me. After my time as an Immortal, where we had to stand through any number of boring senatorial speeches made by Senators who loved the sound of their own voice, addresses are one thing I refuse to attend or listen to over the vids. It's the one thing Hawk and I agree on."

Lily chuckled. "Well, speeches rarely give away important strategic or tactical information anyway. I don't know. But there are some government garrisons and pockets of Central loyalists out here that still need to be won over, or suppressed. And I can't complain about my duties. Besides the couple of hand-to-hand classes I teach, I spend most of my time learning the ship and how it's run, and tactics and strategy, and—you know."

"Does 'you know' include running a few obscure training missions for Callioux? Except for that little mop-up at Jeze-bel, which hardly could be described as a battle, you're the only one of us who's seen any action since Harsh that I know of."

Lily shrugged. "Callioux only had Bach and me run *two* intelligence-gathering missions. That doesn't really qualify as action, although it was nice to get off the ship. You know they only picked me because of Bach's abilities."

"They picked you because they mean to make you an

officer and they're putting you through your paces. Us simple comrades just get drill, no matter what our abilities."

"Or do the drilling." Lily grinned. "I've seen you take your classes through *their* paces. And believe me, I feel sorry for them."

"Necessity breeds," replied Jenny. "I really have to go. Walk me back?"

"No. I think I'll stroll the shopping district."

Jenny waved and left her.

Lily wandered out along the shop fronts that lined the broad hub of Station. She still had not grown used to the perspective in the huge orbiting Stations that served as anchors for the great web of the highroad that spread out through Reft space, windows of passage from system to system. Partly it was the physical oddities: the curve, the constant view of changing stars in the port domes, and the feeling she often got in the smaller Stations of unending movement—rotation, orbit, the shift of the solar system itself in space. It made her dizzy.

But the tiny fleet under Callioux's command only docked in systems that had no landfall, no planetary colonizations: just the solitary stations necessary for calculating the shifting vectors of the road correctly. And in these places Lily felt uprooted.

Born and bred on a planet, however inhospitable, she was used to a home, a center, a place with its own being and purpose. Here, besides the Ridanis and Station-hoppers marooned by poverty, the pygmies living their own strange lives in the low-gravity hub, the occasional merchant or shop-keeping family building their trade, the only purpose of a Station was to move its visitors onward, to cast them through that window of passage to another world. Bleak, indeed, for souls stranded in such a place.

As she walked slowly along the facade of shops, not really examining what was in fact a fairly mediocre selection of goods for sale, she considered that these past months were a passage for her as well. Only she was not sure what destination she was vectored for.

She paused to examine a necklace that, if unstrung, could provide new beads for Paisley to braid into her hair. Jehane's service did not pay well, although it did provide room and board, but Lily spent so little credit on herself that she always had something to spend on her associates.

"Definitely not your color," said Kyosti from so close behind her that she managed not to drop the necklace, balanced across her palms, only by accidently catching it around one finger as she started.

"So much for my training," she muttered as she turned. "I thought I'd buy it for Paisley," she said to him.

He shook his head. "Definitely not her, either. Look at that pattern. Paisley is a—a paisley, after all. This is too geometric. It would do better for Pinto, although Rainbow might—"

"Kyosti! These beads are so small that no one can tell the difference."

He raised one slender hand in a gesture meant to forestall and correct. "A discerning eye can."

The Ridani shopkeeper, perceiving a serious customer, moved forward, discreetly available, as Kyosti began to examine the rack of necklaces.

Lily smiled, watching him. Like all of Jehane's people, he wore white, but his were the medical whites universal to the profession: shirt, long jacket, and loose trousers rather than the close-fitting tunic and slim-legged trousers of the military uniforms. On Unruli, white had never been fashionable; on a mining planet it was impractical. But in the gleaming sterility of space, white proves dazzling and monotonous by turns. After half a year in Jehane's rebellion, Lily had concluded that it was mostly monotonous.

But Kyosti—Kyosti somehow managed in his medical whites always to look stylish. Perhaps it was just his posture, or the long, slender lines of his body, but he wore it, too, with a panache that was practiced and self-conscious, and with an ever-changing array of discreet but colorful accessories that lent a cunning enhancement to his clothing.

And there was also, of course, his hair. Her smile sharpened to a frown as he held up a necklace and examined it with the eye of a connoisseur. For he had, as he had warned Jenny when he boarded the shuttle to escape Arcadia, let it grow out, had given up bleaching it blond.

And it wasn't really that it was growing in more slowly than she thought hair was supposed to grow. It was that the roots were coming in blue.

He offered her the necklace for her consideration, and smiled at her expression. "But I thought it would suit Paisley so well," he murmured.

She gave the necklace a cursory glance and handed it to the shopkeeper. "I'll take it."

Kyosti laughed. "The only saving grace to your complete lack of style, Lily my love, is that you are one of the few people who look stunning in the unadorned lines of Jehane's uniforms." He considered. "Jenny looks good as well, but that comes mostly from her complexion and her magnificent physique."

"But I like uniforms," protested Lily. "It means I don't have to decide what to wear in the mornings."

"Utilitarian to the core," said Kyosti. "There must be a Bentham in your ancestry somewhere."

Lily had long since learned to ignore those of his comments that made no apparent sense, so she calmly paid for the necklace and turned down the corridor to continue browsing along the rest of the shops.

He followed her. She felt him follow her, not without pleasure. And she wondered if Jenny was right—if Kyosti's instability in regard to Finch did not indeed make him a weak link in their team.

"Wait a minute." She halted between shop awnings, jewelry at her back, scarves and tunics before her. "Where's Bach?"

"Analyzing blood samples in the lab," said Kyosti casually, moving ahead to run his hands over a hanging row of scarves with real pleasure, as if the textures alone were a delight to him. His hands had a way of moving that awakened memories in her of other times, alone with him. She smiled. "We seem to have picked up a mild venereal disease at the Mother-forsaken hellhole of a Station so ironically named Renunciate, and it's spreading through the Ridanis like wildfire."

"Kyosti," she began, reproving almost as much for the jolting prosaicness of his comment as for the realization that without Bach monitoring him, Finch was left unguarded.

"Get him transferred to another ship, Lily," he interrupted in a sharp voice. "Do you have any idea of the effort it takes me *not* to seek him out, not to track him down to whatever cabin you've hidden him in? Or the bridge when he's on duty?" He was still examining the scarves, and his voice, low, stirred no farther than her. *"Franklin's Cairn* is not that big a ship."

"Big enough. Finch and Swann are lost enough as it is, and especially now that their mother transferred—at her own request, I remind you—to the *Boukephalos*, to run Jehane's personal Portmastery division. I had no idea she'd turn into such an ardent Jehanist. I'm not going to abandon them now. Why do you have to kill him, Kyosti?" Her voice shook. *"Why is your hair growing in blue?"*

He did not reply, but his hands trembled slightly as he drew out of the row of scarves one bearing a brilliant red pattern. He tied it solicitously around her neck, twisted the ends, and stepped back to survey her.

He smiled. His smiles always disarmed her, and she suspected that he knew it quite well. "Yes. That's what it wanted."

It was at times like this that she most hated it when he looked at her that way—because she loved it. Of course he was a brilliant physician. But she wouldn't force him to leave because *she* didn't want to be without him. Even if it meant risking Finch. Disgusted and exasperated, more with herself than with him, she turned to find a mirror, staring at her reflection.

Her black hair still hung to just below her shoulders, cut absolutely straight around the bottom except for the short riffling of bangs above the oblique slant of her dark eyes. But the almost insouciant twist of the scarf lent her a rather rakish look, otherwise so proper in starched whites, that reminded her briefly of La Belle.

"Someday, Kyosti," she said to the mirror, fixing her gaze on his reflection behind her, "you ought to consider trusting me."

"Because blue is its natural color," he replied without expression.

"You're not used to trusting people, are you?" She turned, struck by this sudden illumination, but he remained remote from her.

"Should I be?" he asked bitterly. "My mother abandoned me when I was eleven. My father's family disowned me when I was seventeen."

"What about your father?" she asked quietly.

"He died before I was born," he replied with an irony so

deep that she knew there was a wealth of unspoken information in those simple words.

"How could your mother just abandon you?"

"An unfortunate choice of words, perhaps. She did what she had to do. I no longer blame her for it."

Abruptly she wanted very much to reassure him that she, at least, would not abandon him so callously. "Come on," she said softly, brushing his arm with one hand, feeling his muscles respond, anticipatory, as she let her touch linger. "Let's go back to the ship."

She began to untie the scarf, but he forestalled her brusquely. "No. I want to buy that for you."

She watched him carefully as he completed the transaction with the shopkeeper, but as they left the shop he turned away from the direction that would lead them back to their berth. It occurred to her that he was avoiding the intimacy that in his present mood might tempt him to reveal too much.

"Kyosti," she began, using the distraction of musical instruments in the next shop as an excuse to continue speaking, "I know that technology in the League is far advanced of what we have here in the Reft, or at least it ought to be by now, after we've been cut off for so long. Just look at Bach. He must have been marooned here when the original highroad fleet came in. And I know, although I still find it difficult to believe, that Master Heredes was far, far older than he looked—than any age extension technology we possess here—and that you are, too—"

"Once the Hierakas Formula was discovered," he interrupted as if at random, "it really proved quite simple, but the actual manufacture is not so easy, especially with the laboratory conditions prevailing here. Quite primitive."

"What's the—never mind. Don't try to distract me. Kyosti, there must have been someone besides your family in all that time that you loved." She hesitated, aware of an ember of jealousy within herself that she did not yet want to examine. "A woman."

He stopped in the shadowed corner of an awning and pulled her to face him, close, hands on her shoulders. "Do you want the truth? There were two women, Lily. One was murdered by a man who thought he could save his own life by killing her. I saw her die. The other"—he paused—"was killed in the Betaos engagement against the Kapellans. I saw her die, too. But I didn't love them in any sense that you mean the word. And I had my comrades in arms, in the fight we terrorists led for the League against the Kapellan Empire. We were close because we had to be, in such circumstances, in such work, but we could lose a friend to death at any moment those years. We knew the risk. It made the experience, and the attachments, more intense."

"No one you loved?"

His face took on an expression almost inhuman in its detachment, yet his voice shook. "So many years ago. I had a friend whom I loved, like a brother. What a terrible, trite phrase that is—the worse for being true."

"What happened to him? Was he one of the League's saboteurs, too. And he died?"

Kyosti smiled, so bitter and so mocking that Lily felt as if she could cry to see such pain in his normally controlled and blithe facade. "I murdered him, Lily."

At first she was too choked to speak, half out of pity, half out of fear at his hands resting so tenderly on her shoulders. "Why?" Her voice was scarcely more than a whisper.

"Because he slept with my—" He hesitated, searching for a word.

"Your lover?"

"Yes." He shut his eyes. She could scarcely hear his voice. "But if he knew—that she was your lover."

"He didn't know. She seduced him, because she didn't believe me when I told her that I would have to kill any man she slept with. So she chose him. She wanted to know that she had that power over me."

The soft conversations of other shoppers flowed past them, rippling around their silence.

"I think it amused her that I couldn't repudiate her, not even after that," he continued, his voice growing more detached as he spoke, as if the memory was too awful to attach emotion to. "But I was glad when she was killed on Betaos."

In the silence following this remark, the shopkeeper approached, looking apprehensive, and after a moment retreated again.

Too shocked to speak, Lily very carefully did not move from underneath his hands, but with deliberation he removed them himself and turned to examine with feigned interest a row of whistle pipes in the shop.

"I trust *you*, Lily," he replied, a murmur, "and someday we are both going to wish that I didn't." And he said something else, fluid as a prayer, under his breath, in a language she did not recognize.

Because she could not decide whether his unqualified statement of trust was a blessing or a curse, she began to walk again, as if movement alone would dispel her troubles, or at least hold them at bay.

Was she better than that woman, willing to risk Finch? Doing everything she could think of to protect him—that, yes—but it still put his life at risk. She did not know what to say to herself. She could not possibly think of what to say to Hawk, and she was suddenly afraid to ask any more questions, because they might reveal the selfishness of her own motives as clearly. Had she really thought she could manage Hawk so easily? Obviously, her first duty on returning to the ship must be to request that Finch be transferred—anywhere.

Kyosti followed her, walking alongside her in a silence that was, perhaps, in deference to her taut expression. They simply walked and, casting a glance at his set, serious face, for the first time she *really* wondered what Master Heredes had known about Kyosti's background that had caused him to oppose Kyosti's interest in her so strenuously and yet acquiesce so abruptly once he knew with certainty that they were lovers. And yet, having been one of the League's saboteurs as well, what more had he needed to know?

"Heredes! Hawk!"

The hail interrupted her thoughts so thoroughly that it took her a moment to recall where she was. Then she saw Yehoshua and his cousin Alsayid sitting at a cafe table under a striped awning that jutted out into the hub corridor. Yehoshua motioned them over with a glittering wave, and as she and Kyosti approached the table, Lily realized that Yehoshua had gained an artificial arm since she had last seen him unconscious and injured on Harsh.

He grinned and lifted the arm up for her and Kyosti to admire. It was metal and plastine, and stiff jointed, with a three-pronged hook apparatus where the hand would be.

Kyosti frowned and reached out to examine it more closely.

Yehoshua looked on with pride as Kyosti slid a hand up to tickle the straps and down again to test the hook mechanism.

"I thought I'd be left one armed, or with a simple prosthetic," said Yehoshua with a grin, "but Jehane values his people too highly to leave it at that. I just got back from Halfway itself. The best surgical and rehab center worked on me, and then I got my reassignment at my request back to my original unit."

Alsayid, who Lily had met on and off the past months in the corridors of *Franklin's Cairn*, grinned at his cousin and ordered two cups of aris for the new arrivals.

"In celebration," said Yehoshua. "Please sit down."

Lily and Kyosti sat, but not before Lily caught Kyosti's sharp whisper: "Mother bless us, is that primitive thing the best they can do here?"

However, he dutifully admired the artificial arm and watched Yehoshua demonstrate its facility: awkward writing, picking up both cup and glass, manipulating wire and string and, even, his pistol—which he had unloaded for the demonstration.

"So you were with Callioux's unit to begin with," said Lily once they had settled in to drink their aris.

"Yes." His smile was softly amused. "Did you discover that Callioux had planned all along on Harsh to liberate the thirties?"

Lily considered him thoughtfully. "I've thought a lot recently about how easy it was to manipulate me, but I suppose I deserved it for being so sure I was manipulating Jehane." She grinned. "I won't underestimate him again."

Alsayid chuckled.

"No," replied Yehoshua. "It doesn't do to underestimate comrade Jehane. How did you find out?"

"Oh, Jehane himself told me. He thought it was serendipitous that a test came to hand so easily. I've never felt so humiliated in my life. Well, at least not recently."

Yehoshua still smiled, but gently. "Well, I'm sorry you had to be taken in like that, but frankly it *was* a rather good job."

"If you were in on it." She shook her head. "But I must admit, it was brave of you to volunteer to come with us."

"Thank you." He used his artificial arm to reload his pistol and slip it back in its sling. "Although as much as Alsayid and I would like to take credit for unselfish courage, I must reveal that we had a back-up plan, in case yours went wrong."

"Hoy," Lily murmured into her cup. She laughed. "I hope I didn't make too great a fool of myself."

Under the table, Kyosti patted her reassuringly on the thigh.

"Not at all," replied Yehoshua. "Why do you think you're with Callioux? And training well, I hear."

"It's more than I hear," retorted Lily. "But I do like getting to know the ship and the various specialties in our—ah—line of work. How *did* you two get into Callioux's unit in the first place?"

Yehoshua shrugged. The glare of Station lighting accentuated the fine white scars on his face and arms. "We'd worked in dangerous conditions before. Cable stripping takes cool and calm and the ability not to hesitate or flinch."

"Exactly the right qualities for a good saboteur," murmured Kyosti.

"Or a good doctor," returned Yehoshua, examining Hawk with interest. "How do you get your hair colored blue at the roots like that?"

"It's its natural color," said Kyosti innocently, and he smiled nonchalantly as Yehoshua and Alsayid laughed at his humor. "I hope," Kyosti continued smoothly, "that you'll let me look at that arm more closely. Perhaps I can come up with some ideas for modification, and then if we can just find a clever mechanic—"

All four of their wrist-coms lit up at the same moment, followed by a single blended aural alarm, brief but penetrating. "All personnel, report to your stations. Repeat, all—"

Lily, Yehoshua, and Alsayid slapped the "received" command and jumped to their feet immediately, leaving Kyosti relaxed in his chair as the message, softened to one-quarter its previous volume, went on.

"—personnel, report to your stations. Unidentified ship in-system and approaching with evasive maneuvers. Repeat—"

Now Kyosti rose, tapping his com to silence. Through the hub district, white-clad soldiers flooded in groups of twos and threes toward the docking sector: Jehane's people hurrying back.

"Action at last," said Yehoshua with relish.

Lily felt abruptly quite mixed feelings: excitement tempered by uncertainty and fear. "I think I'd rather meet face-to-face than locked away in a ship," she said. She had to lengthen her stride as Kyosti broke into an easy lope.

His expression remained neutral. "In the long run, it makes very little difference. In the short"—he smiled—"in the short, you're better off face-to-face."

At the berth itself, one of Callioux's lieutenants met them personally. "Commander wants you on the bridge," she said, motioning them to follow while Yehoshua and Alsayid watched this summons with curiosity. When Kyosti turned to head for the medical, the officer gestured at him. "You, too, comrade Hawk," she added, shrugging to show that she was only the messenger and could not explain this cryptic summons.

The owner of *Franklin's Cairn* had been a prosperous merchanter converted to the cause, and the bridge was spacious and well appointed, even with the obtrusive addition of a large weapons bank in one corner.

Callioux did not look up as Lily and Hawk entered, but spoke immediately after the bridge door shut behind them. "We have the initial specs on this ship. It is *not* a Central military vessel of any design we know. And we have received one cryptic message over comm, while meanwhile they continue to approach with clear evasive tactics. What do you make of this?" Read off the screen lit up on the arm of the captain's chair. " 'There will be advantage in every movement which shall be undertaken.' "

Kyosti laughed. "Where La Belle leads, the rest soon will follow. You've bagged yourself a pirate, comrade."

10 Yi

****

"Comrade Officer Callioux." The soldier at comm tilted his head back to catch a glimpse of his captain. "We have run the intruder's specs through *all* of our data bases, and we have no vessel answering to the description we have here."

Callioux examined Lily and Kyosti with a keen eye. "Now. The dossier on you two transferred to me from Jehane's files suggests that you might know something about an unusual sighting like this." Paused, obviously waiting for their reaction.

Kyosti ran one hand languidly through his hair. "Give me an open line on comm, and I'll guarantee they will consider you for the time being as neutral."

Callioux shrugged and signed to the man at comm. "I don't need trouble yet. Go ahead, but remember, it's on your head."

"Isn't it always?" murmured Kyosti as he walked forward to lean with apparent carelessness on the board.

Lily watched as a composite of the sensor's description of the unidentified ship took shape on the screen. It did not have the massive, graceful bulk of *La Belle Dame Sans Merci*, but Lily recognized the lines of a superior technology and did not doubt that this ship had followed La Belle over the lost way from League space to Reft space. For what purpose—she could not imagine.

As the man at comm opened a clear line, Kyosti spoke. "'It will be advantageous even to cross the great stream.'"

Callioux lifted dark eyebrows in surprise, but turned to face Lily as if she could answer his question.

"I don't know," she said quickly, although the seeming incongruity of the exchange reminded her eerily of Heredes's initial exchange with the *Sans Merci*.

The unknown ship had clearly been waiting for some such reply, because after only a brief pause, a voice crackled out over comm, deeply smooth, and strong as silk.

"Indeed, we hope we are successful in our enterprise and overcome our greatest difficulties." Humor permeated the speaker's tone.

"Unfortunately," replied Kyosti, evidently enjoying himself, "I don't possess ten pairs of tortoise shells, although I can't imagine what you would do with them anyway."

A pause, as the message relayed back, but now the deep voice returned with a sharp tone. "Who is this?"

Kyosti straightened and stepped back from the console, gesturing to Callioux.

"I am Comrade Officer Callioux," answered Callioux, "Commander of *Franklin's Cairn* and her attendant vessels in the Second Auxiliary Fleet of Alexander Jehane's Provisional Armed Forces. I request that you identify yourself and state your purpose in entering without clearance territory controlled by the PAF."

"No," said the deep voice. "The man who spoke first." A pause. "Send him over."

Callioux frowned. "I repeat, please identify yourself and state your purpose."

"I am Yi, of course." The sheer arrogance of his tone carried easily over the crackle and spit of comm. "I am not interested in this local squabble over territorial and governing rights that you are engaged in. Heavens, Commander, there is so little with which I might increase my personal wealth here in this gods-forsaken corner of space that you cannot seriously believe that *I* entertain any notion of conquest or plunder."

The sally left Callioux speechless, caught between shock and indignation.

"No." The deep voice of Yi paused, reflective, on the

syllable. "I am merely engaged, on behalf of one of my employees, in a hunt."

Kyosti stiffened. His reaction was so pointed that, although he quickly controlled himself, forcing himself to relax, most of the crew on the bridge now stared at him.

"Well?" asked Callioux in a low, tense voice. "Shall I send you over, comrade Hawk? Can you guarantee that this—this mountebank is fully able to defend his insolent tone?"

"Fully able," said Kyosti softly. He had always been, and was still, at pains to avail himself of whatever methods were available to darken his skin to some facsimile of a golden tan, but now Lily saw him pale. He rested a hand on the console, as if steadying himself. "It is better that I go over than for you to test his strength."

"I have six ships to his one," exclaimed Callioux. "And three are advantageously deployed even as we speak."

"That cuts down on his advantage, certainly." Kyosti's expression cleared as he controlled himself, somehow erasing that initial reaction entirely from his face and posture.

Callioux cursed in a low voice, jabbed out some command onto the keys of the screen on the chair's arm. "Very well. I'll send an escort with you. Comrade Heredes." Lily saluted. "You will take your robot and go as well. Record as much information as possible. I want every possible detail on that ship. And I will send a ten with you."

"Leave Yi alone," said Kyosti in a quiet voice that brooked no disagreement. "He's been a privateer for longer than you've been alive, comrade Callioux, and even if that weren't true, he's called out on a hunt. Don't even attempt to get between a hound and its quarry."

"All right," said Lily as she and Kyosti buckled themselves into the shuttle that would ferry them over to Yi's ship. "You wouldn't tell Callioux. For a second there I thought you would be arrested for insubordination. What about me? What is a hound, and a hunt?"

"No." He did not even look at her. "Don't talk to me now, Lily." His face bore a set expression that disturbed her far more than his flat tone of voice.

She remained silent for the rest of the brief flight across, wishing she could see the great ship they approached, and increasingly troubled by the frequency with which Kyosti reached up to touch his hair. It seemed to her a gesture either superstitious or self-conscious, and she was not sure which explanation made her more nervous.

At last they ferried in to docking. She and Kyosti were escorted by Yehoshua and Alsayid rather than an entire complement of ten—Callioux's one concession. Bach floated behind Lily as they waited in the lock, nudging up against her back.

The lock opened into the ship to reveal a party of ten men and women clad in dullest grey. This escort showed them courteously, but without smiles, up a series of corridors to the bridge elevator. Compared to La Belle's ship, this vessel had no color at all, although in many places Lily thought she saw some sort of textured ridging at shoulder height, panels as much tactile as luminescent. The ten guards left them to ride in the elevator alone, a journey horizontal and diagonal as well as vertical. When the doors opened, Lily gasped.

The bridge was huge.

She could not hear the speech of the figures at the opposite end. Only a slight undertone in the air suggested to her that they were indeed speaking. At intervals along the expanse of wall, separate stations had been built, peopled now by a few individuals whose uniforms were black. It struck her then that everything on this ship was gray or black or white, lacking color entirely. Without stronger contrasts it was hard to measure the distance between her and the far wall, but she guessed it to be some hundred meters.

She leaned close to Kyosti. "Why would someone build a bridge so big?" she whispered. "The captain can't even see who we are from so far."

"But he can hear you," replied a voice that Lily recognized instantly as Yi's. It echoed in the vast space. "Come closer."

Kyosti walked forward immediately, so Lily followed, Yehoshua and Alsayid close at her heels staring about themselves. Bach rose to drift forward just above Lily's head.

She felt dwarfed and alone on their walk, felt intimidated. Looking behind, she saw that two doors opened onto the bridge on either side of the elevator's terminus. The undertone of speech stilled as they neared the far wall, dissolving into silence as they came to a halt in front of a simple console at which sat a dark man.

Behind him, the walls held a long, curving bank of instruments manned by more black-clad individuals. Only the man directly in front of them examined them, however; the rest continued with their work.

Yi—for surely it was he—did not speak for some moments. His tongue touched his lips several times as he surveyed the four visitors, as if he was tasting the air. Although he did not rise, Lily could tell by the fold of his body in the chair that he was quite tall. At last an expression of interested surprise crossed his face.

"You are the one called Hawk, are you not? I knew—a familiarity."

Kyosti inclined his head briefly. "You are astute."

"Yes." Yi considered the others in a further silence.

Lily realized with a start that he had no irises: he was blind.

He lifted a hand to a small tray attached on the left arm of his chair, picking up a selection of small sticks. Casting them down, he let his left hand trace their pattern while he surveyed Lily intently. Surveyed her somehow without sight.

"The virtue of brightness," he said in his deep voice. "Although one sees also tears flowing in torrents. But tread reverently, and there will be no error."

"I beg your pardon?" asked Lily.

He laughed, amused perhaps at her expense. "You are of interest to the Changes. Your passing stirs the stream." His tone sharpened. "You have with you a rare model. I was not aware that such technology, however dated, was available in this backwater." And his gaze, however sightless, drifted up to fix on Bach.

"Perhaps," replied Lily, not without a hint of irritation, "we aren't as backward as you would like to believe. Why did you want us on your ship?"

"Curiosity," he said, not without smugness. "But now I know that it was the legendary Hawk who spoke so cleverly to me earlier."

"Then why did you take evasive action as you entered this system?" she countered.

Yi sighed, as might a teacher when asked a foolish question for the tenth time by the same student. "I took evasive action because it is always prudent to take evasive action. Furthermore, I have met with several vessels claiming to be official military ships in the course of my—shall we say—wanderings in this benighted region, and all were inclined to be hostile."

"Can you blame them?" Lily asked. "We don't even know why you're here."

Kyosti brushed a hand against her arm, warning, as Yi's expression tightened.

His dark hands fingered a small keyboard on the chair's arm, and after that he seemed to wait, content not to speak but merely to observe them with whatever senses he used. Yehoshua and Alsayid continued to stare around themselves, amazed. Bach whirred quietly above Lily's head.

She only knew something happened because Kyosti suddenly stiffened beside her. Glancing at his face, she saw him shut his eyes, clenching them tight as if to prevent them from opening. His shoulders made the beginning of a movement to turn, a gesture he cut off with a jerk into immobility. Yi's face remained impassive, but his awareness had subtly shifted past her.

She turned.

Across the vast room she saw three people enter the bridge and stop by the elevator. Two of them had blue hair.

Of a different hue than Kyosti's, certainly tinged with green, perhaps—but without a doubt blue. They were tall, seemed pale, but beyond that, at such distance, she could not tell.

"You see," said Yi quietly. "I am indeed called to course on a hunt for some of my employees. I have reason to believe you can give me information." His gaze rested on Kyosti.

Kyosti stood so still he might as well have been paralyzed. He did not respond.

By the elevator, the shortest of the three figures detached itself from the others and began to cross the floor. Yi made a brief, almost undetectable gesture with one hand, and the two blue-haired people left the bridge.

Kyosti shuddered and opened his eyes. He stared at Yi with a look close to hatred. "Why did you do that?" He sounded near gone to rage.

"Is it not allowed?" Yi's tone might have been mocking.

"Don't play your damned games with me," snarled Kyosti, transformed with an anger that seemed to emanate off him.

"I remind you that this is *my* ship. *My* ground."

"Do you think I care?" Kyosti fairly shook with rage. "I

repeat. Don't play your games with me. I'm no longer a piece on this board."

"Of course you are still a piece," replied Yi coldly. "You have merely been transformed into the wild card." He extended a hand, and a grey-clad man passed beside Lily and handed Yi a stoppered vial. "I am called to the hunt, Hawk. What is it worth to you to help me?" He lifted the vial.

Kyosti recoiled from the movement. "Nothing. It's worth nothing to me. Leave me alone with what little I have managed to build out of the wreckage." His voice was hard.

"Ah, I see." Yi examined Kyosti, his face alive with curiosity. His tongue touched his lips three times. "You seek to escape your past by denying it." His left hand brushed at the sticks on the tray, gathered them into his palm, tossed them, traced them.

Kyosti took another step back, almost stepping into Yehoshua.

"I see the abyss." The grim surety of his voice did not change the expression of lively curiosity on his face. "'His endeavors will lead him into the cavern of the pit.' You had do better to strive for wholeness."

"Leave me alone." Kyosti's voice was so soft that Lily could barely hear him.

Yi smiled, ironic and pitiless. "I think it likely that I had far better fear you than you fear me, since you do not. It is the truth you fear." He lifted the vial again. "I will pay you whatever is in my power to pay. Once the hunt is blooded, we will return to League space. Clearly there is no booty worth our while here." He paused, gauging Kyosti's reaction. "Passage back?"

Kyosti shook his head emphatically. "You don't have the entire equation, Yi. That doesn't tempt me."

Yi considered this thoughtfully. "It may indeed be true that I lack certain bits of vital information. It is a small enough thing to ask of *you*, Hawk. I need only to know if you have come across the quarry in your wanderings."

Kyosti hesitated, and Lily could see some debate warring inside him that manifested itself by no larger gesture than the clenching and unclenching of his right hand.

"Your honor," chided Yi. "*Abai'is-ssa*. For your mother's memory, at least."

Kyosti reached out and grabbed the vial. Unstoppered it and, in a movement made stranger by the complete lack of self-consciousness with which he did it, he lifted it to his lips and then simply breathed carefully and deeply, as if he were intent on its smell.

After some moments he lowered it, stoppered it, and handed it back to Yi. His face was now clear of expression. "Yes. On La Belle's ship."

Yi did not reply for a moment. "Difficult," he said finally, musing, "but even La Belle must honor a hunt. Where did you meet her?"

Kyosti reeled off a string of numbers that Lily could not follow. "But that was over two League years ago," he added.

Yi smiled again. He looked pleased. "If it was simple, it would not be a challenge, would it? Why do you think I allowed my vessel to be called out?"

"I can't imagine," Kyosti said sarcastically. "Your magnanimous nature, undoubtedly. I think we may as well go now. You have what you want."

"But you have neglected your payment. I cannot"—Yi paused, repeated the word emphatically—"*cannot* let a debt go unpaid."

Kyosti shook his head impatiently. "I said I don't want anything—" As he began to turn away, he caught sight of Yehoshua, standing perplexed but alert behind him. Kyosti smiled abruptly, a brief chuckle. "Look at that thing," he continued, pointing to the artificial arm strapped to Yehoshua's left shoulder. "That is the most obscene excuse for medical rehabilitation I have ever seen."

Yi raised his winged eyebrows. "Come here, man," he said in a voice Yehoshua did not choose to disobey. Yi reached out and felt the arm from the hooks at its tip to the straps at its base. "Inept and primitive, certainly," he agreed without expression.

"How can you tell from that kind of examination?" Lily demanded.

"It is true that I lack sight, but do not, therefore, underestimate my other senses. Or your own, indeed. As Hawk knows." He waved Yehoshua back and turned to regard Kyosti with his uncanny, sightless gaze. "You wish?"

"Replace it," said Kyosti. "With your best prosthetic."

"If *I* may speak—" began Yehoshua, exchanging a startled glance with his cousin.

"Yehoshua," cut in Lily, "if I were you, I'd take it." The

clear decisiveness in her voice convinced him, and he subsided into a watchful silence.

Yi tapped on the console keyboard, waited, seeming to listen to some voice no one else could hear.

"It would take a watch week, at minimum," he said at last. "That covers only fitting and grafting and the elementary fitness testing. Any further care and rehabilitation would have to be completed under your care."

Yehoshua chuckled. "Well, I certainly trust comrade Hawk's care. But we would have to talk to the Commander."

"*I'll* talk to Callioux," said Lily, forestalling Kyosti's reply.

Yi frowned. "It will mean delay..."

"But it is my price," finished Kyosti sweetly. He lifted a hand to touch his hair. An almost furtive expression marked his face for a moment. "And I'll need some specialized equipment," he added, like an afterthought.

Yi's eyebrows arced, a question. "Will you, indeed?"

"For monitoring his condition, of course," Kyosti continued a bit too quickly. He glanced at Lily, measuring something in his own mind, then carefully returned his gaze to Yi.

"As you say," agreed Yi, and smiled a curiously premonitory smile.

11 *Franklin's Cairn*

****

The *Cairn* remained in contiguous orbit with Bleak House Station for three full fleet weeks. Callioux agreed, after a brief but obligatory, and scathing, denunciation of Lily's presumption in giving orders without permission, to Yehoshua's surgery, and sent on two of his six ships to a further post, expecting to follow them once Yehoshua returned.

But before full preparations could be made to depart, a small merchanter arrived ostensibly for trade and abruptly Callioux announced a delay. Yehoshua came back and was immediately sequestered in Medical, seeing only Kyosti, Callioux, his cousin, and the duty techs, all of whom refused to elaborate. Kyosti told Lily only that he was pleased, if a bit unprepared to deal with a prosthetic of such sophistication. Rumors of all sorts swept the crew deck. None could be substantiated.

"What do you think?" Lily asked Jenny at the end of the third week. They sat in the corridor common room on one of the uncomfortable benches that lined the walls.

Jenny did not answer for a moment, and Lily followed the line of her gaze. At one of the near tables her son Gregori stood at Paisley's shoulder, peering with a seven-year-old's intense concentration at the Ridani game of colored sticks and dice that she was playing with Pinto, Kyosti, and Rainbow. At the table next to them, the Mule painstakingly taught the intermediate elements of *bissterlas* to Aliasing; although it treated Lily with reserved respect, the Mule remained aloof toward everyone else except Paisley, whom it treated with a restrained tolerance that it had only recently begun to extend tentatively toward Lia.

"It's sweet of Paisley to help Lia and me care for Gregori," said Jenny at last, musing. "And you, of course. Otherwise we'd never cover our duty."

"Don't thank me," Lily replied quickly. "Actually, this past two months Kyosti of all people has been spending time with him, letting him tag along to Medical."

Jenny looked surprised, then chuckled. "So that's it. Lately he's been coming home full of peculiar facts and stories and questions I can't answer. And he keeps saying that he's being tutored. I thought he'd snuck into some higher level education program in the computer. I'll have to thank Hawk."

Lily grinned briefly. "Please do. It will discompose him."

"Will it?" Jenny asked with interest. "I don't think I've ever seen him discomposed. Well"—she paused—"except for those two times with Finch."

"Finch," Lily declared with exasperation. "That's what I was asking you about. Callioux has refused all three of my requests that Finch be transferred to another ship. I told Bach to switch from shadowing Hawk to sticking close to Finch. Then he can at least alert me. And possibly stun Hawk—but you wouldn't have seen that. I just don't know what else to do."

Jenny considered this while keeping her gaze on her son, who had reached past Paisley to roll the three dice for her. "I honestly don't know," she answered at last. "Given that you're determined to keep Hawk with you. You're using what resources you have to cover as much ground as possible. Beyond quarantining one of them—or forcing it to a controlled resolution—"

"I have thought of that," Lily agreed, "but I'm not ready yet. I have yet to figure out how to set up a confrontation that I can control completely. Especially with Hawk."

"Yes." Jenny shifted her gaze to Hawk as he sat perfectly at ease with the three Ridanis, playing a game with them that by tradition only Ridanis were supposed to know. "I thought that sticks game was sacred, or something. Why does he know it?"

Lily shrugged. "They're letting Gregori watch."

"Yes, but just watch if any adults go near, or show too much interest. Have you spoken to Finch anymore about Hawk?"

"Only a bit. I never have time to see him, partly because his duty schedule is so carefully set up to match Hawk's, and partly because he won't come *here* when he is free."

"Can you blame him, Lily-hae?"

Gregori clapped his hands in excitement as some roll of sticks or dice came up in his—or at least in Paisley's—favor.

"I'm not sure it's entirely because of Hawk," said Lily. "He still won't speak to any Ridanis unless he has to."

"That's not so different from a lot of Jehane's troops. You know very well that it's a shock to most of these people that Jehane has enlisted tattoos as regular comrades at all. Even if most of the Ridanis are in separate companies, still—it rankles a lot of the soldiers. Finch isn't so different."

"He ought to be," retorted Lily hotly. "I expected better of him. I always thought he was so easygoing, so good-natured. But on the other hand, when did we ever see Ridanis at Ransome House? There may have been some mines that employed them for the worst work. I don't know. But most jobs weren't open to Ridanis on Unruli. And if you weren't tied into one of the House mines, or to the university or the city offices, you had no access to living quarters, which were a true necessity on Unruli. We just never saw them, growing up."

"Then you ought to understand why Finch could be prejudiced."

"Except it doesn't mean you *have* to be," said Lily harshly. "Having nothing personal against them. That was one thing the Sar *never* tolerated at table: Any kind of ignorant prejudice."

"Just informed ones?" Jenny shook her head. "Did he ever try to hire Ridanis?"

"No," Lily admitted. "I don't think he did. But he made it clear to his children that you have to judge an individual on her own merits, rather than on any preconceived idea." Now her gaze moved to the Mule. Jenny, looking with her, nodded slightly. "Yes," finished Lily. "Too bad it's not as easy in practice as in theory. What do you think Callioux's got on the screen, anyway?"

"Void take me," said Jenny with a sigh. "I just had this one out last night with the other form leaders. I don't want to go over it again."

Lily laughed. "All right. Then how about Yehoshua? What do you think Yi's people strapped to his arm? A laser cannon?"

"Speak of the Void, and it enters," said Jenny abruptly, her eyes lifting to the far wall. "There he is."

Preceded by his cousin, Yehoshua had indeed entered the common room. He halted to survey the occupants. Most had not noticed him yet—many, in any case, did not know him—and as his gaze found Lily he smiled and walked across toward her.

"I don't see anything different—" began Jenny.

She stopped as Lily gasped.

Indeed, there was nothing different. Yehoshua held a thin screen in one hand; the other hung relaxed at his side, swinging as he walked. He had two hands, two arms: perfectly normal.

Kyosti glanced up, not with surprise, but more to mark Yehoshua's passage and acknowledge it with a brief nod. Other people glanced at him noticing nothing out of the ordinary. Rainbow stopped playing and stared, an action that attracted Gregori's attention. Alsayid merely grinned.

"Comrade Heredes. Comrade Seria." Yehoshua halted before the two women with a smile. He was clearly pleased with himself, and enjoying their consternation.

"Let me see that," Lily demanded.

He held his right arm out for her. She took the hand, touched the arm, and made a face.

"Stop trying to fool me. The artificial one."

He shrugged, still smiling, and offered her the other arm.

"No," said Lily after a moment, "it *was* the right one that was amputated. Hoy."

"Damn my eyes," breathed Jenny. "I've never seen anything like that in my life."

Yehoshua was not, however, inclined to gloat. "Comrade Heredes," he said as he detached his hand from her incredulous, and apparently paralyzed, grasp. "I'm actually here to call you to a staff meeting with Comrade Officer Callioux."

"When?" asked Lily.

"Now. This time it's not a false alarm: we have an assignment." He smiled with relish, closing and unclosing his false hand that was as real to touch and sight as his true one. "Action at last."

Callioux had already lit up the table in the tac room when Lily and Yehoshua arrived. Three officers from other ships came in after them. Yehoshua leaned on the edge of the tac table, examining the array of lights beneath the surface that represented the placement of systems surrounding the *Cairn*'s current position. Lily, with a last glance at Yehoshua's right hand, moved to stand beside her fellow officers in training and waited.

The tac officer finished entering information into the table's computer and stepped back to let Callioux into the control console. Callioux surveyed the group—about sixteen people— before reconfiguring the display on screen and beginning to speak.

"This model shows approximately the plus x, minus y, plus z oct of Reft space. The red point represents Bleak House." A white light dutifully started to blink red. "Now I'll expand perspective to include the entire plus z duo of the grid. Central, as you know, rests at null. The two blue points of light"—they switched over—"represent Salah-eh-Din, and Tollgate. Jehane has clear control of Tollgate and all points beyond and passive—undercover—control of Salah-eh-Din. Now"—Callioux paused, reading each face in turn before continuing—"we begin to encircle. Our first goal: To control all windows into and out of Salah-eh-Din. With Salah-eh-Din and Tollgate in our hands, Jehane basically controls the major vector routes throughout the plus z duo." A second pause as Callioux widened the perspective to include the entire grid of Reft space.

"Not counting Arcadia at null," commented Yehoshua into the hush, "there are only two major agricultural planets in the minus z duo: Dairy and Blessings."

Lily lifted one hand slightly, catching Callioux's attention. "Dairy isn't *that* productive, comrade. It supplies its own sector, but as far as I remember from school, exports very little outside of that."

Callioux offered the group a brief smile. "Exactly. The pressure builds on Arcadia. Blessings and Dairy then begin to look vulnerable. In any case"—the grid shrank back to focus on the plus-minus-plus oct—"we are moving out in six hours for Landfall."

A kind of collective, unvoiced gasp caught in the throats of the officers present.

"I thought that was garrisoned. Heavily." A voice from the back.

"It was. We have just received word that a diversion planned and led by Jehane personally is on schedule at Bukharin, which as you see has routes out through Landfall and past the sta homeworld to Tollgate. This diversion will pull off a large proportion of the Landfall garrison, who will believe Jehane is beginning an attack on the vector ring that circles Arcadia."

"But what if the diversion fails?"

"There are two back doors out of Bukharin, both of which immediately branch. It's a fairly safe feint for the attacker, and a dangerous ambush for Central's forces. So"—on the grid, Landfall system grew until a planet turned beneath them, lines tracing two small continents marked with two large cities on their surface—"we move in and destroy all the ground emplacements and garrison housing. The two converted merchanters will dock at Landfall Station—which is, as you see, an orbiter—forcibly evacuate the hub, and destroy the second wheel"—the grid narrowed into an image of Station, with its slow rotation blocking their view of star by distant star in turns—"which houses the garrison's regional command. Then we leave."

Callioux waited while the officers examined the screen and murmured comments back and forth. Eventually they subsided and returned their attention to their commander.

"This is strictly a strike. We are not establishing any zone of control. We hit, and leave. Landfall will be crippled for months—we estimate three months—which will give us time to cinch a noose around it and cut it off completely without worrying about its capabilities."

"What about Central?" asked Yehoshua. "Surely they can send out reinforcements from Arcadia."

"When they hear about it. We'll be gone by then."

Lily, studying the curve of Landfall as it turned on the screen, thought again through the grid of the region, and moved forward to put a hand down on the edge of the table. "What about the sta?" she asked.

Callioux nodded. "The sta are neutral in this conflict. Trade will continue to pass through the routes they oversee as long as no fighting occurs. Any other questions?"

There were none.

"Very well. Assignments. We'll start with the ground assault, divided into teams Alpha and Veeta. Team Alpha will run in three groups. Comrade Officer Yehoshua will lead Group One; Comrade Officer Sgambati, Two; and comrade Heredes, Three. Your destination: This city, called Scarce. The ground emplacements there are strong enough that you may run into fire on approach, but we expect to have thrown Landfall's forces into confusion by our quick destruction of their space command. Team Veeta will be in two groups..."

Landfall hung, a brilliant blue against the void of space. At her first sight of it, Lily had wondered if it had any land at all, but it rotated to reveal two irregular masses that seemed scarcely larger than islands, isolated in so much water. Even after living on Arcadia, where she had in any case seen no larger body of water than a lake, she still could not imagine an ocean, much less a planet whose surface was over ninety-five percent water. Callioux had mentioned that there was land besides the two land masses optimistically called continents, but they were a scattering of islands strewn across the vast sea.

Lily shuddered. She studied the vaguely rectangular continent on which the city named—aptly, she thought—Scarce had grown and presumably flourished. As she turned away from this view, the tac officer's voice came alive in her wrist-com, calling the countdown to strike. At least Scarce was not on the coast, but on a plateau in the center of the continent.

She met the others in the shuttle bay. In the space between two shuttles, Jenny stood arguing with Yehoshua. Gregori, tears bright on his face under the glare of harsh light, clutched at his mother's waist as if he meant never to let go of her.

"—we don't have enough people," Yehoshua was saying as Lily walked up to them. Behind Jenny, Aliasing sat on a crate, dressed in Jehanish whites that looked too harsh for her slight frame. "In any case," Yehoshua continued, turning to include Lily, "if you could use your own comm-man on your shuttle, instead of having him go down with *me* because of—" A hesitation as he glanced toward the distant figure of Kyosti, who spoke to Pinto on the shuttle's ramp. Lily, looking that way, could read from Kyosti's posture that he was listening while trying to look otherwise engaged. "Because of *that*, you wouldn't need a second comm. Aliasing's all we've got. So she has to go."

"I can't leave my son alone on this ship for Void knows how long—" Jenny broke off. Her expression was taut with worry, and she frowned and laid a hand on her son's startlingly golden hair as the full implications of her interrupted comment hit her.

"Take him with us," said Lily softly. "There are extra seats, and he'll be with Lia the entire time."

Jenny turned on Lily, angry now. "Take him into fire? Are you *insane?*"

"Jenny—" Lily began.

Jenny sighed and shut her eyes, sinking to her knees and hugging the boy with a tenderness that seemed uncharacteristic in a mercenary of her background. "Oh, Gregori," she murmured as the boy hugged her with one arm and wiped his face with the other, "what a life I've made for you."

Yehoshua moved away.

"I can help Lia," said Gregori in a high, quiet voice, an echo of Aliasing's. "I know that comm pretty good."

"Pretty well," said Jenny automatically. She glanced over at Aliasing, who simply sat looking frightened, but determined. "I forget that *you've* never done anything like this either, Lia."

Aliasing said nothing, as if to say; I am not daunted.

Lily rested a hand gently on Jenny's shoulder. "I'm sorry, Jenny."

Jenny shook her head roughly, shaking off Lily's pity. "What choice do we have?" she asked, not really with bitterness. "We're better off together whatever happens—by this time at least. I can't protect them forever." She gave Gregori a brusque kiss on the forehead and stood up, pushing him firmly toward Lia. "It's just," she said in a low voice to Lily as he went obediently to stand next to Aliasing, "that I'd like for him to have a chance to grow up. And then I wonder, what kind of life would he have anyway? It's a hard world for children like him."

Lily let her hand rest on Jenny's shoulder a moment longer, then lifted it and gave the other woman a light slap on the shoulder. "Isn't that one of the things we're fighting about? Let's board."

Lily had taken on two Ridani soldiers, named Cursive and Diamond, to fill out her fighting ten. With Finch and Swann doing comm-duty on the other two shuttles on their team, it left her only Pinto and Aliasing to cover the shuttle controls once the ground party was left off. She brought up the city grid on her computer screen as she waited for their disengage, studying the map and the emplacements they were to hit. In the seat in front of her, Aliasing fiddled nervously with the knobs on the comm-board as *Franklin's Cairn* comm talked to Landfall Station.

"—request permission to dock at oh five hundred system standard."

"Accepted. We require a full identification string before clearance can be allowed. Acknowledge."

"Accepted. String to follow—"

Aliasing toggled the switch and caught the end of a ship-to-ship transmission, on a tight channel.

"—we are reading a far higher activity quotient here than expected."

"From our vantage, Commander Callioux, we still see a low activity rate on the military hub, with only two ships in docking. What are your further instructions?"

"Maintain orbit as long as possible, comrade, and keep your vantage on strict distance until our approach order is finalized. We expect a six-hour lag for our teams to reach the surface. Move only once we have commenced firing."

"Accepted, Commander. We are holding."

Aliasing flipped back to the main comm-channel, but it was still running the blur of the identification string to Station central.

Pinto moved abruptly, chin lifting, hands shifting on the controls. "Power ready," he announced. "We will be swinging into Station blindside in two minutes. Prepare for disengage." He turned his head to look behind. "You *are* strapped in? We're going to drop hard downside—fast entry." His gaze flicked past Lily to Gregori, but the boy's dark face showed no more emotion than his mother's, seated behind him.

The string played out, and the comm-channel lapsed for tangible moments into the crackle and spit of dead air.

After an ominously long pause, Station's voice came back on.

"We have received you, *Franklin's Cairn*. Docking clearance and approach will be transmitted on your next pass. Please remain in your present orbit while blindside. Acknowledge."

The *Cairn*'s "Accepted" was lost to sudden static as the ship passed blindside. The shuttle rang with the disengage, shook and jarred, and abruptly Pinto cleared his view windows and they could see the wall of the *Cairn* receding as they dropped away from it.

Aliasing fumbled with the head harness that would allow her to communicate with the rest of the team shuttles. In the back, behind the last rank of seats, the Mule and Kyosti had begun the final check and assembly of their equipment.

The wall of the *Cairn*, receding, resolved into the rotund, utilitarian lines of a merchanter. All signs of its military refitting had, at least to Lily's eyes, been cleverly hidden.

"Power up," announced Pinto. "Prepare for entry. One last warning." He did not look up from his controls. "We'll be dropping fast—"

The engines came to life, filling the cabin with their low undertone, and *Franklin's Cairn* lifted abruptly away from them. Somehow, even with the pressure, the Mule and Kyosti managed to keep working.

"All teams clear," said Aliasing, so softly that only Lily and Pinto could hear her.

They hit the atmosphere hard, bucketing, headed down and straight rather than in the more leisurely curve, but they were gauged for time, not comfort.

"What's our count, Pinto?" Lily asked quietly.

He tapped a few keys, bringing figures up on his console. "Five hours, thirty-eight minutes." She nodded, turned her head to survey her team. "I suggest you rest while you can. I'll give you four hours."

Behind her, Jenny was already dozing. Lily shut her eyes, hoping she could sleep. Next to her, Gregori had settled his com-screen on his lap and was doing calculations, talking to himself in a whisper as he attempted to master the intricacies of elementary *bissterlas*. His light voice lulled her.

She woke to the crackle of the comm. Aliasing, trying to pull in Station comm, had turned up the volume.

"Count?" Lily asked, shifting in her seat.

Pinto checked. "On schedule. One fleet hour, twenty-two minutes. Groups One and Two are at point and left."

"Any sightings?"

He shook his head. In the window all they could see was cloud.

Aliasing turned down the static, glancing back at Lily apprehensively. "Nothing on any channel. Tight beam with One and Two confirms that we're on course as scheduled. We'll land four hours after sunset. But the *Cairn* hasn't come back into Station sightside yet."

"Keep it monitored." Lily unstrapped and rose gingerly, testing the shake of the shuttle for balance. She moved back, waking each person individually. Kyosti, in the back, had cleared all the lockers. She did not ask him if he had slept. They ate quickly, strapped into equipment. She went once more briefly over the mission: a communications node, flanked by a military port that warehoused about twenty shuttles, mostly transports.

"This isn't meant to be fancy," Lily finished. "It's demolition. One and Two will be, respectively, striking at emplacements five and twelve kilometers away. We'll take separate courses off-planet and rendezvous with *Franklin's Cairn* beyond Landfall's orbital track. Farther if we have to. Pinto assures me this shuttle can coast to system's edge if necessary." She smiled wryly. "Let's hope we don't have to find out if he's right."

"Lily—" Aliasing's voice, startled but hesitant. "Comrade Heredes. I've got Station comm, but—"

The explosion drowned out her exclamation. The shuttle veered abruptly left, banking sharply. Lily was thrown into a seat. She scrambled up as Pinto righted the shuttle and then dropped it as suddenly into a steep dive. She slid down to her seat, hurriedly strapped herself in.

"Status?" Her voice rang sharp.

"Someone is shooting at us—" he began but was cut off by Aliasing.

"Two's been hit! But they're still—"

A second explosion. The shuttle jerked as if it had been hit.

Pinto banked a sharp left, then right, but the shuttle dropped swiftly, shuddering, until at last he pulled it up.

"Damn," he murmured. "I've lost stabilization in my right wing."

"You'd think," said Jenny in a low voice, "that Jehane would have provided these shuttles with guns." Her gaze rested on her son, who sat staring wide-eyed out the front.

"Who fights in the atmosphere?" Lily asked grimly. "Pinto, who's on us?"

"It's ground fire. They must be tracking us from the com node."

Another explosion. This time the entire shuttle rocked with the violence of the hit. A thin stream of smoke began to leak out from the back into the cabin.

"I'm not going to make it to that field," said Pinto in a colorless voice. "I've lost one engine."

"Can you pull up?"

He was too focused on beginning a zigzag path and consulting his map grid of the surface to even shake his head. "I wouldn't risk it."

"Then land safely. First priority." Somehow Lily kept her voice even, though her legs were trembling with tension. "Veer off from the target. Find us a safe harbor. Once we're on the ground, we'll work from there. Lia." She snapped her head around, was amazed to see tears streaming down Aliasing's face. "Lia! Tell the *Cairn* we're changing to prolonged ground action. Then get me Yehoshua."

"They're not there." Aliasing's voice shook. She gulped, trying to speak coherently. "I can't raise *Franklin's Cairn*, and all I get on the channel is Landfall Station talking about firing on target and some government military receiving. *They're not there.*"

"Get me Yehoshua!" Lily snapped.

The shuttle shuddered violently. A high, ominous whine lanced above the noise of the engines.

"I'm losing number two engine," said Pinto. "There's some kind of open strip at thirty degrees, and I'm taking it for landing."

"Strap in," Lily ordered, not looking around.

They came out of the clouds into night lit by distant city lights, almost on top of a dark sprawl of derelict warehouses ringed by a long stretch of black roadway.

"I think there's something wrong with my console," said Aliasing desperately. She flipped switches frantically. "I can't—"

"—Three. This is One. Can you"—it faded again—"*Cairn* is hit. We are receiving no communication at—losing altitude— must assume that we are on our own without—"

Static replaced the faint, cool voice of Yehoshua.

Pinto said something under his breath, and they touched down. The shuttle rocked and bumped along the strip of road, shaken by ruts and fissures in the roadbed. They slowed and Pinto turned them toward the shadowy bulk of the warehouses.

"With your permission, comrade," he said quietly, "I'll head for cover."

"Granted." Lily unstrapped herself and moved to stand behind him, craning forward to get the best possible view of the sky. Clouds obscured one corner of the horizon—the way they had come—but most of the vault bloomed with stars, clear and bright, echoed by the distant lights of the city, by an occasional lamp beyond the dark warehouses.

"What's that?" asked Gregori, a child's surprise.

Above, far above, color and light blossomed into a great blaze, a flash illuminating the night sky, like fireworks, or the announcement of a ship's death.

And abruptly, the last gasp of Lia's console, the voice of Landfall Station, or one of its military adjuncts, came on with brief clarity:

"Accepted. We have destroyed the vessel *Franklin's Cairn*."

12 Little Boy Blue

****

"It be ya sure I can't fix them, or ya comm," said Paisley, "and I be studying nothing but ya tech, 'cept ya basic combat, all ya time we be on—" She broke off, rubbed a grease-stained hand across a smear left previously on her face, unwilling to say the name of the ship. "Sore luck pass me by," she muttered, and made a brief gesture that was echoed by all of the Ridanis except Pinto.

For a moment no one spoke as they surveyed the crippled shuttle, stowed now in the temporary haven of a derelict, empty warehouse. Then, as if with a common thought, they all turned to look at Lily.

She felt a moment of hideous self-doubt as they regarded her expectantly, faces pale with worry or bleak with grief for comrades presumably dead or obliterated in the *Cairn's* final doom. Kyosti alone had a slight smile on his face, as if he was amused at her predicament.

"Rainbow." She chose action as her refuge. "You and Diamond will secure the area: I want a constant patrol on the roof and an emplaced gunner set to cover the main door. To be relieved at intervals by Cursive and Pinto and Paisley." She paused, considered Paisley for a few moments, remembering their run on Unruli Station through back alleys and forgotten corridors. "No, I'll want Paisley on reconnaissance. We'll set up sweep patrols to recce this area. We need to know what the nearest habitations are. Pinto, I'll need your estimate of where we are in relation to the military target. We'll go in pairs: Jenny with the Mule, Hawk and Lia—"

"Hold on," said Jenny. "Lia is hardly—"

"Comrade." Lily's tone silenced Jenny's protest. "We don't have enough people as it is, and the Ridanis will probably show up like blast storms if Landfall has the same restrictions most other planets have. Until we find out otherwise, Aliasing patrols. I'll trust Paisley to patrol in this area because I know she has experience in not being seen."

Paisley beamed at this compliment, wiping a third streak of grease over the bright pattern of her face.

"Paisley will sweep with Bach and me. Gregori." She turned to the boy, who held tightly to Aliasing's tunic. "I want you to stay on the shuttle and listen on the comm—in case we get a message from one of the other teams."

The boy nodded solemnly.

"Now." She swept her gaze across all their faces, checking each in turn, measuring their resolve. "We need to find Jehanish sympathizers—people here who would be willing to help us. We need to repair the engines, and the comm. If we can also strike and destroy our original target, once we have a clear escape route, so much the better. Jenny and Hawk, take your teams out first. Use your best judgment if you run across any natives. Paisley—I want you to go out solo as far as you can—find me the nearest habitation and get an estimate of how many people, how it's linked to the city itself, and what conditions they live under."

When she stopped speaking, the silence left by the absence of her words seemed to impose a paralysis on her listeners.

"Well?" she demanded, impatient at their hesitation, as if in itself this lack of action might cause her doubts to resurface. "Get moving."

They moved.

In the wake left by the sudden departure of her audience, she sat on the lip of the shuttle's ramp and beckoned Bach closer. The robot floated over to her, lights blinking to the rhythm of the soft chorale he sung

> *Herr, wenn die stolzen Feinde schnauben,*
> *So gib, dass wir im festen Glauben*
> *Nach deiner Macht und Hülfe sehn!*

Wir wollen dir allein vertrauen,
So können wir den scharfen Klauen
Des Feindes unversehrt entgehn.

Lord, if proud enemies rage,
let us then in steadfast faith
look to Thy might and help.
We will put our trust in Thee alone,
so may we withstand unharmed
the talons of the fiend.

She allowed herself the chorale's length just to sit, to let her mind follow the music without dwelling on the task before her. But as Bach closed the final cadence, she sighed deeply, shaking loose her reverie, and rubbed a hand over her eyes as if thereby she could clear them to enable herself to see lucidly enough to get them out of this disaster.

Footsteps rang softly on the ramp as she stood up. Pinto appeared, holding a screen in one hand. Bringing it over to her, he displayed it so that she could see the map grid.

"I estimate that we are here," he said. A flashing bar pinpointed them on the grid. Bach rose to hang at Pinto's shoulder. "That puts the target—"

Another marker flashed.

"It could be worse," said Lily. "Twelve kilometers. We could have landed right on top of them."

"I'm glad you're optimistic," replied Pinto caustically. "You don't really think we're going to get out of this, do you?"

Lily pulled the screen out of his grasp. "Do you suggest we just turn ourselves in? Somehow I don't think you can persuade your *father* to intervene this time. Or shall we ask the local military to call Senator Isaiah at Central and see if his influence extends this far out?"

Pinto's mouth pulled taut. He averted his face quickly and with obvious anger.

"Pinto." She let her voice soften. "When I looked at the damage this boat took, I'm amazed you landed us in one piece."

She paused to let the compliment sink in, but he only made a brief, negatory shrug with one shoulder.

"We have a good crew," she continued. "Just because you think life has it in for you doesn't mean—"

Pinto laughed abruptly. "Doesn't mean that it does? Can you really stand here—*here*, now—and say that?"

"Didn't you tell me something once about your luck? Hoy, Pinto. You can let circumstances rule you, or you can work to change them. I know which life is easier."

She waited, but he choose not to reply. With a sigh, she swung around to lift up the main hand-pack radio that Rainbow had left before setting up her position. "I suggest," Lily finished, more command than solicitude, "that you sleep while we have the leisure."

He gave her a sarcastic salute and disappeared up the ramp.

"Hoy," she murmured, adding a few exasperated phrases of music to which Bach wisely did not comment. She sat down again on the ramp and fiddled with the hand-pack, continuing to whistle. *Bach. We need to contact Yehoshua's team—if they're still out there. And Two, as well. I'll want five-second bursts of the Cairn's codes, at random intervals, at fluctuating frequencies. I don't know how sophisticated Landfall military's detection equipment is. If we get a response, go to the classified code in a ten-second burst. And if it is Yehoshua or Sgambati, compress Pinto's estimate of our position into no more than a fifteen-second burst.* Cadenced with an interrogatory two note.

Affirmative, patroness. If I may suggest a more sophisticated strategy for avoiding detection by surveillance equipment— Bach paused respectfully.

"Bach," Lily answered, rubbing the robot's smooth sheen with one hand. "Do whatever you think is best. Just find out if either of them made it."

Bach sang happily and drifted down to plug into the hand-pack.

Unfamiliar voices carried in from the front, a protest—Lily jumped up, unstrapping her pistol; paused when she heard the sharp bark of Jenny's voice ordering silence. Lily kept her pistol loose as she came forward around the shuttle's bulk and found herself face-to-face with a sullen adolescent boy of perhaps sixteen years and his smaller, female companion.

The Mule had a firm grip on the female's bulky jacket. The girl, seeing Lily, shook herself hard and came up against the Mule's strength for what was clearly the fourth or fifth time.

"She's a slow learner," said Jenny apologetically to Lily. The mercenary kept her rifle trained on the boy. "We found these two skulking around the next warehouse over."

"Told you I heard something landing," said the girl in a ragged but triumphant voice.

The boy, after a cursory and uninterested glance at Lily, had focused on the shuttle. "That's a Gami Ten Eight Two," he said loftily to his companion. "It's got longer range capabilities than the Zu's—and *you* said it was a military crash. But this one is modified." His eye ranged over the shuttle with the eye of a connoisseur. "And damaged."

"If you'll excuse me," said Lily sardonically, "I wonder if you can tell me what you're doing here."

"You're criminals," said the girl with conviction. "We don't have to tell you nothing."

"Oh shut up, Red." The boy's tone rang heavy with an old irritation. "How could criminals have this kind of boat?" Now he looked at Lily, but it seemed still a chore for him to tear his eyes away from the shuttle—despite the several guns trained on him. "What are you—smugglers caught in Security? I thought you all knew how tight it is here. Or haven't you ever been to Landfall before? They won't execute you, though, like I hear they do some places, but they'll take everything you have and leave you stranded in Shanty with nothing more than the clothes on your back. That's punishment enough."

Lily glanced at Jenny, but the other woman had no expression at all on her face. "Is that what happened to you?" Lily asked carefully.

"Nah." The boy shrugged casually. "Me Pap. I been here all my life."

"What?" broke in Red hotly. "You going to pretend you don't hate it here just so you can impress *these*?" Her glare raked Lily, and abruptly she put a hand to her hooded head in a gesture made doubly melodramatic by her sudden and very audible intake of breath. "White uniforms! They're Jehanists! Bet you. Bet you, Blue."

Blue shifted with sudden interest. In the banked lights that ran along the shuttle's wings, Lily could see that what she had thought was a bruise mottling the right side of his face was in fact a pattern of circles and squares and triangles woven together, like a Ridani's incomplete tattoo.

Jenny turned suddenly to level her rifle at the far door. A moment later Paisley entered and jogged over to salute Lily and wait for permission to speak, panting slightly from her run.

"Is that a *real* tattoo?" asked Red. "Are those real, or just painted on like Blue's?"

Paisley turned to look at the girl, taking her measure. After a moment she blinked her eyes innocently and said sweetly: "Do you want to touch them?" She extended a dappled hand.

Red leapt back as if Paisley had offered her the plague, only to collide with the Mule's unyielding chest. She yelped.

"Oh shut up, Red," snapped Blue. "I guess you're in charge here," he said grudgingly to Lily.

"Hold on," said Lily curtly. She looked at Paisley. "Report."

Paisley beamed proudly. "Ya fields be on ya three sides of ya warehouses. Ya fourth be ya street. Sure, and it be ya rundown old place. Reckon ya people there be as poor as ya Ridanis. It be ya quiet so—so late. Or be it early here?"

"She talks funny, too," muttered Red rebelliously.

"How about Rainbow's people?" Lily asked Jenny.

Jenny nodded. "Well concealed. Knowing they were there, I had to look twice to see them."

Lily considered Blue in silence for long enough that he regained his sullen mask and began to fidget, his eyes drifting occasionally to the shuttle.

"What do you know about Jehane?" she asked finally.

He shrugged. "Not much. Me Pap talks about him some with Red's Mam and the other Shanty elders." His lips lifted in a sneer. "Course, if you're Jehanists, I suppose you're going to say you're here to save us."

"No," said Lily quietly. "I'm not going to say that. I'm going to have you and the girl take me to see your—ah—Pap and your elders."

"Lily." Jenny kept her voice low, but it sounded menacing nonetheless. "Shouldn't we keep one of them here as hostage? For leverage?"

"Do you think that will make them trust us? No. I'll go alone." She motioned to the Mule to take the two kids aside for a moment. "Paisley, you're to follow without being seen. Jenny, you and the Mule continue sweeps, but keep in contact with Paisley."

"But—"

"No. We have to get their help without coercion. We can't get out of here without real support, and that will only come if they trust us, and believe in Jehane's cause. Or can be convinced to believe in it."

Jenny frowned, but she sketched a salute to Lily and moved over to the Mule.

"Get going," said Lily to Paisley, and then she restrapped her pistol and waved at the Mule to release the two captives.

"Are you really a Jehanist?" asked Red once they were clear of the warehouse.

"I work in Jehane's cause," replied Lily.

Red whistled appreciatively. "Old Elder Vajratti got thrown in the block last month for preaching Jehane's cause. I heard she's on a hunger strike now cause they won't let her have a terminal or nothing, not to read or write on. And last week this one kid got shot by Security for—"

"What difference does it make?" broke in Blue. "Jai-Vinh just wanted to impress Sosa, and Vajratti's half out of her vector anyway. You don't really think Jehane can win against Central, do you?"

"That sounds familiar," said Lily.

"And who cares, anyway?" continued Blue as if she had not spoken. "I'd love to see the modifications in that shuttle. I'll bet they're disguised so they can't even be read by a cruiser's sensors. I got into a locked file and got to see the specs on the cruiser they brought here last week."

"A cruiser?" Lily asked sharply, realizing now that the feint on Bukharin must have failed, and yet hoping that there might be a different explanation. "Are you sure there's a military cruiser in Landfall system?"

"Yep," said Blue enthusiastically. "It's a beauty. The fire-power is way augmented from the old models."

Lily considered this as they walked along the tarmac that paved the ground between the close ranks of warehouses. It had grown cracked from long disuse, making their footing precarious.

Red squealed abruptly.

Lily dropped instinctively into a crouch, whipped her pistol out.

"That was your ship, wasn't it?" Red exclaimed, a vocal continuation of the squeal. "The one that blew up tonight. It lit up the whole sky."

Lily let out her breath through closed lips and straightened up.

"And I'll bet it can just jump double windows, too," said Blue, oblivious now that he was intent on recalling the cruiser.

"Hoy," murmured Lily as they went on.

Blue's Pap took a bit of rousing, but once he stumbled out into the drab, ill-lit kitchen and common room of his tiny apartment, situated over a junk heap of a small building marked with a sign saying: Blumoris's Repairs and Metals, he greeted her civilly enough. And a clear, although bleary-eyed, look at Lily's white uniform galvanized him into action: within twenty minutes six elders of Shanty sat sipping curdled-looking aris and staring raptly at Lily and her Jehanist accouterments.

Red had pulled down her hood to reveal a wealth of copper-orange hair. Blue lounged in a corner chair, ignoring the proceedings while he scribbled aimlessly on an old, battered screen.

Lily stood up and surveyed the company for a long moment in respectful silence, as much to let them look at her as to study them. But what she saw was hopeful. The room was shabby, sparsely furnished with secondhand appliances and worn, ugly furniture. The elders wore poorly fitting clothes burnished with age. A rash disfigured the pale skin of Red's neck and jawline. Blue's Pap had a puffy eye, and the elder introduced to her as Red's mother kept coughing, a racked, painful sound. One elder had entered with a pronounced limp.

"My name is Lily Heredes," Lily began. "Comrade Heredes, if you will." The silence that greeted these first tentative words was expectant but cautious. "And I'm going to give it to you straight. We're Jehane's soldiers. Our ship was destroyed by Central's fleet, and we need your help. And you look"— she paused to let her eyes sweep the room again, deliberately— "like the kind of people Jehane has been fighting for all along."

Blue's Pap rose from his chair, a bulky man who neverthe-less moved with slow dignity. "I am Elder Blumoris," he said. "This is my shop, and my living, here. I reckon you are what you say you are. It isn't likely you're anything else, unless you're a spy from Security come to roust out a suspected Jehanish nest."

A dry chuckle all around greeted this sarcastic remark.

"But you'll have to prove it," he went on. Lily nodded,

acknowledging this request. "And I reckon we'd all like to hear why you're here in the first place, and what help you can do us."

Looking at them, Lily wished desperately that Master Heredes was here, because he would know what to say, and how to say it. She gave her tunic a self-conscious tug and banished such pointless thoughts. After all, *she* was Heredes now, and sooner or later she would have to truly assimilate that fact. She smiled slightly, thinking of the disparity in experience between her and Master Heredes, and was surprised to see the answering gleam of a smile on Blumoris's face. His sympathy gave her confidence.

"I suppose," she began, "that the easiest way to prove we are from Jehane's forces is to see how quickly the troops here would come running if we gave up our position. But we're not ready to do *that* yet."

She adjusted a sleeve as she got a muffled chuckle from one of the elders, stopped herself from toying with the other sleeve, and lifted her chin a little. "The only proof I can give you is to show you to our shuttle and let you look it over. Otherwise, you'll have to take us on trust. I don't have any credentials, and they wouldn't mean anything if I did have them. As to how we can help you, I'm not sure—" She paused as a thought occurred to her. "If you'll excuse me a moment." She raised one arm and, coding in the tightest possible channel, called up Kyosti's identification code on her wrist-com, hoping he was within range. After a moment, he replied.

"I need you," she said. "Have Lia return to base. And bring your kit. I'll send Paisley back to base to show you where I am."

"That won't be necessary." His voice sounded detached and almost alien over the tiny receiver clipped to her ear. "I'll find you. Out."

She looked across at Blumoris. "Elder, I've sent for one of my people. Perhaps you can set someone outside to watch for him."

"Inocencio." Elder Blumoris nodded curtly at his son. "Go on."

Blue did not respond for a moment, as if judging whether or not this was a fit moment for rebellion. Finally, looking put-upon, he let out a prolonged sigh of adolescent disgust and rose with sullen lethargy to drag himself out of the room.

"I'm not sure what help we can do you," said Lily as the door shut behind Blue. "We need your help if we're to carry on Jehane's fight. But turn comes turnabout—our success helps Jehane, and his will bring the reforms that will lift you out of"—she gestured with one hand—"out of this."

"So Jehane says," muttered one of the Elders.

"Well, Hoang," said Elder Blumoris, "I reckon it's a sight better promise than any Central's given us these past twenty years." He had a slow, almost ponderous way of speaking, but perhaps it was conscious, for he used it to let his words carry weight. "Not like in Rooce's time, when she made jobs for them as hadn't any, and helped those as couldn't work through no fault of their own." He nodded at the Elder who had limped in.

"It's true there was more help, food and decent shelter, and medicine," said Red's mother, stopping after these words for a spasm of coughing to pass. "But Rooce governed here on Landfall, even if she was appointed by Central. Who's to say how much reform will reach us even if this Jehane business does reform Central?"

"Surely it can't get any worse?" muttered Hoang. "Vajratti always said—"

"Vajratti hasn't any nav left to vector from—"

"I hear it's a tattoo religion, this Jehane. Would you trust any tattoo superstition?"

"Central isn't going to help us. They've made that clear. I *still* say we're better off supporting them as at least cares for our troubles."

"Elders! Elders!" Blumoris lifted both of his thick hands in the universal plea for silence. "Let us not *trouble* our visitor with our quarrels. Please continue"—he hesitated—"Comrade."

Lily glanced toward the door, but it remained closed. She looked back at her audience. "Here and now, I can't promise that I can make your life better. But I have faith that Jehane's people believe in this cause, that they have dedicated their lives to bring reform to all of the Reft's citizens. I don't suppose you've heard of a speaker called Pero." But as soon as she said the name, she saw recognition light their faces. "You have?" She could not keep the surprise from her voice.

"All the way out here? Although I suppose it's not so unlikely." She shrugged, a little embarrassed.

"We may be a small place," said Blumoris proudly, "but we're not so very far out as all that."

"But I thought," said Red suddenly and loudly from her cross-legged seat on the floor, "that you rigged up that console specially to receive illicit channels and scrambled broadcasts."

"Absinthe!"

"Do you know comm-consoles well?" asked Lily swiftly, caught by this confession.

Blumoris hedged by going to the counter to pour more of the discolored aris into his cup, and then offered it around to everyone else. "I've a bit of interest in that line."

"He's being modest," muttered Hoang. "And if that son of his weren't hells-bent on getting thrown into detention, he'd be sight-certain to get accepted into tech school."

"Do you think so?" Blumoris for the first time sounded angry. "After twice Council let rents be raised on my shop so that I had to leave two decent locations downtown, and then they used the excuse that my premises were both unsightly and unsafe to drive me out of the third and force me to move *here*? My son will have no truck with *their* schools, not while I still breathe."

Before this tender subject could be enlarged upon, the door opened and Blue ushered Kyosti in. The boy's gaze was fastened on Kyosti's hair with the rapt attention of an acolyte; in this light, in the drab surroundings, the finger's-length of blue roots coming in showed up as glaringly as any painted-on tattoos.

"This is Comrade Hawk," said Lily. "He's a physician."

As if on cue, Red's mother coughed. Kyosti took in the situation at a glance and within moments set up his medical kit on the only clean space on the counter and got to work. Within half an hour, as first Red and then Blumoris left to spread word of this bounty through the neighborhood, a good dozen more people arrived, yawning with sleep yet clearly ill or injured. Two were carried in, too sick to move themselves.

By morning, Lily had Blumoris's assurances that Shanty would support them in every way they could, and that he and his son would do what they could toward the shuttle's repair.

13 Hippocratic Oath

****

Lily stood on the dilapidated roof of the Blumoris shop and watched the sun set beyond a range of red-hued hills. Both evenings she had done so. The sight, even after her year on Arcadia, still astonished her in its beauty. She had traded her white tunic for grubby overalls borrowed from Blue; they fit her reasonably well, although she had to roll up the legs to avoid tripping and the sleeves to keep her hands free.

A scrape of shoe sounded from the ladder. She turned her head to see a crown of blue-tinged hair appear, and after it the rest of Kyosti. He smiled when he saw her and pushed himself easily up to the roof and walked across to stand by her, letting one hand stray to caress her neck. Two days of constant work running a makeshift clinic had left him looking rested and cheerful.

"I was thinking about Ransome House," she said softly, returning her gaze to the sunset, "Paisley once said that sometimes you have to lose your home before you can find it. I had to leave Ransome House to discover what Heredes meant to me. And yet, there are many things at Ransome House that are worthwhile. I just didn't see them at the time, because I was too busy rebelling, trying to get out. I didn't realize how much I learned there that's served me well these past months. So I wonder if what Paisley said can't mean both of those things at once."

"Waxing philosophical, my love?" He sounded both amused and pleased. "'The modest Rose puts forth a thorn, The humble Sheep a threat'ning horn; While the Lilly white shall in Love delight, Nor a thorn, nor a threat, stain her beauty bright.'"

She sighed suddenly, a vocal sound, and rested her head against his shoulder. He did not react for a moment, as if this tiny act of tenderness surprised him, but abruptly he turned into her and embraced her tightly against him. He kissed her hair. When she lifted her head to look at him, equally surprised by his burst of feeling, she found herself caught by the maelstrom of emotions in his face.

"Lilyaka," he murmured, a strange echo of Master Heredes, who alone besides her father ever used her full name. Except the very nature of the address was utterly different here: the Sar had used it casually and frequently, like any parent, and she had never bothered to attempt to trace his feelings any deeper than that; Heredes had spoken it with that stern affection she had come to love. But the music Kyosti made of her name left her dizzy with a longing she had never been able to explain to herself, much less understand.

How long they stayed that way, clasped close, lips a finger's breadth from the other's as they gazed, she was not sure. The sun's rim touched the hills; its glimmering disk sank and hid behind the darkening heights.

As suddenly as his embrace, Kyosti brushed her mouth with a brief, almost mocking kiss, and released her.

"Is the sullen Inocencio making any progress with the engines?" he asked in his usual languid voice. "Or has he thrown another tantrum over having to work with Paisley? One wonders how deep his commitment to rebellion really is when he paints his face to mimic tattooing and thus shock his elders on the one hand, and on the other shows the same boring prejudice that most of these socially backward peoples exhibit."

"Actually," said Lily slowly, "I *was* wondering about rebellions. Mine—and Blue's, which I think is a lot like what I went through at Ransome House. Even Jehane's. What kind of change is the Reft going to see? It's hard to imagine." She paused. The last glow of daylight still limned the hills. "Do you know, it's still hard for me to imagine that you came from across the way—from Terra, from the League. I know a little what Terra must look like. It can't be so different from

Arcadia, I suppose. But I think it's easier to keep it in mind as an abstraction, a place that only has life like Paisley's Tirra-li: A paradise, a memory, not a place that really exists."

She hesitated, reached out to brush a finger over the back of his hand. His was a smooth, supple, long-fingered hand, with that rich, lightly bronzed skin tone that she sometimes suspected was artificially enhanced, although she could not guess how or why. "You once confessed to me that you were sixty-four years old, that Master Heredes was twice that. But that's like Terra: I want to believe it, but it can't possibly be true. And yet, it has to be."

"Just give me more time," he said, not looking at her. Watching him, she knew he looked no older than Jenny. "I was making progress with the equipment I got from Yi, but now that's all gone, with *Franklin's Cairn*. The Formula is simple enough, but without the facilities. . . ." He shrugged.

"What formula?"

He blinked, turning to look at her as if he were amazed to see her there. "The Hierakis Formula. I suppose you would call it life enhancement. Extension. Most people just call it the Formula. The medical term is more complex."

"Kyosti, we have the drug Lipro, but it doesn't make you live any longer, it just holds off the effects of aging for a while."

He made an expressive face. "I got to look at its formula on Arcadia. It's not worth the cost to make it. And long-term use breaks down the bonding—never mind that. That serum is just as primitive as the Reft's outmoded hierarchical political structure."

"I beg your pardon!" Lily jerked her hand away from his. "And Terra, and the League, has something so much better? I remember your bitter words to Wingtuck even if you don't."

He laughed. "Lily, my love, a more advanced culture has never made the individuals within it any less hypocritical, or less prone to exaggerated fears and unreasonable hopes and simple greed. *That's* human nature."

"Are you waxing philosophical?" Lily asked sarcastically. "Life may not be perfect in the Reft, but that doesn't mean you have to denigrate it."

Kyosti dropped to one knee and, availing himself of one of her hands, brought her palm to his lips and kissed it. "Forgive me, my sweet. I perceive I have offended you."

Lily rolled her eyes, although she did not remove her hand from his grasp. "You look ridiculous. Would you get up?"

"Only if you forgive me."

"Hoy. All right. I forgive you."

He rose with dignity and kissed her firmly. "We have time," he said obscurely. "I'll show you the League soon enough."

She glanced at her wrist-com, pushed away from him. "We'd better go. Bach is going to run that new set of signals that Blumoris devised—it's our last chance to raise Yehoshua. If he's still alive." She walked across to the ladder, paused as Kyosti came up behind her. "Is it real, the Hierakas Formula?"

"Yes," he said simply.

"How long does it make people live?"

"About one hundred fifty to one hundred eighty years of relative youth. Then a fast decline of about twenty years."

"Hoy. People will kill for it, you know."

He considered her a moment thoughtfully. "I suppose they would. It hadn't occurred to me. But in any case, the base is the most difficult part of the manufacture, and I'm back to scratch without equipment. We won't be having any wars over it yet."

"Don't we have wars enough now?" she asked, and expecting no reply she turned to climb down the ladder. Stopped, staring at him. "*That's* what you got the equipment from Yi for."

"Isn't that what I just said?"

"But I didn't—it didn't sink in. Why? Why make it now?"

His gaze, resting on her, left no room for any reason but the obvious one. "My magnanimous nature, of course," he said impatiently. "Bringing the ambrosia of semi-immortality to the benighted. For God's sake, Lily, you know perfectly well why."

As the light faded, she could no longer see his face clearly, but the taut intensity of his body was easy to read. "Yes," she said softly, beginning the descent, "You made it for me."

In the shop, Bach was happily ensconced in Blumoris's comm-room, hidden behind a cleverly disguised partition that was in itself partially concealed by a large pile of old metal and rusting pieces of antiquated equipment in the far corner of the work space.

Blumoris looked up as she entered. His coveralls were grimy with oil and unidentifiable stains, but his broad face creased in a grin when he saw her.

"Got your console fixed, I did," he said. She began to

speak enthusiastically, but he forestalled her. "It's a nice piece, but I wouldn't use it here. I reckon that's how they caught you incoming and trained their fire so accurately: it's got what I call a strong pulse. And that hand-pack's got no range, begging your pardon."

Lily smiled slightly. "I'm hardly likely to take offense at *that* truth, especially after all you've done for us. I wonder if the engines—"

He shook his head, a gesture she took for a moment as a complete negative. "I never thought," he began with that ponderous way of speaking that marked him as a man of deep opinions and long patience, "that any good would come of Inocencio's obstinacy about off-planet vessels. I told him there wasn't any good setting his sights on a living he couldn't ever get admittance to, but he kept on. I don't say he's fixed them, or even that he can, but he's in paradise just working on that boat, and if anyone here can cobble up a fix, given the damage she took, I think it's not boasting to say that my boy can."

"I think you have every reason to be proud of him," said Lily carefully.

He considered this seriously. "I won't say he isn't a stubborn boy, just to show he can be, or that he doesn't make trouble just to get attention, or get the Telesford girl into scrapes to prove he can influence her, but still, he's the gift in him for understanding and coddling engines. Here now, that creature of yours seems to be saying we're ready."

He refused to call Bach a robot and had shown a remarkable aptitude for reading the basic messages in Bach's singing speech to Lily. Neither had Bach surprised him, when he first saw the 'bot, a circumstance later explained when he had lifted a similar round globe out of his junk heap and showed it to Lily. The globe had several obvious differences from Bach; slightly smaller, it was also an imperfect sphere, being heavier at the equator. Although Blumoris did not say as much, Lily suspected that he had not given up on fixing it someday.

Lily cleared a space for herself on a stool and sat down, watching the console. Bach had an attachment plugged in, and as one of the unauthorized broadcasts Blumoris had previously mentioned began its brief evening's program, he began a coded transmission to the old man's specifications.

"Now," said Blumoris softly, "if we don't get anything with

this, there's another broadcast we can hide in at sunrise, and that will give us a broader—"

Bach winked red. Through the soft static of the receiver a voice spoke, faint, and desperate enough that it dispensed entirely with codes or identification.

"Thank the Void. Is it you, Heredes? We're in desperate trouble."

Lily had no difficulty recognizing Yehoshua's voice: strained, weak from fatigue, but steady. She grabbed for the switch, almost tripping over her own feet in her haste. "This is Heredes. We are safe for now. Where are you?"

Yehoshua coughed, shuddering the static. "I don't know. But there is an embankment here, studded with five metal poles and three dishes in a Quince configuration. We're dug in at thirty Q seven."

"That's Cemetery Hill," said Blumoris softly. "I know it. It's a good thirty kilometers from here."

"We've got a fix," replied Lily. "We're coming tonight."

"Bring Hawk." His voice shook on the name. Someone spoke behind him, but the words were muffled by static and distance. "Military is still running sweeps, but none through here since last night."

"Any news of Two?"

A pause, and the undertone of the illicit broadcast giving trading prices on the black market. "All dead. Have you had news from the *Cairn*? We can't raise her."

Lily caught in her breath, let it out, feeling choked for a moment. Swann dead, and Yehoshua did not know about Callioux. "We're on our own, Yehoshua," she replied. "I'm going off now. Acknowledge."

Another pause. "I see." The hiss of static. "Accepted."

The connection broke.

Lily stood up. "I need a guide."

After some argument, Absinthe Telesford—Red—was allowed to volunteer. Lily kept her own forces small: herself, Hawk, Jenny, and the Mule—strength and speed. With some trepidation, she left Pinto in charge, giving Lia the job of intermediary between the Shanty elders and the crew.

Elder Hoang had an old six-wheeler van, marked for deliveries, which he claimed was registered to someone on the other continent. Jenny drove.

Red lost her bearings once, but the mistake proved fortuitous. Driving up without lights on the back height of Cemetery Hill, they saw three military vehicles stopped on the road they had meant to come in on. Jenny shut off the engine and let the van drift into the cover of a large satellite dish.

Seated in a front bubble, Lily surveyed the uneven height around them. "Why is it called Cemetery Hill?" she asked.

Red shrugged with the blithe disinterest of youth. "I don't know. Reckon people must have been buried here once. My mam once told me this used to be a courting place when she was a girl. I guess it's lonely enough." She looked out at the lights of the military trucks, sweeping in arced patterns across the series of embankments that shored up the hill itself. "Or used to be."

"Courting?"

"Yeah. *You* know." Red used that tone of voice that suggested that she herself knew quite well and did not want to say, but revealed instead that the opposite was more likely true.

Jenny chuckled softly. "Oh, yes, Lily-hae. *You* know. Hawk once told me—"

"Leave Hawk out of this," Lily muttered grimly.

"*Hawk?*" murmured Red. The way she spoke his name betrayed her conversion to Blue's worship of Kyosti as the pinnacle of rebellion, cosmetic and otherwise. After a suitable silence, she let out her breath. "Gee." She sounded disappointed, but whether that sprang from her judging Lily unsuitable to receive such an honor, or from her own now-shattered dream of becoming the Chosen One—given the competition—was unclear.

"Hoy." Lily loosened her rifle strap and eased out her pistol. "Jenny. Based on my reading of this configuration, Yehoshua should be over—damn."

Jenny echoed the curse. Dark figures fanned out from one of the trucks below: troopers on foot recce.

"Red, *stay here.*" Lily's tone was adamant and not a little threatening. "Let's go, Jen. You and the Mule downside, Hawk and I covering upside."

She soon lost sight of Jenny and the Mule. Her own face was streaked with grime. Fingerless gloves covered most of her hands. Kyosti had a hood pulled down to cover his head and face—all but his eyes and nose, and they both wore the dark night-fighting coveralls issued for planetside missions.

The rough outlines of the hill, the product of much excavation, provided good cover. They reached the Q7 line out from the center and circled out as far along its circumference as they could given the terrain. So far the troopers had not advanced farther than a quarter of the way into the kilo-meterwide configuration.

"Good thing they're cautious," whispered Kyosti as Lily stopped, panting, beside him after her bent-over run across a dark, flat gap between ditches. "I keep expecting to see them move in on the road we came in on."

She did not reply, but let herself relax, grow still, stretching out her senses as far as she could. In the distance, she heard an engine idling; far above, a shuttle passed over the city. Embankments slid away into darkness below them, traced by the nimbus of light coming from the trucks beyond, which they could not see.

Kyosti's hand tightened on hers. "This way." His voice was barely audible. "I smell the blood."

He was off so swiftly and silently that she did not have time to question his comment. The ditch led down, deeper, until their view was restricted to a narrow band of sky. They turned a steep corner and ran up against the stub end of a laser rifle.

Jenny lowered it. "Just in time. We're ready to pull out."

It was not a heartening scene. Four shadowy figures hud-dled over two prostrate ones on the ground, the pitiful remnant of Yehoshua's crew of ten. One of the figures straight-ened to reveal the thin crest of the Mule. Five left from One. Two was gone entirely. Lily wondered what had happened to Team Veeta on the other continent.

Kyosti had already gone forward to kneel beside the wounded. Lily gave a curt nod to Jenny, and the mercenary moved out to establish a more generous perimeter. As Lily joined the group around the casualties, she heard Kyosti's overly sharp rejoinder to someone's suggestion.

"No, I don't need a light. It isn't safe to risk it, which any damn fool would know if—"

"Hawk," she said softly, and then she realized how close the edge on his voice was to complete loss of control. She reached down and touched his neck. He was trembling— shaking—and his head was lifted to look not at the injured but at someone else. He was poised to rise and lunge.

"Finch," she said, knowing who it must be even as her grip

tightened on the nearest thing to hand—Kyosti's hair. "Get out to your left, on perimeter with Jenny. *Now*."

"You're *protecting* him?" Finch's voice cracked and he caught back a sob. "You aren't worth—" He broke off, gasping in pain.

The body that interposed itself between Kyosti and Finch was Yehoshua. He had gotten a hard grip on Finch's arm.

"Out," Yehoshua hissed. "We've all lost loved ones. Go." He shoved Finch out, following him.

Lily knelt beside Kyosti and wrapped her arms tightly around him. He shook in her grasp. "We need you now, Kyosti," she whispered, intense, her face hidden in his hair. "Don't leave us now."

He gulped air, fighting, and slowly his ragged breathing evened and his trembling stopped. She realized how tense her muscles had been when she relaxed her grip on him. He groped blindly forward until his hand came to rest in a damp patch of ground: blood seeping from a hastily bandaged wound. Touching the body, he felt along it with both hands, pausing now and again: at the sticky mess of his abdomen, at the rasping, shallow rise and fall of his lungs, at the pulse under his jaw. It was a peculiar examination, until Lily realized that Kyosti's eyes were closed. At last his fingers brushed along the man's temple, and Kyosti shook his head.

"Even in a hospital, we couldn't save him. It's just a matter of hours."

Lily felt a presence, still and unmoving, at her back. She turned her head to see Yehoshua staring at Kyosti.

"No hope at all?" Yehoshua's voice was so quiet that it scarcely penetrated the air at all.

"I'm sorry."

A wet, warm drop struck Lily's face. She glanced first at the sky, but it was clear and black and studded with stars.

"Do what you must," said Yehoshua above her. "We must be moving." He knelt briefly to kiss the dying man's forehead, rose again to collect his three remaining men.

The other casualty proved to have a shattered femur. The team medic had administered a painkiller, and the soldier was only semiconscious.

"I'll need two people to carry her out," said Kyosti, applying a quick, stiff wrapping to the wounded leg. "And the

Mule to carry Alsayid." He turned his head toward Lily, for her confirmation of his orders.

"Thank you," said Yehoshua softly. "I thought you were going to leave him."

Kyosti rose. "In other circumstances I would, but we can't afford for them to find his body."

Yehoshua did not reply, but rather knelt to shoulder a large, bulky pack that clearly was quite heavy.

"That is?" asked Lily.

"Our shuttle's com-console."

"We have one. Leave it."

"No!" Yehoshua's reply was bitter and stubborn. "Alsayid lost his life saving this."

Lily bowed her head and waved the others on. The line headed back along the ditch the way she and Hawk had come. Hawk walked past her to the bend, stopped, and waited. She gestured him on, but he did not move. As she came up beside him he grabbed her and tugged her in to him, began to kiss her face repeatedly.

Lily got out from under his grasp, broke it, and shoved him hard away from her. "Move!" she hissed.

He hesitated, reached out, but withdrew his hand without touching her. She just walked past him. At the top of the ditch Jenny waited, flat on the ground, her rifle pointed toward the lights of the military trucks.

"I sent Finch on ahead," she whispered as Lily crouched beside her. "One truck has left. They've pulled back the team covering the left side, but the group on this side might intercept the wounded."

Lily nodded. "We'll keep heading up. If they get too close, you and Hawk run rear guard and I'll draw them off."

"But Lily," Jenny began, "you're our commander—"

"No. Yehoshua is senior. Don't argue." Lily rose up and started a careful circuit forward.

They climbed. Once she thought she heard a muffled gasp of pain from ahead, but it did not sound again. Twice, definitely, she heard a shouted command carry all the way from the distant trucks, caught by some current of the air.

Then the firing started. Jenny swore behind her, but Lily was already moving. A moment later she realized that it came from above, from the direction of the van. Had Finch panicked? Or Red?

Without really thinking about it, she scrambled up to the exposed height of one of the circling embankments and charged up toward the dish that sheltered the van. She could reach it and clear the opposition before the wounded got there by their more circuitous route.

Or at least that was her first thought. An explosion of light lit the sky as she ran, almost blinding her with its brightness. A hail of streaked fire and solid bullets rained around her so close she saw it hit and sizzle, or, with that heightened awareness that comes on under stress, the actual spit and spin of dirt as the metal bullets struck the ground, peppering the path of her sprint.

A pause in the firing, as if her attackers expected her to be dead and could not believe she was still running. Behind, far behind now, a voice shouted—screamed—her name.

The dish loomed above her. She felt her lungs begin to gulp air at the strain. Shadows moved in the lee of the dish. She fired, coming on.

Burst over the top to find herself in the very midst of a cluster of troopers surrounding the van. Red lay face down by the front tires.

Lily dropped and rolled as the troopers opened fire, came to her feet with a spin and a sweep of fire across their ranks, and dove for the cover of the satellite dish's thick stalk. A deafening return volley sprayed the base of the dish.

"Hoy," she breathed, checking the charge on her rifle.

Fire opened up from below, but not at her. Troopers fell. Red squirmed forward on her stomach to hide underneath the van.

"Lily!" With the part of her that measured the sound, she did not recognize the voice instantly. It was too desperate, too afraid, too—frenzied to be *his* voice. Except it had to be. And it was Kyosti who burst over the edge—and fell in a barrage of fire from the remaining troopers.

An instant later a ruthless line of fire from just below the top scattered the troopers who had shot him, giving Lily the cover to dash out and drag him back behind the dish. More fire from the other direction, killing in its accuracy.

Kyosti's eyes were open, tried desperately to focus on her. "I thought you were dead," he whispered, ragged. He went limp in her arms.

She felt like the world dropped three meters out from

under her, and then she fell. If the dish had burst into flame above her she wound not have noticed it. She laid her face against his throat.

He was still alive.

Slowly she realized that she could hear the uneven labor of his breathing. The firing had stopped.

"Damn my eyes." At some point Jenny had come forward to crouch beside her. "I can't believe you're still alive, Lily-hae—you were dead lit from above, totally exposed, with every gun in this ten trained on you. You're not—"

"Hurt, no." Lily rose, brusque, turning to see Yehoshua already at work loading his two wounded into the van. "Who's your medic?" she demanded of him.

He paused, reacted. "Caenna."

"Finch." Her voice was low but adamant. "Get over here."

He hurried over to her. "Did Jenny get shot—" Broke off, seeing who lay tumbled on the ground. "Void bless," he murmured. His face shone pale in the night. The Mule came over. He and Jenny lifted Hawk up carefully and carried him to the van. "You can't expect me to—not after what he's done to me."

Lily grabbed him by the throat and jerked him to within a hand's breath of her face. "You save him or I'll kill you myself."

"Let's go!" ordered Yehoshua.

Below, firing broke out, too distant to harm them, but trucks were moving, and one had turned to display the shadowed cylinder of a laser cannon, pointed at the height.

Lily pushed Finch forward roughly, shoved him into the rear bubble, and climbed in after him. The van started up smoothly, backed out, turned, and threw everyone in the back forward with its sudden acceleration. An explosion shuddered the ground behind them. Pieces of shattered metal struck the bubble like the opening onslaught of a hailstorm.

The bubble was cramped, with so many people. Evidently Jenny and Yehoshua were in front with Red. The Mule calmly knelt and rearranged the injured.

Kyosti lay on his side, awash in his own blood. Lily rested a hand on his blue hair, fixed her glare on Finch.

Lips tight, he set to work.

14 Ya Old Ghost Ship

****

In the tiny, hidden room that harbored Blumoris's illegal comm-console, Lily sat slumped on a stool, much of her weight resting on the counter that held the console. Her face she had pressed against Bach's cool surface. As he softly sang, monitoring all bands for military communications, she felt the deeper, virtually inaudible hum of his inner workings as a gentle vibration on her cheek. She felt hot, and utterly tired. Bach finished one piece and began another. Lily did not stir.

> *Können Tränen meiner Wangen*
> *Nichts erlangen*
> *Oh, so nehmt mein Herz hinein!*
> *Aber lasst es bei den Fluten,*
> *Wenn die Wunden milde bluten,*
> *Auch di Opferschale sein.*

> If the tears on my cheeks
> achieve nothing,
> o, then take my heart!
> But let it for the streams,
> when the wounds bleed gently,
> also be the sacrificial cup.

* * *

Behind her, the partition to the shop slid aside.

"Heredes?" It was Yehoshua.

She lifted her head. He looked exhausted, drained of any will left to act except perhaps the primeval impetus of vengeance.

"I'm sorry," she said quietly. "About Alsayid."

He shook his head roughly, as if he meant to shake off her words. "What news?" He looked at Bach.

"Nothing new. If they continue their sweep at their present rate they'll reach this area in about three hours."

He reached for the other stool and sat down abruptly, rather like his legs had given out from under him. "We might as well load now." He lifted up his right hand, studying it with a grimace of pain on his face. "I got hit twice on this arm," he said. "Didn't even leave a scratch. I pulled Alsayid out of the shuttle after it exploded—he'd gone back to get the console out. It was too hot to face. I couldn't bring my left arm near it."

Lily saw now that the streaks on the right side of his face were ash, singed eyebrows, and the dark raised welts of treated burns.

"So I pulled him, with that damned pack strapped to his back, pulled him out with one arm. The fire burned off the sleeve. But there's not a scratch on the arm. I don't really feel like it's mine."

Bach reprised his chorale in the silence.

"The engines?" Lily asked at last, no longer sure she cared to make the effort to escape if the shuttle was unrepairable.

Yehoshua sighed and lowered his arm. "The boy says less than an hour. He's having Paisley run one more test. But he doesn't guarantee they'll work. He's out arguing with his pap right now. He wants to come with us."

That interested her a little. She cocked her head and could, indeed, hear Blue's voice pitched high in adolescent anger. His exact words were impossible to make out.

"What happened to Two?" she asked.

"They crashed almost on top of us, obliterated their ship. And because ours exploded, I think their military thought there was only one ship. We flew in close enough together. That's why they weren't searching very hard, until now. They had dead bodies enough."

Lily tugged at the corner of her mouth with one finger,

caught herself doing it, and clenched her hand on her lap.

"And *Franklin's Cairn?*" he continued.

"I don't know. Blue says a cruiser came in last month. I guess Jehane's Intelligence didn't get the report. We saw the *Cairn* blow up. You must have been under cloud cover."

"Yes," he murmured.

"No!" shouted Blumoris from the shop, his declaration carrying easily through the partition.

"Oh," said Yehoshua absently. "Comrade Hawk was exactly the sáme when I left the shuttle. Unconscious, breathing fairly evenly."

"Oh," Lily echoed. "Thank you."

Silence, except for Bach's aria.

Yehoshua slumped forward suddenly and put his hands over his eyes. For some reason, the hopelessness of the gesture galvanized Lily into action.

She stood up, whistled a quick *Disengage* to Bach, and put her hands on Yehoshua's shoulders. "Come on," she said, brisk now. "Isn't there a rendezvous point out at the edge of the system? There were four ships here. Surely one got out there."

"Past two asteroid belts, with a cruiser in pursuit?" he asked bleakly, speaking toward the floor.

"Well, *I* for one do not intend to stay on this hells-forsaken planet. Do you?" she demanded.

That brought his head up. "I don't think I've ever heard you swear before."

"Who's left here to collect?" she asked.

"You," he replied. "I sent Aliasing and my two crewmen back already."

She removed her hands from him and let Bach precede her out into the shop. Blue sat brooding in the middle of a heap of rusting engine parts. His father stood at the workbench, tinkering fussily with an old-fashioned video console.

"Well, I *will* ask," muttered Blue in a burst of adolescent rebellion.

"You will not!" corrected Blumoris, turning around quickly. "These are people who have important work to do, and they won't want to be bothered by an ill-tempered scrap like you."

"And what happens if the engines—"

"Excuse me." Lily pitched her voice low. It had the desired

effect: Both father and son whirled to gape at her. "The fact is, Elder Blumoris, that we haven't anyone trained in mechanics as well as your son. We could use him, given that he will, or can, learn to submit to army discipline."

Blue began to speak. She waved him to silence.

"But I also understand," she continued, "that you haven't any other family but the boy, and no one else to help you run your shop. And further, that if he goes with us, it isn't likely you'll see him again for years. Or perhaps not at all. I won't ask you to let him come with us."

Blumoris surveyed the scattered mess of his old shop. "But you say there is a place for Inocencio in Jehane's army? Hope for advancement? Training and work after Jehane wins?" His words came slowly, as if he was weighing his shop against such prospects.

"A place in Jehane's forces, certainly. If he works; yes, he'll advance. What lies beyond that lies with Jehane's success. I can't promise you more than that."

The old man examined her, his lips creased in a careful frown. He lifted a hand to encompass the shop in a brief gesture. "It's a better promise than what I have to offer him."

Blue seemed to be holding his breath.

Blumoris sighed abruptly, looking tired. "If you'll excuse us, comrades, a moment."

Lily nodded in understanding. She and Yehoshua and Bach went outside into the suspended half-light of predawn. From inside, they heard Blue's yelp of joy.

"I hope that boy understands the sacrifice his father is making," said Yehoshua.

Lily just shook her head.

They waited. A short while later Blue emerged carrying a large bag stuffed full of whatever items such a boy thought indispensible. He looked recklessly happy.

"Well, come on!" he demanded, seeing them. "Let's go. Scrag this dump."

"That looks like a heavy bag," said Lily. "Comrade Officer Yehoshua will help you sort through it while I go in and speak with your father. We have weight limits, you know."

Blue's yelp was now one of protest. "But this is all important," he argued, beginning to look sullen again. "You can't just make me get rid of any of it."

"Comrade Blumoris." Yehoshua looked grimly amused, and not at all forgiving. "Set that bag down and open it up."

"But *I* said—"

"*Now.*"

Blue did as he was told.

Lily went inside. Elder Blumoris stood again at the workbench, hands busy at the video console, but the effort looked half-hearted.

"Elder?"

He turned.

"I want to thank you. I'll take care of him as well as I can, and send you news when it's possible."

He nodded, to show he understood. There were tears on his face, just a few. "Please go," he said brusquely. Lily nodded, echoing him, and left.

Outside, Yehoshua ruthlessly discarded a full half of Blue's possessions. Each time the boy began to protest, Yehoshua cut him off with a few well-chosen, barbed words, usually in reference to his immaturity. Blue flung the discarded things with disgust into the alley trash bin and followed them, complaining all the while, as they set off for the shuttle. After about one hundred meters Lily, without even looking back at him over her shoulder, told him to shut up or go home. He shut up, but his sour expression deepened, could perhaps even be said to curdle. Bach began to sing, softly:

> *Wer hat dich so geschlagen,*
> *Mein Heil, und dich mit Plagen*
> *So übel zugericht.*

> Who has buffeted Thee so,
> my Salvation, and with torments
> so harshly used Thee?

Coming up to the warehouse, Blue at last, as if he could hold it in no longer, burst out, "But I reckon anything that Red's going to try to stow away."

And indeed, they found Red squeezed into the very locker Blue was assigned to store his bag. Jenny marched the girl off, and as Paisley's test ran down, Lily could hear Jenny's scathing denunciation of Red from outside.

"—and what do you expect your Mam to do? Who's she got to look after her?"

Red gulped an incomprehensible answer through her noisy sobbing.

"Is that so? Do you really suppose you have skills so necessary to us? I suggest you get home and see what you can do to help your Mam."

Paisley showed the test results to Blue. He pulled them from her and, turning his back on her, studied them intently. Lily stepped out onto the ramp. Below, she could see two figures in the gloom.

"And anyway," continued Jenny in a lower, more confidential voice, "I'm sure you have better plans for helping the revolution on Landfall than Blue ever did. Now you're free of him."

Red's sobs snuffled to a stop as she considered this aspect of developments. "An' there's a couple of younger kids he never could stand that *I* like well enough, and they'd listen to me—"

"Exactly." Jenny gave her a comradely slap on the back. "Now get."

Red ran off with a hasty good-bye.

"I'm beginning to feel sorry for Security on this planet," said Lily as Jenny walked back up the ramp.

Inside, Blue had decided that the test was positive. Lily glanced at Yehoshua.

"It's your ship," he said to her.

"Then we strap in. Call in our guards, Jenny. How soon can we lift, Blumoris?"

Pinto keyed in Blue's stats and began to fix a course. Within minutes, they were secured and ready to lift.

The old roadway that girdled the warehouse district, although pocked and ragged with age, proved sufficient for a runway. Once the shuttle cleared the ground, Pinto headed away from the city, keeping low, running the contours of the slopes and ridges for almost an hour until they reached the shoreline. Then he banked steeply up and cut for orbit. The pressures in the cabin grew heavier, plateaued, and at last diminished slightly as Pinto leveled the shuttle into a smooth curve. Radio traffic gave no sign yet that their flight had been noticed.

Lily rose and checked all their passengers, including the

silent, sheeted corpse of Alsayid. She paused longest by
Kyosti. He had been given the single stasis chair, to ease the
pressure of the lift on his wounds. He was unconscious, but
he breathed with the same slow evenness of a sleeping man.

Next to him, Yehoshua's injured crewwoman moaned in a
low, semiconscious voice, only half-aware of their flight. Yehoshua
sat in the front, lips turned down, his face expressionless in
grief, as he watched the changing view out the plastine
without any interest Lily could discern. In the very back,
Blue was busy calculating on a screen, calling up schematics
of the shuttle's amplified engines, and tampering with them.

Everyone else, except Aliasing and Bach at comm and, of
course, Pinto, had fallen asleep. Jenny cradled Gregori's bright
head on her lap.

Lily returned to her chair and sat down. Yehoshua glanced
at her, nodded, and she sank back gratefully and went to
sleep.

When she woke, they were drifting in the dark, empty
field of space. The brilliant spray of stars surrounded them.
She blinked and sat up. The stocky figure at the pilot's seat
did not seem familiar, and she realized that Pinto sat sleeping
in the chair beside her, body straining against the straps.

She felt the familiar, quick curl of nausea in her stomach at
weightlessness and then controlled it. "Yehoshua?" she asked,
recognizing the person at the pilot's board finally.

He turned his head, all his acknowledgment.

"How long? How far out are we?"

He checked the red numbers soundlessly clicking off on
the clock. "Nine fleet hours out. In this boat, another thirty-
one to the rendezvous point. We're on auto until the next
asteroid belt—then Pinto will come back on."

"And Landfall?"

"Nothing. Either they didn't see us, or they didn't care, or
they're following now hoping we'll lead them somewhere."
He sounded equally apathetic about all three options. "Although
I doubt any ships would negotiate two asteroid belts to chase
a limping shuttle. Our charts aren't even complete for the
edge of this system."

"Have you slept?" she asked.

"No."

"Shouldn't you?"

"No." He did not raise his voice, but something in his tone made her decide not to pursue the question. He went back to staring out at space.

Lily retrieved her screen from her belt and started a log of the Landfall expedition. Eventually she finished it. Others had awakened. Rainbow unstrapped and handed out rations. The shuttle reached, and Pinto negotiated, the second asteroid belt. It was the only interesting part of the trip.

Lily dozed, studied engine schematics with Blue, watching closely as Finch examined a still-unconscious Kyosti, and spoke reassuring words to the crewwoman with the broken leg.

At last they reached the rendezvous point. Finch went on comm. Pinto yawned at the pilot's board. Instrument sweeps showed nothing. Comm picked up no traffic.

They altered their position. Nothing.

Altered it again. By this time everyone was awake on board, except of course Kyosti. Even the injured woman had refused her painkiller in order to listen: their alternative now was to limp on quarter power six days back to Landfall and turn themselves in.

In the overpowering, expectant silence, the faint hiss of static sounded more like a person whistling through teeth. One small, frozen planet unveiled its stark and lonely curve at the very edge of the transparent shield.

"Wait," whispered Finch. The quiet word electrified the cabin. "I've got movement on another band, barely there. But it's not any band I've ever used before." He tweaked knobs, buttons, careful and sure in his domain.

A loud scratch of static startled them, faded, and then there it was, a whisper lost in the depths of space, barely caught by Finch's expertise.

"This is the *Forlorn Hope*. This is the . . . *Forlorn Hope*. Do you . . . copy? Do you—"

Paisley shrieked. "It be ya ghost!" she cried, terrified. "It be ya old ghost ship. We got to run!" She fumbled at her straps.

"Paisley!" Lily's voice shocked the girl into silence.

"Idiot tattoo!" hissed Finch, fiddling madly with his controls. "Now I've lost it."

Paisley, huddled in her seat, made a warding gesture with one hand that all the Ridanis but Pinto echoed.

Silence on comm. Static crackled.

"No, wait," said Pinto softly. "I got a fix on the trail. I think it must have been caught by that planet."

"And I'm willing to bet that was a mechanical hail," said Finch, glancing at Pinto with comradely agreement—until he recalled that Pinto was also an idiot tattoo, and jerked his gaze back to comm.

Pinto's lips curled up into a self-righteous sneer.

"Well?" Lily demanded. "What are we waiting for? Set a course."

15   The Mule Balks

****

They found the hulk of the vessel calling itself the *Forlorn Hope* locked in a high, stranded orbit around the frozen planet that rimmed the edge of Landfall system.

"I get nothing but the same signal, looped," said Finch. "I don't think there's anyone aboard."

"Bring us alongside, in contiguous orbit," ordered Lily. "We'll board. Do you think it's really the *Forlorn Hope?*"

The answer came, surprisingly, from Blue. He had keyed frantically onto his screen as they approached, and now, with a crow of triumph, he lifted up his arm to display a fine-detailed line drawing.

"It does!" he cried. "It conforms to the exterior specs for the old highroad fleet. Central impounded the four that reached here, but this one got away. And there's none left operational that I know of. Central never could build any boat as good. If this is really her—"

"It be ya sore hard luck," muttered Paisley with determination. "Sore, hard, terrible luck, to tamper with such as were cast adrift from ya pattern so long since. It be wrong o' them to try to find ya way back to Tirra-li 'afore it were ya fated time to travel. And it be wrong o' us—"

"That's complete nonsense," exclaimed Pinto, forestalling the comment that seemed about to emerge from Finch. "A lot of superstitious nonsense."

"Sure, and be it your hard luck to say so," answered Paisley darkly. "I reckon your mater be sleeping ya poor tonight to hear you say so."

"Well, she can't hear me, can she?" said Pinto in disgust. "*Being* as there's Void knows how many windows between us."

"It be not fit to scorn ya pattern," Paisley continued, undeterred. Her confidence was clearly beginning to have an effect on the other three Ridanis, who cast nervous glances by turns at the pale hulk of the ship, at Paisley, and, last, at Lily.

Lily unstrapped herself, keeping one hand gripped to the armrest. "That's enough, Paisley. I'll take three to board. Jenny, the Mule, and—" she hesitated. "Yehoshua."

"No," said the Mule.

Finch gave a snort of disgust. "What, are you superstitious, too?" he asked, happy to include the Mule in the circle of contempt he otherwise reserved for the Ridanis.

"I suggest we keep this civilized," interposed Lily quietly, well able to read the Mule's body language as it reacted to Finch's comment. "Do you have any objection to the orders, comrade?" she asked.

The Mule's lank crest lifted slightly, as if a breeze stirred the cabin. The gaze it shot at Lily might have seared cold steel. No reply was forthcoming.

"Then if you have no objection—" began Lily, but even as she said it she saw the curl of the Mule's hands, the set of the face, as it settled into a stubborn posture. It looked as if it were digging in for a long, determined resistance. She could see that the Mule would not explain itself publicly, and certainly not when all attention was focused on the conflict. "If you'll come with me," she finished, "we'll discuss this privately."

"But where—" began Finch, knowing full well that this cabin was the only compartment on the ship that held atmosphere.

"In the suit airlock to the cargo hold," replied Lily, cutting him off. "Just don't vent us, please."

The Mule let out a brief hiss that was too sta-ish for Lily to interpret, but rose and followed Lily back to the airlock. Lily keyed it open, waited a few silent minutes, and then stepped inside and shut it behind them.

"Well?"

"You are unfamiliar with sta, are you not?" said the Mule. The tiny chamber and thin dusting of air swallowed the words.

Lily shrugged.

"Have you ever seen any sta doing suited work? In vacuum?" When Lily did not reply, the Mule gave a sibilant sigh and arched its crest again. "I am sta enough, comrade," the Mule continued, stiffly formal now, not a little offended, "that I too am unable to work suited in a vacuum, despite my human half." Here the Mule's voice descended into all-too-human sarcasm.

"All right," said Lily. "You'll stay here, for now." She paused, began to ask why the Mule had forced this private audience, and immediately thought better of it. That pride could stick on even such a seemingly innocuous subject was no surprise to her, and certainly not with the Mule, who would have no desire to express such a—failing?—in front of people who already had cause to be prejudiced against it. She keyed the airlock open instead to reveal the expectant silence of the cabin.

"Lia, take comm," Lily ordered. "Finch, you'll board with us."

The four of them suited up, hooked on lines, and left the ship via the cargo airlock. Yehoshua and Jenny, inured by practice to the experience, fired up immediately to cross the thousand meters between the shuttle and the bulk of the *Forlorn Hope*.

But Lily and Finch hesitated, side by side, caught in the exhilaration of freedom and the vast emptiness surrounding them. All the soldiers in Jehane's forces were trained in suits, but for those still new to it, like Lily and Finch, there had not been enough training to dull the sheer wild rush of adrenalin.

Lily clicked on her mike with her tongue. "After all those years on Unruli, this is hard to believe, isn't it?" she said softly.

She heard Finch sigh. With an old instinct for his thoughts resurrected from their closeness on Unruli by the intimacy of their link within such immensity, she knew that he was thinking of his sister, so newly dead.

"Yehoshua wants to bury his cousin in the Void," he said at last, his voice quiet. "Just vent him. It seems strange to me."

Lily stared at the infinite depth of stars, at the grey curve of cold planet beyond the *Forlorn Hope*, at the slow, bright rise of the distant Landfall sun above the shuttle's top vane. "I don't know," she answered. "It's not such a bad place to rest." She moved to catch Yehoshua and Jenny in her line of sight, discovered that they were almost halfway to the derelict. "Come on, Finch. Let's go."

"Do you suppose it is a ghost ship?" Finch asked as their packs fired them across the gap.

"What do you mean?"

"I'm not sure. That Paisley sure seems certain about her superstitious—" He broke off. "Why are you laughing?"

"Just surprised. I didn't know you even knew her name. Paisley, that is."

"Why shouldn't I?" he asked, defensive. "Sure, she's a tattoo, but you have to admit she's uncommon pretty no matter what her—" He stopped speaking abruptly, as if he had said something overly revealing.

"I was just surprised, Finch," Lily replied. "You haven't been exactly friendly to the Ridanis."

"I still don't see why I should be," he muttered. "Bunch of damn—" The rest of the comment was lost to indiscriminate static across the line.

"Anyway," said Lily. "If it is the *Forlorn Hope*, the original, there can't be anyone left alive. It's been far too long. I'm amazed we stumbled across it."

"So am I. That signal is so weak it's incredible that we caught it." Finch sounded almost irritated, but it was hard to tell over the mike. "But you've always been lucky."

"I *have*?" She had no time to debate this point because they reached the ship. Yehoshua had already located an outside seal, halfway around the curve of the ship, and he beckoned to them. By the time they arrived at his position, he had managed to open it, revealing an airlock that led inside.

"Maintenance shaft, I'd wager," said Yehoshua over the mike. There was easily enough room for all four of them, and once the outer lock shut, Lily felt an immediate shift in her balance, a tug toward one wall.

"This place gives me the spooks," said Jenny abruptly as the inside lock sighed slowly open onto an empty, silver-walled corridor. "You'd think it was still alive..." She trailed

off as Lily took the first, hesitant step into the *Forlorn Hope*,
paused, and read the narrow screen on her lower suit arm.

"We still have atmosphere," Lily said. "That's incredible,
after all this time." She glanced at Finch. "Maybe there are
ghosts on board."

But they found no one living, and no bodies, dead, decayed,
or otherwise. What signs of human habitation there were had
the look of tidy, shipshape readiness, as if a crew was about to
board, not as if it had carelessly or hastily abandoned the
vessel.

At first they wandered, rather lost, through a seeming
maze of silver corridors. The barest gleam of light heralded
their path. Eventually Lily relayed on the hand-pack back to
Bach, and discovered a fact that somehow did not particularly
surprise her: the little robot was completely familiar with the
design specifications of the so-called highroad fleet. She used
his rather convoluted directions to lead them along more
silver corridors to an elevator that, at his directions, carried
them to a new deck.

This one was gold, textured, and patterned, glowing with
an incandescent gleam, like the ghost of the ship's past life.
The way to the bridge proved almost deceptively simple.

The bridge itself had a refinement, an efficiency of design,
that in a subtle way put the ostentatious command centers of
La Belle's and Yi's ships to shame. Streamlined and sleek,
like the *Forlorn Hope* itself, it was easy to find and bring to
life the various consoles, to identify their purpose, even in
the gloom of minimum lighting.

Finch discovered the comm and quickly sat down and went
to work. In minutes, he had opened a line to the shuttle.

Jenny found and studied weapons. Yehoshua settled in at
life support and began to bring up an array of functions on
the console. Lily, on her way to the engineering link, paused
beside the captain's chair.

On impulse, she keyed in for the log, tried once, twice,
three times. Used the relay to Bach, and tried his new
commands.

The log had been wiped clean. There was no sign if the
damage was deliberate or accidental. Thoughtful, she crossed
to the engineer's link and, with Blue kibitzing through Bach,
pulled up the function banks.

Suddenly the lights came on, brilliant, glaring. Softened

abruptly to a smoother brightness. She turned to see Yehoshua removing his head gear; gasped—like the lights coming on—and then caught herself as Bach sang a question, and she relaxed.

After a few minutes, when Yehoshua did not die, she took her own head gear off, quickly followed by Finch. Jenny, with a grimace, kept hers on at Lily's command.

"Well?" Lily asked, gesturing toward the consoles, which had come to life at the hands of these interlopers.

Yehoshua shook his head. For the first time since Alsayid's death, his face bore a look of animation. "It's as if," he began, slowly, careful of his words, "they shut it all down, all but the absolute lowest level maintenance and drive functions, just put it on hold and then left. I can't imagine what would cause them to do such a thing, or where they might have gone."

"Or how," added Finch, his voice an echo of Yehoshua's astonishment. "If this *is* the *Forlorn Hope*."

"Can you doubt it?" asked Yehoshua.

Finch shook his head in agreement. "How could they just leave—" He set his lips together, thinking. "Unless there are bodies in cryo on one of the lower decks. Or just plain bodies."

"I hope the channel to the shuttle is closed," said Lily cautiously. "We'll never get the Ridanis on the ship if they hear that. Yehoshua, we need a working hold that can bring in the shuttle."

He made an affirmative noise and began keying through the systems files.

"All right," said Lily, when he had found what she needed. "You and Finch relay through Pinto and Lia, and bring them in. Jenny, you and I will go down to meet them."

Lily sealed her head gear back on for the trip down to the holds level. They took their time, wandering as they went, this time armed with a tight relay to Bach, who kept them oriented.

The gold deck had only two other sections besides the bridge: a three-room suite comprised of tac and computer centers and a two-room suite that evidently had belonged to the captain.

"Look at that bed!" Jenny exclaimed as they keyed open the lock into the inner room. "Four people could sleep on that bed, and it's freestanding! Do you suppose all the quarters are like this?"

Lily stared. The two rooms seemed huge to her, at least five meters square each. She shrugged, tonguing her mike switch. "It was an exploratory vessel, wasn't it? They might spend years on this ship without ever making landfall."

Below gold they found the silver deck they had entered onto. Here were far more corridors, but this maze was quickly explained: this deck held the crew's quarters, the medical, the mess and rec sections, and a few areas Lily thought might be labs.

After silver, the color of the walls changed again, this time to a copper sheen. Labs, a small detention suit of cells, and a second and larger rec suite, filled about half of the deck. The other half they did not explore: a single door labeled Green Room led into it.

A large freight elevator took them to the lowest deck.

"Well," said Jenny, examining the iron-grey walls of this deck with a practiced eye. "Now I feel more at home."

Lily suspected that there was some pattern to the decks, as there had been on La Belle's ship, a pattern that Kyosti would have laughed to see, although she could not possibly guess why. They hurried past cargo holds, the weapons and engineering access, a maintenance lab, a second computer center, before they found the triple airlocks giving onto the great hangar.

The shuttle had arrived before them. After almost half an hour of misunderstanding Bach's answers to her questions, Lily finally discovered that it *was* possible to connect a pressurized tube to the shuttle hatchway and funnel the passengers off to an atmosphered overlook without having to put them all in suits.

Blue, of course, emerged first, followed by Bach and Lia and Gregori, in a clump, and then Yehoshua's crewman wheeling the stasis couch in which Kyosti lay, still unconscious, and last the Mule carrying the injured woman. After a pause Pinto emerged, looking disgusted.

Lily had taken off her head gear. "Where are the others?"

"Where do you think?" Pinto said. The geometric lines on his face emphasized his derision. "Paisley was telling stories about the third cursed merchanter when I left. You know, hailed by the ghost ship and didn't cut and run fast enough. I think this one ends up trapped in the gasp between windows."

"Oh." Lily looked at Kyosti's still form thoughtfully, wondering what he would think of such a fate. "I'll deal with them."

Blue had gone to the overlook plastine and stood, face pressed against the plastine, staring out across the vast hangar. "Look!" he exclaimed. "Two other landers. But just small ones. You'd think a ship like this would have had some larger shore-boats, or recce yachts, at least."

Lily lifted her gaze from Kyosti to consider the group assembled before her. A motley collection, without a doubt. Most of them gaped out the overlook glass at the hangar, at the fine, impressive interior of a ship older than their great-grandparents and yet still as advanced—still *more* advanced— than any that Reft space, Central or Jehane, possessed now.

"First." She waited until they all looked at her. "Comrade Blumoris." He turned, reluctantly. "Bach will have to give us a quick guide to the ship, before you head to your posts. Keep in wrist-com, in case you get lost. Blumoris, I want you to engine-access. You're what we've got right now for engine tech."

Blue's mouth dropped open, leaving him looking young and foolish. He was clearly too stunned to speak. "*I* get to—" Almost too stunned. "*I* get to run these engines?"

"Not yet," said Lily with patience. "Familiarize yourself for now. I'll send Paisley along after you—"

"That grimy tattoo—"

"Blumoris." The sharpness of her tone cut him off. "Who gave you leave to speak?"

Under the censorious gaze of all the rest, Blue looked for the first time a little shamefaced, or at least sullenly acquiescent.

Lily transferred her gaze to the crewman holding onto Kyosti's stasis couch. "I'm afraid I've forgotten your name, comrade."

He gave her a brief salute, a gesture that surprised her. "Jorge Zia Nguyen, sir."

She coughed behind her hand to hide her embarrassment at being called sir. "Well, comrade." Hesitated, having forgotten for an instant what she meant to ask him. "Yes. Do you have a specialty that might help us here?"

"I have some experience in weapons systems, sir."

"Good. You and Pinto go straight to the bridge. I don't suppose your comrade..."

"Wei, sir."

"Thank you—has any experience in navigation?"

Nguyen shook his head. "Soldiering, mostly, with a little training in comp and tac."

Lily sighed, feeling lost again. Without nav, they could fill every other seat and still remain stranded in Landfall system.

"If I may?" The Mule's fluid question was surprisingly deferential. Lily nodded, looking at him curiously. "I have some experience in nav."

"But in Jehane's fleet—on *Franklin's Cairn*—you weren't ever training in nav, were you? Why wouldn't Callioux have assigned you there?"

"You forget, comrade," hissed the Mule with a sardonic edge, "that in Jehane's fleet there are sta running nav. Sta have not taken sides in this so-human conflict, but they are always willing to accept pay for services. Sta will not work with me."

Blue stared in repulsed amazement at the Mule, his nose puckered up as if the air had suddenly brought him a bad smell. The others, all but Pinto, looked down, or away. Pinto, however, looked at the Mule with acute interest.

"Why didn't you tell me this before?" asked Lily.

"You didn't ask," replied the Mule.

"Hoy. And you're good at *bissterlas*, too, aren't you?"

"*Damn* good at it," said Pinto so sharply that the Mule shifted its gaze to meet the pilot's eyes. They seemed to measure each other, two whose work had to mesh perfectly in order to guide a ship safely through the precise limits and angles of the vector drive. After a moment, as if satisfied, they both looked at Lily.

Lily shook her head. "I think we've got the absolutes covered," she said, not quite believing it herself. "If this boat still runs, and we can figure it out. Jenny, you take these two to Medical. Do what you can to make them comfortable until Finch can come down and check them. Then you—and Gregori, I think—just roam the ship until you feel familiar with it. That should cover everyone except the Ridanis."

"What about me?" Lia's soft voice barely stirred the air. She had managed to lose herself in one corner of the overlook, hidden in swathes of loose fabric and the dark cloud of her hair.

"Relieve Finch while he's in Medical."

"I could," said Aliasing tentatively, "but there is one thing you've forgotten."

"There is?" Lily asked, surprised not by this revelation but by its source.

"Food." Aliasing pursed her lips, giving her fragile features a remarkably practical cast. "Maybe I should go find the mess."

Lily glanced, startled, at Jenny, but the mercenary merely lowered her eyes in a uncharacteristically demure gesture that Lily abruptly suspected hid amusement.

"By all means," agreed Lily. "You've just been appointed Steward."

For some reason, this made Lia laugh, but she went after the others without further comment.

16 Aliasing Takes Charge of the Kitchen

****

Lily's first act on reaching the shuttle cabin was to order Rainbow, in her most military voice, to stand guard in Medical over Finch's examination of the wounded. Rainbow's reflexes got the better of her superstitions, and she snapped a salute, called up her ten—consisting of Cursive and Diamond—and marched them out of the shuttle before they could think twice about setting foot on the decks of ya ghost ship itself.

Paisley did not budge. Her expression stiffened into one of mutinous resolve.

"It bain't right," she said stoutly. "It be *poor* of you, min Rans—min Heredes, to play sore and fast with ya cursed ground."

"Paisley." Lily let the girl wait while she peeled off her suit and stowed it in its locker. When she sat down beside the Ridani girl, she unclipped her screen from her belt and keyed it on.

Paisley regarded her with a stubbornness that would have put the Mule to shame.

"I'm going to tell you some things that most of the people on this ship—and most people in the Reft—don't know."

Paisley's lips twitched. "Be it ya secret?"

"Not quite. It's something people here have forgotten, and I found out just by accident."

"I remember," said Paisley slowly, "'bout ya time we be

trapped in ya spook's ship, and min Bach showed us ya star map."

Lily nodded. "Think about it. Say it's true, that long ago colonists from the old planets—what they call League space now—traveled out here and lost the way to get back. That later the highroad fleet, just a few ships, stumbled onto colonized Reft space, and that the government impounded most of them, but this one wanted to go back, and got lost—"

"Sure," interposed Paisley. "It be ya punishment for trying to get back over ya way when it weren't meant yet."

"Paisley." Lily sighed. "Maybe it just happened. They lost their nav functions, or got vectored wrong by a miscalculation or—I don't know—there are gas clouds and solar flares and I don't know what else that can throw a system off. And somehow ended up lost and drifting, and abandoned ship."

"Or all died, and ya corpses be still haunting on board," muttered Paisley darkly. "Sure, and they be wanting ya companions on ya bleak way, waiting out ya belly down day til Jehane come tae lead them back."

"But Jehane *has* come," said Lily, abruptly giving up cold logic for the warmer climes of legend. "We're part of his forces. We're the ones who stumbled on this ship after so much time. Don't you think it's time we took it back, to help Jehane take ya people back over the way to Tirra-li?"

"Sure," breathed Paisley, rapt in the sudden illumination of her great prophecy, "and glory. I never thought of that." She stood up. "We mun go, then."

"Hoy," murmured Lily to herself, an exhalation of breath. "I want you to go help Blumoris. You've got to see what you can do with these engines."

Paisley made an expressive face. "He smells," she said succinctly.

Lily laughed. "I think he'd be surprised to hear you say that."

"Sure. But it more likely he says that 'bout us tattoos."

Lily rested a hand, briefly, on Paisley's shoulder. "Yes, I expect it is. Just remember that he comes from a very—ah—limited background."

"Be it so," murmured Paisley with a skeptical frown, "though at least he knows no better. It be ya cruel o' Finch to say ya low words about tattoos when he knows how sore sad it makes Pinto feel. A'course," she finished, looking thoughtful, "that be certain sure why he says it."

"You can't judge everyone by Finch," said Lily hastily, feeling both protective and angry over Finch at the same time.

"Nay." Paisley lifted a finger and traced, unconsciously perhaps, one of the curling figures that decorated her face. Like Pinto, all her gestures held an inherent grace that accentuated her beauty. It was, Lily thought idly, some trick of fate that had thrown two Ridanis of such particular and unusually striking looks together. "I reckon," continued Paisley in a considering tone, "that your min Hawk be from over ya way, bain't he?"

"What makes you say that?"

"He be different. And ya blue hair. And anyway," and now Paisley's voice took on the accents of a proven argument, "he be ya only one o' all o' you, even you, begging pardon, min Heredes—and excepting min Bach, being as he be ya 'bot—as treats us Ridanis absolute no different than ya others. Bain't no one I ever met done so, 'cept him."

"Well, and say it's so, for the sake of argument. Then that means there is a way back, doesn't it?"

"Sure," agreed Paisley cheerfully, "but he be ya strange, be min Hawk. So sometime I reckon we be better off here anyhow."

Lily chuckled. "We'll leave it as a theory. Promise me not to mention it to anyone."

"You don't reckon they guessed it for theyselves?"

"Well, then, just wait until they ask you."

"Ah," said Paisley wisely, and confined herself to that comment.

Lily left her in the huge, and confusing, engineering hall with an ecstatic Blumoris, and made her way to Medical.

Comrade Wei was awake, looking haggard but optimistic. Finch had managed to find her a mobile chair, so Lily sent her, with the Ridani soldier Diamond, off to gold deck to see what sense she could make of the computer and tac centers.

Rainbow stood at the foot of a stasis couch, looking solemn. Finch examined Kyosti with prim reluctance and pronounced his condition unchanged, and unchangeable.

"Look at those stats," he said, pointing to the readout above the couch. "I got him transferred to this couch, figuring it was better than that makeshift business we had him in before. I even got most of the functions to work. This ship is remarkably well designed. All the systems follow along logically from your entry points, and—"

"What about the stats?" Lily asked sharply.

"Oh." Finch shrugged. "They're all skewed. Somehow I just haven't got that functioning properly. It'll take some time, working with it."

Lily frowned. "I think we're better off with you on com on the bridge, for now. Learn the system as well as you can in the next four hours, and then I'll send Lia up for a quick survey of it so that she can relieve you when necessary."

"What about—*him*?"

On the couch, Kyosti looked not so much asleep as closed in, as if his essence had been pulled tight in around and into himself.

Lily said nothing for a moment, gazing at him, at the sheen of paleness underlying the bronze tone of his skin. "Our first priority has to be to get out of this system, to find Jehane's fleet and report this disaster. And anyway, what more can we do?" She looked at Finch as if daring him to say that he had deliberately not done as much as he could to bring Kyosti back, but he merely ducked his head and backed away from her.

"I'll get back to the bridge, then," he said, and left.

"I can stay and watch him," said Rainbow unexpectedly. "Be I've got ya bit o' medic training—not as makes ya real difference, mind you, but I can tell ya clean bandage and ya signs o' distress, or if he be coming round." She paused, went on in a lower, more deferential voice. "Min Hawk, he be ya fair to us Ridanis."

"Thank you," said Lily. She motioned to the other Ridani soldier, Cursive. "I want you to find comrade Seria and send her to the bridge. Then continue with Gregori to familiarize yourself with the layout of the ship. We're going to need to know this boat backward and forward. Take a verbal log as you go."

Cursive nodded. He followed Lily out, separating off from her outside Medical. Lily, on her way to gold deck, got lost once, but she forced herself to patiently retrace and reroute her path until she found one of the elevators. It brought her to gold deck, where she found Yehoshua loitering in the corridor. He looked up, hearing the quiet fall of her feet on the soft flooring.

"Comrade," he said, formal. "I would like permission to bury my cousin. I think he would have wished this kind of—solitude."

The words brought her up short. "Yehoshua. Comrade *Officer* Yehoshua." It was not the nature of the request, but the request itself that stunned her. "You outrank me. You don't have to ask *me*."

In the softening glow of the golden walls, she saw that he had aged in these few days. The stark white lines, the legacy of his years of hard work in deep-space asteroid mining, showed more sharply on his face than before. Streaks of gray sprayed a fine mist of silver across his black hair.

"I don't want charge of this expedition," he said curtly. He paused, mulling over the words, and started again. "You were being trained by Callioux for ship's command. My rank is purely soldiering—and by that measure, on this ship, you outrank me. It's in your hands, comrade."

"Hoy," Lily muttered. "I need to go sit down."

A brief smile curved Yehoshua's lips, perhaps sympathy, perhaps the merest distracted response. "And my request?"

She shook her head, wanting for the moment to be free of him, to consider what she had to do now. "Do you want any company?"

A slight, negative shake of his head. "I would prefer to be alone, with your permission."

"Then granted." He began to walk away. "Wait," she added. "Who is monitoring life support?"

"The 'bot," he said with another wisp of a smile. "He seems to have the system well in hand."

Motionless, she waited until he vanished into the elevator before she took slow steps toward the bridge, as if by delaying her entrance she could somehow put off the moment when she had to face squarely that *she* was responsible for this tiny, fugitive crew, stranded on a ghost ship in enemy territory.

Well? she thought, lifting her hand, pausing before she set it on the panel that would trigger the door mechanism, and send her, all retreat impossible, into the bridge. What would Heredes have said?

She smiled. Heredes, at least, never let circumstances throw him off-balance. Always maintain your stance, and stay centered. Wasn't that the first thing she had learned? And yet one never stopped learning to deepen that center.

With the briefest of touches, she opened the door and entered the bridge.

Finch glanced up at her as she paused beside the captain's chair. "I think I can bring up the in-ship com now."

"Let me see."

He explained the basics to her. She watched him engage the system and begin calling through the ship. As surprised responses filtered back, she went over to Bach. The robot was singing happily, deep into the life support systems, which he proclaimed in glorious counterpoint to be working perfectly as he brought each one out of manual call-up and into auto-function. Lily shook her head and walked across to weapons.

She spent some time with Nguyen, puzzling through the array of screens, and finally recommended he bring Bach over once the robot had finished engaging all full-support systems.

Last, and most apprehensively, she crossed to stand between pilot and nav stations. Seeing her, Pinto peeled back the stillstrap and stretched his arms and legs. He looked tired.

"Well?" she asked.

He shrugged. "Just like any other boat. If this really is the last of the old highroad fleet, this harness is the model on which every Reft spacer is built. If I had to make a comparison, I'd say that the vectoring alignments are a little more fluid here—not a problem for me, but a less accurate pilot might slide too far and miss their angle." In the chair, and despite the profusion of tattoos covering every millimeter of exposed skin that under any other circumstances of birth would have proscribed him from entering such a prestigious profession, he looked relaxed and completely at home.

"Pinto," she asked abruptly, but quietly, "why did you decide to become a pilot?"

He considered her, his expression turning suddenly caustic. "Why do you think? A deep-seated hunger for freedom from that part of my heritage that has marked me for life." He lifted a slender hand to touch the geometric patterns that defined and accentuated the lines of his face.

"Pinto," said Lily drily, "your martyrdom has long since ceased to make me feel uncomfortable. Most people go into piloting because they score very high on those particular aptitude tests."

"Do you suppose that anyone bothered to give *me* aptitude tests?"

"I don't know. I always thought that was the one profession that didn't allow exceptions."

Pinto levered himself out of the chair and stood with one hand resting on the blank panel that separated pilot's nest from the nav bank.

He smiled, still caustic. "That's right, and I got the highest scores they'd seen in a generation. Now, if I may, I'd like to go off-shift."

Lily nodded slowly. "Take four hours. We'll do a complete status check then."

He left, and she turned to the nav banks. The Mule was busy, keying in numbers, testing screens and logistics, all with a studied air of ignoring what took place just beyond its shoulders. Lily watched it for a while.

"You seem comfortable here," she said finally. "And you certainly seem to be taking well to the system."

The Mule stopped and carefully turned to give Lily the benefit of its full attention. It wrinkled up its muzzle in what she recognized as a sta-ish grimace of approval: not a smile as humans might know it, being both more comprehensive of approval and less specific of humor.

"I thank you," said the Mule, surprising her. "For giving me this opportunity. I have long wished to invest my talents where they are best utilized. Before now, I have only had intermittent opportunities to be allowed at nav. And this system!" Its crest lifted and subsided at some emotion she could not name. "A pleasure. Simply a pleasure. Clearly made for the less agile human abilities and yet curiously without the rigid framework necessary to sta calculation and implementation. For instance, the preliminary *ought* calc function—"

Lily stood stunned by this uncharacteristic effusion. Fortunately the Mule seemed oblivious to her speechlessness and continued with great vigor of expression and tone to illustrate the details of the system to her. She was further amazed by how much it had dissected of the nav bank in so short a time, but she thought it prudent not to interrupt, even for praise.

Eventually, the Mule paused, fingers splayed across a monitor, half-hiding the scroll of numbers that coursed along underneath. "That is the basic system. I fear that to one untrained in navigation the rest of the bank might seem inexplicable."

"I think it might." Lily allowed herself a brief smile. Some instinct for the Mule's uncertain temper made her keep her voice neutral. "You seem well in control here. We'll do a status check interlinking all systems in four hours."

The Mule nodded, a little absently, already engrossed in a new set of functions coming up on the monitor.

Lily turned away and saw Finch regarding her. He followed her as she walked to the door of the bridge, where she paused, looking at him expectantly.

He glanced at the Mule across the long width of the bridge. "How did he get to be a pilot?" he asked in a low voice. "That tattoo?"

"His name is Pinto," said Lily in a tired voice. "'And while you're under my command, comrade Caenna, you will stop calling them 'tattoos.'"

Finch stiffened. "What happened to *our* friendship?" he asked, tight. "I knew you long before any of these people did. I used to think I was your closest friend."

"You were. But I have different responsibilities now."

"Yes," he answered bitterly. "Now you have a psychotic lover. And more important associates in higher places. But I still can't understand why you favor a filthy tat—" He broke off. "A damned Ridani so much. But I suppose *he* must be some Senator's son."

His sarcasm was too obvious to be lost on her. At that moment, the door sighed aside to reveal Jenny, poised to enter. The mercenary's eyes widened, taking in the little tableau, and she hesitated.

"Actually, he is," said Lily, and walked through the door. It exhaled shut behind her, leaving her in the gold deck corridor with Jenny.

"What was that all about?" Jenny asked mildly.

"Robbie Malcolm, known as Pero to you, once gave me a lecture on something he called 'the redistribution of wealth,' which I didn't pay much attention to at the time. But thinking back on it, I wonder if it doesn't have something to do with what that was all about."

Jenny shook her head. "Don't start in on trade averages to me. You House miners are all alike—everything is economics to you."

Lily laughed. "Please. Don't accuse me of *that* particular virtue. Although I expect I absorbed some through no fault of my own. It's hard not to when it's the main topic of every clan supper conversation."

"Was it really?" Jenny sounded sincerely curious. She smiled. "No wonder you ran when you had the chance. What did you want me for?"

"Actually, I confess that I've forgotten. But I'd like to spend some time just walking the ship to get the lay of her. I feel very uncomfortable not knowing my physical ground."

"At your orders, comrade."

They stopped first at comp/tac, and found comrade Wei ensconced beside Diamond, working slowly but stubbornly through the top layers of the system, trying to get a feel for their structure. They had not made much progress, but Lily felt they could be trusted to be careful and as thorough as their limited experience allowed.

"In any case," she said to Jenny as they left, "we won't get any real progress there until we hook back up with Jehane. He'll have experts. We're doing well to have cobbled together as much of a qualified crew as we have now."

They took the elevator to the lowest deck and worked their way back up.

In engineering, Paisley and Blue had established an uneasy truce based mostly on their mutual desire to gain a working knowledge of the engines. The Green Room, on bronze deck, proved to be a vast jungle of vegetation in a chamber whose dimensions and shape Lily could not measure from inside of it. She chose not to venture far. On silver deck they stopped first at Medical—Kyosti showed no change—and then explored the warren of crew cabins: although small, each cabin was cleverly designed to give the illusion of more space.

They finished their circuit of silver deck with a stop at the galley. Entering the empty but markedly well-appointed mess hall, they could hear voices raised in some kind of argument from the kitchens beyond. Lily recognized Pinto's voice first.

"—and anyway, I *still* say it's unnatural."

"Unnatural!" Lily could not quite place this second voice.

"You don't believe that anymore than I do, Jonathan. You just say that because—"

Jenny chuckled.

Glancing at her, Lily realized that her eyes were bright with unshed tears, looking both happy and sad at the same time. "What is it, Jenny?" she asked softly.

"—and you know you would never have had the chance if your own mother hadn't been faithful all those years," continued the second voice, forceful and definite as a self-confident orator. "So you can't tell *me* that—"

"I think Lia's finally found a home—no—a place that she can call hers. Her—her ground, if you will."

"That's Lia?" But even as she said it, Lily realized that it was indeed Lia scolding Pinto in a tone of voice Lily herself had only once or twice dared take with the sulky Ridani.

"You ought to be *thankful* that you've fallen in with people who treat you decently, instead of complaining—"

Lily could not possibly imagine what expression Pinto might be wearing under this assault. "But Lia is so—quiet." Lily looked hopelessly at Jenny, shrugging to make the statement a question.

Jenny grinned. "You never saw Lia lecturing the other Senators' daughters, the other rich girls, on the unfairness of them using illicit birth control while other women went without, or held willingly to the laws and did their civic duty. Not that those girls didn't have every opportunity open to them in any case, no matter how many, or how few, children they had."

"Even on Unruli you only had to have two children to qualify for university, given that you passed the basic test scores."

"I still don't understand why you, coming from such a well-to-do House, didn't just opt for that choice."

"I don't know." Lily considered. "Perhaps it *was* always fated that I'd someday meet and bond, however symbolically, with Pero. I always thought it was unfair that my brothers and male cousins had to work so hard for a chance to get in. Even Finch once confessed he'd have liked to go to university, but he never got high enough scores."

"There you are," said Jenny.

"It's all very well for you to call it decent," said Pinto from the other room, "because no one sneers under their hands at you, or calls you names in whispers—"

"I'm sorry, Jonathan, but you are so self-centered, so—*spoiled* from growing up, that you think every action any other person makes is directed at you. When in fact most people don't even notice you're around—I've learned that these past seven odd years, very clearly."

"Are you trying to tell me that *you* weren't spoiled? The Honorable Aliasing Sephor Feng?"

"Of course I was spoiled," said Aliasing quietly in a voice more recognizable to Lily. "We all were, in Central. But at least I tried to look past myself to other people's problems."

"Well, I confess myself surprised," said Lily to Jenny.

"About Lia?" Jenny shook her head. "She always had her opinions. She spoke out without any self-consciousness. Her mother thought it was a sign she'd inherit the Senate seat, that she'd give up her radical leanings when she grew up, but I'm not so sure. Anyway, after Mendi Mun betrayed us, and Lia got uprooted from the only home she knew, she grew into herself."

"As if she no longer had a center on which to focus from?"

"I suppose. Some people can find that center within them-selves, and carry it with them, but I think most people are still rooted in that sense to planets: they need a ground, a physical place to call home."

"Do you?"

"I don't know. I've been wandering for so long I've lost track."

"—oh, Jonathan," said Lia from the galleys in a tone of utter disgust. "Why shouldn't Lily wonder why you became a pilot? You know perfectly well you're the only Ridani pilot there is. You also know very well that the only reason you did it is because it was the most expensive and infamous way to humiliate your father publicly, after he threw your poor mother off his estate when he decided to seal a bond with that fluff-head Arabinthia."

"How do you know? You'd already gone by then—you and Jenny and that Mun fellow."

"Yes, but I know you perfectly well. After that time you managed to get into the Senate chambers and embarrass your father because he wouldn't let you sleep with Mafecta's daughter—"

"It seems to me," said Lily quickly, "that this is beginning to get personal."

Jenny nodded, and they left.

Returning to the bridge, they found Yehoshua sitting at the auxiliary tac bank, trying to get the scanning system up. Lily discovered that Bach had long since brought on-line all the support systems and was now busy tinkering with the temperature readings of individual cabins, none of which were occupied or likely to be in the near future. She whistled him off and escorted him, while he protested in elegant four-voice harmony, back to the computer center, where she had him take her and Jenny and Yehoshua through the main outline of the ship's functions step-by-step. Pinto turned up eventually, looking none the worse for his heated discussion with Aliasing, and he paused to watch. Wei and Diamond wandered in from tac.

"We're late for the status check," said Lily eventually. "Bach, as from now, you run comp."

Patroness, Bach sang happily, *it would please me most exceedingly to serve you in such wise. This vessel beareth indeed a fine, if rather unintelligent, network. I confess to you that at my previous station when we began to discuss systems protocol, I was sadly disabused of my belief that this system went beyond the lower functions—*

She whistled an interrupt, and Bach ceased singing. "*After* we're settled. For now—"

Affirmative, patroness, replied Bach respectfully.

"Then everyone else to the bridge," said Lily, "except Wei and Diamond."

They filed out, took positions in silence at the bridge. After a brief hesitation, Lily sat down gingerly in the captain's chair. It did not bite back. She called up the monitor and opened the log.

"This is Lilyaka Ash Heredes, commandeering the *Forlorn Hope* for Jehane's Provisional Armed Forces. We will now attempt to bring all systems on-line. Comrade Blumoris." From the depths of the com, his voice answered her hail. He sounded nervous. "Give me the engines."

The pause that followed seemed, like a window, infinitely long, and yet the merest instant.

And then the *Forlorn Hope*'s engines came to life.

17   Bloodhunt

****

Yehoshua was adamant. "We hunt down the cruiser that destroyed *Franklin's Cairn,* and destroy it." Glancing at Lily's impassive face, he added, tactfully, "That's *my* recommendation."

"You just want revenge," said Jenny.

They had gathered in the tac room, whose layout and large conference table was designed for such meetings. Only Rainbow and Kyosti were not there. Bach had been left on scan on the bridge. Even Gregori sat next to Lia, hugging his knees to his chest as he stared solemnly at the proceedings. The *Forlorn Hope* rode at the very fringe of Landfall system, broken free of its frozen captor's grip, thrown through all of its paces except the window itself, and proven functional on all levels that the inexperienced crew could cobble together for testing.

"Yes," agreed Yehoshua vehemently. "I want revenge."

"If you'll consider," said Lily slowly, tracing the monitor's graph of Landfall system with a pointer of light, "we have to return to Landfall Station in any case, or here, to Landfall Far Horizon, to get vector stats so that we can get out of this system."

"But is it worth the risk of testing this ship in action when we hardly know her ourselves?" asked Jenny.

No one ventured to answer this question.

"If I may," said the Mule at last. Lily nodded. "Our nav

bank is woefully inadequate. We possess incomplete coordinates for Reft space, and a curiously complete set of coordinates for an area of this galaxy that I do not recognize. And linking the two regions, contradictory information, which leads me to believe that this vessel got lost trying to navigate from Reft space back to the place I can only deduce it must have come from in the first place."

"Sure," said Paisley, "and glory. Tirra-li."

Lily surveyed the group, seeing astonishment on every face except Gregori's.

"Then it's really true," said Finch. "There really is a lost way to get back to the home planets. They really do exist back there."

"That may be," said the Mule fluidly, "but this ship has little chance of making such a journey given the lacuna in its bank."

"It came close enough," Jenny remarked.

Yehoshua tapped the tabletop thoughtfully with his real hand. He looked at Lily. "Jehane will want those coordinates."

The words, simple enough, brought back to Lily a vivid memory of her first meeting with Jehane: he had been convinced—perhaps still was—that she herself was from across the way, was from the place she knew now as the League, and that she could tell him how to get there.

Then she remembered Master Heredes's warning: That a man like Jehane wouldn't like knowing that such power existed. And she wondered if perhaps Jehane wanted not to go there himself, but rather to prevent others from going, or from coming into the Reft.

The sudden flash of memory subsided as abruptly as it had come. She shook her head, doubting the veracity of her insight. Jehane could only benefit from opening up the route back to the League.

"Yes," she said to Yehoshua. "Jehane will indeed want to know." She looked back at the Mule. "But I think you have something more to say?"

The Mule hissed, affirmative. "It is necessary that we gain a complete nav bank, one as complete as any Reftwide merchanter can purchase. Or a better one, if we can get it. Even with Station-provided coordinates, and restricting ourselves to small hops, it will be risky running the highroad."

"All right," said Lily. "Then we're decided. We follow the

route of the cruiser, disable it, lift its nav banks, which by
definition must be the best Central can supply, and then
destroy it."

Yehoshua smiled, grimly satisfied.

"But shouldn't we try to take the cruiser intact?" asked
Blue plaintively. "We could take it back to Jehane. It's got an
incredibly sophisticated engineering setup. Nothing to this
boat's," he added hastily. "But still. . . ."

Lily shook her head. "We haven't got enough people to
cover *this* ship. It's settled. Four hours rest shift, and then
we head in for Landfall Station."

Landfall Station did not argue with the *Forlorn Hope* when
it appeared and easily blasted out of orbit the military cutter
that was all that was left of the government ships that had
destroyed Callioux's tiny assault fleet. Station officials did not
know that it had taken comrade Nguyen three tries to get
weapons locked on and firing accurately.

They also did not know that the scathingly tight beam of
fire that severed the Station second wheel's main stabilizer
vanes was the accidental product of Blue shifting the engine's
rate of fire at the same moment as Yehoshua, at steering,
canted the vessel's placement to allow Nguyen to pick off an
empty cargo drone, as a warning measure.

But as a result of the maneuver, Station officials evacuated
the second wheel and hastily broadcast the last vector coordinates of the cruiser.

Lily delayed their departure long enough to complete
Callioux's directive: carefully, because of the obvious inexpe-
rience of her crew, she directed fire at the second wheel until
it was irredeemably shattered. That the painfully slow pace of
the destruction might, to the terrified thousands on Landfall
Station, seem like deliberate sadism did not occur to her until
Stationmaster came personally onto comm and begged her to
either finish them all off or cease the game. She regarded the
ruins of the military wheel with distaste and ordered the
Forlorn Hope on its way.

The Mule rechecked the vector coordinates at the autobeacon
beyond Landfall Far Horizon and, finding them honest,
began the countdown to window. A sta-ish whistle flowed
from under its breath as it worked, calling out coordinates
that either Pinto or Yehoshua seconded. Velocity, angle, shift:

they got clearance from the beacon, and a concentrated silence froze the breathing of the bridge crew as they came up to "Break."

They went through.

In the void, the hunter awakens. First, the slight movement of the face, breathing in the flavor of the air. The eyes open. The head lifts, the body rises, and a single hand brushes the skin.

And came out.

A hand, slender, long-fingered, closed on her wrist.

She reacted blindly: pushed up, twisting loose, and punched. Pulled it, barely, so that he could deflect it with a quick snap of his arm.

"Kyosti!"

Whatever congratulations the crew on the bridge meant to give themselves on negotiating their first window successfully died as every head, every chair, turned to face this new and utterly unexpected occupant of the bridge.

Ship's com lit up on the arm of the captain's chair. "Comrade Heredes. This be Rainbow, in ya Medical. Min Hawk hae vanished, comrade. But he were here, unconscious as he ever were, when we hit ya window, and now—"

"It's all right, Rainbow." Lily laid a trembling hand on the com. Her voice sounded far more calm than she felt. "We know where he is. Stay at your post. Heredes out."

"Damn my eyes," breathed Jenny. "Where by all the Seven Hells of Gravewood did you come from?"

Hawk surveyed his audience with a slight, disdainful smile. "'For it is no easy undertaking, I say,'" he said softly, "'to describe the bottom of the Universe.' Although that seems a bit melodramatic under the circumstances."

No one spoke, giving perhaps the impression that it did not seem so melodramatic to them. The audio signal from the system autobeacon looped over and over on comm. No one paid it any attention, not even Finch, whose hands, which had been gripping convulsively the arms of his chair, rose now slowly to his throat. He made a noise that was more shriek than gasp.

Jenny stood up. Lily took two steps to stand between Kyosti and the com station.

With shaking hands, Finch attempted to untangle from around his neck a long, thin strand of hard plastine cord. He could not control his trembling, gave up, the black cord still ringing his throat.

"I could have killed you," said Kyosti in a languid voice. "But I did not. There." He shifted his gaze to Lily. He looked relaxed, but the grip of his hand on the arm of the captain's chair betrayed him. "Are you satisfied?"

"Get out of here," she said.

He smiled, gave a mocking bow in Finch's direction, and left the bridge.

"What in—"

"How did—"

"Void bless, he must be—"

"Silence," Lily snapped. "Comrade Seria, get that—that junk off Caenna's neck. The rest of you—plot our course. We can't afford to lose any more time tracking down that cruiser. Is that understood?"

There was a brief pause. Then the Mule began to call in the beacon's calculations, and Yehoshua got Blue on com and asked for a new velocity.

Lily left the bridge. Kyosti was waiting for her in the corridor. She marched past him, on into the empty tac conference room. He followed meekly.

When the door shut behind them, closing them into the half-lit, still room, she turned and abruptly flung her arms around him and embraced him tightly.

"Lily, my love," he said softly as he cradled her against him and kissed her dark hair. "This is the first utterly spontaneous gesture of affection you have ever made toward me."

She pushed away from him as suddenly as she had hugged him, and paced the length of the room to stand at the far end, the unlit table between them. "I thought you might die," she said harshly.

He pulled out a chair and sat down, leaning his elbows on the table, his chin on steepled fingers, regarding her with a mocking expression. "What? Are you sorry I didn't?"

"You know damn well—" she broke off. Stood quietly a moment and just breathed, willing herself to relax. A tumult of joy and fury and sheer shocked fear made it difficult for her to think clearly. The dim shapes of chairs and table seemed

like unanswered questions: she could make out their substance, but none of their details.

Kyosti watched her, but did not speak.

"Don't you *dare* mock me!" she cried. "After your second
attack on Finch, I could have gotten you transferred, or
detained. And no one would have blamed me had I done it."

He lowered his hands, looking abruptly serious. "But you
didn't," he said softly.

Since there was no answer to the truth, she did not
attempt one. "You must know," she said at last, "that no one
on this ship is going to feel safe, not after that."

He dismissed the comment with an impatient gesture.
"Tell them to lock their doors."

"Would it make any difference?"

"No, not unless they can lock-code it on manual. But how
are they to know that if you or I don't tell them?"

"I refuse to lie about something this serious. Is it true?
Were you still unconscious when we broke into the window?"

He shrugged, untroubled. "I suppose I must have been."

"You were badly wounded."

He put a hand on his tunic, over the spot where he had
been shot. "Was I? I'm not now. Do you want to see?"

"No. I don't." She stood perfectly still. "How? Not only did
you somehow get off the stasis couch and somehow walk all
the way from Medical to the bridge without knowing the
layout of this ship—"

"Oh," he said easily, "it follows the standard layout for
League exploratory vessels. They're very efficiently designed."

"—*but*," she continued more forcefully, "you are evidently
completely healed of a potentially mortal wound."

He considered this thoughtfully. "No, I don't think it would
have been mortal. Bloody, yes, and quite a bit of damage to
the outer tissue, but I expect that loss of consciousness came
from blood loss rather than—"

"Kyosti!"

"Lily." He stood up. "I told you once that I no longer
experience windows the way others do. Temporality as you
understand it does not exist inside a window; thus I can heal,
or walk, or love—"

"Or kill."

"Or kill," he agreed pleasantly, "in a space of time that to
you is only an instant."

"Why?"

"I don't know why." He went to stand by the door. "And that is the truth. I will remind you again that I did *not* kill Finch, when I could have. Now if you will excuse me."

"Where are you going?" she asked sharply.

It was too dim to see his expression, but she thought he smiled. "There's a magnificent lab attached to Medical. I think it's time that I begin serious work on the Hierakis Formula. I don't intend to lose you, Lily, not before *I* die." He made a gesture toward her, thought better of it, and left, his words hanging almost like a threat behind him in the quiet room.

Lily sat down. The soft cushioning of the chair seemed to shift, to mold itself to her contours, altering each time she moved. She contemplated the darkened room for a while, torn between a fierce joy that Kyosti was well enough to be maddening, and the growing fear that she was far out of her depth in trying to deal with him. And if it was his unpredictability that endeared him to her—or bound her to him, rebelling as she had against the predictable living and lines of Ransome House—

I must be sick in the head to find that quality attractive, she thought. She had brought a man on board this ship who could walk through windows, and whose very unpredictability could be a threat to the entire crew. And yet, he *had not* harmed Finch, this time. And he had never threatened anyone else.

"And I'm already making new excuses for him," she muttered to herself. Grimacing, she called up the charts in the tac table and began to consider their options.

In this system it was easy: there was one way in and one way out. Over the next two fleet days, much to her surprise, they passed through four more such systems—single roads that led in one direction. The cruiser had left Landfall on an obscure but direct route toward the fringes of Reft space. Because the *Forlorn Hope*'s charts for the Reft were incomplete, it was difficult to estimate where they were headed, but the beacons and tiny manned stations they hailed and left behind gave them one piece of inadvertently welcome information. They were gaining on the cruiser—and they had a name for it: *Heart of Lion*.

Jenny laughed, hearing it. Even Pinto found the irony

moving enough to smile, briefly. Blue spent most of his off-shift hours reconstructing the specs of the cruiser that he had managed, more by luck than by skill, to get a look at on Landfall's computer net. Lily studied them with Yehoshua and Nguyen, formulating a plan.

To the unspoken, but unsubtle, relief of the bridge crew, Hawk spent most of his time in the medical lab, and he carefully sealed it when he was gone, letting no one, not even Lily or Bach, enter. He put comrade Wei in some modified form of traction; in five days he declared the broken femur cleanly knit and let her out to walk, albeit gingerly. When others professed amazement at this swift recovery, Paisley going so far as to start a rumor among the other Ridani that he had supernatural powers of healing, Kyosti merely looked indignant, and let Lily know in scathing terms what he thought of the medical technology of the Reft if it had fallen so far as to have no better means of dealing with fractures than to let them heal at the agonizingly slow rate of unagonized osteogenesis.

And after six days following *Heart of Lion*'s trail, the Mule turned to Lily and informed her, with a slight, sardonic, and very human inflection of the brow, that the next window would bring them to Remote.

"Remote!" A rush of memory engulfed her: the escape from the ship of the alien Kapellans; her separation from Paisley; her brief conversation with the strange sta imprisoned next to her whom she now knew was not truly a sta at all.

"We're receiving contradictory information from the beacon here," said Finch. "Evidently there's some kind of strike on Remote downside. I'd guess that *Heart of Lion* was sent in to put it down."

"What's the contradictory information?"

Finch frowned. "Central seems to have slapped a cease trade order on Remote system. I would suppose they're trying to cut it off by stopping supply. But embedded in that loop is a second message asking for help, with two references to Jehane."

Lily tapped her fingers on the console, measuring her crew with a sweeping glance around the gold sheen of the bridge. "Looks like help is coming. Let's go in at the highest velocity we can run."

They came into Remote system screaming, alarms on,

comm silent, cutting close as only Pinto could so that they emerged far closer to Remote planet itself than any normal vessel would, and covered the remaining distance at accelerated in-system speeds.

They shifted course when they got their first fix on *Heart of Lion*, and plotted a close targeting run past her orbit. But after three unanswered identification hails, and two threatening ones, *Heart of Lion* pulled out of orbit and ran.

They chased her past Dairy system, braking hard for hours in-system to try to match velocities. *Heart of Lion* eventually banked and tried to shake them by veering at the last minute into an unexpected vector, but Pinto caught a sharper angle and they came through the window close enough behind her to corner her just sunside of the asteroid belt that ringed Unruli system.

Heart of Lion banked for fire, but Lily watched this show of force dispassionately as she set her plan in motion. It came down to three tangible aspects; even after factoring in an inexperienced and overtired crew, the *Forlorn Hope* had better shields, better speed, and more firepower.

"Take out their engines," she said as she wondered what, after more than two centuries, the so-distant League fielded as battle cruisers these days. With this ship, she might someday be in a position to find out. Except that the *Forlorn Hope* belonged to Jehane's revolution, not to her. She smiled, fingering the smooth ends of the console arms, and wondered at her own presumption in sitting in this chair.

"They have returned fire," said Jenny from scan. "I'm tracking it—damn, I lost it."

"I've got it," said Finch.

On the screen above, Lily could see a faint, magnified image of *Heart of Lion*; between them—only the void of space, and the drifting bulk of an asteroid. The sight of it, rough-hewn, tumbling like a mote in a vast, unseeing eye, reminded her to her surprise of the asteroid miner who had been her lover for one season. He had not been unlike Yehoshua, burly and cheerful and a little short of temper, a quality she had mistaken at the time for unpredictability— and to her disappointment he had proved as predictable as the other men she knew. What had his name been? Evan something? She could not now remember.

A distant flare, an explosion.

"Number two engine disabled," said Nguyen.

"We are receiving fire—now," said Finch, sounding nervous.

"Evasive," ordered Lily. She felt a shudder through the hull, but it was slight.

"Number four engine disabled. Number three engine—"

"We are receiving on comm," said Finch. "*Heart of Lion* wishes to surrender unconditionally."

"Tell them they have one fleet hour to evacuate their vessel. Unconditionally." Lily pushed herself up to stand. "Yehoshua."

He stood also, nodded at her, and left the bridge.

"I still think," began Jenny, "that at least one more person ought to go with him."

"I can't afford to risk more than one. I already had to argue down Blue when he wanted us to carry the boat intact to Jehane. And anyway, this was Yehoshua's idea. Something to do with an old Filistia House custom."

Jenny looked skeptical. "For what? So he can revenge himself personally for Alsayid's death? I've always thought revenge a ridiculously impractical notion. Or maybe I've just been too busy surviving all these years to have the leisure to indulge myself in it."

"*Heart of Lion* is complying with the evacuation order," said Finch. "They request that their shuttles be allowed to set a course for Unruli Station."

Lily walked across to the console Yehoshua had vacated and sat down in the chair. "Tell them affirmative. Give them the coordinates Bach plotted. That should give us plenty of time."

"I don't understand," said Finch darkly, "why we have to stop at Station. Or why you want to go downside."

"Unfinished business," she replied, short, concentrating on the information flowing across the three screens controlled by steering that she only imperfectly understood. "Are you *sure* you don't want to go downside with me to see your father?"

"No." Finch's voice was hard and unforgiving. "I don't want to see my father. Why should I?"

"But I'm—"

"Your father didn't betray you. Don't expect me to be generous. Not after Grandmam. And—Swann."

Figures tracked on across the screens. She waited a silent, pensive moment before turning to Nguyen. "Fix on those two asteroids in quince quadrant. I need a better feel for this. Let's do some target practice."

The first proved a sloppy job, but the second they pulverized neatly just as the signal came in from Yehoshua that he had gained *Heart of Lion* in the two-man short-hop bus whose controls he and Blue and Bach had figured out between them.

"*Heart of Lion* is fully evacuated," he said across the delay of space. His voice faded in and out, caught in a loop of static. "I have dismantled their nav bank and loaded it into the bus, together with three duplicates copied onto wire for backup. Detonators are set for point three two."

Lily rose from steering and returned to the captain's chair. "You are cleared to return, comrade. End transmission. Jenny, what about *Heart of Lion*'s shuttles?"

"They're in pattern and heading sunward at the specified course. They should arrive in, let me see—damn, I'm no good with this stuff."

"One fleet week, I believe, comrade Heredes," the Mule interposed in a soft hiss. "Do you need more specific figures?"

"No. Let's intercept Yehoshua and head in ourselves."

They picked up Yehoshua's bus just as *Heart of Lion* blossomed, a brief, brilliant star among untold others.

Unruli Station had adopted a practical course of stoic neutrality. Some of the malcontents from Remote had made their way here and been exiled to the Ridani sectors of Station, but none had been arrested. Faced with a large and clearly destructive vessel bearing uncounted numbers of Jehanish partisans, Station officials prudently reminded its commander of system policy: all downside shuttle trips must be cleared through their offices, or else activate automatic defense systems. They assured her that opinions on planet were not nearly as sympathetic to Jehane's cause as they were in the out-system mines and on Station.

"They're lying," said Finch harshly. "At least about that automatic defense system. Bootleggers went back and forth all the time."

"Unless they set up a system after you left," replied Lily. "Maybe Central forced them to. In any case, Finch, don't you think it behooves us to make the best possible impression on them? As Jehane's representatives? To at least attempt to sway the downsiders? The House miners?"

Yehoshua looked at her curiously. "Do I scent a conversion to messianic Jehanism in you, comrade?"

"Do you know, Yehoshua, that I find that after all this time, and despite the circumstances under which I left, I would still like to protect my parents' House from the worst of the fallout should Jehane triumph and they're left still supporting the old government. Perhaps this is my way of helping them—try at least to make them see their way to professing neutrality."

"What," asked Jenny, "if Station is lying and they're just sitting in wait to throw you in prison?"

"That's why you're coming with me, both of us fully armed, and we leave everyone on board except a shuttle pilot and one other soldier, so that if they do arrest us you can run for Jehane's fleet."

"But we need Pinto—"

"We have another *shuttle* pilot." Lily tapped the com on her console. "Medical? Rainbow? I want you to meet comrade Seria in bay one, in full rig, in one half hour. Tell comrade Hawk that we need his services as well."

The corridors of Unruli Station, rather inevitably, seemed less impressive to Lily than they had during her previous visit. An escort met them at their berth. She left Rainbow and Kyosti on the shuttle, and she and Jenny walked along the familiar corridors to Portmaster's office.

They waited almost one hour before the Assistant Portmaster could see them, and after a long and pointless discussion, were sent on to a nicer chamber to wait for the Portmaster herself. After another hour, and just before Lily guessed they were to be shown into Portmaster's office, Lily demanded they be given dinner.

Portmaster's aides obligingly ushered them off to a nearby plush bar, and Portmaster arrived at the same time their food did. Jenny looked tolerably amused, but said nothing.

Lily kept the talk politely neutral until they had finished their meal. By its end she felt that she and the Portmaster understood each other fairly well. The Portmaster suggested they move to a private room in the back of the bar, and it was as they were crossing to this refuge that Lily happened to glance at the vid screen superimposed above the flask rail.

A familiar face. It took her a moment to place it, and as

she paused, the voice-over and her recollection hit her at the same moment.

"—the victim was strangled and mutilated, and found less than one hour ago in corridor Q7, a little-used warehouse sector adjoining Q8, where the victim was said to habituate the string of bars well known to that sector. Security has no current leads, but all traffic in Station is now subject to search and screening. According to the latest report, the victim was last seen engaged in a fight in QuaNon's with an unidentified assailant. The two men were pulled apart by on-lookers, and both left the establishment separately. Security is now searching for a man answering to the description of—"

Jenny had turned back and tapped a quick, unobtrusive warning touch on Lily's elbow. "Portmaster's waiting."

The picture on the vid had changed, to an exterior of QuaNon's, but Lily knew who the victim was: the asteroid miner who had, some five years ago, been her lover for however brief and insignificant a time.

18 Dinner at Ransome House

****

She ignored Jenny. It took her a moment to trigger her wrist-com; she had not meant to use it while in Station. Another moment to sort out the voice replying from the general hubbub of the bar.

"Rainbow? Is that you?"

"Rainbow reporting, mim Heredes. I be at ya com."

"Where's Hawk?"

A pause. "I bain't ya certain, min." Even over the com-link, Lily could hear the apprehension in Rainbow's voice. "I told him we were meant to stay on ya boat, but he were certain sure he meant just tae stretch his legs, so he said, min. Nay, he said he meant tae take ya flavor of ya air. And ya sudden come he back again and tells me tae stay on com, and off he goes again. I knew it be ya wrong, but what could I do tae stop him?"

"Nothing, Rainbow," said Lily dully. "You've done fine. Stay at your post."

"I reckon he were ya tired o' shipboard, min. It sure be true that—" Rainbow broke off. "Wait. That be min Hawk at ya lock now, min. Be you wishing tae talk to him?"

"No." Through the sharpness of her voice, Lily became aware for the first time that Jenny, the Portmaster, and her aide were watching her speculatively. "No, Rainbow. That's what I wanted to know. We should be done fairly soon. Heredes out."

"What was that all about?" asked Jenny in a carefully loud voice. "I couldn't hear the crewman."

"Just checking the shuttle's status. They relayed that the *Forlorn Hope* is maintaining orbit." Lily spoke as she walked up beside Portmaster, knowing that the elderly woman would be listening.

"The *Forlorn Hope*? But surely that's the name of the old ghost ship of legend—"

Lily changed the details but not the essentials of the story, and with a ruthlessness she had not previously realized she possessed, she altered the course and tone of the conversation so that it took fifteen minutes and not one hour. She and Jenny left with full clearance from a bemused Portmaster for shuttle access downside.

"Damn my eyes," said Jenny as she and Lily outdistanced the cautious escort. "You made minced cable out of her, Lily-hae. What brought that on—"

"Jenny," interrupted Lily sharply. "Let's just get out of here."

She keyed into their berth, locked and sealed it behind them. In the cabin, she at first saw only Rainbow, seated forward.

"Where is—" But now she saw him, stretched out on a row of seats, asleep. She simply stared at him for a moment. He was deeply asleep, relaxed, breathing evenly. There was no evidence on his clothing, his hands, anywhere on his person.

"Did I believe there would be?" she said aloud.

"That there would be what?" asked Jenny, trying to make sense of Lily's humor and only growing more bewildered.

"How long?" Lily asked Rainbow.

The Ridani soldier shrugged. "He came in when I be talking to you, min. He be in ya sleep sure as soon as he come in." She looked perplexed.

"Wait a minute," began Jenny. "I thought you were both on board the entire time."

"What the Hells am I going to do?" cried Lily in horrified frustration.

Kyosti opened his eyes. He found Lily immediately, but he did not immediately sit up. When he did, into a sudden and lengthening silence, he did so slowly, as if he was not so much tired as aching and ill.

"I'm sorry, Lily," he mumbled. "I'm sorry." His tongue seemed to trip over the words. He got to his feet cautiously and stumbled forward to the pilot's seat, sank into it unsteadily, fumbled at the straps. Rainbow, looking shocked, had to help him fasten the straps; he shrank from her touch as she did so.

"Damn my eyes," breathed Jenny in an undertone that only Lily could hear. "Is he a secret ambergloss addict? Hawk? I just can't believe it."

"That's right." Lily flung herself at this fiction as at a safety line—the only one in sight in a void of empty space. Even were she inclined to prove his guilt, she knew that hanging proof on the Hawk who had once saved Master Heredes from death, whose name was evidently still a minor legend among those folk who ran the highroad in regions remote from the Reft, in League space and wherever else privateers of La Belle's and Yi's ilk roamed, would be virtually impossible, no matter how impulsively he had acted. And were it proved, and he imprisoned: she did not doubt that it would be the work of a moment to escape whatever prison the Reft might devise for him.

"That's right," she echoed weakly. "It happens sometimes." She sank down onto a seat, belted herself in automatically, and let Jenny take her astonishment and her questions elsewhere.

It was a rough ride back to the *Forlorn Hope*. Hawk managed to dock them, barely, and more by force of will than by skill. Lily let Jenny and Rainbow leave the shuttle before she unbelted and rose. And took one step toward the silent, slumped figure still strapped into the pilot's seat.

"Leave me alone," he said harshly.

"Did you?" she asked, sick to be asking. "I didn't really believe—I didn't want to believe—that you would *kill* someone. Tell me the truth, Kyosti."

"You know the truth," he replied in a low, bitter voice. He rested his head in the cradle of his hands, a gesture so typically human that for a moment she thought it strange, in him.

"If I turned you in?"

"No." The overhead lights flicked off abruptly, leaving his head haloed by the soft glow of the lights illuminating the shuttle's controls. His shadowed figure was bent in the age-old pose of true suffering. Instinct told her that it was not feigned.

"No." His voice came stronger on the second negative, although he did not lift his head. "Even if they could prove it, which they can't, I will never let anyone put me in a cell again. Never."

She found she had squeezed the cushioning of the seat back under her hand until it gave no further. The fabric seemed rougher than she recalled. She had gambled, and she had gambled wrong. Certainly, Finch was safe. But someone else had paid the price for her indulgence, and for Kyosti's—what else could she call it?—Kyosti's obsession. "Void bless," she murmured. "I don't know what to do."

"Leave me alone," he repeated, but this time it was less threat and more plea.

She turned and left him. Went to the bridge. Arranged for a message to be relayed to the Ransome House comm. Arranged for shuttle and crew and scheduled departure: herself, Pinto to pilot, Jenny and Yehoshua for escort. Went to her cabin and cleaned up. Showered twice. Cleaned her clothes again. On her return from the washing cubicle, she found Bach floating just about the bed she usually shared with Kyosti. He merely blinked lights at her, but strangely enough did not sing.

"Oh, yes," she said. "You ought to come with me as well. But rekey the lock before we go. Manual. To admit you and me only."

His affirmative was subdued and monochromatic. After a moment, he began to sing a pensive aria.

> *Ach, mein Sinn,*
> *Wo willt du endlich hin,*
> *Wo soll ich mich erquicken?*
> *Bleib' ich hier,*
> *Oder wünsch ich mir*
> *Berg und Hügel aug dem Rücken?*
> *Bei der Welt ist gar kein Rat,*
> *Und im Herzen*
> *Stehn die Schmerzen*
> *Meiner Missetat,*
> *Weil der Knecht den Herr verleugnet hat.*

Ah, my troubled mind,
where shall I find comfort?
Shall I stay here,
or hide beyond the hills and mountains?
In the world there is no counsel
and in my heart
stands the pain
of my shameful deed,
because the servant has broken faith with his Lord.

She knew that she would have to go eventually, but she waited passively, expecting that sooner or later Jenny would come and prod her into action. For once, she could not find the impetus within herself. It had never occurred to her before now that not only was she truly out of her depth—not with Kyosti perhaps, but with Hawk—but that she had now locked herself into an impossible situation.

Her thoughts wound pointlessly on in this manner until the door chimed an "enter" request. She accepted it automatically and was surprised to see Paisley.

"Min Heredes." Paisley examined her thoughtfully, astute in the way only a child grown to adolescence on harsh streets can be. "You be heart tired, min. I reckoned I ought to tell you that min Hawk be right sore ill. It were only 'cause I and Pinto helped him that he even got to ya Medical." She paused and waited for Lily's reaction.

Lily sighed and stood up. "Is Pinto ready to leave?"

Paisley said nothing for a moment, frowning, and then shrugged. "Sure, min Heredes." She turned and left the cabin.

Lily followed her, Bach coasting along behind in her wake. Someone had refueled and cleaned the shuttle. Lily boarded in silence, sat without speaking as the others came on board. Once they detached from the *Forlorn Hope*, she slept, waking only as the tearing winds of Unruli shook the shuttle as Pinto brought them in for landing on the Apron Port strip.

She had forgotten what it was like, and when she stepped outside, she realized that she had never truly appreciated it.

Unruli had a terrible beauty: the wind raged and tore at her clothing, almost knocking her over until she remembered to balance for it. One of the ways Master Heredes had taught her stance was to send her outside into the worst gales until she could stay upright and relaxed against them. A riot of colors filled the air, shading up and down the spectrum in a wild kaleidoscope, a pattern as busy as that covering the skins of Ridanis.

Jenny and Yehoshua came out after her, struggling. Both lost their footing more than once, although only Yehoshua actually fell to his knees, knocked sideways by a furious gust of wind.

Jenny tugged at her breathing plug and pulled on Lily's arm. "Isn't there an inside?" she shouted.

Pinto had parked the shuttle on the far edge of Apron Port's berthing field, and now Lily stood staring at the sheer cliffs that sheltered the port, at the glittering whir of the wind generators, powering the town, and at the faint, far flash of beacons marking in the wilderness of Unruli's turbulent surface that safety could be found here.

"Look," she breathed, unaware of the growing apprehension of her two companions. "Look!" She froze, slightly crouched for wind balance, and stared at an apparition scudding down the near cliff face, thrown in scattering sheets in front of the wind. "I've never seen one so close to built-up areas before. See. There. It's blowing this way."

"What—that—it looks like white filaments woven together?" asked Jenny.

"It's a ghost." Lily gazed, mesmerized, as the white being drifted closer, and closer yet. "There's an old legend that the souls of people lost in storm become absorbed by them." She gasped as a sudden sharp gust brought the ghost past her. Jenny and Yehoshua both took quick steps back.

A thin, sticky filament brushed across the back of Lily's hand, like a gesture, or a fleeting wisp of affection, and then wind caught it and it streamed upward, pulled into the maelstrom of cloud above.

"Hiro," Lily said, to no one.

"Cursed to the Seven Hells." Jenny stared up at the turbulence above. "What did you say?"

Lily shook herself. "Nothing. I just thought of my cousin Hiro. I don't know why. We never got along—always fought. I didn't really like him. In fact, it was some story he told that made me go that night, the night I left Ransome House for good—" She broke off. "Let's go. Where is Bach?"

On the ramp, behind, Bach was still valiantly trying to adjust his equilibrium to compensate for the force of the gale. She waited. They set off together.

Harbormaster's office was expecting them, but had cautiously not sent an escort. Lily did not know the young woman at the desk. She did not ask after Finch's father. After registering and paying the berth tax, one quick call ascertained that the Sar had already sent an ore train in on the tunnel to pick her up and transport her to Ransome House.

"I seem to be coming home in rather better style than I left," she murmured, more to herself than to her companions.

As in all ore trains, the passenger compartment was cramped and crude. They sat out the rough, noisy ride from Apron Port to Ransome House without more comment than the occasional question from Yehoshua concerning House protocol and the low singing of Bach: *Wie soll ich dich empfangen?* (*How shall I receive thee?*), which was mostly drowned out by the rattle and hum of the train.

At last they slowed and bumped to a halt in the loading breaches of the House mines. Lily eased open the compartment door and found herself face-to-face with her father. Her first, and most damning, impression was that he looked old. Old, worn, and yet, when he saw her, took in her actual physical presence, lit suddenly from within by a rejuvenating energy. He waited alone on the broad platform.

"Lilyaka." His voice had the same neutral cast she remembered, but his hand, lined and veined with age, trembled slightly as he reached out to greet her. "I was sure you must be dead. I am—" He hesitated, whether out of deference for her reserve or simply out of emotion. "I am very happy to know you are not."

"I'm sorry, for the way I left." She reached out and took his hand, feeling as if she were meeting a stranger in a familiar guise. His skin was cool and damp, but his clasp on her hand was firm. "I didn't think—" Suddenly she chuckled, and as if that released something in him, he let go of her hand and ventured his characteristic, calm smile—indicative not so much of humor as of approval.

"No, Lily," he agreed. "But then, you rarely did." He looked past her, and she quickly introduced Jenny and Yehoshua. The Sar, not much to her surprise, recognized Yehoshua's House affiliation, and greeted him rather more warmly than he did the imposing mercenary. But his real surprise came when Bach emerged from the compartment.

"Why I remember that piece of—equipment!" he began. "Not even Shiro could get it to work." He turned a suspicious eye on his youngest child. "Perhaps we all did underestimate you, Lilyaka," he finished, with a comprehensive glance at her composure and her uniform. Then, reading her discomfort, he turned to Yehoshua and discussed mining and ore with him as they walked the half a kilometer to Ransome House itself.

Various representatives from Unruli's House concerns had already arrived, but the Sar took his three guests to a small suite to let them clean up before he led them to the formal dining hall. This was not the room in which the Ransome House clan had their family meals; Lily had in fact seen this hall rarely, never being of sufficient age or importance to merit inclusion in any formal functions.

But now her own mother greeted her formally as she came into the room. Held her hand a moment long, looking at her with that prim disapproval that was the expression Lily best remembered of her, and said in a low voice, "You are looking well, Lily. I see that your stubborn wildness has found a suitable channel at last."

Lily was too astonished to do more than reply limply, "You're looking well yourself, Mother."

It was true enough. The intervening time had left no apparent mark on the Saress. She wore the same tightly coiled hairstyle, precise to each strand, and the smooth ebony of her skin concealed her age far better than the paler brownness of her husband's complexion.

At her father's urging, Lily passed on to meet the other guests: wealthy men and women, elected counselors and university instructors, other House functionaries. She was grateful when they sat down to dinner, and she could escape from enforced conversations that had no meaning into the safety of eating.

In such company, Jenny too remained quiet. When the talk turned to Jehane, and the rebellion, Lily found herself at a loss to convince these passive observers in the kind of reasoned, uncontroversial dinner talk that was their social forte. To her immense relief, Yehoshua's years in Filistia House, before he had joined Jehane, had accustomed him to such niceties and evasions. He quickly became the spokesman while Lily, sitting next to the Sar, could relax and watch him field questions and gently rebuke the prejudiced and ignorant.

"He's a good man, this Yehoshua," said her father softly under the cover of the conversation. "I know of Filistia House—mostly asteroid mining, of course, but still a large and well-run operation out in the Salah-eh-Din belt. Any kind of alliance, or a bond, with that House would certainly be valuable to us."

It took her a minute to catch his insinuation. Her first reaction was horror. "That's out of the question," she began hotly, thinking of Hawk, and then diverted her agitation into a quick change of subject. "During times like these, I mean. But I'd never heard of Filistia House until I met Yehoshua." Once voiced, the thought made her regard the Sar with sudden, and keen, interest. "You must collect a great deal of information on the mining and House operations across the Reft."

"To be successful, one must stay informed." He returned her regard evenly, giving no clue as to what he thought of her brief and impassioned outburst on the subject of bond alliances. "Yes, it's true that I collect a lot of information. Though you've never shown any interest in such things before, Lilyaka."

She did not answer immediately: she was thinking of Bach, whom she had left back in the suite, idle but for whatever activities such a robot might choose on his own initiative. Already she was planning how to get that information out of Ransome House's computer net and into Bach, to transport back on the *Forlorn Hope* to Jehane's people. Perhaps Jehane already had access to such files, but whatever twists put on the collation by the Sar's active and penetrating mind might reveal some valuable grain of a detail otherwise lost. Lily smiled, taking in her father's bemused expression. "No, I hadn't shown much interest before, had I?"

"Is this the influence of Jehane that I see?"

"No." She felt the old pain—muted now, true, but still hard beneath the surface. "Perhaps a little, but it was mostly Master Heredes's influence. But he's dead," she added quickly, wanting to forestall further questions.

"I'm sorry," he answered gravely. "Then he was indeed in danger that day."

"Yes. But it was Central that killed him."

He pondered the bitterness of her voice for a few moments in silence, while farther down the table Yehoshua kept the guests busy with his passionate, but not unreasonable, defense of Jehane. "Some months after you left, the Caennas were arrested—all but the father—by the government on charges of harboring seditious material and tampering with port logs and trade regulations and tax collection. I could discover that they were sent to Harsh, but nothing more."

"I know. Old Grandmam Caenna died there. And Swann, the daughter, was killed in a raid. Finch is with me now. His mother, not surprisingly, is on Jehane's staff on his flagship."

"Everyone has suffered, Lilyaka. Your cousin Hiro died the day you disappeared."

"Hiro?" The name caught in her throat, and she felt with vivid clarity the trailing strand of the ghost's tendril across her hand, back on the flat grounds of Apron Port.

"He blamed himself for your precipitate departure. He followed you, much against my wishes, in another surface truck. He was not as lucky as you."

She did not reply, stared at her plate for a long while as, half-heard, Yehoshua discussed the meaning of Jehane's name and assured the guests that Jehane was not a Ridani, in disguise or otherwise, nor yet a fool who did not understand the problems inherent in dealing with the Ridani population sprawled across every grimy corner and rundown corridor of Reft space.

A long ripple of repercussions spread out from her impulsive choice to follow Master Heredes, and yet she was herself just one link in a larger chain that led back across unimaginable distances to its hazy beginnings in a war fought through regions of space that her people—the citizens of the Reft—had long since been exiled from and ignorant of. And yet the *Forlorn Hope* itself might hold some key that could unlock the route that could lead them across the uncharted and confusing wastes that had stranded such a population here in the first place.

"Do you think Jehane will win?" asked the Sar, breaking into her musing.

She saw that this of all questions was the one that truly concerned him, planning for the future of his House. However much he might care for her—and she understood now that he did—his was a conserving soul, and his overriding goal was one of preservation, to which all other affections must come second.

"I think it likely," she said carefully, "given that he is what he is. If Central rallies enough to break him, still I think he'll have come so close to succeeding that things will change in any case. One way, or the other."

He nodded. Already she could see in the way his attention retreated from her that she had lost him to the calculations necessary to keep Ransome House protected from the upcoming storm.

Dinner adjourned soon after. Lily excused herself from the more casual after-dinner salon, where, surprisingly, Jenny found herself more comfortable than Yehoshua, having experienced at close hand the informal formalities of senatorial society on Arcadia.

A few words to Bach in the silence of the suite, and he was set busy with the House computer, digging up facts. Lily retraced her steps of that day two years since to the old warehouse, recalling the procedures with breathing plug and helmet, the codes on the doors, the cold stillness of the lock that gave suddenly onto the rough wilderness of Unruli.

She felt the same exhilaration, battling those winds as she made her way across the familiar route to the Academy. Old habits came back to her: listening for the snap of rock, the heightened wail of a changing gust of wind, the sudden shift of color in the roiling clouds that might presage new turbulence.

But coming over the rise to the narrow, sunken plateau that housed Master Heredes's Academy, she saw that it had changed utterly. It was nothing but bones, now. A few wind generators still clacked repetitiously, but most had long since shattered, or else flapped aimlessly in the gale. She went as far as the elevator shaft that led down.

Sand silted the door, half-concealing it. After extensive digging she got enough purchase on the door to shove it open. Sand poured down into darkness.

Cool, stale air wafted up from the deep shaft to commingle with the violent whip of wind around her. No command, no combination of keys, lifted the grounded elevator from its grave. Empty and abandoned, the Academy lay in ruins in the harsh landscape of Unruli.

Thoughtful, but not despondent, she returned to Ransome

House. Soon after, she gathered her companions and they left.

"So," said Jenny when they were back on the shuttle and lifting for the clear veil of space beyond Unruli's storms, "we've accomplished our revenge and succumbed to our nobler impulses of familial solidarity. Now what?"

"What do you think?" asked Lily absently. Hooked by her screen to Bach's memory, she paged through the wealth of information stolen from Ransome House's computer net. "We track down Jehane."

"Oh, Jehane," said Jenny, sounding a little disappointed. "I thought, with that boat falling so providently into our hands, that we might set up as a bootlegger. I think we could be pretty successful."

Lily looked up from her screen. "I don't think the next couple of years are going to be very fruitful for bootleggers. If—when—Jehane succeeds, he knows too well how useful they can be in clandestine operations against the government. And if Central wins"—she hesitated, casting a glance at Yehoshua—"they'll want their own revenge against the people who aided and abetted the rebellion."

"And in any case," said Yehoshua easily, but with a surprising touch of sarcasm, "we're all Jehanists, aren't we?"

"'Jehane will come,'" said Lily slowly. "'He will bring justice. But, comrades, it is up to us to prepare the ground on which he will stand.'"

But she thought of Robert Malcolm as she said it, not of Jehane.

19   Gregori Meets His Father

****

The *Forlorn Hope* slunk along the littlest used interstices of the Reft's vector net for two months before a chance encounter with a terrified merchanter gave them the *Boukephalos*'s last known location. They had taken out two military cutters with their guns and had scared off any number of less aggressive vessels with the faded, looping distress beacon that was the last vestige of the *Forlorn Hope*'s previous crew.

A long two months, but fruitful for Pinto and the Mule, Finch and Nguyen and Blue, and even Paisley when Blue cooperated with her; with Yehoshua acting as an *ad hoc* first, they began to grow comfortable with the ship's systems, so that their lack of qualified people on many of the posts was a problem they learned to work around, even as their ability to respond to the ship became more complex.

On returning from Unruli, Lily had told Hawk that he was no longer welcome in her cabin, and that she would prefer he stay confined to Medical. He did not press her for an explanation, just disappeared into Medical's lab. Only Rainbow saw him with any frequency, which suited the rest of the crew, although Lily suspected that both Paisley and Gregori spent time in the lab with him. Now and then he requested through formal channels the assistance of Bach. She always agreed, although she did not inquire into his doings. Aliasing brought him meals from the kitchen, and Jenny, mercifully, asked no questions.

Rumor led them past Salah-eh-Din by circuitous routes to Timbuktu. Good hard facts directed them back toward that sector of space that Jehane had come out of in the first place.

They found the *Boukephalos* at Tollgate. After a tense hour during which Lily finally managed to convince a massed fleet of twenty ships that she was with them, not against them, she received a sudden order to report on board the *Boukephalos* in person in two hours. She sent Pinto and Jenny and Finch to prepare the shuttle, left Bach in her cabin with the usual instructions to be cautious, and went to docking to discover Hawk already strapped into one of the last row of seats.

"What are you doing here?" she demanded, annoyed to find that her hands shook and her breathing quickened at the sight of him.

He smiled, mocking. "It occurs to me," he replied softly, "that it is time that I met Alexander Jehane. I am curious to see what kind of man he is."

"I would have thought you'd have plenty of opportunity to do that by watching the vids of his speeches."

He had cut his hair short. It gave him an almost normal look, as if he were just any other person, except that his hair was now entirely blue: all the blond ends had gone. His expression was still mocking, and he glanced, briefly, toward Jenny at the front. "Ah, but it is the one point on which comrade Seria and I agree: being both uninterested in messiahs, neither of us have bothered to follow the exploits of our glorious leader except through what we hear from others, or inadvertently over the comm."

"Then what's your interest now?" She found herself getting more annoyed because he seemed so distant from her. Had he no reaction at all? No explanations or even a plea for forgiveness? He had never even sought her out in the past two months—

The mocking look on his face changed abruptly, as if he could read her thoughts, to one of amused complicity. She blushed: there had been dreams, and stranger, more erotic ones still when she had slept through windows, until at last, this past week, she had scheduled her sleep to periods when they did not traverse the highroad itself.

"You wouldn't dare," she hissed in an undertone. "Not

during a window—" She stopped, infuriated by the look on his face. She could not tell if he was laughing at her for her fantasies, so revealing, or if he was pleased with himself for having found so underhanded a way to circumvent her decision to reject him.

Abruptly he frowned and turned his face away from her. "I will thank you," he said in a low voice, "not to insult me by believing that I would touch you without your consent."

Instead of replying, Lily spun and went forward to strap in beside Jenny, just behind pilot and comm.

"Let's go," she snapped.

Much to Lily's surprise, she found Kuan-yin waiting with ten white-clad soldiers to escort them at the *Boukephalos* docking bay. Lily had intended to have Jenny accompany her, but seeing the hard face of Kuan-yin, she felt it might be wise to leave Jenny with the shuttle and go alone with Hawk, who she doubted she could persuade to stay.

"Comrade Jehane wishes to see you alone," said Kuan-yin harshly, seeing Hawk emerge from the shuttle behind Lily.

Before Lily could reply, Kyosti stepped forward. "Don't you remember me?" he drawled.

She glared at him, but without a word turned and motioned them forward. As they filed along the white corridors of the *Boukephalos*, Lily wondered if comrade Kuan-yin had changed at all in the intervening time, or if she had perhaps forgiven Lily for the injury she had dealt Jehane. The belligerent set of Kuan-yin's shoulders seemed to indicate that she had not.

She left them in the same office that Lily had met Jehane in some nine months ago. Lily sat down in what might well have been the same plush chair, but Kyosti prowled, touching each surface, each texture, in the room, including Jehane's desk and chair. Lily watched him move, the familiar posture, the smooth grace with which he completed his exploratory circuit of the room. He returned to stand just behind and to one side of her chair.

A door sighed open, and Jehane entered.

He paused as the door slipped shut behind him and simply gazed at them. His brilliance had neither dimmed nor, Lily thought, changed in its essence, and yet she felt he was measuring her in a new way. She stood up.

As if her movement was a cue, Kyosti stirred beside her, and spoke.

"'And he stood in his own Light that surrounds him who is the eye of the Light that gloriously shines on me.'" His voice was so neutral that Lily could not tell whether he was being sardonic or sincere.

Jehane cocked his head to one side, a curiously mortal gesture. "Have we met before?" he asked.

"Not personally, I think," replied Hawk.

As much as Lily wanted to turn her head to see Kyosti's expression, she did not think it prudent.

"Ah," said Jehane, the exclamation encompassing an entire universe of understanding. "Yes. I remember you." He walked with deliberate steps to his desk and stood behind it, finger-tips resting lightly on the plastine grain of its surface as he examined the blue-haired man. Lily could not decide whether he approved of what he saw or not.

"Shall I wait outside?" asked Kyosti in a tone both languid and amused.

Jehane did not reply immediately. He sat down instead and tapped onto the keypad of his desk, until a shifting of the light that radiated up toward his face from the screen imbedded in the desk revealed that he had called up some information. His gaze flicked over it, but whatever it said either did not surprise him or was entirely unrelated to his scrutiny of Kyosti, because his expression did not alter in the slightest.

"Yes," he said softly, at last. "I think you might."

Hawk offered him a negligent bow and left by the other door.

Lily remained standing.

"I sense," said Jehane, "that you have rather a lot to report to me, comrade Heredes. Perhaps you would be more comfortable seated."

"Thank you, comrade." Lily sat down.

He acknowledged her thanks with a patrician nod and simply waited, then, for her to begin.

She started with Callioux's final instructions, with the death of *Franklin's Cairn*, with their time on Landfall, and moved from there to the discovery of the *Forlorn Hope*. As she spoke, his fingers moved lightly over the keypad, so that she wondered what notes he was taking. His gaze remained on her, as narrow and tight a channel as that between two ships in a crowded port who wish their conversation to go unheard by any other comm. The effect was so disconcerting that she faltered once or twice, but always she found her balance again and went on with her story. When she finished, his fingers continued tapping for a time and eventually ceased.

He considered her in silence. She felt uncomfortably like a transparent slate, all motives and desires clear to the eye, under his scrutiny. But she held still in her chair and returned his gaze.

Finally he touched a panel on his desk. The wall screen behind came to life: the slow circle of systems and star fields that marked out Reft space.

"You have learned," he said slowly, "a few methods besides brute force. You have information for me from Unruli."

"I'll transmit it to you as soon as I return to the *Forlorn Hope*."

On the wall screen, she saw that the shifting of stars traced her journey from Landfall to Tollgate.

"How long have you been with this man, Hawk?" Jehane asked abruptly.

This diverted her interest from the map behind him. "Since—on and off since Nevermore. You saw him there."

"Yes, I did," he replied, as if that answer ought to remind her of some significant detail she obviously had forgotten. He glanced at his wrist-com and flicked off the wall screen, pulling out from the desk a slim screen that he handed across to Lily. She had to stand and come forward to get it. "I would like you to confirm that this is the current manifest of the crew of the *Forlorn Hope*."

She scrolled through the file, names with faces: Hawk; Yehoshua Akio Filistia; Heneage Finch Caenna; UnaDia Vitales Wei; Jorge Zia Nguyen; Inocencio Blumoris; Jenny Seria; Gregori Seria; Aliasing Exul; Ridanis known as Rainbow, Cursive, Diamond, Pinto, Paisley; one putative sta called "the Mule."

"Yes." She laid the screen on the desk in front of him. "It's complete except for myself and my robot."

He rose. At the same time the door sighed open and the white-clad figure of Kuan-yin appeared in the doorway, her basilisk eye fixed on Lily. Behind her stood her usual escort of ten soldiers and behind them—but Lily could see no trace, no blue flag of hair that would indicate that Kyosti had been allowed to wait nearby.

"No," said Jehane gently, conveying by his expression and

tone that her mistake was merely the prelude to a greater honor. "The acquisition of the *Forlorn Hope* to our fleet is of incalculable benefit to our cause, comrade, as you know. Experienced crew will be added to those already familiar with the vessel, to bring it up to its full complement. But you will be of more value to our work elsewhere. That is why I am reassigning you to my personal staff."

He smiled magnificently and came around the desk up to her, extending his hand in a gesture so common that he made it laudatory. "Welcome to the *Boukephalos*, Comrade Officer Heredes."

She shook his hand because it would have been idiotic to do anything else. Kuan-yin's obvious and hostile presence made it impossible for her to protest, and as an officer in Jehane's army she was in any case subject to his orders. That was the choice she had made when she had joined his revolution.

"Now." He turned. "I am to address a large assembly, to be broadcast across the fleet. It is time for the final offensive to begin." He offered her a brief, apologetic smile. "I hope you will wait for the specifics of your assignment until I am finished."

"Of course," she said, not knowing what else to say.

Kuan-yin, waiting for just such a cue, swept him out of the room. In the eddy left by their exit, Lily discovered a single white-clad man waiting by the opposite door.

"I am comrade Vanov," he said. Lily disliked him immediately. He reminded her of a compact and cruder version of Kuan-yin. He grinned at her, recognizing her dislike. "I know you will be anxious to hear comrade Jehane," he continued, as if he was doing her a great favor. "There are several rooms above the docking bay in which his personal staff can listen in some privacy—"

"Excuse me," interrupted Lily. "But I came here with some people—"

He smiled again. He had particularly small eyes, which lent his face a sly, mean look. "I suppose I could arrange for them to meet you there," he conceded reluctantly. He waited, as if expecting her to offer him something in exchange.

"I would appreciate it," she replied.

"Remember one thing, Heredes," he went on, putting a little threat into his voice now, enjoying it. "Comrade Kuan-

yin has asked me to keep an eye on you, for her. I'll be doing
so."

"Does comrade Jehane know about this—arrangement?"
Lily asked, unable to picture Jehane confiding in this man.

Immediately Vanov looked annoyed. He walked to the
door. "Come on," he snapped. She followed him without a
word to a plastine-sheathed bubble of a room overlooking a
huge docking bay that had been pumped full of air and
populated by cameras and a huge contingent of Jehanist
troops, all shifting and seething in anticipation of the speech
of their leader. Other rooms and bubbles overlooked the bay.

Comrade Vanov left her there alone, but soon the door
sighed open again and much to her surprise Jenny and Kyosti
came in.

"Where is—?" Lily began, casting a quick, almost accusa-
tory glance at Hawk.

Jenny shrugged. "I thought it best to leave them on the
shuttle. They didn't mind. But Hells on Gravewood, Lily, is it
true that Jehane has transferred you?"

Lily set her elbows on the sloping wall of plastine and
stared morosely out at the mass of humanity below. "Yes. I
don't see that there's anything I can do about it."

Kyosti chuckled. He did not seem at all distressed that they
were about to be parted. "Our Heliogabalus knows which
fires to keep close by him, to stoke his own flame."

"Our *what*?" asked Jenny.

Lily turned back to look at Kyosti. "Why *did* you want to
see him? 'See what kind of man he is,' indeed. What does
that mean?"

"Look," said Kyosti. "Here he comes. They must be preparing this for broadcast illicit and otherwise across half the
Reft."

A file of men and women, clearly notables or officers of one
kind or another, marched out and lined up on the platform. A
pause, and then the unmistakable figure of Kuan-yin emerged.
She halted behind the podium.

From the bubble, they had an excellent vantage point.
Some trick of the com-system muted the noise of the assembled troops.

"There," said Kyosti, and he laughed under his breath.
"Oh, marvelous. What an entrance."

Somehow the sudden appearance of Alexander Jehane,

golden hair gleaming in the harsh lights of the bay, the commonplace lines of his brown tunic and trousers marking him both as humble and yet, in the sea of white, as rich in color, brought silence rather than tumult to the waiting crowd. They stilled as if each was touched by Jehane's hand in passing, and stood in a hush so deep as to be almost eerie.

Jehane walked slowly to the podium, his deliberation seeming somehow necessary so that he might have time to mark and approve each individual in the vast bay.

As he halted at the podium, paused to sweep his gaze once more round the assembled thousands—and not perhaps coincidentally to allow the assembled cameras an opportunity for a few more precious seconds on the careful beauty of his face—Jenny leaned forward and splayed one dark hand on the plastine, staring.

"Well damn my eyes," she breathed. "If it isn't Mendi Mun."

Jumbled together with her amazement that Alexander Jehane was the man who had abandoned Jenny and Lia on Arcadia, only one clear impression of Jehane's speech remained with Lily afterward: That she recognized immediately that the bold and stirring phrases he spoke were not *his* words, but Pero's. Some of them she had actually heard Robbie Malcolm compose, speaking in his sonorous and deeply sincere voice as Bach recorded them and then spilled a copy through the printer so that Robbie could both listen to and read the speech again and make what changes he thought best.

But Robbie had always possessed the gift of brilliant extemporization in great measure, and had rarely needed to change much. His belief in the plight of the people fueled his words, and they flowed from him as smoothly as lava, red and hot, from a split seam in the earth.

Pero's words: they brought the image of Robbie back to her so vividly that it was some time before she realized that Jenny was still standing next to her, staring down at Jehane with an expression blending anger and amused resignation.

"Come on," said Lily abruptly, pulling Jenny back from the plastine. "By the time he finishes, we'll be back on the shuttle and halfway to the *Forlorn Hope*."

Jenny tugged Lily to a stop, blinking and not a little confused. "What do you mean? You've been reassigned."

"Yes, and I need to pick up all my possessions, don't I? We'll pick up Gregori as well and *then* we'll see what Jehane has to say to that."

"Now wait." Jenny's lips curled down. For an instant she looked as stubborn as Paisley. "Whatever fantasies I might have had about confronting Mendi with his—" she hesitated.

"Betrayal?" suggested Lily.

"I don't think that under the circumstances, it would be a good idea—it's been almost eight years. Why bother it now?"

"How am I supposed to trust someone who would do that?"

Jenny glanced back, at Jehane speaking: passionately, forcefully; the entire crowd—indeed the entire audience made up of uncounted millions watching him in this system and in systems to come when the tape would be sent out on every ship leaving Tollgate—rapt in his spell.

"Maybe he's changed," Jenny said, meaning it. "Void knows we saw enough corruption on Central to be changed by it. Hawk." She extended a hand, a pleading gesture. "You agree with me?"

"Not at all." He looked amused. "I wouldn't dream of missing this reunion for the world."

Jenny grinned abruptly. "Well, I must say I've always wondered what excuse that squirrelly bastard would come up with. But, Jehane. . . ." She shook her head as she followed Lily out.

Lily easily bullied her way through the ship to the shuttle. By the time they reached the *Forlorn Hope* an urgent call had come in from the *Boukephalos* asking—not quite demanding—that Lily report immediately for duty on the flagship.

So she did, but with three companions and one 'bot in tow. In some confusion, a staff officer showed them into the empty office, and left.

A moment later Kuan-yin appeared, Vanov at her back. Her diamond-hard glare swept over the group and came to rest on Lily.

"You were to report for duty, comrade," she snapped. "What does this mean?" Her gesture, encompassing Hawk, Jenny, and a wide-eyed Gregori who had a strong hold on his mother's hand, was just short of being insulting.

"I have a last piece of business to finish with comrade

Jehane," said Lily without raising her voice. She was beginning to realize that if she remained calm, Kuan-yin's belligerence would have nothing to act on. "You must understand that I still have some responsibilities to the people who are remaining on the *Forlorn Hope.*"

"I understand that you are disobeying orders, comrade," Kuan-yin barked. "And I have the authority to—"

"Joan." The softness of his voice permeated the room as easily as the coarse energy of Kuan-yin's anger. He stepped into the office, alone, and she retreated with abrupt meekness to leave him in solitary splendor, still in his plain brown clothing, facing Lily and the others.

He acknowledged Lily with a nod of his head. Bach and Kyosti he merely remarked with a glance. His gaze rested longer on Jenny.

"Eugenie," he said, and though it was not a name Lily recognized, she knew immediately that it must be Jenny's real name. He said it a little sadly, as though its memory filled him with regret.

Last, he looked at the boy.

In such close quarters, the golden hair clearly linked them. Lily had never seen hair with such a metallic sheen in any other human. Beyond that link, Gregori was more his mother's child, or at least the intervening years had made him so. Dark-skinned, with a square-jawed, narrow face, he had none of Jehane's charisma. So solemn, solitary, and quiet a child had little scope in which such a trait might blossom, even if it had been encouraged under the hard circumstances of his day-to-day life.

Gregori stared with somber curiosity at his father, but did not venture to speak. He kept a tight grip on Jenny's hand. She, too, said nothing.

"I wish," Jehane began, and stopped. He looked back at Jenny, direct, sad, but unashamed. "I'm sorry I had to abandon you and Aliasing, in such straits. Her child?"

"She miscarried," said Jenny bluntly. "Too many windows, too fast, getting away from Arcadia."

His expression was impossible to read. "I had to make the choice, between you and the revolution, which I had only then realized I was called to lead. Sometimes duty exacts a harsh price."

"Yeah," said Jenny, looking uncomfortable. "Well, we managed." She looked over at Lily. "We'd better go now."

"Please." Jehane crouched, putting himself more on a level with Gregori, and extended one hand. "If I may."

Slowly, Gregori detached his fingers, twined in among his mother's, and took first one, than two, then three steps toward his father, so that he stood in the gap between the two, looking small and hesitant. He glanced over his shoulder at Jenny, seeking permission.

"Perhaps we might have a few moments alone," said Jehane in a gentle voice, but it was clearly an order, not a request.

Jenny nodded once, short, and turned quickly to leave the room. Lily and Hawk followed her.

Outside, Jenny halted and set one hand, palm resting on the wall, to hold herself up. "Damn him," she muttered. There were tears in her eyes. Lily put an arm around her. Kyosti, mercifully, kept his thoughts to himself.

The interview lasted about ten minutes. Jenny did not speak the entire time, not even when the door opened and Jehane personally showed Gregori out, and then went back inside.

Gregori regarded his mother with a child's solemnity. "Is he really my father?"

She nodded, still not trusting her voice.

"He's nice. He invited me to visit him once the war is over."

"Do you want to go?" Her voice was choked.

He shrugged, conveying his indifference with the gesture, but his eyes remained fixed on his mother, gauging her reaction. Her relief was obvious. He smiled and went to take her hand.

20 Gordion Knot

****

Lily said good-bye quickly to Jenny and Gregori, and Hawk, when they left for the *Forlorn Hope,* because to linger over farewells would have been too painful. In the three days before the fleet broke up to begin Jehane's new offensive, she dreamed of Kyosti often.

Worst, when they did at last cast off from Tollgate system in their designated groups—the *Forlorn Hope* receiving her assignment far from the *Boukephalos*'s projected field of action—the first window they departed through brought her such a vivid, disquieting image of Kyosti that she could almost believe he had actually been with her.

And within the hour, she was ill. Quite ill. So bad that they admitted her to Medical and even let Bach stay with her, day and night.

She lapsed into delirium—could not gauge time—forgot the name of *Boukephalos*'s physician and the others who attended her sporadically; now and then surfaced enough to hear the physician telling a presence she thought must be Jehane, because his being there brought her at least partway back to consciousness, that it was either psychological strain or else some disease she had not seen before.

Lily was moved to a white, enclosed space. Only Bach's singing remained constant.

Bach's singing, the occasional glowing memory of a visit from Jehane, and the windows.

In every window she went through she saw Kyosti. For that instant, with piercing clarity, she felt his pale hands and recalled the coarse curling blue of his hair. Then the ship would come out of the window and for a few hours the delirium would fade and she would recover enough to understand that she was sick.

This occurred with such regularity that the physician once told the visiting Jehane, not aware that Lily was aware enough to listen, that she could only speculate that some unknown property of the windows was curing comrade Heredes, and that if they had not been traveling so far and so fast along the highroad, they would have lost her.

Finally, the delirium faded and disappeared all together. Lily found herself lying on a stasis couch in a white isolation chamber in one corner of Medical. Bach floated at the foot of the couch, linked by one of his attachments to a terminal built into the wall. He seemed to be doing calculations. Lily lay quietly and did not bother him.

Almost immediately, the isolation unit door popped aside and the physician came in. She was outfitted entirely in quarantine gear, but Lily could still make out deep brown eyes in a broad, dark face beneath the clear mask. She stopped beside the couch and stared first at Lily and then at the readings on the couch's monitor.

Her lips pursed tight, she took a blood sample from Lily and left as abruptly as she had come. An assistant came by, also outfitted in quarantine gear, and gave Lily a clear liquid to drink, seeming pleased by Lily's hunger. By this time Bach had detached himself from the terminal and drifted up to wink lights happily about an arm's length from Lily's head.

Bach Lily whistled as soon as the assistant left. *How long have I been sick?*

Patroness, thou has been ill indeed. Even I have despaired of thy recovery. A full eighteen days, in the day periods designated by this fleet's systems, have passed since thou didst fall ill.

She lifted a hand. It looked no different. Swinging her legs over the side of the couch, she sat up carefully. Her head seemed light, but sound. She stood up. Reeled and grabbed at the couch until she could balance herself. Then she waited a few moments.

"Eighteen days," she muttered. "No wonder I feel weak."

The door popped open behind her. She felt it prudent not to attempt to turn, yet.

"Comrade Heredes." The physician's voice had that vigorous cheeriness that is so often annoying to convalescent patients. "You ought to be lying down."

Lily began to reply, but felt a hand on her arm before she could speak. It exerted the slightest pressure, to ease her to sit, and she began to resist as she glanced to that side.

And did sit.

Jehane smiled and released her arm. His hand, all of him, was encased in the thin sheath of quarantine gear, like the doctor. "Thank you, comrade. We have been concerned about you."

The very intensity of his concern as he stood next to her made her doubly dizzy. "What happened?" she asked, pulling the back of her hand across her forehead. Her fingers strayed in the loose ends of her hair; to her relief, she could feel that it was clean.

Jehane turned his expectant gaze to the physician. "Comrade Doctor Prachenduriyang? Have you any more clues?"

The doctor's shrug was eloquent of ambivalance. "Oh, yes," she said tartly, "I have clues, comrade, but they don't lead me anywhere." She examined the vital signs on the monitor again and shook her head. "Have you any idea, comrade Heredes?" she asked. "Were you exposed to any disease? Some kind of poisoning?"

"Not that I know of."

"There. I'm not sure I would even call it a disease in the medical sense, but perhaps rather a reaction. You are in quarantine because I have come to the only conclusion I can: that this is some sort of mutated plague that you picked up from the abandoned ship that you commandeered. We have sent messages to the—" She paused.

"The *Forlorn Hope*?" Lily asked abruptly, pathetically eager to hear news of the ship and its crew.

"Yes, the *Forlorn Hope*, to see if any other outbreaks have occurred similar to yours. Until we get such news, I fear we will have to leave you in quarantine, comrade. Your readings here"—she pointed to the monitor—"indicate that you have recovered, so I'm afraid that your convalescence may feel confined."

Lily made a slight shrug with her shoulders. "I don't suppose it can be helped. Can a—a plague of such kind linger on a ship so long?"

"Presumably," replied the doctor, but she frowned.

"I feel," said Jehane slowly, "that there is something still disturbing you, comrade. Some piece to the puzzle that does not yet fit."

For an instant, Doctor Prachenduriyang's gaze at Jehane betrayed the depth of feeling with which she regarded him. "Of course, comrade," she answered, the three words conveying how strongly she believed in his powers of perception. "As a matter of course we take blood samples of any person admitted with an unidentified illness, and do a detailed analysis. I won't go into detail, but in any case we can if necessary break down the sample to the genetic level in some areas. In the course of your illness, comrade Heredes, according to our analysis, a very small segment of your genetic material has altered."

Bach winked a single blue light, but otherwise remained motionless and silent. Jehane studied Lily with a gaze whose thoroughness, even wrapped beneath the quarantine sheath, seemed capable to Lily of piercing through to that altered segment that so disturbed the doctor.

"But what does that mean?" Lily asked.

The doctor's lips were pursed tight again. "I don't know. That you now harbor this plague in a form that is impervious to vaccines. That in an unspecified number of months or years, or in your children, you will manifest a further sequence of events, or illness—one can only speculate—that has come about because of this alteration. We can't be sure. It might be a harmless, if virulent, physical reaction. It might be—more serious. I can't give you reassurances, comrade, because I don't know."

"Hoy," said Lily, feeling very tired.

Jehane put a hand, slick in plastine, on her shoulder. It was a deeply comforting gesture. "Would you like me to remain with you a while, comrade?" he asked.

She looked up at him. He appeared utterly sincere, and concerned, and yet she was reminded of Jenny's face—indeed, her entire expression—as she waited outside Jehane's office while he spoke with his son Gregori.

"No," said Lily, and looked away. "I'll just rest a bit now."

He nodded, removed his hand, and left.

The doctor lingered. "I'm sorry. But I hate to lie to my patients. I wish I knew more."

"You looked after me well enough. I can see you have a problem, doctor—" She hesitated.

"Call me Duri. I never insist on the full syllabary, unless I'm being formal. I understand you are capable of drink and food."

"I'm starving," replied Lily with some force. "I feel weak, but perfectly fine otherwise."

"Yes." Duri sighed. "Your signs are completely normal. Your color, your blood—everything is fine. Except . . ."

"Except."

Duri waited a moment, but Lily did not continue. At last she reached out to pat Lily on the shoulder, a pale echo of Jehane's gesture, and retreated to the door. "I have other duties, but I'll send one of my assistants with a meal. You might make a list of anything you want. You have a terminal built in, of course."

"Thank you," said Lily. When the door sealed shut behind the doctor, she turned immediately to Bach, who still winked blue.

Bach? she whistled, interrogative.

Patroness. He prefaced his remarks with a little prelude, as if, like a child, he had been asked to memorize lines to recite. *Comrade Hawk instructed me—*

"Oh, he did, did he?" Lily muttered under her breath.

—to engage thy attention as soon as your vital signs had returned to normal.

"But how could he know—" She broke off. *Go on.*

Bach waited a moment before he continued, as if her interruption of his carefully crafted melodies distressed, or insulted, him. *Comrade Hawk instructed me to let it be known to thee that he has inoculated thee with the Hierakis Formula, and that once thou hast recovered from the initial reaction, that there will be no recurring symptoms.*

"The Hierakis Formula?"

The Hierakis Formula. Bach winked through a sudden, brilliant pattern of lights, as if showing off. *A term I had not*

the fortune to be conversant with previously, so I must
assume that advances in human life extensatory research have
progressed since I was first commissioned.

"Hoy." She lifted a hand again and stared at it: fingers,
skin, the same lines at her knuckles. It looked no different. "I
don't believe it."

Patroness. His song was slightly dissonant now. *Surely thou*
dost not suggest that I would practice to deceive thee?

"No, Bach. Of course not." She amended the words with a
reassuring whistle. "But—" She shook her head.

A brief chime signaled the entrance of the assistant with
her food.

"Are you all right?" he asked, checking the monitor as he
levered out the tray for her to eat on.

"I'm fine. That food smells delicious. Thank you."

The assistant smiled and left.

Patroness.

"Yes?" she asked between bites.

Comrade Hawk also instructed me to request that thou
dost not yet reveal this information to anyone else.

"That's all he said?"

Affirmative.

She speared a strip of protein and considered Bach's gleaming
surface thoughtfully while she chewed. "Leaving me stuck
here for the present, of course," she muttered as she hunted
for the next strip. "All right. I'll play his game a little longer."

Patroness?

I mean, Bach, that I trust that comrade Hawk has good
reason to say what he did.

Affirmative, patroness. Indeed, it is my belief that he has
devised a larger plan which he would have confided to thee
had he not been sundered from thee so abruptly.

"Let's hope so," murmured Lily, and got back to her meal.

Over the next seven days Duri visited her assiduously
every five hours. Nothing changed, except that Lily began to
recover her strength by moving the couch to one wall and
doing kata slowly to break herself in. She discovered that she
was weaker than she expected to be, and was grateful that
she was allowed this respite to convalesce.

Jehane did not visit again. Lily had no more dreams of
Kyosti, or at least none inside windows.

On ship's morning, eighth day, Duri sighed and shook her head over her screen. Lily watched her attentively.

"Under any other circumstances I would proclaim you well and let you return to duty," Duri said. The plastine quarantine sheath gave a sheen to her dark skin and silver-flecked black hair. "But we've gotten news from the *Forlorn Hope*. I'll let you review the records on your own, but unfortunately there's been an outbreak of this 'plague' on the ship. So far it's confined to the people who found the ship—the people you were with—but there's no knowing how long an incubation period there might be."

"Have they *all* been quarantined?"

"No. They're understaffed as it is—you'll see why—and in any case the rest of the crew had already been exposed. At least there have been no fatalities. That gives me hope." She checked her wrist-com and clicked her lips in dismay. "Void bless, I've got to go. All the reports are accessible through the medical folders, program three lest eight. I'm sure you have the clearance."

"Yes," said Lily, glancing at Bach. "I'm sure I'll have no trouble getting access to them."

As soon as Duri was gone, Lily plugged Bach in to the terminal and sat next to him, watching the screen. He quickly accessed the files detailing the most recently known movements of the fleet.

It took a while, scrolling, indexing, and trying to make sense of schedules and route maps, but eventually a pattern emerged: the *Forlorn Hope* had been sent into a string of obscure systems whose allegiance was still heavily to Central and had engaged in a far higher percentage of battles and running actions than any other single ship in Jehane's fleet. It had lost two companion vessels, and had taken, so far, eleven casualties out of a crew of forty-seven.

"Too high," said Lily, tense as Bach found the lists of reported dead. She let out her held breath when she found no familiar names among them.

The plague on the *Forlorn Hope* was also recorded, as well as a complaint from Captain Machiko about the difficulties he was experiencing integrating the old crew with the new people who had come on board with him. His final suggestion was to transfer, as a body, the old crew to some new assignment, or else break them up. His report did not mention the ship's doctor except in the most general terms, referring to his work in dealing with the plague, and what injuries the crew had sustained during fighting.

"Let's see the *Boukephalos*'s movements, Bach," she said.

Jehane's flagship, with seven escorting vessels, had swung a long arc out from Tollgate past Jenny's birthplace Unity and back in toward Cold Comfort, approaching the central region of Reft space from a different quadrant.

"There," said Lily, pointing at a highlighted three-dimensional map of the central Reft. "From here we can move in either on Gravewood or Blessings, although I can't imagine that Central would give up Blessings without a fight. Is there any news of Arcadia?"

She shut her eyes, resting them, as Bach searched. The robot had transposed all of his pieces so that he could use the quiet hum of the ventilation system as a pedal point as he sang.

"—I urge you to restraint, citizens, for the promised day will come. And come soon."

The voice, achingly familiar, caused her to start up before she recalled where she was. After glancing once, a little embarrassed, toward Medical—but no one was watching—she focused on the screen.

It was Pero.

An old tape, surely, but no less vivid for that. There were lines by his eyes that had not been there before, but the open, intent expression that marked him so clearly was unchanged.

"Our task now must be to give Central no leverage on which to break our backs. Walk quietly under their illegal laws, their illegal curfews, their illegal restrictions. Buy only what food you must from their dispensaries, but do not give them cause to arrest you for stealing. Do not use the illegal identification clips they have forced on us by boycotting the transportation they control, and the stores they police. Will this condemn us to a life of scarcity? Or hardship? Yes." His face shone with the glory of such a burden. "But this crisis will pass, because Jehane is coming."

The screen flickered and faded to static as the tape ended. Lily pressed her lips against her fingers and smiled, thinking of Robbie. How wonderful that he had not changed at all— that his beliefs, and his passion, remained constant.

Abruptly she thought of the Hierakis Formula. What would Robbie do if he knew of it? But the answer was self-evident—for Pero there could be only one action: the Formula belonged to the citizens of the Reft, all of them, impartially, and all should share it, without cost, without qualification. The only question he would have would be how to get it to them all.

It took her a moment to realize that there were still voices on the terminal—coming from the speakers, that is, although no image registered on the screen.

"—nevertheless, comrade, despite Pero's invigorating words, the fact remains that Arcadia continues well supplied while we are struggling to keep our fleet manned, fed, and repaired. The Mun House bankroll cannot keep us solvent alone. We no longer have the leeway to conduct our campaign on the fringes and slowly cut Arcadia off."

"Hoy," breathed Lily. "What have you found, Bach-o?"

Thou sayest, patroness, that thou desirest news of Arcadia. After indexing the computer's memory, I also accessed the ship's internal com-circuits and discovered this conversation underway in the tac room adjoining the bridge. Dost thou wish me to access a different channel, or return to the internal files?

"No, no," Lily murmured. "Let's listen." She lifted one hand, slightly, and Bach subsided into silence. A single red light gazed, a steady, brilliant eye, out from the surface of his attached keypad.

"—and your suggestion that we bring the fleet together and risk one total assault on Arcadia is absurd. Perhaps even treasonous." *This* voice Lily recognized: the hard, brittle tones of Kuan-yin. "We'll never get in without sustaining impossible losses."

"How many windows open onto Arcadia?" argued the first voice, defensive now. "Sixteen? Eighteen? How can Central garrison every point of possible entry?"

"Now, now, comrade Fon." A third voice. "We can't possibly send the fleet in piecemeal like that." After a moment, to her great surprise, Lily realized that the voice belonged to Finch's mother.

Kuan-yin said something undecipherable, but clearly uncomplimentary.

"And yet, comrade Kuan-yin," continued Finch's mother,

"comrade Fon's concern about our fleet being overextended is in my opinion quite legitimate."

There was a pause, during which Lily imagined that Kuan-yin wanted to give her opinion of comrade Caenna's opinion, but was constrained by another presence.

"Then we are caught." Even over the terminal, Jehane's voice had a compelling magnetism. "Between the necessity to strike now, and the still overwhelming advantage of force possessed by Central's military. Comrade Fon, brief me again on the situation at Blessings."

"Why Blessings again?" asked Finch's mother.

"Blessings remains, comrade Caenna, the single largest agricultural resource in Reft space. A jewel worth risking much for. Comrade?"

"Yes. Yes." Comrade Fon's heavy voice sounded the slightest touch nervous. "According to our most recent reports, Blessings is still wavering. A large Centralist party still controls their legislature. And there is a small but active core of rebels loyal to us. But"—he coughed—"evidently a new 'Independence' movement is gaining strength—they wish to secede entirely from Central, and from our revolution, and declare Blessings's complete independence. They're the strongest faction right now."

"And that, I submit," said Jehane in a softly dangerous voice, "is the real threat to our cause. We need—we *must* have—unity in Reft space."

There was a silence, made longer by the sound of people shifting uncomfortably in their chairs. Lily understood clearly for the first time that Jehane did not like or approve of Hawk: Hawk would always be, as Yi had said so many months ago, a wild card.

"Blessings," said Jehane, "is the key. Give me Blessings, and I can take Arcadia. I must consider this." A pause. "We'll meet here again in eight hours."

The shuffling and movements and low chatter of people leaving scratched out over the speaker. The chime on the isolation unit door sang out, and Lily quickly punched to an innocuous text of Pero's most recently received speech as one of the assistants brought in her breakfast.

"Feeling better?" he asked reflexively.

"Yes. I expect I'll be back on duty any time now."

Eight and one half hours later Lily was startled out of her

continued perusal of the movements of the fleet by the sudden appearance of Kuan-yin outside the isolation unit. The doctor was arguing with her, but the dispute was settled in short order as Kuan-yin shoved past Duri and opened the isolation door. Without a suit.

The inner lock popped aside, and Kuan-yin stormed in, looking thunderous and on the edge of some great outburst.

"Get up, Heredes," she ordered. "You and the 'bot are coming with me."

Lily stood up, not liking to meet someone such as Kuan-yin sitting down. "What's going on?"

"I don't need your insolence. Jehane is gone. You're going out tracking. I've called in every available ship. Now let's go."

Lily stood her ground. "What do you mean, Jehane's gone? Just hours ago he was—"

"Don't you think I know that?" If Kuan-yin could have sent out sparks, she would surely have kindled several fires by now. "But he was pushed into a corner by those damned idiots who don't understand him."

"That's why he's gone?"

"You don't understand him either." Clearly, to Kuan-yin's mind, this was an insult. "He'll have gone straight to the heart of the matter. He'll have gone to Blessings."

21   The Battle for Blessings

****

They came skating into Blessings ten days later to find armed revolt broken out across the beautiful blue-and-green jewel of the planet. The comm-signals emanating out from downside were rife with panic and exhortation.

No fleet met them, no one except a strengthened garrison, which was wiped out by the entrance, one after the next, of the large bulk of Jehane's fleet. No fleet, because Central had either not yet heard, or was not yet able to respond.

"They will," said Kuan-yin ominously from her station on the bridge of the *Boukephalos*. "They will."

Lily stood beside her, staring at the huge screen that showed the image of a planet as brilliant as Arcadia, suspended in the dark void of space. "But if Blessings is so valuable, why hasn't Central guarded it better? They doubled their space garrison, but—" She shrugged.

Kuan-yin glanced at her, at the two other soldiers who had been called up to the bridge with her: the three leaders of the tracking expeditions.

"Look," she said harshly, pointing to her console, on which a map of the largest continent shone across the screen. "They didn't choose to strengthen their space defense by much. But according to comm-traffic, five centuries of Immortals were posted in the capital and outlying cities three months ago. That's one piece of information Central kept hidden from us."

"Jehane is down there, somewhere." Lily looked up from the map to the globe of Blessings, turning slowly on the screen. "Alone."

"Not alone," said Kuan-yin scornfully. "Jehane is never alone once he makes himself known."

At comm, a woman turned in her chair to address Kuan-yin. "Comrade, we have confirmation that the former Blessings 'Independence' movement has now allied itself totally with Jehane."

"But there is still no sign of comrade Jehane himself?"

"No, comrade. He has not spoken over any medium that we can track, nor has any broadcaster referred to him as being with him."

"I can't imagine," said Lily, beginning to feel impatient with this fencing, "that he wants government troops, and certainly not the Immortals, to know where he is. Does he know we're here yet? He could very well be trapped in one of the cities and unable to move."

"Precisely." The intensity of Kuan-yin's regard made Lily uncomfortable. "That is why you three are to choose teams, find him, and get him back here."

"What if he doesn't want to be found?"

Kuan-yin dismissed this possibility with a cutting gesture. "He has obviously accomplished his purpose by galvanizing the entire Blessings resistance into open revolt."

"By galvanizing it under *his* name," Lily murmured under her breath; then, louder: "I can't believe that Jehane—comrade Jehane—would act so impulsively and put himself in such danger."

"Then you don't understand him. The unexpected feint wins the engagement. In any case, comrade"—Kuan-yin's stance seemed threatening as she stared at Lily, one hand resting on the immaculate tuck of her tunic's collar—"he knows that *I* can be counted on to safeguard his interests. And his person."

Lily inclined her head, but refrained from comment.

"So?" Kuan-yin swept her scathing gaze over the three soldiers. "You have your orders."

"Comrade." The woman at comm turned again. "We have another ship coming in." A pause while she listened. "The *Forlorn Hope*, attended by *Zima Station* and *Savedra*, has just entered Blessings system and awaits orders."

"There," said Lily quickly. "Let me get my team from the *Forlorn Hope*."

Kuan-yin regarded her speculatively. "Weren't you just transferred from that boat?"

"Yes, and I've worked before with a team now assigned there. Twice. Successfully. Surely that's in Jehane's interest."

Kuan-yin hesitated. Lily realized in that hesitation that Kuan-yin was reluctant to countermand Jehane's previous orders, but could think of no good reason, under the circumstances, not to.

"Very well," she said. "Go on. Your team will put down near the capital. You others—"

Lily waited to hear the other team assignments and then left, Bach trailing after her, at a brisk walk from the shuttle bay.

"Wonderful," said Jenny. "It sounds like we're headed for another disaster like Landfall."

"No." Lily rested her palms on the table in the tac room; Captain Machiko had let the team meet there while one of the shuttles in *Forlorn Hope*'s bay was readied. "That plan was flawed from the start. Callioux was overconfident."

"Are you sure you're not?" Jenny asked. She stretched her long legs out and rested one boot, the other crossed atop it, on the table. Her hands she slipped behind her head, elbows out.

Lily grinned, acknowledging this. "Jehane's no fool. And he's not impetuous, either. If anything, he calculates every move down to the finest detail."

"Then what?" asked Yehoshua. He traced the curve of his dark hair around an ear with one finger of his artificial hand. "You're not suggesting that he wants *you* to get in trouble downside?"

"Jehane doesn't trust you, Lily, my love," said Kyosti, drawling over the endearment. Since her sudden and hurried arrival on the *Forlorn Hope*, punctuated by enthusiastic, if brief, greetings from everyone else, he had maintained a studious distance from her. "You've been a bit too successful for him, I think."

"What do you mean?" asked Yehoshua. "I'm not sure I like the tone of your voice, comrade."

"Come now, comrade." Kyosti waved a negligent hand.

"Why else do you think he transferred our Lily from a post where she was clearly doing a great deal of good to one where she would inevitably be lost among an already established chain of command?"

Yehoshua frowned, but said nothing.

"Why else," Kyosti continued, "send us into a series of engagements that was surely designed to rid him of a few people he had cause to believe might prove more loyal to her than to him?"

"Like yourself," said Yehoshua, but he rubbed one lip absently as he said it, as if his thoughts were elsewhere.

Kyosti shrugged eloquently.

"All right," interposed Lily, not wishing to continue such speculation. She paused a moment to take stock of her team: Jenny, Yehoshua, and Kyosti; Pinto, Paisley, and the other three Ridani; the Mule, Finch, Nguyen, and Wei. Blue was still too valuable in engineering to risk, and Aliasing had agreed to stay with Gregori on board the *Forlorn Hope*. Lily suspected that Jenny did not, in any case, want Lia along on such a mission.

"Let's make some cautious assumptions," continued Lily. "For instance, let's assume that Jehane accomplished exactly what he meant to do in getting Blessings to combine with him against Central's forces on the planet. Let's assume that he has something further planned that we don't know about. Let's assume that he in fact did *not* know that Central had garrisoned Blessings with five centuries of Immortals."

Jenny whistled. "*Five* centuries?"

"Finally, let's assume that Kuan-yin really does want him back on the *Boukephalos*. Any arguments?"

"That's pretty general," objected Yehoshua.

"Well, yes, but we haven't got much time. Now I'm going to make one final assumption: he's stuck in the capital, which is being patrolled by one or two centuries of Immortals who either don't know he's there or only suspect it. He's got to get to the countryside to get a shuttle off planet. He has to risk the Immortals to get out."

"Risk the Immortals?" Yehoshua shook his head. "You don't *risk* Immortals. How can even Jehane hope to fight past them?"

Lily looked at Jenny.

Jenny smiled. "Doubtless comrade Jehane is full of surprises," she said sardonically. "Where's your faith, Yehoshua?"

"Levity is all very well. I'm talking about the *Immortals* here."

"Yes, I know you are," replied Jenny. "I was one."

His eyes widened. So did most everyone else's around the table. "But—I thought Immortals couldn't retire."

"They can't." Jenny said this in a tone that sounded tired of the subject. "So there you are. Listen, Lily." She turned her attention back to the other woman. "I've a good idea how they'll post patrols. Especially if they're looking for one person."

"Good." Lily nodded. "I was hoping you might. Bach has a map of the capital and a précis of all current and recent comm-traffic out of that area. Finch, you'll assist Bach in trying to use that information to trace the most likely locations Jehane might be holed up in."

Finch nodded.

"We'll need two shuttles. One will aot purely as a decoy. Pinto, can you find me a volunteer who is willing to risk their life—"

"I'll do it," said Kyosti casually.

"No, you won't. You're staying on board this ship, comrade. The work you're doing with the Formula—as a *physician*—is far more valuable to the citizens of the Reft right now. Don't you agree?"

At first he was too stunned by her fiery stare to retort, but after a moment he laughed.

"Lily, my heart," he said softly. "Our old friend Robbie must have inoculated you with his idealism." He smiled, gently mocking. "I bow to your superior charity."

"Get your gear," ordered Lily. "We leave in one half hour."

The room cleared quickly, except Kyosti, who did not even bother to rise, and Paisley, who stood, but supported herself on her chair back as if she could not stand without aid.

"Paisley?" Lily went across to her and rested a hand on the Ridani girl's shoulder.

"I were sore ill," whispered Paisley, looking fragile for a moment. "You know I bain't scared, min. You know it. But I fear I be ya right sore hindrance to you if I go."

Lily glanced at Kyosti. He studied Paisley, measuring the

girl, but said nothing. "Very well," said Lily. "Then you're better off staying here."

Paisley dipped a brief curtsey and left, head down.

"I wonder what that was all about," said Kyosti. He stood up. "Lily."

She went to the door, put her hand on the pad, but did not open it. "Why did you give me the Formula?"

"I can't imagine," he said, sounding disgusted, "why you feel the need to ask that question. The answer *must* be obvious."

"Only if you assume that I can possibly forgive you for murdering that man. He never threatened you."

His face shuttered: lips drawing straight and tight, eyes half-closed, breath caught in; lifting his chin, for an instant he looked impossibly alien to her—framed all by the startling blue of his hair.

He did not reply.

"Wish me luck," she murmured as she pressed the pad. The door slipped open behind her.

Still, he did not reply.

Only after the door slid shut behind her, leaving him alone in the dimming room, did he sigh, echoing the door's soft hushing close: "Luck."

Lily was in no mood to discover an argument at the shuttle, but she did so anyway.

"—and who is going to take care of Gregori, pray tell?" Jenny stood on the ramp, effectively blocking Aliasing from boarding the shuttle.

Lily halted in the boarding walk, staring at Lia. The two women remained unaware of her. The rest of the corridor was empty.

Somehow, somewhere, Lia had cobbled together a white Jehanish soldier's uniform that really fit her: she had always been too petite to meet any standard soldier's issue. Most of the splendid dark fall of her hair still hung loose, but in the front it had been cunningly braided to keep away from her face.

"Paisley," Lia replied, hands clenched tight as she stared stubbornly up at Jenny. "It's true enough she was sick later than the rest of us, so she said she'd plead sick and stay here with him."

"You idiot!" hissed Jenny. Lily had never seen her so angry. "Whatever training you've had in the past year hasn't begun to prepare you for this kind of action. You can't go."

Lia sucked in an obvious, big breath of air, like resolve. "It's not your choice. I'm taking Paisley's place."

"You can't go," repeated Jenny.

Lily was shocked by the violence of Jenny's tone, especially directed at Lia, whose frailness under this attack, enhanced by the cleverly ornamented lines of the white uniform—like, yet unlike, Jehane's people's uniforms—was beginning to dissolve away to reveal something unyielding underneath.

"You don't want me to meet Jehane," said Lia, shifting her ground so abruptly that the expression on Jenny's face immediately betrayed the accuracy of the hit.

"You're afraid," Lia continued, sounding anything but fragile now, "that I'll leave you for him when I find out who he really is. But I knew all along, Jenny. After all those years as a Senator's only daughter, do you think I don't watch every face that pretends to power? Do you think I don't measure them, and wonder, and predict? I grew up with politics. I can't ignore it like you can."

She paused, but Jenny merely stood, hands motionless at her side, stiff with an emotion Lily could not name.

"I don't know how long you think you've been protecting me. I thought you knew me better than that, that just because I'm so small you didn't treat me like everyone else does: something to be protected. Void bless, how my mother and aunt laughed when I said I wanted to join the Immortals. Size requirements, you know." Her voice held a bitterness that Lily would never have guessed existed there, under the cloud of soft hair and the sweet piquancy of her face.

"I've known who Jehane was ever since his revolt really began to threaten Central's government. Yes, he's changed the timbre and pitch of his voice a lot, and he looks a little different—it's mostly his carriage, I think—but still. *Still*, Jenny."

She stopped. Paused, and turned her head to see Lily standing some twenty paces behind her in the empty corridor. Turned back. "Let me by," she said softly.

Jenny moved to one side and let her board the shuttle. Just stood there, as Lily came up to her.

"Jenny."

A single tear snaked down one ebony cheek. "She loves him," Jenny whispered. "Void and Hells. You saw him. How can I compete against *him*?"

"By not competing," replied Lily softly. "Anyway, do you think Jehane wants the burden of her love?"

"Do I think I care if he wants it or not?" Jenny demanded in a low, harsh voice. "I care that I've lost her. I care that she never once told me what it was she did to break the fabled chastity of the man who was Mendi once. Don't you think she can do it again? That she doesn't have some power over him? That even if he doesn't want her love, he'll be able to resist it?"

Lily could think of nothing to say. She did not dare attempt to touch Jenny, standing there taut and tense as a strung cable.

"She even made a uniform," said Jenny at last, almost inaudible.

"The uniform?"

"Yes. Oh." Jenny glanced at Lily, a spark of irony showing in her expression. "You probably didn't notice. The differences are subtle. That's not a Jehanist uniform—Jehanish whites, like ours. Look at the ornamentation, and the cut. That's an Immortals uniform."

A face in the shuttle door: Finch. "Oh," he said, relieved. "There you are. We're three minutes late."

Jenny whirled and went inside the shuttle.

"Oh, Hells," said Lily under her breath, and followed her.

"Bach and I are picking up some new comm," said Finch as Lily strapped into the seat directly behind him and Pinto. "There's troop movement in the capital—the Immortals are setting up some kind of ring around the very center of the city. *I* think, from what we can piece together, that they've isolated one of the 'Independence' movements' strongholds, or meeting places, in one of the downtown buildings."

Lily looked at Pinto. "Let's move. Whether or not it's Jehane, there's somebody down there worth saving—if only because they might know where Jehane is. Is the decoy ready?"

"Affirmative." Pinto flipped through his controls. "We have engines, detach sequence counting down."

Finch handed Lily a headset as the shuttle detached and,

after separation, canted with a flash of engine to begin the descent.

"How many centuries are we up against?" she asked. "Can you give me an estimate?"

"Two, Bach guesses. Do I transmit to the *Boukephalos*?"

"No. For now we maintain silence. If we locate Jehane, Kuan-yin will send in backup, probably on our tail, to pick him up. We've got to find him without alerting Central's people that we're looking."

Finch glared at Pinto, who sat intent at his controls, then leaned back in his chair. "We're not really going in twenty meters up, with that decoy riding in two hundred meters above us, are we? Even Pinto—"

"Finch. We've got to get in undetected. We don't have time to go overland. By this time, you ought to know that if anyone can do it, Pinto can."

Finch's lips twitched as if he felt he had to say something, but could not bring himself to. "I suppose," he said at last, grudgingly.

Lily chuckled. "I'll bet that hurt."

His lips tightened, and he turned stiffly back to his console. Lily listened in.

"—we have achieved complete command of the ten-block circumference. All civilians are now being evacuated through our points of entry. Acknowledge."

"Accepted. Lieutenant, give me an estimate of time remaining to clear the area before your troops can move in. Acknowledge."

"Accepted. Due to the necessity of careful search procedures and the opportunity to close the ring as each building is cleared, we estimate the operation will take over six hours. Acknowledge."

"Accepted. Commodore Byrd wishes a complete disposition sent by courier before—"

Lily plugged her screen into Bach and plotted out what she could deduce of the Immortals' positions around the central hub of Blessings's capital. Behind and to either side of her, Jenny and Yehoshua leaned forward as she showed them her map.

"They've trapped some people in here," she said. "We'll have to send ourselves in if we get no clue before that whether Jehane is among those trapped."

They discussed alternatives as the shuttles streaked downward through the atmosphere. From the main cabin behind, she could hear only a bit of desultory talk between the Ridanis.

"Two minutes to split," said Pinto. "Hold on to your seats."

Lily, glancing up, thought she caught him smiling. Then the shuttle banked hard and the green fields of Blessings screamed past a seeming hand's breath beneath them. She could just make out the decoy shuttle above, running slightly before them.

Jenny, Yehoshua, and Finch all shut their eyes. Lily forced herself to watch as the far suggestion of hills transmogrified into a distant city, approaching fast.

Antiship fire exploded out of distant emplacements still hidden from her eye.

Bach whistled, and she turned up her headset.

"—inform Commodore Byrd that we have *vende patria* confirmation that the traitor calling himself Jehane *is* among those still within the ring. Advise. Acknowledge."

"Accepted. Absolute imperative. Jehane must not escape. You know your orders. I want all civilians out of there and a full assault to—"

"All stations. All stations. This is post A-seven. We have a breakout assault in progress. Repeat—"

"Finch! Get me their exact position and feed it directly into Pinto's grid. Pinto. Can you get there—through the city?"

Pinto paused long enough to cast a quick, controlled glance across at the fire peppering the decoy above. The city grew, doubled, quadrupled in size as they raced toward it.

A sudden explosion from above, and a spray of light and fire.

"Braking," said Pinto tersely as he glanced at the grid that now showed the intricate lines of the capital's layout, and the winking light that pinpointed post A-7's position. "We're going in."

"I hope he got out before his boat blew," Lily had time to say before Pinto targeted them for the first high buildings. After that she had to concentrate on her grip on her chair.

"Damn my eyes," whispered Jenny as Pinto's light hand on the controls took them scant meters above, and sometimes scant meters between, the maze of Blessings's capital. "I wonder how many windows we're shattering."

It took eight harrowing minutes, each one pulled into an agony of stretched-out time, before they drew their first fire.

"I'm going street level." Pinto's voice sounded calm and strangely detached.

"Four minutes to rendezvous," gasped Finch, so taut with nerves that he could barely speak. "Reinforcements coming from B and C areas, not the adjacent postings. I get constant assault readings still from post A-seven. Aren't we supposed to wait for the backups?"

"We don't have time." Lily glanced to either side. "Jenny. Yehoshua. Get your squads. We'll hit the ground running."

It proved easier, despite the sharp, hard maneuvering of the shuttle, to get squads arrayed in the back cabin, because they did not have to watch walls whip past the canted wings, so close that it seemed impossible they did not crash. Once a heavy object shattered against the hull, rocking them, and throwing half the people to the floor, but with a brief flare of engine the shuttle went on.

Three minutes—four—they could hear the muffled ricochet of firing above the roar of the engines. Small shudders shivered through the hull.

Finch: "We—are—down."

Jenny's team went first, crouched, running down the ramp, followed by Yehoshua, and last, Lily, leading Aliasing, the Mule, and Rainbow.

They used the bulk of the shuttle's belly to cover them as they sprinted to the edge of the street. The shuttle itself took up most of the street span. For an instant Lily could marvel at Pinto's incredible piloting, and then the first spray of fire shattered windows above her head, and she waved her group forward.

Post A-seven was situated to guard in toward the city's center, the cordoned-off area, but Immortals were never unprepared for any actuality. Already two large guns yawed around to face the new threat and white-uniformed soldiers scattered to adjust their shielding.

A hot explosion obliterated one of the guns. Lily pressed her people forward to the next scrap of cover under the protection of the boiling cloud of fire and steam that heaved up from the hit.

She threw herself down on the pavement and sprayed covering fire across the position as Jenny and her pair darted forward. Beside her, Rainbow swore. Lily glanced back to see blood streaming down the Ridani's leg.

The other gun leveled and aimed.

"Break forward," Lily shouted. They dived ahead as the masonry four meters behind burned and shattered under the gun's fire. "Rainbow, cover from here when we move forward."

Fire arced through the post, and several Immortals fell, but Lily could not tell the direction it came from. From the building above Jenny, a new rack of shooting opened up: Yehoshua had gone up, to add a third angle to their fire.

His firing pinned down the far corner of the post. Lily ran forward and crouched; the Mule and Aliasing split behind her, and broke into a sprint to hit the nearest opaque shielding of the post.

She flung herself around it without a break and had the briefest glimpse of a grim-faced man lifting his rifle before she shot him. Fire ricocheted around her. She caught a glimpse of Jenny grappling with an Immortal, fighting for his gun.

The second big gun exploded. Searing waves of heat flooded over her, and she yanked the dead Immortal over her to shield herself. After a moment she shoved her rifle out and fired at the next rank of shielding.

"Wait," hissed Aliasing, appearing abruptly beside her, crouched, eyes intent ahead. "He's broken through."

An Immortal fell, shot with scathing accuracy through the head. A second came tumbling backward. An instant later a new, brown-clad figure appeared and shot with dispatch the struggling Immortal.

Brilliant gold hair. Several figures materialized behind him. To the right Lily saw the white uniform flash out of concealment, but Jehane had already launched himself into the attack in a manner so reminiscent of Jenny that Lily wondered how anyone could ever mistake his fighting for anything but Immortal trained.

Lily lifted her gun, but could not trust herself to shoot. Beside her, Aliasing calmly aimed and fired and the Immortal fell at Jehane's feet.

He turned. Looked across the gap—not so great, Lily realized now in the fleeting lull afforded by this tiny victory—between him and Aliasing.

And stared.

It was an instant's reaction. Across fifteen meters Lily

could see his face clearly, even as heat simmered across it, melding with wisps of steam; she could see the lines of his posture transform as he recognized the tiny figure staring back at him.

For that instant, Lily knew without question that Jehane was too stunned by this vision of Aliasing—small, fragile-seeming, and yet utterly at ease in Immortal whites—to speak.

More figures, perhaps Jehane's entire group, stumbled into the relative security of post A-7's shielded center. Most were wounded. Lily rose and moved forward.

She found Jenny beside her. A welt, oozing blood, scored the dark woman's hand.

"Tupping idiot," she swore. "He isn't even wearing a helmet."

"He looks prettier that way." Lily hailed the nearest refugee, grasping his arm. "Get your group moving!" she snapped. "Board the shuttle just past here—Move!"

A few glanced toward Jehane, but most hustled past her, crouching as Yehoshua in his position above began firing past them.

In the muddy swirl of their retreat, wounded dragged or carried along, Jehane still stared at Aliasing. Even when a huddle of refugees crossed his line of sight he stared, as if he could see right through them.

A black-clad man came up to him. "Comrade. How can we thank you? We would never have gotten out of there without you. You were magnificent."

With a visible effort, Jehane returned to himself and transferred his gaze to the man before him. "You leave now to continue the battle here?" he asked, smooth as if nothing had interrupted his drive out of the city.

"Yes. Thank you. Thank you. We will carry on the fight." The man grasped Jehane's hand, pumped it, then took a step back and gave him a half bow more worshipful than respectful.

"Fall back," said Lily. When Aliasing did not respond, she gestured to the Mule. "Carry her if you have to. We've got to go *now*!"

Above, Yehoshua kept up a steady stream of fire, but through it Lily could hear the movement of heavy ground vehicles and a new echo of fire nearing them.

The black-clad man hurried away into a narrow alleyway, and Jehane jogged gracefully forward to halt beside Lily.

"It seems," he said, "that I am in your debt."

"Jenny," said Lily quickly, "get back in covering position and call Yehoshua down."

Jenny acted immediately, waving back the two Ridanis with her, but flashed a brief glance of vivid anger back over her shoulder at Jehane as she retreated.

Lily turned back to find Jehane still regarding her thoughtfully.

"I'm not waiting for the reinforcements to show up," she snapped, "and after all of the trouble I've been to, I'm damned if I'm going to let you either."

A final barrage from Yehoshua's gun triggered a shuddering explosion down the street.

Jehane smiled, but it was a wistful and surprisingly vulnerable expression. "I had forgotten how beautiful she is," he said softly, "gracing that uniform that was once a badge of honor."

"Hoy," breathed Lily, feeling a sudden cold prickle of misgiving run up her back. "If I'd known, I wouldn't have brought her."

But he was already off, sprinting for the shuttle, and did not hear her.

22   The Hounds

****

With effortless efficiency Jehane got his refugees strapped in by the time Yehoshua and his pair came pelting up the ramp.

Pinto had the shuttle off the ground before Finch could begin retracting the ramp, and above the buildings just as Jehane strapped into the seat behind him, Lily sitting where Jenny had on the trip down.

"Hold on to your seats!" shouted Finch, and then Pinto took them up at an angle and velocity that brought screams from the wounded and gasps from everyone else.

Black engulfed Lily's vision as a vise gripped her chest, faded to a haze of spots and grey, and then she could see again: the back of Pinto's head and the stark tattoos visible between his throat and collar; the curving gleam of Bach blocking her view of Finch; Jehane's profile: golden hair brushing along the sculpted line of his cheek, lips parted slightly under the strain of their climb.

No one spoke for minutes as Pinto, body relaxed and yet entirely focused, guided the shuttle up. From the cabin behind, Lily could hear weeping. She could not tell who it was. Beside her, Yehoshua cursed softly under his breath, mostly imprecations about "damned tattoos."

Slowly the vise lightened as Pinto slacked off their climb. Lily found she could take real breaths. Yehoshua let out a long sigh.

"Cursed Ridani," he swore in a good-natured voice. "If you weren't such a cursed good pilot we could have gotten blown up on the way in and not had to suffer through these damned Gs. I'm too old for this."

In the clear plastine of the shuttle's windshield, Lily could see the ghost of Pinto's reflection, all geometric lines etched in faint traceries, and she thought the corners of his mouth quirked up—although she could not be sure.

"I have a signal from the decoy pilot," said Finch. "He is downside, and still alive. That's all I can tell."

"Good. Monitor the full range of comm—" Lily broke off and glanced at Jehane.

"Interesting," he murmured. "A Ridani pilot."

Lily watched him watch Pinto. He blinked once, twice, as if there was a clue here that he was missing, and wished to find.

"Ah," he said suddenly. "Senator Isaiah's son."

Nothing in Pinto's body betrayed his reaction to that statement. Lily glanced at the windshield, but the angle of light had erased his reflection.

"Where are we going?" asked Finch.

Jehane turned his head to look at Lily—not at all as if he were deferring to her, but rather as if he were wondering why Finch needed to ask that question. He noted each occupant of the forward cabin: Pinto, Finch, Bach, and Yehoshua, and then, of course, he understood.

Lily wondered, suddenly, if he was angry at her appropriation of her former crew from the *Forlorn Hope*. She could tell nothing from his expression.

"To the *Boukephalos*," he said. Then he unstrapped himself and went into the main cabin to check on the wounded.

Jehane kept Lily and Bach with him when they left the shuttle bay. His first words, coming onto the bridge, were to Kuan-yin.

"Have you positioned the fleet as I directed?"

For a fleeting moment she looked irritated. "Yes."

"Then." He sat in the captain's chair and swiveled it around to face Lily. Tapped the com on his console. "Send shuttle and crew back to the *Forlorn Hope*," he ordered, watching her.

She did her best to keep her face and stance expressionless.

"The Hierakis Formula," he said. "What is it?"

Surprise betrayed her. She simply stared at him, unable to answer, or not to answer convincingly.

He lifted his hands, palm to palm, and rested his lips on his thumbs as he studied her. She was aware of Kuan-yin staring at them until a slight movement of Jehane's head sent that woman back to her duties. At the other stations, the crew remained intent on their work.

Tapped the com again. "Contact Captain Machiko on the *Forlorn Hope*. Have him send his physician here. I have casualties I want him to look at."

He resumed his study of Lily.

She had recovered herself, somewhat. Bach winked silently at her, neutral yellow.

"Request permission to change out of battle dress," she said formally.

He smiled. His brown tunic and trousers were soiled with grime and stained with dried blood, but he looked perfectly at ease in them. "Granted. Although I will want you back on the bridge once you have—"

"Comrade!" The woman at comm, her tone urgent. "*Savedra* reports two ships not ours entering low and fast in sept quadrant—no—and two more in terce, reported by—wait" —she frowned as reports began to flood the comm—"Another three—" Broke off again.

Jehane dismissed Lily with a wave of his hand as he settled a headset over his golden hair. "All fleet on red. We have contact. Open fire."

Lily left the bridge, but she felt it wise under the circumstances not to change out of battle dress. Having no cabin, she went to Medical. Duri let her clean up and had one of her assistants go to Armory for a full refit and reload of her rifle and oxygen package.

Bach monitored the battle on screen over the next hours. The *Boukephalos* did not even fire a shot.

"Void bless," murmured Lily as Central's incoming fleet took scathing fire and shattered under its concentration. "He must have planned this out from the beginning: the entire Blessings revolt must have been the decoy to lure the fleet in here piecemeal, in a hurry."

Duri regarded her, puzzled. "What did you expect? He is Jehane. By the way, would you mind if I took a new sample of your blood? I still have no idea what that illness was. Although I did get a suggestion to—"

She looked up as the door to Medical sighed open. Stood up, startled.

Lily turned and rose as well.

Jehane had entered, followed by Hawk.

Kyosti took in the room with a comprehensive glance, not giving Lily an instant's longer glance than Duri or the bank of medical equipment. And yet Lily knew that he somehow savored her presence, carefully and completely, in some way that the others could not detect—not even Jehane, who kept his watchful gaze on Hawk and seemed ever-so-slightly displeased that the blue-haired man had no stronger reaction to Lily.

"Comrade Doctor," Jehane said to Duri, embuing the title with a wealth of praise. "Would you leave us a moment?"

She nodded and retreated into the adjacent ward.

Jehane looked first at Lily, and then at Hawk. "I'd like to repeat something to you," he said, not a request.

"Good gracious," drawled Kyosti in his most aggravatingly foppish tone, "then I hope you'll let me sit down."

Lily gave the barest shake of her head, warning him, but Jehane merely waved at a nearby chair. Kyosti sighed and brought it forward and seated himself in it with ostentatious fussiness.

Lily stood, still, hands clasped behind her back. For the first time in her life she tried consciously to efface herself, just as, she realized, Heredes had long ago learned to make himself inconspicuous or unthreatening, if circumstances warranted.

Jehane kept his face carefully neutral, and yet the brilliant intelligence that animated his charisma could never be disguised or hidden.

" 'Oh, he did, did he?' " Jehane said without inflection. " 'But how could he know—' 'The Hierakis Formula?' 'I don't believe it.' 'No, Bach. Of course not. But—' 'That's all he said?' 'Leaving me stuck here for the present, of course. All right. I'll play his game a little longer.' 'Let's hope so.' "

Lily said nothing.

"Lily, my dear woman," Kyosti drawled, deliberately provoking. "You ought to remember that on a ship like this your every word will be taped and played back."

"What is the Hierakis Formula?" Jehane asked smoothly,

not rising to the bait. "What game are you playing, comrade Hawk?"

Kyosti hooked his hands behind his hair and leaned back into the cushions of his chair. He smiled. "That would be telling, wouldn't it?"

"My thought, exactly," replied Jehane. Although his voice was gentle, the threat was clear.

Jehane's wrist-com beeped, and a breathless woman's voice spoke.

"Comrade Jehane! Please return to the bridge!"

He lifted his wrist. "Is there some trouble? I thought at last tally that all was in hand."

"We have a new ship, comrade. It came in at oct quadrant, where there isn't even a charted window. And she's—Void bless us, comrade"—even over the thin speaker, the tremor in her voice was obvious—"she's huge. I've never seen a hull that size. She doesn't answer to comm. So far cautious fire has made no penetration whatsoever."

"Has the cavalry arrived at last?" Kyosti murmured obscurely.

"What the Void is 'cavalry'?" Lily demanded, shaken out of her stance by the sudden instinct that she knew who had just arrived.

Jehane lowered his wrist and raked them with his glance. "Come with me to the bridge," he ordered.

Kyosti shrugged, and rose as if it would be too much trouble to resist, but the gesture was lost on Jehane because he had already turned to walk to the door, expecting their compliance. Lily followed him silently, Kyosti at her heels.

The atmosphere on *Boukephalos*'s bridge was taut with uncertainty. As they entered, the man on scan looked up.

"Comrade." His face was creased with worry. "I've had tac running through all our records. Central's battle fleet has nothing this big listed in our files."

"Status?" asked Jehane as he sat down in captain's chair, slipping on his headset and levering out the chair's console and screen to display over his lap.

"The ship has halted at the following coordinates." Scan reeled off a list of numbers. "She's currently making no movement whatsoever, hostile or friendly."

"No response to our overtures on any channel," said the woman at comm.

"We're scattershooting fire from three ships, close enough

to warn but not to hit. There has been no reply or action of any kind," added the officer at weapons.

"I don't think," said scan abruptly, "that ship cares one whit about us. We could just as well be flak on entry: something just to fly through."

Jehane's face was a study in disapproval crossed by the intense interest with which he studied the specs unfolding on the screen before him.

Beside Lily, Kyosti sighed and shifted his weight from one leg to the other.

Jehane glanced up. "Do you know anything about this?" he asked mildly.

"Is there some reason I ought to?" Kyosti retorted lazily.

Jehane sighed, as ostentatious a gesture as any Kyosti ever used, but toned down for all that into an expression of long-suffering patience. "I won't bother to insult your intelligence by replying directly to that question, comrade. I somehow doubt that you are unaware that we met, albeit not personally, at Nevermore Station some time ago. I haven't time to fence as I'm in the middle of a rather large and important engagement."

As if on cue, comm spoke up. "*Aberwyn* reports that the cruiser *Singh* has taken a disabling hit and officially withdrawn from the action. *Suffrage* reports that the cutters *Manticore* and *Gryphon* are in retreat, heading for a quince quadrant window, and *Forlorn Hope* reports the cruiser *Lion's Share* dead in space, and its attendant *Zima Station* is in full pursuit of an unidentified cutter-class ship. *Nova Roma* reports it has sustained irreparable damage to its weapons systems. *Bitter Tidings* reports it is evacuating the merchanter *Disenchantment*, whose hull has blown." She paused. "Shall I go on?"

"No. Let comrade Kuan-yin coordinate the data for now." He returned his attention to Kyosti. "Now, do you?"

Scan swore, a long, obscene oath. "Another ship just appeared in oct quadrant. It'll take time to analyze its spec, but we've got no immediate match on our long-range—"

"Comrade!" Comm broke in. "I have com traffic on a narrow beam between the incoming and the resting vessel. Transmitting both ways."

"Can you break in?"

She shook her head. "It's too tight a channel. We're too far away in any case. I've got—I'll put *Nova Roma* on it. They're closest."

Lily took a step forward. "Comrade Jehane. Let me try. I think I can get a reply from the first ship."

Jehane cocked his head to one side to examine her. The careful line of his mouth lent his stare a preciseness that seemed piercing. "Ah." One side of his mouth quirked up. "You've finished observing our little sparring match and have decided to act, I see. Thank you."

"Lily," said Kyosti in an undertone that spoke volumes.

"Someone has to tell her about Heredes," replied Lily. "I intend to do it—in person, if comrade Jehane will let me."

Jehane smiled and waved her toward comm. His eyes sparked with interest as she walked across to the station and, after waiting for the woman to set her channel, leaned closer to the mike and spoke.

"I am calling from the—the—" She hesitated, trying to recall Heredes's words on the tiny bridge of the *Easy Virtue*, caught in an isolated backwater of space facing an imposing ship which they could not possibly outrun. "The region of the summer stars. I am calling for La Belle Dame."

For a long moment only the hiss of the channel answered her.

Then, *her* voice.

"Who is this?"

Jehane's eyes narrowed as he took in the brevity and unself-conscious authority of the question.

Lily glanced at Jehane, returned to the mike. "This is Taliesin's daughter. I have a personal message for you, if I have your permission to come aboard."

"Wait," commanded Jehane. "I want to know who you are speaking to, and what intentions they have here."

"Who I am does not concern you, Alexander Jehane," said La Belle, across the channel, as if Jehane had spoken directly to her and not to Lily. "My intentions have nothing to do with your revolution. You need not fear that I intend to interfere in any way. I am merely here looking for someone."

Lily felt with sudden numbing certitude that she knew who La Belle was looking for: Heredes.

"That is all very nice," said Jehane conversationally, "but what assurances can you give me that it is true?"

La Belle laughed, shattering the crackle of static. "I don't give assurances. But neither do I expect my word to be questioned."

If Lily had not been glancing that way at that moment, she would not have seen the look of absolute, utter fury that transformed Jehane's face for an instant. Then she blinked, and it was gone, obliterated into his usual bright, controlled intensity.

"Go, then," he said calmly. "Give her what information she seeks, and return. Your robot will remain safely with me, here, while you go."

"I don't think—" objected Lily, and stopped. After all of her protestations of not knowing League space, she had just given him ample reason to disbelieve her—and to distrust her. There was no room in his revolution for a La Belle Dame. Lily still had responsibilities to the people on the *Forlorn Hope.* So if Jehane chose to hold Bach as hostage for her safe return—

Signing off comm, she gave Bach brief instructions to remain behind and, with a salute to Jehane, left the bridge. Kyosti followed her.

"What are you doing?" she asked as she waited for the elevator.

"Going with you."

"Did Jehane give you permission?"

"I wasn't aware I had to ask for it," he said languidly. "Ought I to?"

"Well, he didn't stop you," she muttered, "so he must know what he's doing."

Kyosti laughed. It was not a complimentary sound. "Jehane is seething with rage in there, my heart. If he hates me because I am nothing he can control, then what do you suppose he feels about La Belle, who could blast his revolution out of the sky with her single ship?"

"But La Belle isn't interested in the revolution."

"Very true," he agreed. "But La Belle is a link back to the League, and if the League rediscovers Reft space officially, and arrives here in all of its advanced technological glory to welcome the Reft back into the community of humankind, then where is Jehane?"

"Maybe he's exactly where he wants to be." Lily frowned at Kyosti, too angered by his presence to admit that she had had the same thought herself. They stepped inside the elevator and she keyed in the sequence for the shuttle bay. "*If* the government of the League is as representative and equal as you claim it is."

"Oh, yes," said Kyosti with a tone much like sarcasm in his voice. "Oh, it is. That's why they hunted down people like me and Heredes and Wingtuck. They dislike being reminded of what humanity once was, before the golden age: 'villains, vipers, damn'd without redemption. Dogs, easily won to fawn on any man.'"

"And murderers." Lily closed one hand into a fist and set it with deliberate weight on the wall beside the elevator keypad, turning her head away from Kyosti. The thought of what that miner's body must have looked like, after death, impinged with awful clarity on her mind. She shut her eyes. Evan. Evan something. Still—*still*—she could not remember his entire name. That only made it worse.

"Lily." The word seemed forced from him. "Lily?" The door opened and he followed her out of the elevator. "At least let me try to explain."

She kept walking, did not turn even as she spoke: "You should have explained a long time ago."

Kyosti said nothing. Continued to say nothing the rest of the way to the shuttle bay, on the boarding, the detach, the long trip to La Belle's ship. Lily whistled under her breath, wishing Bach were here to talk to—but he was not.

Kyosti shifted, with an almost inaudible sigh, in the seat behind her. She realized that although she could not hear his breathing, she could feel it, like the pulse of her own heart and breath. She had not spent so long a time in such close proximity to him since Unruli Station, and she cursed herself for letting him come along now, when there was no reason for it.

Duty impelled her to tell La Belle face-to-face about Heredes's fate. Duty, and her instinct that Heredes would not want his Bella to discover this truth in any cold and impersonal manner. But there was no reason for Hawk to attend her, except to pretend that he was finally going to explain what he had all along avoided explaning, in order to dissolve her adamancy.

No reason for him to sit so close and with every slight movement remind her of his presence, his soft breath, the

feel of his skin and the light, clean scent of his hair, and the
satisfied shuttering of his eyes while—

"Damn it," she swore. Behind her, Kyosti chuckled, the
way he did when he—

She clenched her hands on the chair rests and held on tight
for the remainder of the flight.

Adam met them at the docking bay. He welcomed them
graciously, even gave Lily a brotherly hug, but a suggestion of
a frown tightened the lines at his eyes and mouth, and he
seemed preoccupied.

"Just in time," he said obliquely, glancing at Kyosti, as he
led them to an elevator that took them somehow straight to
the bridge. Lily remembered how far they had had to walk
the first time, and she wondered if La Belle's business was in
fact not what she had initially expected it to be: not news of
Heredes, but someone else—and this hurried shortcut to the
bridge an indication of a preoccupation that extended beyond
Adam to the entire ship. Whose ship had come in behind
her? And she remembered that Yi had been looking for La
Belle, on his "hunt."

As the doors sighed open onto the bridge, Kyosti took a
step out after Adam, stopped, and took an audible breath in,
as if he were scenting the air. "Just in time for *what?*" he
asked sharply.

To their right, a second elevator door opened and a man
tumbled out and rushed forward to fling himself at the foot of
La Belle's dais. "I've worked for you—good service!—for
seven years!" he cried. "It's your sworn duty to protect me!"

The man's stark fear permeated the bridge like a rank smell
as La Belle's chair swiveled slowly around, revealing her: face
set as in stone, black hair braided tight and lapping in its fall
her knees. She regarded the man at her feet in awful silence.

"What did he do?" whispered Lily.

Adam shrugged, answering her in a low voice. "It's the
typical story: asteroid miner comes in to some station on
leave, runs across a sweet adolescent je'jiri girl in full raging
heat who'd slipped her clan for a night on the prowl. And of
course all intelligent people are avoiding her like the plague,
and trying to get calls through to whatever ship has hired out
her clan. But people like him usually figure that as long as
the je'jiri isn't already mated, they're safe. Brainless idiot.
And then of course once he realized he was marked, he

ran—and tried to cover his trail by pretending it had never happened."

At last La Belle spoke. "You lied to me." Her anger was bone deep and implacable.

"Oh god, oh god," the man wept. "What else could I do? I had to leave. They were on my trail already."

"You knew the law." Her voice hardened with each word she spoke. "'No human will mate or have intercourse in any sexual or sensual fashion with je'jiri.' Code ex-eleven-oh-four of the Codified Law of League space. Which even a privateer acknowledges."

He stammered something incoherent, lifted a hand to his hair. His forehead bore a brilliant red scar, like a brand, puckered across his dark skin.

"'In dreams you hunt your prey,'" murmured Kyosti in an expressionless voice, "'baying like hounds whose thought will never rest.'"

But Lily, glancing at him, saw that he was strung so tight that the merest touch might shatter him. The usual bronze of his skin had washed out to a ghostly pallor, accentuated by the unearthly color of his hair.

"But she was still an adolescent—and she consented—" the man gasped. His gaze darted to the elevator doors, halted for a frozen heartbeat on Kyosti's still, taut form, and skipped back to La Belle.

"Then you are either uncontrollably libidinous or simply stupid. The je'jiri *are not human*, man. Their ways are not our ways."

"They're savages," muttered Adam under his breath. "Little better than animals."

"You have violated every tenet, the very foundation, of their culture, as admittedly alien and atavistic as it may seem to us. Yi took the hunt on, and now they have caught up with you. *I* cannot stop it."

He lay in crumpled anguish at her feet, weeping with noisy and awful terror. The bridge crew stood utterly silent, watching him without compassion. "But you are La Belle Dame," he sobbed. "*You* could stop them."

She stood up. "I am La Belle Dame Sans Merci," she said with the bite of diamond, "and I do not suffer fools gladly."

To Lily's left, the third set of elevator doors opened.

23 Je'jiri

****

In that first instant, she could have believed that Kyosti had somehow moved from her side to the elevator without her knowing, and emerged again onto the bridge; a kind of vivid double entrance made possible by some quirk in his character.

He took two sprung steps out of the elevator and stopped. He had the same tall, slender form, crowned by startlingly blue hair. Then he turned, and she saw his face.

The shock of the absolute inhumanity of the man's—the alien's—features shook her: first, the strange, unearthly pallor of his skin matched against brilliant green eyes pierced by an acute and vital intelligence. The features of his face had a delicacy that lent it an almost angelic cast, a beauty that might be said to surpass human beauty, but for—

But for its contrast with the alien's behavior. He froze, like any hunting thing, and cast his head about, eyes half-shuttered, as if he were smelling out the room, scenting and placing each individual. The movement repelled her: it seemed grossly primitive, as violent as Unruli's unpredictable storms, tied by tide and wind and gravity, and the unbreakable bond of the gross senses to the cycles of earth, to the unforgiving grip of the deepest, oldest part of the brain.

The man on the steps of the dais had ceased weeping and now groped up to a crouch, gathering himself in like an animal driven to its last, desperate fight.

More of them emerged from the elevator—two, four, seven in all. Each scented the room. The male who had first come in had locked his gaze on his prey, and he trembled, as if the wait was unbearable. He lifted his hands. Lily saw that each finger was tipped with a pale, sharp claw.

A strong, bitter smell permeated the bridge: *their* scent.

Except for the trembling male, the rest, having finished their scenting, stood stock-still. One stepped forward—Lily thought it was a female, although it was hard to tell.

When she spoke, she spoke directly to La Belle in a voice deeply accented with alien sounds. Her teeth were a carnivore's teeth: pointed and deadly.

"Do you contest the kill?"

La Belle did not move. "No," she replied.

A sigh rippled through the je'jiri. The male lunged forward. Beside Lily, Kyosti gasped, a strangled sound, and collapsed to his knees.

The man fought, at first—some instinct for survival that humans had never lost—but ranged against this inhuman lust for the kill it did not avail him long.

The je'jiri male set claws into his face and chest and ripped open the man's throat with his teeth.

Blood pooled out and dripped in streams down the steps of the dais. The last rattling sigh of the dying man echoed across the bridge.

Adam swore under his breath.

Lily felt her knees sag as bile rose in her own, intact, throat. She put a hand out to grip Kyosti's shoulder, to steady herself, but he was shaking, trembling, and he had thrown a hand up over his eyes as if it could protect him from what they had just seen.

Someone in the far reaches of the bridge was vomiting. The noise cut off abruptly as, escorted by two other figures, they fled out another door.

The je'jiri male waited a count of ten, and then sniffed, scenting for a smell now eradicated from the universe. He set his hand, palm down, in a sticky puddle of blood, and brought it up to his face, marking each cheek and his forehead, and last his lips, with red.

Then he rose, and retreated, clothes stained with brilliant, wet scarlet. And the others came forward, one by one, and repeated the gesture: hand, palm down, in blood, and the precise, ritualistic marking of their faces.

The female went last. As she rose, all of them turned and looked at Kyosti until because of their scrutiny the attention of all the people left on the bridge was on him.

The female spoke directly to him; alien words, but her meaning was clear: It is also your obligation to mark the kill.

Kyosti shuddered, a tremor that passed through his entire body. He shook away Lily's hand on his shoulder and stood up.

Took one step back.

"Abai'is-ssa," hissed the female. As if he was being pulled forward by a force as powerful as gravity, he walked to her. Each step seemed agonizing, torn out of his will to stay where he was.

Lily began to move after him, but Adam grabbed her by both arms and held her back. "Don't be a fool," he muttered. "You can't stop this."

Stiffly, Kyosti crouched by the mutilated corpse. His hand shook violently as he lowered it—stopped it a finger's breadth above the pooling blood, and then shut his eyes and pressed it down. And marked his face: both cheeks, his forehead, and last, his lips.

The female je'jiri turned her feral gaze on La Belle, expectant.

La Belle had not moved during the entire time. Her gaze rested dispassionately on the corpse. "I and my crew witness this kill, fulfilled under the specifications of the Gabriel Treaty, and we now declare that this course is finished."

Like ghosts, the je'jiri vanished into the elevator without a word or gesture of acknowledgment. The door sighed closed behind them.

There was silence on the bridge.

Kyosti still knelt by the corpse.

"Adam," said La Belle curtly, and she looked pointedly at the corpse.

He let go of Lily's arms and, signaling to two other crew members, walked over to the corpse. He had clearly come prepared: they bundled the body into white sheeting, sopped up the worst of the excess blood—although a few deep stains and the acrid scent lingered—and carried the dead man off the bridge, vanishing like the je'jiri into an elevator.

Lily watched it all with an intensity brought by the realization that once this act ended, she would have to react to what she had just seen. Kyosti still knelt on the steps, his face streaked with drying blood.

La Belle stood, her feet incongruously bare, on the top step. As Lily raised her eyes to look at her, she met La Belle's gaze. It was not unmixed with pity. Perhaps she saw the storm rising in Lily's expression, or perhaps she just knew enough of human nature, but she moved her hand slightly, not more than a twist of the wrist, and the rest of the personnel cleared off, leaving the three of them alone in the hushed cavern of the bridge.

"You had something you wished to tell me," said La Belle.

"I can't believe it." Lily's voice emerged hoarse and ragged. "You let them murder him. You let them just mutilate him as if he was no better than"—she shook her head roughly—"No one, no *thing*, deserves that. I thought the League was supposed to be civilized."

La Belle stepped carefully around Kyosti's motionless form and descended the steps to come stand a body's length from Lily. Their eyes were on a level. "Do you tell the cat not to kill the mouse? The owl not to hunt at night? The eagle lives by killing rodents. The wolf drives down and butchers caribou. But unlike humankind, they only kill what they need. Je'jiri are not indiscriminate killers, as we humans are. They are driven, they are fueled, by instincts that we have long striven to transcend or deny, but I, for one, respect the absolute predictability of their honor."

"Honor!" Lily cried. "You call *that* honor?"

La Belle smiled, but it was the smile of grim truth, not of sympathy. "How many men and women have you killed, Taliesin's daughter? And for what cause, and whose honor? Can you say it was for as compelling a reason as the iron law of je'jiri mating: one mate, for life, no exceptions. It is in their bones—in the very fabric of their being."

She paused, but Lily stared, silent, at Kyosti's frozen pose: kneeling on the steps as if he were praying to a god who had long since forgotten him.

"A linguist once told me," La Belle continued, softer, now, "that there is no word for 'love,' or 'adultery,' in the je'jiri language. Love is a human construct for fleeting ties. *Their* bonds are burned into every cell of their bodies. And adultery does not exist, except among the aberrant. If you sleep with a je'jiri, their mate *must* kill you. It is as simple as that."

"It's horrible," she breathed, still seeing the clean ripping of the man's throat.

"We live in a great, vast universe," said La Belle calmly. "We must accommodate those to whom our ways seem equally alien, and unspeakable."

"Kyosti," Lily murmured, lifting her anguished gaze to the clear sanity of La Belle's pale face. "Hoy. He's one of *them*. I thought he was human. No wonder he's so—" But she could not bring herself to identify what it was in words whose spoken permanence might mark him forever.

"No, Lily," said La Belle with abrupt, but real, compassion. "He is indeed half je'jiri, on his mother's side. But that is not the root of his particular crisis. Je'jiri are too prosaic to harbor insanity in their minds. It is his human half that curses him."

"What do you mean? That murder—it was so savage—and that awful ritual of marking themselves with the blood. *That* was the horrible part."

"Oh, and I agree, even though I may understand why it is so. But I can look at it from a distance. I can intellectualize it, as we humans do so well. I cannot be forced by birth and instinct to partake in a deed that the rest of me finds cruelly and bitterly repugnant."

Lily shut her eyes. The searing pain that shuttered Kyosti's face as he knelt unmoving was too terrible for her to look on. And she wondered what kind of death his father had died.

"There *was* a message, I think," said La Belle, coolly changing the subject.

Lily's throat was choked with anguish, but she managed to force out the words anyway. "I'm sorry. I don't know how else to say this." She opened her eyes, because it would be cowardly to tell in any other way but face-to-face, seeing her. "Heredes is dead."

"Yes," La Belle agreed, with no change in her expression. "Joshua Li Heredes is dead. I came to Reft space to discover what had happened to him. We have just been to Arcadia, where I found out." She paused. Still, her expression did not change.

Because Lily did not know if La Belle would welcome

sympathy, she found refuge in an awkward question. "But how did you end up here, at Blessings?"

"Curiosity impelled me to follow the sudden flurry of military activity, but—" She dismissed the Reft's political turmoil with a wave of her hand. "I see nothing here to interest me. The *Sans Merci* will return to League space. Now. I think you will need a few moments alone with Hawk before you return to your ship. Farewell, Lily Ransome." She lifted a white hand to touch Lily's forehead, a benediction, and turned and walked, soundless across the expanse of floor, to an elevator.

"But"—Lily stammered, confused by her abrupt dismissal, and by her complete lack of reaction to the news of Heredes's death—"but you can't just leave the bridge deserted."

La Belle smiled. "Like Mephistopheles, the bridge is where I am." Without explaining the comment, she disappeared into the elevator.

Lily stood, feeling dwarfed and alone in the vast silence of this strange, almost alien, bridge.

Kyosti's voice, soft, brushed against the quiet that hung so heavily over him. "'Hell hath no limits nor is circumscribed In one self place, but where we are is Hell, And where Hell is there must we ever be.'"

She took fifteen deliberate steps forward and halted three steps from him. Where the blood had streaked his face most thinly, it was already dried and beginning to flake off.

"I don't know what to say to you." She extended a hand toward him, tentative, and withdrew it without touching him.

He did not look up at her, but his voice was low, compelled by an inner pain she could not even imagine. "Say you forgive me for murdering the man on Unruli Station."

She felt dizzy, having forgotten to breathe, and she knelt beside him. "I forgive you." She put her hands on his shoulders.

The urgency and force with which he embraced her caught her by surprise, and the strength of his grip scared her—until she realized that he was holding on to her as if she were his anchor. Not even so much for his life, but for his sanity.

24　Arcadia Falls

****

Kyosti did not speak at all on the return trip back to the
Boukephalos. He sat next to Lily, eyes shut. The slight rise
and fall of his chest, and the barest, shifting presence of his
fingers brushing her leg, were the only signs that he was
alive.

When Doctor Prachenduriyang met them at the shuttle
bay with Jehane's orders that they were to be returned
immediately to quarantine, Hawk acquiesced without protest. Duri had taken careful precautions from the shuttle bay
all the way to Medical, and installed them swiftly and efficiently
in a two-room suite somewhat larger than Lily's original
quarantine room.

As soon as they were sealed into the suite, Kyosti lay down
on a couch in the second room and turned his back to them,
effectively leaving Lily alone with Duri.

"He isn't feeling well," Lily said, feeling obliged to explain.
"I don't understand, after my quarantine was broken so
thoroughly by Kuan-yin, that you're bothering with this."

Duri shrugged, watching Hawk's back with the measuring
eye of a healer. "Jehane's orders. What are his symptoms?
Lethargy? He seems pale. I'd better take his readings. I don't
mean to alarm you, but I've finally gotten in the medical
records from the *Forlorn Hope*, and he is the only member of
the entire crew who has not yet come down with this

mysterious plague. And evidently we have a new rash of cases on *Zima Station* and *Savedra*, the two ships which accompanied the *Forlorn Hope* the past month."

"Maybe he's immune," suggested Lily.

Duri shook her head. "Unlikely. So far we have one hundred percent contagion. Why should comrade Hawk be immune?"

"Why, indeed?" asked a new voice.

Lily whirled to see Jehane, sheathed for quarantine, enter from the other room—she had not heard him coming in through the quarantine lock. He waited, examining her, expectant.

"I wouldn't know," she said smoothly. "I'm not a doctor."

"No, you aren't," he agreed. His gaze moved to investigate Kyosti's still form. "Doctor Prachenduriyang, do you think comrade Hawk might be coming down with this illness?"

"I can't say yet." She took a step toward the couch, hesitated. "Of course I'll have to take a blood sample. I haven't had time to study in depth the analysis of the illness's course on the *Forlorn Hope*, although"—she pressed her lips together with a brief tightening of disapproval—"I must say there are a few irregularities in the report."

"Which was, I believe, compiled by comrade Hawk himself," interposed Jehane neatly.

"Yes. For instance, he took no blood samples at the onset of the disease, only midway through and during recovery."

"Which suggests?"

Duri glanced at Lily, then at the unreadable line of Kyosti's back. "I couldn't say. Poor procedural methods could account for it. Although all the other medical records from the *Forlorn Hope* show a meticulous thoroughness in keeping records. Lack of time due to the sudden and virulent outbreak of cases. But again, battle casualties show no such lack of precise record keeping. He might have thought he knew what he was dealing with, and then realized midway through that he did not."

"In which case," Jehane said softly, "would he not have changed his procedures with the later cases?"

"Well, yes. . . ." Duri cast another glance, this one worried, at Lily.

"Perhaps you ought to ask comrade Hawk directly," Jehane suggested in a tone of utmost reason.

"He's asleep," Lily said sharply.

Jehane smiled, making her feel suddenly as if she had given something away. "I meant, of course, when he is feeling better. Meanwhile, Doctor," and he transferred his attention with effortless smoothness back to Duri. "I wonder if you have dealt with all the inquiries on wounded that have come in from our fleet? Has a complete compilation of casualties been made?"

"No, comrade, but it should be finished within six hours. I have two technicians at work on it now. There were twenty-eight casualties that I did not have sufficient expertise to advise treatment for beyond what the medical teams on board their respective ships had already done, so I'm afraid that they may not recover—"

Kyosti sat up. So smoothly and abruptly that both Lily and Duri started. Only Jehane did not register any obvious change of expression.

"Let me see those files," Kyosti said harshly. The extreme pallor of his skin gave him a look of desperation, or desperate illness. "My specialty is triage, and specifically combat injuries."

Duri was too startled to do more than look helplessly at Jehane for guidance.

For an instant Kyosti looked right at Lily. He was so pale that she had a sudden blinding flash of *deja vu*, seeing, not him, but one of his ghostlike cousins, hand immersed in blood. A tiny smudge of red decorated his cheek: a bit of blood he had missed when he had scrubbed his face with the white towel that Adam had offered him as they had boarded the shuttle for the trip back. She looked away, feeling sick with the memory.

"By all means," Jehane said. The plastine quarantine sheath muted his expression and his tone. "Doctor Prachenduriyang, if you can set up an interface in here?"

Duri frowned. "I don't like it. You look and act ill to me, comrade."

"I won't leave this couch," he promised. Even just sitting, he had an edge of fine-honed exhaustion about him, as if the couch lent him a force of will that alone, at this instant, sustained him. "It will give me something to do."

"Well." Duri hesitated, then walked forward decisively. "Let me examine you, and take some blood, and then I'll set you up."

Under any other circumstance, Lily would have been amazed at the meekness with which Kyosti submitted to Duri's orders, or even to her plastine-sheathed—and thus scentless—touch. But now she was amazed he had the strength of mind to insist on what little he did demand: a task to immerse himself in, one that would keep him free of having to think.

"Very good, Doctor," said Jehane. "Now, comrade Heredes, I would like to speak with you in the other room. If I might."

She allowed herself a brief, exhausted smile as she reflected, following him into the other room, that his habit of asking permission for things he well knew he could demand tended to disarm his followers into believing that they controlled their own actions far more than they actually did.

She seated herself on the other bed, allowed herself a sigh, wishing she could sleep. Jehane did not sit, but turned to face her, standing light and relaxed, his golden hair and brown tunic—given an unearthly sheen by the plastine sheath—set off in rich contrast against the stark white expanse of wall behind him.

"We have routed Central's fleet," he began in as matter-of-fact a voice as if he were announcing dinner, "and I have given orders that we advance on Arcadia. I expect to meet very little resistance there, except in the walled precincts of Central itself."

"Because of Pero," she said. "Robbie will have Arcadia entirely committed to you. He was halfway to that goal when I left there."

"Indeed," agreed Jehane. "Pero has been a tireless worker for our cause."

For some reason the comment irritated her. "He's the most honest man I know," she said abruptly. "I hope you appreciate that."

"Rest assured," he murmured, without a smile. "Meanwhile, comrade, both of the unidentified vessels which caused us—some alarm, have left Blessings system." He paused.

She simply watched him, without speaking.

"You must understand that I need to know what transpired on that ship." Again he paused.

This time she shut her eyes, not wanting to remember, but the vision bloomed unbidden in her mind's eye. She opened her eyes quickly to the soothing monotony of white walls and Jehane's impassive and implacable face.

"And why both ships left so abruptly."

Because they aren't interested in you—or us—at all, she thought, but she refrained from saying it aloud. "Because," she said instead, "they had finished what they came here for. Business"—she had to suppress the image of Kyosti dipping his hand in blood—"that was purely between themselves."

His lack of reaction was so pronounced as to be a strong reaction in itself—a man like Jehane could not like being dismissed so easily. "The ship you were on, where did she hail from?" he asked, cool now.

"You know where she's from," said Lily flatly. "She's not from the Reft. She's from the League. As was the other ship."

"As are you. As is your robot, and comrade Hawk."

"Where *is* my robot?" she demanded.

"In time." He pitched his voice to be soothing, but continued his questions nevertheless. "You were saying, comrade?"

"I'm not from the League. I grew up—" She hesitated. Could she be sure that Ransome House would never be blamed for her actions, in some form or other? And changed what she was going to say. "I grew up in Reft space just as you did, comrade Jehane. I just happen, like you, to have seen stranger things than most people have, and been influenced by them."

He smiled, a surprisingly sweet expression. "Well spoken, comrade Heredes. Nevertheless. Say it is true, about *your* birth and upbringing. That still leaves us with—the League. How does one get in touch with them?"

"I don't know. La Belle Dame might, but she's gone now, and you'll never catch her." She saw the flash of annoyance flicker across his face before he controlled it, and she knew it had been the wrong thing to say.

"Then that leaves comrade Hawk, does it not?" he replied calmly. "Convenient that he who was so well before visiting this La Belle Dame is now obviously suffering some illness. How did you escape from my people at Nevermore, Lily Ransome?"

She had forgotten how much he knew of her—again, she had let distance and time allow her to underestimate him. It seemed to her now that she was walking down a long, but finite, corridor in which all the doors were being shut one by one before her.

"I happened to be traveling," she said slowly, "with a man who is now dead."

"And the three representatives from the League? One of whom was, though I shouldn't have to remind you, our comrade Hawk."

"Hawk came with us. The other two—I don't know. Perhaps they went back to League space."

"Presupposing that the route that the ghost ship called the *Forlorn Hope* once haunted has now been rediscovered."

Lily cupped one hand over her eyes, rubbing the ridges of her eyebrows. "I don't know. I suppose it must have been—"

"If La Belle Dame and this other ship are now running the roads in Reft space, I suppose it must have been, too," he answered for her, perhaps a little sarcastic, now.

Lily lowered her hand and regarded Jehane with the cool carelessness of utter fatigue. "What are you afraid of?" she asked. "I'm not a navigator, but I think—I suspect—that a road that long lost, or so difficult to run that it was left and forgotten, is not so easily opened again. Does that satisfy you?"

"Comrade, you do me an injustice," he replied in his most persuasive voice. "This is not an interrogation. But the safety of the Reft—if the safety of the Reft is at risk, then there is no investigation I will not pursue to ensure peace and the restoration of a true and responsive government."

"Blessings worked well for you. Did you know it would?"

He cocked his head to one side, a gesture both endearing and modest. "I had faith. Now I had better leave you to your well-deserved rest. Events press on, comrade. I will not talk to you again until Arcadia is ours." As he finished speaking, he stood up and walked to the door.

"Comrade." She, too, stood up. "Why are we being held in quarantine?"

He smiled gently. "As long as the risk remains." And left the room.

She reached the door just as it sighed closed behind him. It was locked, of course; a means to ensure quarantine from the inside. She laid a hand on it, felt the unyielding metal cool her palms as she leaned against it as the hope that the pressure of her hand might open it cooled as well with each passing second. He had trapped her as neatly here as he had manipulated her into risking herself and her friends in the liberation of the Harsh 30s mine. That he no longer trusted her seemed obvious; the question now that she had to consider was whether he had ever trusted her, and whether her belief in Robbie Malcolm had caused her to be blinded to his suspicions. But she could not reconcile Pero's belief in Alexander Jehane with her own misgivings about him, and knowing Robbie as she did, could still only conclude that Robbie knew of him something she did not, and had still to learn.

"I will be patient, Robbie," she murmured to herself, and stepped back from the door.

"Did you want something?" asked Duri, coming from the other room.

"No," said Lily hastily. "Nothing."

Duri smiled warmly and perhaps apologetically as she walked past Lily to the quarantine lock. The door opened to produce an exchange of partners: Bach's high, exuberant trill as he was restored—at Jehane's pleasure, Lily reminded herself bitterly—to his mistress. Duri gave a slight, self-conscious wave and vanished as the door slipped to.

Which left her still trapped, Lily thought as she turned. To face the door that led into the second room. And she realized that yet another door in that long, finite corridor had closed, shutting her in. Because Kyosti had trapped her just as neatly. And in his case she had not even been, however naively, a willing accomplice.

She sank onto the couch, preferring, for the moment, to let Bach sing her to sleep than to deal with the consequences of that realization.

But waking unknown hours later, nothing had changed. And after all, when in doubt, she had always chosen action as her first resort.

She cleaned up a little, because it helped clear her mind, plugged Bach into the terminal that graced the front room, and ventured into the second.

"Kyosti." She paused in the arch that separated the two rooms.

The second room, in which Kyosti lay, was dim. Unlike the outer room, which looked directly out on the pristine counters of Medical, this tiny chamber had opaque walls, the only concession to privacy. The corner lighting had been muted until it was more a suggestion than a glow. The only real light came from the screen levered out over Kyosti's recumbent form. She knew he was not asleep because now and then he would lift his right hand and tap a few keys, coding some message or instruction.

Alien. He was—not human, or not fully human. Yet he looked human to her, lying there, not like some fantastic and dreadful creature that haunted the highroad on its inexorable path of vengeance. The idea of making love to that alien male who had lunged for the man on La Belle's bridge, had ripped his throat out—had scented the air when he entered, like an animal.

Like Kyosti did. The gesture, familiar then, was familiar because she had seen it before, not because of some deeply rooted memory from her ancient predecessors. And the thought of loving a je'jiri male appalled her.

Except that, even knowing what she did, he simply looked like Kyosti to her. As if she had known him too long to see him as anyone—any*thing*—else. She felt bewildered by her contradictory emotions, and still, above else, furious that he had trapped her so completely. Without ever telling her why he had done it.

"Have you slept at all?" she asked harshly, finding that her anger confused itself with a concern for his well-being. She sat on the edge of the couch, resting her hand in his hair.

His breathing altered slightly in reaction to her proximity, but now she could read what his response really was: he was taking in her scent. He did not need to look at her to make contact. She recognized finally that touch and smell and taste had always been the most vivid senses for him. She shifted her body just enough that his arm and chest settled into contact with her leg where she sat sideways beside him.

"Kyosti," she began again after it became clear that he was not going to answer her—or at least not in words. "You knew all along what would happen if you slept with me."

This time she waited him out. Information scrolled past on the screen until he lifted a hand to press pause.

"Yes."

"You knew, and you did it anyway."

"Yes," he repeated.

"Without asking, if I had had other lovers. Without explaining anything to me, about the circumstances of such a—partnership. You forced me into a—a contract whose terms I was ignorant of. Whose terms I didn't even know existed!"

"Yes." He did not move.

All her breath came out in an angry rush. "No wonder Master Heredes was so furious! When I think—" She had to pause for a moment to let the full implications of just what it was that he had done to her sink in.

"Would you have slept with me, had you known?" he asked quietly.

"No! Of course not."

"Well." He flipped off the "pause" button and let the information begin to scroll across the screen again. "There you are."

She reached past him and flipped the terminal off completely. "Just give me your attention for one damn second," she snapped. "It may be perfectly easy for you to dismiss this with a blithe 'there you are,' but it's a far different question for me. I'd like to know just how you thought you had any right to subject me to your kind of—partnership."

He winced, reacting to the caustic tone of her voice on the word *partnership,* but he did not reply immediately. His fingers brushed the controls of the terminal, but he did not turn it on.

"Well?" she demanded.

"I had no *right,*" he said softly. "The truth is—" He faltered.

"The truth is?"

For the first time, he looked up at her. In the luminescent glow of the corner lights, his skin seemed as pale as hers, but it was a human pallor. "You aren't going to like this."

She laughed, a truncated noise that was more pain than humor. "You've said that to me before, but this time—Sit up, damn it. How can I talk to you when you lie there like an invalid?"

He sat up obediently, the thin blanket that covered him rustling down around him with a whisper of sound.

"This time, you'll tell me."

He lifted one hand to brush the curve of her throat. "I was running," he continued at last in a low voice. "Running from what the League did to me—locking me away. I was afraid they were trying to drive me"—he hesitated—"insane. By the time they allowed me to recant, I would have said anything to get out of that prison. When I saw you and Master Heredes..." He trailed off.

"Yes?" she asked, with more patience now, because she remembered the first time he had told her that she was beautiful.

"I could tell there was a link between you. A bond of—family. Then he told La Belle that you were his daughter."

"I remember," she replied, but she was thinking of the locked room on La Belle's ship where they had first made love.

"Oh, Lily," he murmured, moving his fingers along the tracery of her jawline. His gaze was agonizingly somber. "I realized that if I slept with you, I would, by linking myself to you, automatically get Heredes's protection."

She hit him.

"You bastard!" she yelled, jumping up.

He gasped, clutching his abdomen. "Did you pull that punch?"

"Of course," she said scornfully. "Not that you deserved it." Hot, angry tears, as yet unshed, scorched her eyes.

He tried to laugh, but all he could manage through the gasping, short breaths occasioned by her blow was a kind of shuddering chuckle. "Lily, my heart." He leaned forward while she was still surprised by his laughter and pulled her against him. "I love you."

"You *what?*" she asked, standing very still.

He murmured something into her clothing which she could not understand.

"I once told Finch," she muttered, exasperated, "that I was looking for someone unpredictable. I thought you were traumatized by what happened on La Belle's bridge."

He moved his head back to look up at her, and he frowned. "I am," he said irritably. "It just occurred to me that this entire conversation has probably been taped for the edification of our friend Jehane. I can't *believe* I let that slip—"

"Damn Jehane." She found herself inordinately pleased by the very humanness of his annoyance at himself, and she used the leverage of her standing to push him down onto the couch. "And anyway," she added, kissing him on the lips, "I told Bach to interrupt any recording mechanisms."

Kyosti smiled and traced the soft angle of her lips with one finger. "Lily," he began, then shook his head and let her kiss him again.

Jehane followed Central's routed fleet to Arcadia. Lily watched their progress on the terminal hooked into the suite, alternating time with Kyosti's monitoring of the condition of the patients injured in the battle at Blessings. Of the forty-two worst cases, all but four survived, a statistic that led Doctor Prachenduriyang in to visit more frequently and at greater length than she ever had when Lily had been in quarantine alone.

And when Kyosti, rather than falling ill, quickly recovered, Duri gave up trying to make sense of his blood sample and instead enlisted his aid in coordinating the report on the plague itself. Lily did not venture to intervene in this project, although she recognized immediately that Hawk had no intention of giving the game away—yet.

The *Boukephalos* swung into orbit around Arcadia without any resistance: whatever station garrisons had not surrendered had already been taken by force by the advance assault teams. Kyosti spent more time relaying treatments to physicians on the other ships, and convinced Duri to send the worst casualties to the *Forlorn Hope,* where a specific ward could be set up to treat them.

And one by one, across Arcadia's great metropolis, the ward councils of each district repudiated Central's rule and welcomed Jehane, until the only place left that remained armed, garrisoned, and defiant was Central itself, surrounded by the walls that had always separated it from the people it had governed.

Jehane came to Medical. Kuan-yin trailed like a hound at his heels.

"Comrade Heredes," he said, while Doctor Prachenduriyang dismantled the quarantine and freed Lily and Kyosti from its sheath. "I would like you to accompany me downside."

"Of course, comrade." She whistled to Bach.

"Comrade Hawk will serve our cause best by transferring back to the clinic on the *Forlorn Hope.*"

Kyosti merely nodded his head, not glancing at Lily, without any attempt to argue or be even mildly sarcastic.

"Well," said Jehane. Lily wondered if he was surprised at

the meekness with which Kyosti received his orders, but he had only paused to glance at his wrist-com. "Let it be so." He swept out.

Kuan-yin paused in the doorway to look at Lily, a glare replete with dark warnings. In the hall beyond, comrade Vanov waited.

Lily turned as soon as Kuan-yin left, but Kyosti was seated at Duri's main terminal and seemed intent on his work, ignoring her.

Duri came forward and offered Lily a little bag in which to stow her few possessions.

"So the quarantine is off again?" Lily asked negligently.

Duri shrugged, but she looked troubled. She glanced toward the door to Medical, as if she were afraid that one of Jehane's lieutenants might be listening in. "It does seem a little abrupt," she began, and then she turned away quickly, as if she had said too much.

Lily went across to stand beside Kyosti. Although he did not look up, she knew he had followed her every movement around the room. Bach hovered an arm's length above the terminal.

"Kyosti," she began, because this time Jehane's separation of them seemed to her determined to keep them divided for a period she could not divine the end of.

He glanced up. Although he smiled, she detected in it a warning to say no more. When she did not, he gave her the briefest of winks and then turned back to his work. With a brief good-bye to Duri, Lily followed the trail of Jehane's procession down to the shuttle bay. Comrade Vanov, silent, accompanied her.

To find, to her astonishment, a familiar face waiting in docking.

"Robbie!" she cried. She flung herself forward and hugged him enthusiastically.

Remembered the bridge of La Belle Dame, and pushed him away.

"Robbie." She realized that she was grinning like an idiot, partly out of the pure joy of seeing him, and partly because he was the perfect solution to her problem: if anything happened to Kyosti, Robbie would see to it that the Hierakis Formula got out. All along, she had known that he would be the most important person to tell. "But how did you come *here?*" she demanded, flush with knowing that she could in this way put to rest her worries about Jehane.

He, too, was smiling, but with a gravity that reflected the seriousness of the situation. "I came to escort Jehane to his people. As is my part as his representative on Arcadia."

"Oh, Robbie." Lily chuckled. "You haven't changed at all. It's so good to see you."

"I knew it was right to send you to Jehane," he replied, his voice resonant with the depth of his sincerity. "I knew you would prove valuable to his cause."

Lily could not help but frown slightly. "Yes." She was saved from having to say more by the entrance of Jehane himself. He had perfected the art of pausing at exactly the right moment to draw attention to himself without overtly seeming to seek it.

Robbie's face shone with the illumination of the converted as he gazed on Jehane, oblivious to the rest of the group clustered around that man. He took two steps forward and thrust out his hand. "Comrade. I am Pero. I am honored to be the one chosen to escort you to our people."

For the barest instant Jehane hesitated, at this rather brash assumption of equality. Kuan-yin advanced quickly to brush aside this impudence, but Jehane moved smoothly forward to circumvent her action, and clasped Robbie's hand.

"Comrade Pero," he said warmly. "The honor is mine. Shall we go?" He motioned for Pero to precede him up the ramp into the shuttle and followed him like any humble acolyte.

Left behind, standing beside Lily, Kuan-yin scowled.

25 The Hierakis Formula

****

"But Robbie," began Lily for the third time. "I don't think you quite see."

Robbie shook his head with the same conviction that informed all of his actions. "It's exactly because I *do* see, Lya, that I see the importance of telling Jehane about this miraculous discovery."

Lily sighed, because it was impossible to argue with Robbie when he was in one of his righteous moods. But the sigh also provoked a smile, because she could as easily have been having this conversation one year ago as now, so little had things changed with him.

She and Robbie stood at the kitchen wall of his tiny apartment, washing dishes. His way of living seemed to have altered not at all, except that this apartment was in Anselm District instead of Zanta, closer to the walls of Central. A nameless benefactor had provided it for him when he had been forced by the closing net of Central Intelligence to move from his last residence some two months previous.

"*I* still don't see," Lily said in an attempt to change the subject, "why you didn't attend Jehane's council this afternoon."

"I have done my part," said Robbie, taking the dish she handed him. "I have delivered Arcadia to Jehane with the least possible violence. Councils of war are not a place where I have any expertise."

"But for all you *did*," Lily insisted. "I'd think you at least deserved a place there, whether or not you spoke."

Robbie regarded her solemnly. "Lya, I did not work all these years for some material reward that will prove as fleeting as the day is short in winter. I worked for the people."

Lily laughed. "Hoy. You're the only person I know who can say that with such perfect sincerity that I believe it."

He narrowed his eyes, puzzled. "Have you grown so cynical in so short a time?" he asked, sounding almost pained. "I hadn't thought to see that quality emerge in you."

"Cynical?" She rested her elbows on the flat edge of the opaque plastine sink. "I hope not cynical. That's a rather ugly philosophy. But clear eyed, I hope, enough to distinguish sincerity from the trappings of altruism that often disguise purely selfish interests."

"The ability to read the human heart without error is a talent that not even *I* can claim," said Robbie with the briefest of smiles.

"No," said Lily softly. "I'm not sure anyone can."

"In any case," continued Robbie with the unerring scent of a hound, "I believe we were not talking about the human heart, but about this Formula that Kyosti has discovered."

Lily sighed again, realizing that she would not divert his attention so easily. And yet, it was right that Robbie be told. Behind them, Bach sat plugged into the apartment terminal, monitoring the various nets, official and unofficial, that had sprung up to accommodate the chaos on Arcadia. All transmissions into and out of Central had been blocked so thoroughly that not even Bach could access them.

"No," she replied. "He didn't discover it. Remember he's from the League—"

"Yes. It's still difficult for me to believe that the League exists, or at least that we can have been in contact with the home worlds at long last. But it seems also to me appropriate that Kyosti's gift—for it is a gift, a gift for all humanity—to the citizens of the Reft springs out of the journey of a few intrepid explorers from the place that birthed us, come to find their lost children."

"And stuck here when they couldn't go back," Lily murmured, but replied in a normal tone, "What I'm trying to explain, Robbie, and why I'm telling *you*, is that we have to make sure that *everyone* gets this gift. Not that it's reserved for a privileged few, like the old drugs that only rich people like the Sars, or the Senators, can afford."

"There." Robbie lifted a hand as any orator does when the point returns to their favor. "As you say. The Hierakis Formula will be the crowning glory of Jehane's triumph. *He* can see that it is disseminated to all the people, even to the meekest and the poorest and the most insignificant."

"Even to the Ridanis?" she asked caustically.

"Of course to the Ridanis."

"Even with the terrible prejudice there is against them?"

"But not in Jehane's forces. He has decreed it so."

"Decreeing it so doesn't make it so. You know that."

"Yes, but the example must begin somewhere. Then, like throwing a stone into a pond, the ripples begin to spread out until they have thrown waves up on every shore."

"Oh, Robbie," Lily said, exasperated. She handed him the last dish. "Remind me not to argue with you. You're impossible."

"Then you see the necessity of informing Jehane?"

"No, I don't." She considered. "Not yet. Let me talk to Kyosti first."

"Lya." He was stern, now. "This Formula is not some possession you own, to dispense at your will."

She took her hands out of the water and turned to face him. "Would you tell Jehane even if I ask you not to?"

He bowed his head, raised it to gaze at her with the fierce honesty that invested his entire being. "Yes. This is too important."

"I'll see if I can reach Kyosti now." She dried her hands off and went across to stand behind Bach. "The council won't be out for a few hours, I hope," she added to herself before whistling for Bach to get a channel to the *Forlorn Hope* with all haste.

All haste still took over half an hour, as it involved several illicit relays patched through planetwide nets and at least two satellites out to the perihelion orbit beyond Arcadia's moon in which the *Forlorn Hope* and several smaller ships circled the planet. Most of the rest of the fleet, minus their ground mercenaries, had been sent out to patrol the outer system and the web of shifting windows that gave access to the rest of Reft space beyond.

Finch was on comm.

"No," he said, his replies delayed by the distance. "Our mercenary tens have *not* been transferred downside. We're the only ship that didn't have ours sent. But we're on a skeleton crew in any case, so it isn't a strong complement. Why? Is the assault beginning?"

"Finch." She rested a hand on Bach's cool surface as she spoke into the terminal. "Please recall that despite the blocking, Central may be able to monitor this."

"Oh." A longer than usual pause. "I've got the com linked through to Medical. Do you want to go ahead?"

"Just one question, Finch." She hesitated and glanced back at Robbie, but he was cleaning up the rest of the counter. "Have you—I mean you, personally—had any problem since Hawk came back on board?"

This time the pause was so long that Lily thought the connection had been cut. Finally Finch's voice crackled back over the terminal. "Lily. I swear to you that that man is—maybe he's not insane, but he's not—normal. If you mean, has he tried to attack me, no, he hasn't. But every time he comes into the same room I'm in, he insists on coming over and"—even though disembodied and strung out across uncounted hundreds of kilometers of atmosphere and empty space, the slight shake in Finch's voice was discernable—"and putting a hand on me, touching me, like he's proving something to me, or to himself. I don't know. It's *weird*, Ransome. I'm doing my best to avoid him."

Lily had not realized that she was holding her breath. She let it out now. "Thank you, Finch," she answered, aware that her voice also shook slightly as she spoke. "Thank you for—forgiving him."

"Oh, certainly not." Distance muted the sarcasm—a quality, she noted bitterly, that he had not possessed those years ago on Unruli. "Consider it my pleasure. I'll put you through to Medical now."

There was no identifiable shift as Kyosti's voice superseded Finch's. The change came so abruptly that for a startled instant Lily thought that Finch's voice had suddenly been altered by some trick of comm.

"Lily? Is there a problem? Are you all right?"

"I'm fine, Hawk. But I need to talk to you about the Formula."

"Is this line screened? Is it being monitored?"

"Kyosti. I told Robbie."

A break in sequence as Kyosti took in this information. Robbie walked out of the small common room into the tinier sleeping chamber, and shut the door discreetly behind him.

"Lily."

Another break. She could not tell from the single word whether he was furious, exasperated, or thrilled.

"Well, Lily. This limits our choices, I think." The tone reminded her fleetingly of Master Heredes. "I suppose he wants to tell Jehane."

"Of course. But considering where you and I are now, I thought it best to bring one more person in on the—facts."

"Yes." Static spit and hummed as he considered. "I wish I had gotten the opportunity to speak privately with you— under circumstances in which I could speak." A pause while she—and perhaps he—considered the last circumstances under which they had been truly private.

"You've had a plan all along," she broke in, scattering the static.

"Yes." Another break. "We'll have to act fast. It's time to bring in accomplices up here. We have no choice. I don't trust many people, Lily—" He let the comment hang, without finishing the thought.

"Sometimes you have no alternative."

"Damn," he said, but she thought there was a smile in his tone. "I might even be surprised by their trustworthiness. When is Jehane's council?"

"It's going on now."

"Why aren't you there?"

"I wasn't invited. Robbie wouldn't go."

"Lily, my heart, then we must *really* act fast, if you weren't invited. I'm going to send Pinto down with a shipment and some instructions. Where can you meet him?"

She whistled. *Bach, where is the nearest port?* Watched as Bach pulled up a zoning map on the screen and flashed a location. "Merrimet Port."

Crackle studded the quiet stillness of the apartment as Kyosti did calculations on his end of the transmission. "Meet him there in seven hours. Give me a berth number."

"Hold on." She whistled, and waited while Bach scrolled through Port records. "Berth One-five-two." Behind, Robbie came back into the room. "I'm signing off, Kyosti. Acknowledge "

"Be cautious, my heart," he replied. "Accepted."

The connection dissolved with a flare of static that dissolved in its turn into the soft hum of the terminal. Bach set to work to eradicate all evidence of the transmission.

Robbie had put on his overcoat. "I'm going to the council. Do you want to come with me? In good conscience I cannot keep this news from Jehane any longer. I'm sorry if that pains you." He regarded her seriously, intent on her feelings and yet, she saw, always ready to disregard the individual for the sake of the whole.

"Oh, Robbie." She shook her head, unable to fault him for the philosophy that drove his entire being. "I may argue with your choice, but I can't fault your nobility of purpose. I want the Hierakis Formula to be distributed to everyone. You know that. But the fact is that I don't trust Jehane to see that it is done." And waited, because she had not wanted to say it.

Robbie blinked, uncomprehending, at her. "I don't understand you."

"That's why you're Pero," she replied, feeling that now that she had set the machine in motion, the inevitable would come. "And yes, of course, I'll come with you."

Jehane's people had taken over one of the rail hubs, built underground, as their headquarters. Even with identification, Lily and Robbie had to pass through two security checkpoints—at the second of which Lily was relieved of her pistol—before a small woman in Jehanish whites ushered them into an empty suite of offices outside the concourse that had been set up to serve as the council of war.

Through two sets of open doors they heard the chaotic murmur of many voices. Lily edged forward to look, but as if in response to her presence, Kuan-yin appeared in the far doorway like a fierce warden and, seeing Lily, leveled her intense and challenging gaze on the smaller woman. A moment later movement fluttered behind Kuan-yin. Several soldiers flooded the corridor, driving Kuan-yin before her until she came out into the suite and stared at Lily and Robbie as she took up a position at the far door.

Two people Lily did not recognize entered, followed by two fleet mercenary captains she knew by sight, and Jehane. The small woman who had ushered Lily and Robbie into the suite spoke in a low voice to Jehane as he halted.

He acknowledged Lily with a brief nod, but his attention focused on Robbie.

Pero came forward and with his usual neglect of ceremony he addressed Jehane without any formality but a brief shake of hands.

"Comrade. I have great news." Pitched to suit the small chamber, Robbie's clear voice filled it to the corners and ceiling without seeming strained or overloud. "A gift of incalculable value for the citizens of the Reft, one that, hand in hand with your restoration of a government for all people, will crown the glory of your triumph."

Lily slowly edged backward, effacing herself, until she stood against one wall, as unobtrusive as possible.

"Comrade Pero." Jehane glanced briefly at his wrist-com, but without seeming impatient, and glanced up once to check Kuan-yin's position. "I am sorry that you did not choose to be present at this council. You know how highly I value you, and how important your work has been, but I wonder if the council would not have been a better platform for your news. We have made our decision, and now have little time in which to implement our plans."

Robbie smiled humbly. "Comrade, I would never have interrupted you had I not thought the cause urgent. In any case, I only learned of it an hour since. Have you ever heard of the Hierakis Formula?"

The effect of these words on Jehane was electric. Although he did not look at her, Lily felt the full force of his awareness center on her for a brief and searingly uncomfortable moment that made her question seriously for the first time the wisdom of telling Robbie about the Formula. But to her astonishment, Jehane's answer, when it came, was delivered in the mildest of tones.

"I have heard the term, yes, but I know neither its origin nor its meaning."

Robbie's face betrayed the simple pleasure he felt in being the bearer of such momentous tidings. He hesitated only long enough to glance at Lily, as if to offer her the privilege, but she shook her head, a minute gesture in keeping with her effacement, and he went on.

"The Hierakis Formula, comrade—comrades—is a life-extension serum developed and perfected in the home worlds. It is a simple draught administered to each individual, and with the slightest of side effects: about two to three weeks of flulike symptoms. And it effectively alters human"—he shook his head—"I am no physician or geneticist, comrades, to describe the physiological workings of such a treatment, but the end result is that humans can expect to live upward of one hundred eighty years."

In the silence created by this speech, the echo of a distant rail lumbering through some subterranean corridor could be heard, the deep core of human interchange bound for further destinations.

Jehane stood poised as if on the edge of a precipice, but it was a man Lily did not recognize who spoke first.

"We haven't had reason to disbelieve you before, comrade Pero, but even if such a—a formula exists, we were long since abandoned by the old worlds, and the ways back have long since been lost. So how are we to benefit from this now?"

"Because some people from the old worlds have gotten through to Reft space. Just a few, mind you," he added quickly, seeing the stir that this additional revelation caused in his audience—all excepting Jehane, of course. "Not any wholesale migration, and more by accident than design, I suppose. But one of them has the Formula and has begun to manufacture it. Here. In Reft space."

Several people began to speak at once. Jehane lifted a hand, and silence descended again.

"Comrade Pero." His voice was soft. "What are you suggesting?"

For the first time, Robbie looked taken aback, but he recovered quickly. "According to this physician, the Formula is easily manufactured except for the minute components of its base. The base is what he has been making, with a view toward distributing it to the entire population. Comrade, as soon as Central has surrendered—which they will inevitably do—you can announce this great boon at the same time you announce the restoration."

Jehane shook his head slightly, as if saddened by some thought that only he could comprehend. "My dear Robbie. Only consider. There will be *riot* if such news gets out. First we must consolidate our government. Then manufacture this Formula. Then we must develop a system of dissemination, and work out the mechanics of the administration of its distribution."

"But I didn't explain," Robbie continued, breaking into Jehane's cool recitation of these difficulties. "The beauty of the Formula is that once the base is widely available, *any* dispensary can blend the correct ingredients. Any clinic—even those in the poorest neighborhoods. It needs no centralized distribution. It truly can be available to all."

Jehane sighed. "And what of people who manufacture it incorrectly? Who hoard it and sell it at increased prices? Poor clinics may not have the facilities. Such a valuable"—he hesitated—"such a gift *must* be controlled from a central source that will assure that it will be doled out fairly, and judiciously."

"No," said Robbie.

The force of that simple word permeating the room gave Lily a sudden shudder of fear. Kuan-yin took a step forward, but some infinitesimal movement by Jehane stopped her from coming any farther.

"No," repeated Robbie. "I appreciate the difficulties inherent in distributing something that people so desperately want. That is exactly the reason that the information must be made available to every person—over the net, broadcast, sent to every terminal, every clinic, available to be bought in every store. Surely you of all people, comrade Jehane, understand that this Formula must never become a privilege, restricted to those who can pay enough, or who line up for rewards. The Hierakis Formula is a right, one each and every citizen of the Reft possesses, and I will do everything in my power to see that the knowledge of it, and the base that is needed for manufacture, is disseminated through every means *I* have at my disposal."

Jehane smiled, looking a little tired. "Of course you are right, comrade Pero. Your argument has convinced me."

But Lily noted that his eyes took careful stock of each person who stood in the room, or near enough to have heard Robbie's news. She eased herself two unobtrusive steps along the wall toward the door, but Jehane's soldiers stood as intent as ever—if not more so, now—at their posts.

"But first," Jehane continued to Robbie, "before we send you off to begin your task, perhaps you will accompany us to Central."

Robbie bowed his head in acknowledgment of the honor accorded him by this offer. "I have no talent for such methods of war, comrade, or I would gladly accompany you. I ask that you excuse me."

"Ah, but there ought to be very little fighting. I long since determined that the cost in lives of our soldiers to storm the walls of Central would be prohibitive. Violence is not always the most expedient solution."

"Then?"

"*Vende patria*, comrade. A man who knows when the time is right to shift allegiance." Jehane glanced at the doors that lead into the concourse. "Where is our new colleague?" he asked. "He was supposed to be with us now."

"He's coming now, comrade," replied one of the soldiers.

There was a rustle of movement, and a slight reordering of positions, as two new people entered the room. Lily recognized the tall, white-haired man immediately: Pinto's father, Senator Isaiah.

26 Death by Water

****

Isaiah did not recognize her: that became apparent when the
Senator, looking carefully around the room, did not give Lily
a second's glance, dismissing her as unimportant. At Robbie
he paused, but then dismissed him as well and came forward
to stand beside Jehane.

"We'd best go," he said to Jehane, sounding both impatient
and, surprising to Lily, respectful. "The override program I
installed in Central's main computer won't wait, and we have
to strike as soon as it goes into action."

Jehane nodded at Kuan-yin to precede the party out of the
room.

"Then it *is* true," Isaiah continued in the pause while
Kuan-yin reordered the soldiers to provide what she considered adequate security. "That you personally led the breakout
on Blessings against two centuries of Immortals—and made it
out alive." The awe in his voice gave Lily a sudden understanding of the obvious respect with which he treated Jehane—
not a politician's respect, but the giddy fear that a true man of
action and physical power instills in a man of more sedentary
habits.

"I was not alone," said Jehane. He checked his wrist-com.
"You are right, Senator. We have very little time."

"We're ready," said Kuan-yin, consulting comrade Vanov,
who had just appeared from the corridor. "A number of

270

vehicles are leaving this area now. Our truck is waiting to take us to the tac center."

Senator Isaiah seemed about to ask a question, but Jehane efficiently swept him out of the room, leaving the rest of his retinue to follow behind. Robbie did not even pause, but followed out the two Arcadians Lily did not know. The two commanders hurried after them, but Lily hung back. Robbie's decision she could no longer influence; now she needed to meet Pinto and put into motion whatever plan Kyosti had devised. It would be easy enough to fall behind, to slip off undetected.

"Comrade." Comrade Vanov, flanked by four soldiers, halted behind her. "We've orders to be sure that everyone here goes on to headquarters."

Lily eyed him speculatively, but he had too much backup, and he was too aware, and too well armed. All the doors but one in that long corridor had now closed before her: she followed Jehane's party.

The truck in which they traveled had the exterior of a common cargo van, but inside it had been redesigned to carry passengers in comfortable padded benches. She sat in silence in the back row, Vanov on one side, a soldier on the other, and listened to the quiet flow of conversation from the seats in front. Several conversations intertwined, eddying around Jehane's silence: The Hierakis Formula. Jehane's single-handed routing of the Immortals on Blessings. The disposition of Jehane's forces surrounding Central, poised at every gate in the huge wall that would soon be opening, unbeknown to those besieged inside, at the command of one of their own, turned traitor. How Jehane had had to be talked out of leading the first assault himself.

Robbie sat with a distant, intent look on his face that betrayed to Lily that he was thinking very hard about something or, perhaps, planning a speech. Jehane sat perfectly still, face impassive, in that way that only honed fighters perfect: conserving their energy. Now and then he shifted his gaze, examining his retinue.

Without realizing it, she discovered that she was looking directly at him, and he at her. An instant, where he was perhaps as unguarded as she, and the kind of communication that is always wordless, and the more profound for it, passed between them.

He did not trust her. She knew it from his gaze. Felt it. But more than that, worse by far, she had a deep glimpse of what her instincts had felt all along: he was a genuinely dangerous man—not because he did not believe in the revolution, but because he believed he was the only person fit to lead it. It was her trust in Robbie that had blinded her; Robbie's idealism that blinded him. Of course it had been right to tell Robbie about the Hierakis Formula—but by doing so, and by coming along with him when he made the inevitable and—she saw now—misguided choice to tell Jehane, she had forced Jehane's hand.

He smiled at her, softly mesmerizing, and she knew without a doubt that he did not intend to let her or Robbie out of his zone of control until things had fallen out as he wished them to. All the doors were shut now. Hawk, and whatever allies he chose to trust on the *Forlorn Hope*, were alone, because she always acted before she really investigated her gut feelings.

She wrenched her gaze away from his hypnotic one and did not look up again for the rest of the ride.

Headquarters proved to be one of Arcadia's large net centers: broadcast headquarters for several image and sound nets. From the outside, little distinguished it from the rest of the buildings surrounding it, but inside, the security measures were both obvious and brutal. Everyone but Jehane and Kuan-yin was searched twice. Lily was relieved of even her com-screen. The soldiers under Kuan-yin's command entered fully armed.

Again, when she lagged behind as the others swept into the elevator, Vanov prodded her forward, not very gently. He was enjoying himself.

They came out of the elevator into another security checkpoint, and then walked down a long corridor studded with white-clad soldiers at every branching and door. Eventually they came to a huge room filled with screens and consoles and banks of computers that all served to coordinate the flood of information and images and transmissions that intersected in this chamber.

Lily came up beside Robbie as they entered and paused, taking in the melding of images and sound and the quiet intensity of the people staffing the consoles.

"Perfect," said Robbie in a strangely normal voice. "I'll get to work right away encoding and positioning the message about the Hierakis Formula so that it can be broadcast as soon as Central has surrendered. But I'll need additional information from you, Lily."

Lily glanced to either side, aware that although Jehane had gone forward to greet the staff, Vanov stood less than four paces from them. The soldier glanced across at Kuan-yin, who had followed Jehane. *Her* gaze was fixed on Robbie.

"Robbie," Lily said slowly. "I don't have any more information."

He glanced at her, clearly puzzled by her tone of voice, and then looked straight at Vanov. "Comrade." His gaze, as always, was open and direct. "Perhaps you can ask your commander to introduce me to whichever of your staff here can assign me a free terminal."

"What for?" asked Vanov rudely.

If his bullying tone startled Robbie, he did not show it. Jehane had circled around the room quickly and now returned efficiently to their side. "To encode and position a message about the Formula," Robbie answered, leaving the *of course* unsaid but clearly understood.

"Of course," interposed Jehane smoothly as he came up to them, as if he were echoing Robbie's unspoken words. "Comrade." He looked at the green-clad civilian beside him. "Comrade Pero needs a console. Do we have one free?"

"Yes, comrade Jehane. Certainly." The man bobbed his head enthusiastically. "This way, comrade Pero. I have heard your speeches many a time, and my own cousin was swayed by your 'waters shall not rise' speech last summer when before she had nothing but scorn for the movement. And the 'I see this system' speech, too, I recall with great pride, although perhaps"—his voice lowered a note in respectful sorrow—"those were your predecessor's words."

"Yes," said Robbie simply. "They were."

Both Jehane and Kuan-yin watched as the green-clad man led Robbie away. Lily tried to drift unobtrusively away, to escape into the maze of consoles that littered the floor of the chamber, but Vanov continued to trail her at a distance. She roamed slowly through the activity, marking the three exits from the room—each heavily guarded—watching Kuan-yin's brisk circuit of all the soldiers stationed at doors and on the balcony that led to a plastiglassed booth overhead. Jehane had halted beside the large central console and now spoke with a nervous-looking Senator Isaiah and the two mercenary commanders.

Across the array of screens, Lily saw images of units massing for the strike, or else static screening whatever existed inside Central's walls. Many people spoke in the room, collating or processing the deluge of knowledge and communications that collected in this chamber, but overall it came to her as a hushed buzz, anticipatory and controlled, not frantic.

Lily strolled back to stop behind Robbie. At first, consumed in his work, he did not notice her, but eventually he paused and glanced up at her, questioning. Vanov had stationed himself about eight paces away.

"Robbie," she said in an undertone. "Do me a favor. Let Bach know where we are. But don't do it overtly. Just let a few of the old codes we used to use to run the underground nets creep in. Bach will trace us."

"Lya," he began, and stopped, glancing first at Vanov and then up.

Looking up, she saw that Kuan-yin had ascended the stairs to the balcony and now stood staring directly down at them. "Just do it, Robbie," Lily said quietly. "While you're at it, see that Bach gets a complete transcript of whatever it is you're writing, and set the transmission codes to activate automatically at a preset time as soon as you're finished."

"You're wrong, Lya," he replied. "But I will do as you say because I have too much respect for you to refuse you."

"I hope so," she murmured, and she touched his shoulder, a brief contact. She eased away from him and repeated her circuit of the room. This time she went toward each door and was neatly circumvented by Vanov before she could reach the exit. Not threatened, really; but he clearly relished this game. He finally told her that he had received orders to let no one enter or leave until the operation was over.

Kuan-yin no longer stood on the balcony. One possible, final exit. Lily turned away from Vanov and climbed the stairs. This time, to her surprise, he did not follow her.

The control booth at the top of the stairs held five large consoles and five technicians, each strapped into a chair much like Pinto strapped into his pilot's seat. They were too intent on whatever processing they were involved in to be aware of her. She walked past them and found, around a corner, another door. It was unguarded. And it opened to her touch.

She came out onto twilight.

The sun set into a rippling flow of land that trembled under each lance of light. Wind whipped her hair back, tugged at her clothes. She stood on a balcony, wrist-thick metal rods fencing in a rectangle of balcony some three meters wide and twenty long. The building rose about twenty meters above her, sheer and pocked with light-reflecting windows that gave back the sun's red glow, and at least twenty meters below, she estimated, running into a barren sheet of land that extended to the horizon where the sun melted down into it, seeming to dissolve in its undulations.

Immediately she knew: get Robbie, get some kind of rope, divert Vanov, and they could escape.

Then she walked to the waist-high fence and gripped it with both hands, staring down.

It was not land. It was water.

She tightened her grip on the rod and fought a searing swell of dizziness. Waves shattered and dissolved against the walls of the building below her. The building itself thrust out far into this—sea.

For that was what it was. She had thought the pond in Zanta District park immense; she recalled the vast, terrifying depths of the irrigation lake that she and Master Heredes and Kyosti had entered into—a foreign, dark substance.

But from space, one saw the unimaginably vast stretches of blue surrounding the lands of Arcadia: this was the ocean, and it surrounded her now on three sides.

What need for the white-clad soldiers who guarded the other doors now? What need for comrade Vanov?

Sun rippled in water. Endless kilometers of water stretched out before her, an infinite expanse of depthless sea. Awe and terror poised like equally matched opponents on the edge of her thoughts.

She unfastened her hands from the railing and walked to one end of the balcony. The building stretched out on either side, at least twenty meters on each side, if not more, and only far away could she see the dark, solid bulk of land, lapped by the white foam of water spilling onto the shore.

"Where is my son?"

The quiet voice surprised her. She whirled, cursing herself for letting anyone come so close without her knowing. Whatever she meant to say died on her lips.

Senator Isaiah faced her. The last rays of the sun bleached his hair and skin so that he looked quite old. His hands trembled as he set them with deliberate effort on the railing.

"Where is my son?" he repeated. "Or is he dead?"

"I didn't think you recognized me," she said.

He shook his head, still imperious and impatient although he had so recently betrayed everything that was his. "But Jonathan—"

"He's alive. He's a pilot in Jehane's fleet. He's found friends, or at least people who think of him as a friend when he's willing to let them."

His hand steadied on the railing. "But he's alive. Does he still owe you his life?"

"Owe me his life?"

"The Ridani debt of honor: kinnas. He told me when—when I last saw him. I'm sure you remember it." His voice cracked with bitterness. "He never would accept that his mother marked him irretrievably. I tried to stop her, but those damned tattoos are fanatic about their markings. Once he understood that he could not be my legitimate child he threw it in my face—forced me at every opportunity to confront that fact publicly. What was I to do?"

"Are you asking me for absolution?" Lily asked quietly.

"No." The wind seamed up the deep creases etched into his face. "I neither want nor would accept anyone's pardon. But if he is still bound to you, by that debt, I ask that you take care of him."

The sun melded at last with the sea. Stars began to show one by one in the dark dome above. In the distance, light flashed on the black ridge of land, and a moment later they heard an explosion, echoed by more distant ones.

"It's started," said Senator Isaiah. "Central is falling." He turned and walked back into the building, his step as soundless on the smooth surface of the balcony as the passing of the mantle of power from his shoulders to Jehane's.

Lily stood alone on the balcony and watched the distant play of light and sound. Stars bloomed above her, each appearing brighter than the last as the dusk shadowed into night. On the horizon, where the last dim remains of the

sun's light edged the far line of the sea, a single blazing star
came to life like an echo of the fire and explosion illuminating
the land. The wind brought the muted sounds of the assault
to her and, occasionally, as it shifted, stripped them away.

She felt a peculiar detachment, gazing at this tumult that
touched her so deeply and yet did not touch her at all. The
storms of Unruli could never be experienced abstractly. Every action on Unruli stemmed from an awareness of their
danger; each foray into the outside sprang only from dire
necessity or a reckless urge for adventure.

If Jehane had not decided, years ago, to foment his revolution, would the natural course of events have driven her to
this ocean, this shore, anyway? Or was this his storm, artificially constructed and set into action by his desires and his
hand?

Movement at the door. She shrank back into the corner,
back pressed against the cold railing.

"—that Formula is too valuable to us to waste by letting it
be uselessly dispersed to every worthless smuggler and poor,
ignorant Ridani when instead it can be a tool. An invaluable
tool." He paused. Because it was Jehane, the pause itself was
redolent with unspoken communication. "But I know of no
way to convince Robert Malcolm of this, while he prepares
even as we speak to broadcast this discovery to the entire
Reft."

"I do," said Kuan-yin.

"Do you," replied Jehane without any intonation at all.

Kuan-yin turned and left the balcony. Lily held her breath.
She could see Jehane's outline silhouetted against the lighter
backdrop of sea and sky, his golden hair showing as a pale
reflection of the lost sun. He moved along the balcony, face
turned to the ocean. Lily wondered if Halfway, the planet
Mendi Mun had grown up on, had oceans as broad as these,
and if it was such oceans he was remembering now in his
seemingly aimless stroll down the length of the railing.

Except that he was Mendi Mun no longer. He shifted
abruptly and with the decisive bolt of a trained fighter
obliterated the distance between him and the corner in which
she hid.

For an instant, she thought of breaking for free ground.
But there was no free ground here—she had seen to that—
and in that instant's hesitation he had her.

With both arms pulled uncomfortably up behind her, she could not move without giving him greater purchase to hurt her. He held her as close as any lover might, his face a hand's breadth away. So close that his body pressed the medallion—the one Master Heredes had given her—into the skin below her throat. She had lost her breathing when he had grabbed her; now she struggled to calm herself, to center and relax. But even as she relaxed, he kept his grip perfectly balanced to counter any move, any break, she might make.

"Never let an Immortal get the jump on you," she said, not a little disgusted with herself.

Jehane smiled. "Now. Give me the Hierakis Formula. "His voice was soft as a caress.

"I don't know it."

His expression did not change. "Not good enough, Lily Ransome. I know where to get it. I've already put in a call to the *Forlorn Hope*, ordering Captain Machiko to use his contingent of marines to keep order on his ship and to detain one comrade Hawk under absolute top security. Well?"

Lily sighed. Even the breath seemed something she shared with Jehane, they stood so close, so intimately intertwined in this dance. "I ought to sleep with you," she said finally, because she could not help but wonder what it might be like, caught under the ardent intensity of his gaze. "It would serve you right. I really don't have the Formula, and I don't know what its components are. *And* I don't understand why you aren't going to do as Robbie says: give it to everyone. Now. Unless you really are planning to use it to buy people's loyalty, and to reward their service. But that would make you no better than—"

She broke off, gasping, as he tightened his grip on her arms. "No, you don't understand. Sometimes difficult choices have to be made in order to bring about necessary changes."

"Duty exacts a harsh price," she muttered, echoing his words to Jenny those weeks ago.

"Yes. Believe me, I would far rather give the Formula to all, but it is naive to think that such a radical change won't alter every facet, the entire fabric, of our society—"

But she thought she was beginning to understand, finally, and far too late. "I thought that was what this entire revolution was supposed to be about."

He examined her with minute thoroughness, like a lover

studies his beloved. The beauty of his face was not, she saw now, so much in the perfection of its features as in the single-minded desire he had focused and honed to such a fine point that it now engulfed his entire being. And woe betide, she thought, whatever—or whoever—came between him and his goal.

"Change takes time," he murmured. "It can't be hurried." He stopped, shifting his head slightly as three figures came out on the balcony, bringing with them a brilliant stream of light through the door from inside. Lily recognized them immediately: Robbie, with Kuan-yin and Vanov two steps behind him.

Robbie, who would not have come here if she had not told him about the Hierakis Formula.

"—and it will give all people the chance," Robbie was saying as he came out and laid his hands on the railing, lifting his head to take in the cool slap of the air and the dark blanket of stars above, "to sit back at some point and simply be with the world, and the stars, and see their beauty as an end in itself—"

Kuan-yin, still behind him, reached for the pistol at her waist.

If *she* hadn't told him.

"Robbie!" Lily screamed.

She wrenched herself free for an instant from Jehane's grip.

Robbie turned his head, surprised, at her voice. The open lines of his face gleamed briefly in the last light of the closing door.

Jehane tackled her. They fell to the ground, grappling. She arched her back, to throw him off, and watching in that split second as Kuan-yin grabbed Robbie by the shoulder and shot him in the back of the head.

Jehane slammed Lily's head against the floor of the balcony. She lay, stunned but still conscious, staring. Kuan-yin stepped back, and Vanov hoisted Robbie's legs and tipped him over the railing.

Lily heard her own breathing like a storm raging around her. She felt Jehane's pulse where his throat lay pressed on one arm. Faint and far down, a splash shuddered the quiet. Even the distant sounds of the assault on Central seemed to have ceased for the moment, in deference to his passing.

Only a soft drone drifted across the cool air, pitched low and steady.

"Just remember one thing," said Lily in a hoarse whisper. Jehane shifted his head so that she could see the pale luminosity of his face suspended above her like one of the stars. "The Hierakis Formula has a side effect. For ten to thirty days you are sick. Delirious." She bent her neck enough so that the gesture was clearly seen to include the silent, white-clad form of Kuan-yin, flanked by Vanov, standing at the railing, looking down at the gift she had given to the sea. "Who do you trust to watch over you?"

A bar of bright light splintered the darkness, began to close back in on itself as a new figure came out onto the balcony.

"I'm sorry," said Senator Isaiah to Kuan-yin, obviously not yet seeing Jehane and Lily tangled on the ground at the other end of the balcony. "I thought I heard someone shouting out here."

The fighting for Central had started up again. Lily could hear the muted sound of laser cannons, but over it all, beginning to drown it out, the high rumbling drone increased in volume. Even the night on the balcony seemed to lift slightly, as if the moon was rising. A wind rose off the sea, swirling Lily's hair where it lay spread out on the hard, cold surface of the balcony.

"Tupping Hells," swore Kuan-yin. "Whose tupping ship is *that*? Vanov, get back inside." Into her com: "I want a ten up here at once!"

"Kill them both," said Jehane. He released Lily and sprang with preternatural speed to his feet.

Kuan-yin nodded. Vanov spun and with cool dispatch shot Senator Isaiah, who was standing stock-still, staring out to sea.

Lily lunged for Jehane's legs, caught one ankle, and brought him down.

Wind screamed over them, tearing at her clothes. She could not even hear Kuan-yin's curses over the pounding roar of engine. Blinding light shattered the last vestiges of darkness across the balcony, giving her a brief glimpse of Kuan-yin striding for the tangle of her and Jehane's bodies as they fought, of Senator Isaiah lying in a pool of blood.

A voice shouted her name.

"Min Ransome! Lily! Be quick!"

Kuan-yin grabbed her shoulders and jerked her up. Lily used the motion to drive back into her, and Kuan-yin lost her balance and her grip on her gun. Lily broke free of her and dove for the pistol.

Came up to find Jehane already at the door, which opened to admit a group of startled soldiers. Behind her, she felt rather than saw the bulk of one of the *Forlorn Hope's* shuttles, coming in toward the balcony, an excruciatingly slow maneuver that had the engines screaming in protest.

Jehane grabbed a rifle from one of the soldiers and tossed it with unerring accuracy at Kuan-yin.

Then he said, quite clearly and with sincere feeling, "Damn, I could have managed it better." And escaped inside.

Laser fire burst out from the shuttle, raking the soldiers in the doorway.

Lily leaped for the railing, shooting at Kuan-yin as she moved. But even as she swung her leg over the cold metal fence, the shuttle a vast rising wall behind her, Kuan-yin and the soldiers remaining in the doorway opened up on her.

It was like being shattered into pieces. A web of light, and she fell.

And then—nothing.

27   Jehane's Triumph

****

The world ran in waves, melding with the sky until both were one. She found the far horizon, became it, really, and melted into the sun's rising across the lap of the waters.

Far below in the depths, she could see Robbie's face, paler than in life, but at peace. He seemed to be breathing. Each slight opening of his lips let escape a tiny current that spread, rising and rippling, until it became the waves that moved the ocean itself.

She would have waited, to see how far the waves rode onto the far shore of hills, but the brilliant whiteness at the heart of the sun drew her, and she drifted toward it, letting herself go as it drowned her in its light.

Except that somewhere out on the waters someone was singing. The sound, plaintive and achingly beautiful, caught her, and she paused.

Even as she paused the sun dimmed, its edges curling in as it sank into the waves, and she could make out the words of the song.

> Ich will bei meinem Jesu wachen
> So schlafen unsre Sünden ein
> Meinen Tod büsset seiner Seelen Not
> Sein Trauren machet mich voll Freuden.
> Drum muss uns sein verdienstlich

Leiden recht bitter und duch süss sein.

I will watch beside my Jesus.
Then our sins go to sleep.
His soul's distress atones for my death.
His mourning makes me full of joy.
So his meritorious Passion must for
us be truly bitter and yet sweet.

It was dim, in this room, except for the gleaming curve of
Bach. He floated next to her, singing softly. A single light
shone on his surface.

For a long moment she just lay, staring at him, and then
she realized that she was breathing, and alive, and that her
eyes were open.

She blinked. A face appeared.

"Lily!" Soft, but triumphantly intense. "Lily-hae. You made
it."

"The Formula." Lily gasped, fighting for breath against a
vast pressure that weighed on her chest. "Got to get it out.
Got to get the broadcast out—" She struggled to sit up, but
could not manage it, too numb—or perhaps it was Jenny's
hand on her torso holding her down.

"It's been done," said Jenny. "Don't worry, it's been done."

"You're sure?" Her voice sounded harsh and muted to her
ears. "The Hierakis Formula, I mean. It got out?"

"Yes." Jenny's voice had faded from its initial cheerfulness
to something more soothing. "Yes. Hawk has been distributing the base for months, you know. Everywhere the *Forlorn
Hope* traveled for Jehane. I sent Pinto down with a crate of
the base, and we set up a message to go out on every net, but
one got there ahead of us. Of Pero's making, I believe."

Robbie.

"I shouldn't have told him." She could feel enough now to
clench her fist in frustration. "I shouldn't have told Robbie
about the Formula, but it was the right thing to do. Hells,
Jenny, if I hadn't told Robbie about it Jehane wouldn't have
had him killed. I should have shot him that first time. I
shouldn't have saved his life on Blessings. I should have—"

"Hold on, Lily. Hold on. Hold on." Jenny put a warm hand
on her forehead and then Kyosti appeared abruptly beside
Jenny and rather unceremoniously shoved her away. He laid

a hand softly on Lily's throat and just stood silent, breathing, for a long space.

At last he sighed and removed his hand. "Let me give you something to drink," he said, and disappeared.

The entire ritual confused her enough to sidetrack her thoughts. As sensation returned slowly to her body, she discovered that her throat was already dry from talking. "Where am I?" she asked, feeling lost.

"You're on the *Hope*," replied Jenny, reverting to cheerfulness. She grinned. "And am I glad to see that you're going to live. When they dragged you in here so shot up that your clothes were half-burned off you, we all thought Hawk was going to go berserk on the spot. He hasn't left this room since you came in. He even slept at your feet."

"When I came in?" Lily coughed. The movement racked painfully through her body, but it was sweet pain, because it proved finally to her satisfaction that she was alive, and whole. "But—Jehane—"

Jenny gave a quick, furtive glance around. "Finch was on comm when a message came in to Captain Machiko. He saw to it that it was acknowledged, but that the captain never got it, and then sent Nguyen down to alert me and Yehoshua and Hawk."

"Got to think," said Lily desperately. She tried to move, but she was encased in some kind of soft, clear plastine, like a wrapping.

A hand touched her cheek gently. Jenny moved aside to admit Kyosti again. "No thinking," he said. "Drink this."

The liquid was cool and tart. He moved away, busying himself at the couch she lay on, and she felt the touch of his hands as he examined her. The drink acted rather like a catalyst, clearing her mind.

"That's better," said Jenny, coming back into her restricted line of vision. "The only reason you're not dead is because you picked the right friends. You were shot up this side of all Seven Hells. If Hawk wasn't the best damned emergency doctor I've ever seen work....He dragged you single-handedly back from the edge."

Lily smiled, as well as she could. "I don't doubt it." She attempted to turn her head, and did. "Bach." She did not try to whistle.

Patroness! His cadence in reply was brilliantly resonant with joy. *I despaired, but I did not give up hope of thee.*

"How did you find me?"

Patroness, indeed I waited, as thou instructed me, but when thou didst not return and I received a message from Herr Pinto that he had arrived at the port and awaited us there, I grew anxious. I then discovered several messages from thou on the net, relaying thy position. So did we find thee.

"Thank you," replied Lily in a muted voice.

Kyosti returned to the head of the couch. "Out," he ordered Jenny. "Give me a few moments in peace, please."

Jenny glanced at Lily, for confirmation, and Lily managed to tilt her head slightly. Jenny snapped a salute, and retreated.

For a long moment, Kyosti just gazed at her.

"I guess I was shot up pretty badly," Lily said. The fact of it seemed remote to her now. In the back of her thoughts, she kept seeing Kuan-yin reaching for her pistol and shooting Robbie. Vanov dumping him over the side.

"We won't talk about that," he replied, brusque. She saw a kind of wild desperation inform his face, and she shivered, wondering what kind of havoc he would wreak if he ever thought she *was* dead.

"All right." It was better to think, to plan, than to dwell on the events that had led to Robbie's murder. "What kind of communications are coming up from Arcadia now? Jenny told me that Finch intercepted. Wait." She paused to catch her breath, went on. "How long has it been?"

"About forty-eight hours."

"And Central?"

He shrugged. "Ask Finch. I think Central put up more resistance then Jehane expected. It's kept him busy enough to neglect us for the moment. We've kept you well hidden here from Machiko. For now."

"Min? Min!" Movement blurred the edges of Lily's vision and then Paisley appeared, triumphantly furtive. "Sure, and glory, but we thought you had found ya kinnas for certain." She reached past Hawk and grasped one of Lily's hands in her own tattooed one. "Be it weren't for Pinto catching you on ya wing as you fell—"

"And here I heard," interposed Kyosti drily, "that you were

the one who ran out on that convenient wing in the middle of all that fire and dragged her inside the shuttle."

Paisley shrugged, a deprecating gesture. "Be it weren't much, min. But have you heard? Central surrendered!"

She let go of Lily's hand and moved away to switch on the com. Abruptly, Jehane's voice permeated the tiny space.

"—and I am grieved to inform you, citizens, that in this moment of our greatest triumph, we have lost a man without whom we never could have won. Comrade Pero—and, yes, this time indeed Pero is gone, never to return—was murdered in a last act of defiance by Central. Even as we struck against their last stronghold, they sent a traitor into our midst, and *he shot Pero.*"

A long, potent pause brought about by the tremor of emotion in Jehane's voice. "He was trying to prevent Pero's last, greatest act. It is no consolation that this traitor is now dead, that his name will never again be spoken—but remember, citizens, Pero died a martyr to bring you what will prove to be the crowning glory of our triumph. The Formula that even now is being broadcast from every net to every planet, every habitation, in Reft space—"

"Wait." Tears burned down Lily's cheeks as she listened. "He's lying. *He* never meant to broadcast the formula."

"Then he was too late. Robbie set it in motion. Jehane can't stop it now. Although it's lucky you reminded me that in a place like this, people would still use that kind of gift for their own ends, instead of for the common good. Or I'd never have made the provisions I did."

"—in every clinic, because this Formula is not a privilege, citizens, to be granted to a few, it is your right, each and every one of you, to—"

"Turn that off," Lily snapped. Jehane's voice vanished just as Jenny stormed back in.

"Paisley!" she muttered. "I told you no visitors."

Paisley shrank back against the couch, seeking protection from Lily even though Lily was basically immobile and completely without strength.

"You'd better go, Paisley," said Lily gently. "But thank you, and thank Pinto. You saved my life."

Paisley shrugged, embarrassed. "Be it kinnas returned, min. Weren't nothing." She cast a scorching glance at Jenny.

"But it be poor o' her not to even let Pinto in to see how you be, seeing as he were ya one as saved you."

"Paisley," Jenny began, warning, but Kyosti intervened.

"She's right," he said unexpectedly. "Pinto ought to come in for a moment."

Jenny glared at him, but acquiesced. Paisley left with a grin.

"The very last thing he did," Lily murmured.

"That who did?" Jenny asked, coming closer.

"Robbie. It *was* right to tell him about the Formula. And yet Jehane will get the credit for it. *And* the martyr he needs to seal his victory. Damn him." She coughed. But it did not seem to her that Robbie would have blamed her for any part in his death; remembering, back to their days on Arcadia, she wondered if he had not expected—or even hoped—to die for the cause. "And you know," she continued slowly, realizing only now that it was true, "Jehane would have had to kill him sooner or later, because of what they both are. And if Jehane didn't, Kuan-yin would have."

Instead of an answer, she got a sudden influx of company, all of them quiet as they crowded into the room: Paisley, Pinto, Yehoshua, Lia and Gregori, the Mule, Rainbow, Cursive, Diamond, Wei, and Nguyen, and even Blue, looking sullenly pleased to be included in the conspiracy.

"Finch would'a come," murmured Paisley rebelliously, "but he be on ya comm, and he got to stay there for now."

"I'll give you five minutes, collectively," said Hawk in a tone that no one would dare argue with.

But no one even spoke. They just gazed at her as if they were astonished that she was alive.

"Well?" she snapped when the silence grew long enough that it fueled her with enough energy to transfer the anger she felt at her own actions in leading them to this pass to the people now watching her. "What are you waiting for?"

Everyone looked at everyone else, and then back at her.

"I don't know, my love," said Kyosti. "What are we waiting for?"

"You don't think Jehane isn't going to track us down the moment he has a free hand to spare? We need this ship."

"Mutiny," breathed Jenny. Her eyes lit with sudden glee.

"Yes," said Lily. "We've got no choice. Will you follow me?"

This time the silence was twice as deep and twice as long.

"You know I'm with you," said Jenny finally, breaking the paralysis that had evidently gripped everyone else. Kyosti had the barest grin on his face.

"Min Ransome!" said Paisley fiercely, unable to restrain herself any longer. "It be *wrong* o' you to even *think* I wouldna' follow you, down ya haunted way if need be."

"Need might be," said Lily. "Because I don't intend spending the rest of what is evidently going to prove a very long life running from Jehane, even in a fine ship like the *Forlorn Hope*." She paused to catch her breath, finding even such a short speech more taxing than she expected, but she had enough energy to find and meet each pair of eyes and, meeting them, read their assent.

"But what else is there to do?" asked Jenny. "Besides turn bootlegger and run?"

Lily looked at Kyosti. He merely looked up at the ceiling, leaving Lily to sigh and regard her ragtag collection of conspirators.

"We're taking this boat back where she came from." She grinned, seeing, by their expressions, that it was the last possible alternative they would have thought of.

"Sure," breathed Paisley, "and glory."

"But no one has been that way for centuries. No one even knows—" began Yehoshua, and then he faltered. Everyone looked at Kyosti.

"Exactly," replied Lily, gathering a burst of strength from the sense of anticipation that abruptly charged the air. "Don't worry. Master Heredes always used to tell me that when you've tried every other attack, the one you're left with, however unlikely, must be the right one."

"What if it doesn't work?" asked Jenny, evidently giving up hard on her bootlegging dreams.

Lily smiled. "It has to work. Otherwise you're dead. And I'm not dead yet, am I?"

"Not for lack of trying," muttered Pinto.

"Pinto," she began, suddenly sober. "Your father—"

"Is dead. I know." He turned and left the room.

"All right," said Lily decisively, before his departure could cloud anyone's resolve. "Get back to your posts. Jenny. Yehoshua. Stay."

They dispersed quickly.

Kyosti went back to a careful examination of her readings. "You're going to need to rest soon," he warned.

Lily ignored him. "Jenny. How many people on board can we count on?"

She frowned. "Captain Machiko has rubbed more than our people the wrong way. All the Ridanis on board. Some few others"—she paused to count—"I'd say twenty-three." Glanced at Yehoshua, as if for confirmation. He nodded.

"Which leaves?"

"Thirty-six supporting the captain. That leaves us with the advantage, I'd say."

"With a large advantage. Good. Now, to begin with—"

"Lily." Kyosti laid a hand on her wrist, a soft pressure that seemed far away to her. "You *must* rest."

"But Jenny—"

"If Jenny and Yehoshua can't manage a simple mutiny with these odds, and surprise, on our side, then you're better off not commandeering this vessel in the first place. I'd estimate that in two hours this boat will be ours."

Yehoshua chuckled. "Somehow, life never gets dull around you, Lily Heredes."

"No." The name no longer fit—and not just because La Belle Dame, and Jehane, and even Paisley, had named her differently in recent days. "Not Heredes. Master Heredes is dead. Any purpose his name had in living on died with Central, and with Jehane's triumph." She failed to keep the bitterness from her voice, but her anger was being slowly washed away by a spreading lassitude that methodically engulfed her body as she spoke. "I don't think he would have wanted me to disinherit my own family forever. Not when they gave me as much as they did. And not when I'll always be in his."

Yehoshua looked surprised. "Heredes isn't your real name?"

She smiled, fighting against her fatigue. "It's Ransome. Lily Ransome."

"Lily," said Kyosti, beginning to sound impatient.

Jenny laughed and rose and snapped a smart, jaunty salute at her recumbent commander. "We'll wake you up, captain," she said, half-laughing still, "when the ship is fully at your disposal."

"Not that soon," said Kyosti.

Jenny grinned. "Come on, Yehoshua." She tugged him by one arm from the room.

"There's too much to do," insisted Lily, looking up at Kyosti. "You can't make me sleep." But even as she said it, she yawned.

"Yes, I can," replied Hawk coolly from away down a deepening well of distance.

Somewhere, echoing up from the depths, Bach was singing:

> *Ich will dir mein Herze schenken,*
> *Senke dich, mein Heil, hinein.*
> *Ich will mich in dir versenken,*
> *Ist dir gleich die Welt zu klein,*
> *Ei, so sollst du mir allein*
> *Mehr als Welt und Himmel sein.*

> I will give my heart to Thee;
> sink Thyself in it, my Salvation.
> I will submerge myself in Thee.
> And if the world is too small for Thee,
> ah, then for me alone shalt Thou
> be more than world and Heaven.

Lily went to sleep and dreamed of Robbie's body washing up on a white shore, whole and untouched by the ills of the world.

About the Author

Alis Rasmussen was born in Iowa and grew up in Oregon. She graduated from Mills College, in California, having spent her junior year abroad studying at the University of Wales. She is currently living in San Jose, California, with her husband, three children, and two newts. She has a brown belt in Shotokan karate and occasionally practices broadsword fighting in the Society for Creative Anachronism. In addition to the *Highroad* triology, she is the author of a fantasy novel, *The Labyrinth Gate*, and is at present at work on a new novel.

From multiple Hugo and Nebula Award-winner

DAVID BRIN

comes his most important novel to date

<u>EARTH</u>

When a laboratory experiment goes awry, allowing a microscopic black hole to sink into the Earth's core, scientists search frantically for a way to retrieve it, only to discover that another black hole already exists there—one that could destroy the entire planet within two years.

But **Earth** is much more than an edge-of-the-seat thriller. From an underground lab in New Zealand to a space station in Low Earth Orbit, from an endangered-species conservation ark in Africa to a home in New Orleans, it is a novel peopled with extraordinary characters and challenging new ideas, set in an incredibly real future.

With **Earth,** David Brin has provided us with a profound testament about our responsibility to our planet—a message so stirring it transcends every genre to embrace and inspire us all.

EARTH

A Selection of the Book-of-the-Month Club
and the Quality Paperback Book Club

♦

**Now available in hardcover
wherever Bantam Spectra Books are sold**

His first short story collection in seven years!

TALES FROM
PLANET EARTH
Arthur C. Clarke

♦

From the author of **Childhood's End, 2001: A Space Odyssey, Rendezvous with Rama,** and **Rama II,** comes an unparalleled collection of some of his finest short fiction, speculating about the fate of our world in the years to come. Included in this dazzling array are classic works such as "The Lion of Comarre," "The Deep Range," and "The Wall of Darkness," along with some stories which have rarely seen print since their first publication. Illuminating the volume are illustrations by Michael Whelan, the most honored science fiction artist of all time.

A major collection of stories filled with bold ideas and startling imagery, **Tales from Planet Earth** will be a landmark addition to the libraries of Arthur C. Clarke's fans the world over.

A Bantam Spectra Trade Paperback
Coming in May, 1990

The extraordinary novelization of the landmark TBS series.

VOICE OF THE PLANET
Michael Tobias

"This book is a cry in the fading light of Earth. Michael Tobias has written a book that must be read by every person interested in continuing to eat and to breathe. Believe me, you will be excited to know that there is a chance to save ourselves from the apocalypse and astonishingly, Michael Tobias weaves his story through the stark facts entertainingly and irresistably. This book is a must read."

—William Shatner

♦

An ecology professor travels to Nepal to track down the source of persistent and inexplicable messages urging him to write a book about the fate of the Earth. What he discovers is an ancient monastery is nothing less than the incarnate spirit of the Earth herself—*Gaia*. Her message is urgent and compelling. Humanity and all our world are at risk—through pollution, overpopulation, extinction of species and other critical concerns.

Voice of the Planet—now a major TBS miniseries starring William Shatner and Faye Dunaway as the voice of Gaia, scheduled to air in the Summer of 1990—takes the reader on a spiralling odyssey to the farthest reaches of our world, past, present and future, to explore what we've done—and what we can do—to the only world humanity calls home.

A Bantam Spectra Book
Coming in July, 1990